Her Frozen Wild

Also by Kim Antieau

Novels

*The Blue Tail • Broken Moon • Butch
Church of the Old Mermaids • Coyote Cowgirl • Deathmark
The Desert Siren • The Fish Wife
The Gaia Websters • Jewelweed Station
The Jigsaw Woman • Maternal Instincts • Mercy, Unbound
Queendom: Feast of the Saints • The Rift • Ruby's Imagine
Swans in Winter • Whackadoodle Times • Whackadoodle Times Two*

Nonfiction

*Answering the Creative Call
Certified: Learning to Repair Myself and the World
in the Emerald City
Counting on Wildflowers: An Entanglement
Old Mermaids Book of Days and Nights • The Old Mermaids Oracle
The Salmon Mysteries:
a Reimagining of the Eleusinian Mysteries
The Salmon Mysteries Workbook:
Reimagining the Eleusinian Mysteries
Under the Tucson Moon*

Collections

Entangled Realities (with Mario Milosevic)
*The First Book of Old Mermaids Tales
Tales Fabulous and Fairy • Trudging to Eden*

Chapbook

Blossoms

Blog

www.kimantieau.com

Photography

www.kimantieau.smugmug.com

HER FROZEN WILD

Kim Antieau

Green Snake
PUBLISHING

Her Frozen Wild
by Kim Antieau

ISBN: 978-1-949644-21-0

Cover image by Tyler Olson | Dreamstime.com.
Cover and book design by Mario Milosevic.
Special thanks to Nancy Milosevic.

http://www.kimantieau.com

Electronic editions of this book are
available at your favorite ebook store.

Published by Green Snake Publishing
www.greensnakepublishing.com

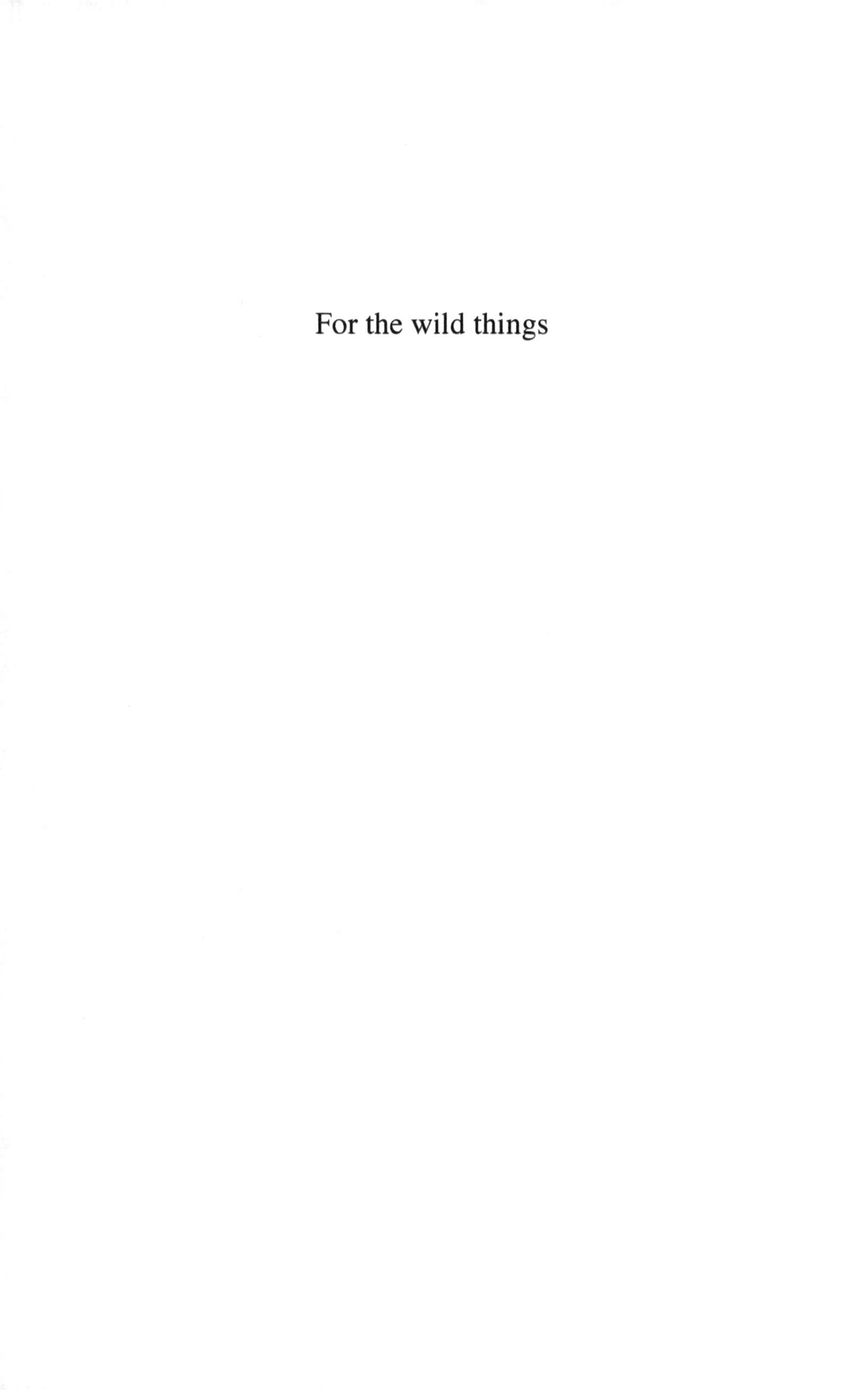

For the wild things

Part One

BEWILDER

1

The Altai, Siberia ca. 500 B.C.E.

The needle slipped out of her arm, and Ulla kissed the spot where it had been, tasting her own sweet blood, her salty sweat, and the clay, horn, and mountain mixture that now bubbled beneath her skin as part of a swan the embroiderer was creating. A deer grazed on her thigh; a spider made her fingers part of her web; a snake crawled up her leg; a bear's claw pricked her heart.

Outside the timeless cave, the others danced and sang. Ulla sat at the edge of the cave while the women needled her. She tried not to sway to the beat of the horse-hide drums. The broad sky was amber and rose with dusk. She felt the roaring inside herself, bubbling, gurgling, tearing at her. The dancers undulated and shook, each moving in such a way that Ulla did not know what she saw, no matter how often she blinked. Was that an eagle or a girl? A fox or a man? A leopard or a woman?

The fire burned her face, and the embroiderers hummed. She was becoming. Was . . .

She smelled him in this cave that reeked of humus and bear before she heard him, felt his hand on the small of her back. His fingers always found her soul. "You don't have to do this. You are already one of the People." He kissed the sweat from the back of her neck. Then he was away again, becoming one of the dancers, twirling the night into existence.

She felt the needle go into her skin, deeper and deeper, and she wanted to roar.

The coriander-colored dirt, heated by the fire—or was it by her own body—tickled the soles of her feet.

She gasped as the needle came out again.

"We are finished," the embroiderer whispered.

The drums sounded like horse hooves.

War was coming. Or war was leaving.

"One more," she whispered, pressing her hand against her buttocks. "Right here. A wild rose. A tiny red wild rose."

"But it isn't like the others," the embroiderer said.

The dancers whirled faster. Everything pulsed.

"I want it anyway," she said. "It's a message for someone back home."

The embroiderer picked up the needle and pushed Ulla's message through time.

2

The Altai, Siberia ca. 1930

Asya hurried to catch up with the men, but the October snow was deep, each flake a tiny mirror reflecting the sun into her eyes. The landscape quivered. She wondered when they would find the bear. They had already passed one timeless cave, but they had not stopped, and somehow the men had gotten ahead of her. She followed the map their footprints made in the snow. In the distance the white hills wavered, as if they were part of a giant heat mirage.

Suddenly Asya heard the cries of the men, "Come out, Old One! The sun is warm enough for you to come out now!" She ran until she saw the men and boys from her village, dark figures on a plain of white standing in front of a snow-covered cave, its opening matching the darkness of the men. Asya walked closer to them. She no longer cared if they saw her. The men continued to chant and pound their spears on the icy ground in front of the cave.

The bear did not come out.

Two men—one of them Asya's brother—stepped away from the group and ducked into the cave. The others stood quietly, their foggy breath steaming the cold. Asya heard drums and looked around for the *kam*, but he was not there—it was only her own heart she heard.

Then a rumble came from the cave. Or the ground shook. Something cried out: a baby's wail? The men raised their spears all at once, as if they were one being with many arms. Asya's brother and the other man rushed out of the cave. A dark blond darkness followed. The darkness roared, a sound that shook the snow mirrors and cleared Asya's vision. The men stepped back from the bear.

"Old man!" someone called. "We are sorry. We are not the ones who do this to you!"

The bear tipped forward. Blood matted his chest. His mouth opened, and they fell upon him, plunging their spears into his flesh easily, as if he were a Christmas duck and their spears were forks and they were all fighting for the best piece.

Asya felt dizzy. The landscape was moving. She stared at the steam rising from the bear's gaping wounds and wondered why her father and brother were killing this man. Why were the villagers carving up an old man for their next meal?

The air stank of sweet sticky blood.

Asya screamed.

The men stopped—shaken from their blood lust—and saw Asya for the first time.

She ran toward them, slipping on the bloody melting ice.

"How can you!" she cried. "Daddy! Why are you killing this man?" She dropped to the ground and cradled the bear's head in her lap. She leaned closer and tasted his breath; as he died, he whispered secrets to her.

Her father pulled her up; the bearman's head thudded against the frozen ground.

Blood soaked Asya's clothes.

"She's the bear's wife," one man said.

"You told me we didn't kill the People," Asya said.

"We didn't know," her father said.

"It's only a bear," another man said. "Take her home. She will soon forget."

Her brother reached for her, but Asya turned and ran. Her feet deftly took her over the icy snow; she heard someone behind her trying to catch up, but he kept falling through the snow. She ran until she reached the edge of the birch tree forest, her tears mixing with the bear's blood. Her chest hurt too much from the cold air to go on. She hung on to a birch and tucked her chin into her coat until she breathed air warmed by her own body. A magpie stood on a branch above her, watching. Asya, the magpie, and the forest breathed together until she grew calm.

Then a breeze whispered to her, bringing the smell of bear. She looked up. Amongst the trees, a thick tall yellow-brown figure walked. The slender white trees almost looked like the bars of a cage, only this being was not contained. Asya blinked. It was a woman striding through the forest, wrapped in fur, walking on the ice-snow without slipping.

A woman who was not caged or contained.

Asya glanced in the direction from where she had come and then over her shoulder at the hill which hid her village from view. Then she looked through the trees again. The woman watched her.

Asya released the birch from her embrace and followed the woman deeper still into the wild.

3

Washington State, 1975

The bear had Ursula in her sights. Ursula sucked in her breath and looked down at her hands. She had sprouted claws.

She gasped and opened her eyes to a darkness too deep to be real. She felt the dampness of a cave in her bones. Something leaned over her—something darker than her dream on this New Moon night. She reached her child's hand up and up until she grasped fur. So it hadn't been a dream.

"What is it?" Grandmother Asya growled; Ursula's fingers now caressed flannel.

Asya sat on the edge of the bed. The smell of cave was gone, yet the scent of musk lingered.

"I'm an old woman," Asya said. "I need my sleep."

"I dreamed a bear was down at the bottom of the yard." Ursula pointed in the darkness. "In the woods. She watched me."

"You cried out because of that?" Asya asked gently. "You are a country girl, *duscha*. You've seen bear."

"She spoke to me, Grandmother," Ursula said. "She told me that I was hers and she'd come to get me."

"Go back to sleep," Asya said. "That old she-bear has no power here. It isn't time yet."

"Time for what?"

"It isn't time to be awake," Asya said. "Now go to sleep." She brushed her lips against her granddaughter's forehead.

"Can you leave a light on?"

"She frightened you that much?"

Ursula slipped deeper under her covers. "I want her to know where I am," she answered.

Asya did not turn on the light, but she left the door open. She walked quietly into the kitchen, then out the back door, stepping into a night that smelled of snow. She sighed deeply and wished she could breathe, once again, that achingly cold air of the Altai. Wished she was a girl watching the delicate patterns in the ice that formed on the small window in the room she shared with her brothers and sisters.

She shook herself. This was not a time for wishes. She glanced up at the dark clear sky, looking for Ursa Major and Minor—Big Bear and Little Bear. When she found them, she looked down again.

"You can't have her," Asya shouted into the dark. "It isn't time!"

Nor would it ever be, if she could help it.

She went back into the house and closed the door. She hesitated, then locked the door. It was a useless gesture. A dead bolt could not subvert destiny, but it was the best she could do tonight.

Asya tiptoed into her granddaughter's bedroom and stayed until the sun came up.

4

The Altai, Siberia, 1999

The tomb smelled of rotting meat and pine, but Miriam no longer noticed. Neither did she pay any attention to Pasha bailing water from the chamber floor or acknowledge Ivan when he handed her a small bucket filled with water that someone above had taken from a nearby lake and heated with a blow torch. She was focused on the woman she knew lay within the opaque block of ice that now filled the larch tree coffin.

Miriam carefully guided the hot water over the ice. The darkness within the frozen water was taking shape as the ice melted. The entire crew watched Miriam quietly, all but three of them on the plateau above looking into the tomb. The silence was almost reverent. She knew they felt as she did: They had discovered something extraordinary. It was as though a door had creaked open and they were allowed to glimpse—what? Heaven? This place that looked out at the Altai Mountains was called the Pastures of Heaven, after all.

Miriam continued to pour water, to melt ice, and she felt like a healer bringing a body to life. Or an artist restoring a masterpiece. Then suddenly—even though hours, days, years had passed—suddenly, ice melted and revealed a jawbone without skin. Miriam did not stop. They were so close! Ivan swore in Russian and furiously waved away mosquitoes. Water trickled from the bucket, down the jawbone, and exposed a section of fur. Miriam handed the bucket to Pasha. Then she reached out, touched the sodden fur, and gently moved it aside.

Everyone gasped. They had found their treasure. Their grail. Their mother lode. Beneath the fur blanket was the woman's shoulder and arm; her skin was olive-colored; and on her arm was a bright blue tattoo of a swan.

"This one," Ivan said, tapping the ice. "She will have much to say to us."

Pasha leaned over to look more closely at the swan. "I think there are more tattoos. Right there, see, there's a piece of one. I wonder what they mean?"

"We'll have time to think about meaning later," Miriam said. "First, I have to get her out of this ice coffin."

Someone screamed.

"Who was that?" Miriam asked, looking up.

"Nothing," Leonard called down. "It's only a vulture."

Miriam could just make out a bird circling high above them.

"Vultures don't scream," Miriam said.

"Scream?" Pasha said. "I heard a growl."

The women looked at one another.

"I heard the lady," Ivan said. "She said let's get going before I freeze to death!"

Miriam laughed. "All right. I get the message. You'll be free in no time."

5

Ursula stared at the twisted figures strewn across the top of the long workroom table. As she ran the tips of her fingers over the flat reproduction of the body tattooing, she marveled at the detail. She could almost smell the fish diving down the right leg of the man from Barrow 2 and hear the rams' hooves as they charged up the same leg. A ram on Barrow 2's right forearm appeared to be running—or falling—and the rear half of its body was twisted around and up. Bob called them animal pretzels. The horns of the ram were massive, curving nearly heart-shaped around the head. From the animal's chin down the chest to the legs, the skin seemed to hang loose. Ursula had found a twin to this creature in a recent photograph taken of the arkar, wild sheep who now lived in the central deserts of Asia and who could have roamed the Altai 2,500 years ago.

The door opened, and Ursula looked up, blinking.

"You look like a deer in headlights," Peter said, closing the door again. He glanced around the room, and Ursula followed his gaze: wooden shelving that went to the ceiling filled with various types of containers, all with tags indicating site number, description, unit, quadrant, level, elevation, name, and date. Inside the boxes and bags were bones, stones, and the moans of those whose past they had dug up, or so Bob often joked.

"You all need to get organized," Peter said.

"Just because you couldn't find anything on your desk to save your life, doesn't mean we all have to be follow suit," Ursula said.

Peter rattled the box of wooden stakes at the end of the table.

"Did anyone ever tell you these look like something vampire hunters would use?" He pulled one out, turned the dirty pointed end toward his chest, and pretended to push it in.

Ursula smiled. Peter had accompanied her on enough digs to know the stakes were pounded into the ground to mark off the sites and the grids within the sites. The screens next to them were used to sift dirt in search of something meaningful. Ursula glanced at the pile of dirt drying on another screen across the room. That was what she did: looked for meaning in the earth.

"It's a dirty job, but someone's got to do it," Ursula said.

Peter dropped the stake back into the box and came around the table. Ursula pushed the paper tattoos into a pile. When Peter reached Ursula's chair, he bent down and kissed the back of her neck.

"Hi stranger," he said.

"Hi yourself," she answered. "I thought you had a test tonight."

"I had the TA administer it," Peter said, sitting on the edge of the table. "So you want to make out?"

"Sure." Ursula laughed.

Peter pulled her up toward him, drawing her between his legs. He kissed her lips. "Really, let's do it here. There are some advantages to having no windows."

"Yeah, it's like working in a tomb."

He put his hand on her breast. "Come on. It'll be fun."

Ursula glanced around. Having sex in a room where someone could walk in at any second was not her idea of a good time.

"Bob is going to be back from dinner soon."

"Won't he be in the lab with his bones? Come on."

His hand tightened on her breast. Ursula pushed away from him.

"That hurt."

"You're so sensitive," he said.

She watched him.

"You have the emotions of a tight-assed accountant," he said, straightening up. "You know, you used to be adventurous."

"No, Peter," Ursula said. "I've never been adventurous. You knew that when you married me. This is who I am. Dull, boring me. If you don't like it, go fuck your TA. Oh wait, that was last semester."

Peter stared at her. She gripped the table. Where had that come from?

Peter cleared his throat. "I thought we might—I got off early so we could be together, but I see you've got other plans."

He turned and walked quickly out of the room.

"Peter!" she called.

The lab door on the other end of the workroom opened. Bob leaned his head in.

"Just got an e-mail from Miriam," he said.

Ursula hesitated, then went into the lab. She preferred the workroom to the lab—even though the latter had computers and more microscopes. The workroom always smelled of dirt, and she liked that. Tonight, the connecting door from the lab to the archaeologists' offices was dark. Because Ursula only had a Master's degree and Bob was still working on his Ph.D., they were not considered "real" archaeologists so they had no other office besides the workroom.

Bob would soon get to use Dr. before his name; those two letters would garner him an office with a small window overlooking not much if he chose to remain at Cascadia University, a second rate school on its brightest day. His specialty was faunal analysis—the study of bones. Ursula admired Bob's tenacity. He once told her about a site he had worked on in Africa where they found fragments of more than 195,000 animal bones and were only able to identify a little more than 2,000 of them.

Ursula preferred her artifacts less fractured. She studied ancient body ornamentation, including clothes, jewelry, and tattooing. In a way, she was following in her mother's footsteps. Her mother had studied cave art—a kind of ornamentation on the skin of the Earth, Ursula sometimes thought. Her mother, whose name was also Ursula, had disappeared in Siberia thirty years earlier during an archaeological expedition to study rock art.

Ursula knew she was not as good as her mother had been; she lacked the single-minded dedication to a particular area of study. Peter said she was lazy; if she had really wanted her Ph.D., she would have hunkered down and chosen a specialty whether she was interested in one or not.

Bob asked her once why she had studied archaeology.

She told him, "I like history."

He shook his head. "No, that's why someone studies history."

"OK then, I like touching the past, holding it in my hands, imagining what life was like way back when."

Bob nodded. "Yup. We're a kinesthetic bunch, aren't we? If I can't dig it up and touch it, I don't believe in it."

Ursula had laughed. Bob was one of the more balanced people she knew. He loved his work, but he did not spend an inordinate amount of time in the pursuit of it. His wife and two daughters came first.

Now he motioned Ursula over to his computer. She sat at it

and read Miriam's message. "Hi guys! We uncovered part of the woman today. OK, we still don't know for sure that it's a woman but since nearly everyone here has had a dream about her, we're saying she's a she. Anyway, she's in fantastic shape. And get this, Ursula, she's got tattooing. We've uncovered a swan and a deer so far. Tomorrow I'll try to send pictures. Our electronic equipment doesn't seem to like these climes. More tomorrow."

Ursula looked up at Bob. He smiled.

"You should have gone to Siberia with them," he said.

"Yeah, yeah, well, I'm going home now," she said.

"Good night."

Ursula went into the workroom and grabbed her backpack. Bob was right: She should have gone. Her stupid fear of flying had kept her stateside. Or maybe it was her fear of following too closely in her mother's footsteps: She did not want to disappear—die—in that frozen wasteland her grandmother used to call home. When she had told James Paddock, the head of the department, that she could not go on the expedition for personal reasons, he had looked at her as though she were from Mars. She knew he was thinking, "One more nail in her professional coffin."

The only reason they kept her on at Cascadia was because she taught the 101 classes no one wanted to teach and because she had a peculiar—and unexplainable—gift with languages. Ursula understood most languages, spoken or written, and she could speak any language after brief exposure to it. Her mother had had the same ability. When faculty members came across publications in languages other than English during their research, Ursula translated for them. She saved Cascadia University time, but Ursula believed they kept her on staff mostly as a kind of freaky trophy. They enjoyed showing her off to foreign visitors.

Ursula turned off the workroom lights and went out into the hallway. She walked down the corridors, squinting at the institutional glare from the too shiny polished floors below and the fluorescent lights above.

Soon she stepped out into a warm summer night and breathed deeply. Cars sped by on the street out front of the Columbia Building. Students walked to and from night classes. Ursula smiled. Hardly anything better than a night like this in Portland. Maybe she'd walk downtown to Powell's Books. Or have a late dinner at Thai Orchid. Or—

Or go home to Peter and try not to argue.

She walked to a bench under a ginkgo tree and sat on it. She pulled a veggie burrito from her pack, unwrapped it, and bit into it. She sighed and closed her eyes as she chewed. She had waited too long to eat.

She opened her eyes. A woman loped by her; she was walking, yet her strides were so long she seemed to be running. She wore hip-hugger shorts and half of a ripped T-shirt. She slowed and smiled at Ursula.

"Are you one of us?" the woman asked. A swan tattoo floated on her right arm.

"One of you?"

"I thought I saw—while you ate." The woman stared at her, then smiled. "I must have been mistaken."

She continued walking. Ursula watched her until the woman went around the corner. Then Ursula finished her burrito, wondering what the woman had seen in her.

6

The kam stirred and took a long deep breath. She opened her eyes and gazed sleepily at the undulating walls of the cave. Perhaps they did not actually undulate, but they did change color—from light pink to lavender to violet to light pink—in bands of light similar to the aurora borealis. Perhaps the aurora borealis was timeless, too. Like this cave. Or time *full*.

She sat up and yawned. She always liked waking up to the sight of the rock paintings. They seemed to move as one color bled into the next. The deer danced in a group. Swans flocked in the indigo cave sky. Marmots dug out of the ground together. Only the big old Siberian bear was alone.

This was the difficulty with some of the Old Ones: They had forgotten how to be together.

She shook herself and stood. She had started down the mountain just in time. Something had changed. They had found the grave, she was certain.

The kam walked to the entrance of the cave and looked out upon a sky mauve with dawn. Early morning sunlight falling on the snow-covered mountain tops caused the snow to glow slightly gold and pink. The alpine meadows were orange, blue, and purple with wildflowers. The valleys, still dark with night, seemed to be in a different time zone.

The cave was up high enough that she was not bothered by summer insects. But she was going to have to go down. She would have to leave her beloved Altai.

She needed to go to Novosibirsk, find Ursula, and bring her back.

First, she growled, she had to find something to eat. Then she would save the world. Or at least her part of it.

7

Miriam sat up in the darkness and pulled the blankets and thick comforter closer to her. It might be summer, but they were still in Siberia. Often they awakened in the morning to find that a thin layer of ice had formed on the nearby lakes overnight.

Miriam held her breath. She wished it was morning. Something was snuffling outside her tiny—and flimsy—cabin. The something sounded like a bear and if it wanted to get inside, the walls would fall over like dominoes—only dominoes would give more resistance.

"Who's there?" she called.

No answer.

"Well, that was lame," she said.

She picked up a book from a crate next to her bed and threw it. It barely made a sound as it hit the dirt floor.

She sighed in exasperation.

Today one of the border guards had told them that some local Altaians were upset with the expedition because of "the lady."

The Altaians said the archaeologists were desecrating their graves. As leader of the expedition, Ivan went to talk with them, but he was Russian, and they were suspicious of "foreigners." Perhaps one of the Altaians was outside Miriam's door now. No, that was paranoid. She closed her eyes.

They had uncovered more of the lady's body today and had found a spider web tattoo on her hand. And a tall conical felt headdress lay near the lady's head. This most likely meant she was some kind of shaman or priestess. She wore white felt boots decorated with animals, a long dark skirt, and a blouse. Next to her in the coffin was a hand mirror with a swan on the back of it. Her clothing was similar to that of the woman Natalya Polosmak had uncovered several years earlier. At first glance, the tattoos seemed similar too. But Miriam would have to ask Ursula. Six horses had been sacrificed and buried with Polosmak's woman; none had been buried with Miriam's lady.

Miriam sighed and rubbed her face. The darkness seemed to vibrate around her. She had not been sleeping well. She kept waking up with her heart racing from some nightmare she could not remember.

Now she thought angry Altaians or bears were outside her door. Most likely marmots.

She would feel better in the morning when they brought the lady up into the sunshine.

8

Asya sat on the cinammon-colored dirt pulling weeds near the
yellow and gold marigolds that circled her vegetable garden.
The marigolds kept away harmful pests from her vegetables, plus
she liked looking out her kitchen window and seeing the colorful
circle of flowers.

Panda, her black and white cat, rubbed up against her leg. Asya
pulled off her gloves and rubbed Panda's stomach. The cat purred
and kneaded the air with her front paws. Asya smiled. She had
lived on this piece of land for many years before domestic animals
would come anywhere near her. Perhaps they had sensed the wild
in her. Now, every stray cat, dog, or goat was drawn to her. Did
that mean the wild was gone? Tamed?

Panda suddenly sprang up and ran away, chasing some thing
Asya could not see. She had decided long ago that every cat was
one of the People. Except maybe for that lazy tabby over at the
General Store. He had never hunted further than the cupboard
for his dinner.

Asya tilted her head back to face the sun. This would be a

perfect day to drive to Mount Rainier. Breathe in the mountain spirit.

She had dreamed of the lady last night. She knew what the lady wanted, what she had always wanted.

Asya squinted down her driveway, watching for Ursula's car. She had kept Ursula from going to Russia once; she could do it again. She had lost her daughter to the past. She was not about to lose her granddaughter, too.

She got up and stood with her hands on her hips. She wished she could go back and undo her mistakes. Not follow the men on the hunt or the woman into the woods. She had never been sure what had happened to her that day. The world had shimmied and shifted as she matched the woman stride for stride.

And then what? What had happened to her?

Her heart had slowed. She remembered that. The sound of it had deepened in her ears, and she had felt, *yes, this is how it is to be*. She became certain of her body and her place in time.

Then the woods changed. She looked at a birch and saw more than a tree.

And the magpie. Had she winked at Asya?

Then the woman had stopped and faced her.

Hadn't she?

And they were surrounded.

By whom? What?

Had the woman said, "We are the People"?

Had someone stepped out of one of the timeless caves? And was he the most beautiful man she had ever seen? Had he smelled of bear? Or was that his coat? Or the blood on her own clothes?

Had he taken her hand?

They ran through the woods. Or danced.

Asya blinked.

And ended up in a timeless cave. Naked on a bearskin rug?

Asya felt sick. She dropped to her knees and dug her fingers into the earth.

No. I don't want this.

The cave was filled with them. Or was it just the two of them? She sank into her body and into his and found the wild.

No. I don't want this. Memory.

Then she had known what the future would be. To be with him—with them—meant to be without all she knew. She could not do it. Could not be separated from—

She had howled.

The howl became a scream, and the world disintegrated.

She had come to her senses—or out of them—on the floor of the bear cave. Alone. She stumbled home with the bear's blood turned black on her clothes. Nine months later, her baby girl was born. She called her Ursula. Soon after, she moved them both to Moscow.

Asya heard her granddaughter's car door slam. *Ursula*—she looked so much like the mother she was named after.

"Grandma!" Ursula ran to her side, her voice frantic. "Are you all right?"

Asya leaned against her granddaughter. "I'm fine," she said.

"What happened?" Ursula searched her grandmother's face.

"I was remembering," she said. "Something I had thought was only a dream. Maybe it was. Who knows?" She squeezed Ursula's hand, then stood. Her knees shook.

"Come on, Grandma. Tell me what happened."

Asya looked at her grandchild. She could still see in her face the ten year old who left her light on for the she-bear and the four year old who sat by the window waiting for her mother to come home.

Ursula had lived such a long time in the shadow of Asya's fears.

"I was remembering your grandfather."

Over the years, Asya had only told Ursula lies about her grandfather. "He was a soldier," Asya had always said. "He died in the war. We didn't have cameras, so no, *duscha*, I have no pictures of him."

"From the look of you, Grandma," Ursula now said, "it was not a pleasant memory." She took her grandmother's arm and helped her up. They walked up the stone path to the house. "Is there something you want to say about your husband? You can tell me if gramps was an asshole. I can relate. I'm married to one."

"*You* married Peter," Asya said. "I don't understand why you girls choose the men you do. In our village, we picked the bravest, the best hunter, the most beautiful. We picked good men to be the fathers of our children. At least we tried to." Asya laughed. "At the end of the choosing, I suppose some ended up with lazy drunks who beat their wives."

"And how did you choose? Which end of the spectrum was Grandpa at?"

For the first time, Asya let herself remember the feel of him in her arms. The ecstasy of it. Indescribable, as all truly sacred moments are. How could she have let that go? She felt her knees shaking again. Such cowardice.

"I don't remember much," Asya said. "But look at you. You turned out well, so your grandfather would have to have been a wonderful person!"

"Smooth, Grandma," Ursula said. "You're almost as good at avoiding a straight answer as my husband."

"Someday I will tell you more," Asya said, opening her screen door and stepping into the kitchen. "I promise. But for today, let's eat sugar and drive to the mountain."

9

They carefully lifted the woman out of her coffin and onto a metal stretcher. Miriam's fingers cradled the woman's shoulders as they moved her. She was surprised at how human the lady felt—still a body after twenty-five centuries.

When the lady was safely on the stretcher, Miriam stepped away to allow them to maneuver her up onto the plateau. Miriam was rather appalled by some of the methods Ivan employed; none of them had used protective gloves when they moved her, and now they were going to store her in a shed while they awaited the helicopter. The mummy should be in a sterile temperature-controlled environment.

But it was not Miriam's show; she had to hang on for the ride and learn as much as she could.

She watched as they raised the stretcher up out of the kurgan. Then Miriam climbed out of the grave. They all looked at the lady on the stretcher now on a piece of plywood. She seemed smaller up here, turned on her side as she had been in the grave. She looked fragile. Vulnerable. Pasha unfolded a white gauze-like cloth. She took one end, Leonard the other, and they lowered the makeshift pall onto the corpse.

A north wind blew clouds across the sun. Miriam looked around the plateau. Purple and maroon wildflowers danced in the breeze, a pair of marmots watched the humans, and three swans floated gracefully on the lake. It was a beautiful place to spend eternity.

Pasha pressed tacks into the cloth and the board to hold it down at the edges. Beneath the gauze, darkness huddled.

Without a word, six of the crew bent down and lifted the platform onto their shoulders—modern people becoming ancient pallbearers—and headed toward the cluster of cabins in the near distance, each stepping over the rocks that circled the burial chamber—the kurgan—they had spent several summers uncovering. The wind fluttered the cloth, the air moving between it and the lady, and for a moment, it looked as though life was struggling to be set free beneath the gauze. Then the wind died away, and the lady was still.

Later, Miriam went into the cabin. Ivan and Pasha stood over the lady who now rested on a rickety wooden table. They both wore surgical gloves and masks. Miriam put on gloves and a mask and went to the lady's side. Pasha carefully tweezered off pieces of detritus from the corpse and dropped them into a plastic box. The contents would be analyzed later. Traces of pollen or flora could help determine what time of the year she had been buried.

Miriam started to reach out to the lady, to work alongside her colleagues, then stopped and gazed at the dead woman: her long dark tangled hair, the curve of her breasts visible beneath the delicate yellow blouse, the dip of her waist just before her body curved up into her hip. It was almost as if she were asleep.

"Look," Ivan said, peering through a magnifier. "The fibers on this blouse. It is silk, isn't it? But the fibers are so large. Wild silk?"

Miriam stepped forward again. Something about this dig made her sentimental—or superstitious. It was the Russian influence, she decided. The Russian archaeologists looked at their work with more emotion—more passion perhaps—than their American counterparts. The Russians were acutely aware that they were grave robbers, counting on the benevolence of the neighboring forces of nature not to punish them for their desecration.

"Maybe from India," Miriam said. "I think the woman they found on the other side of the Ukok plateau had a blouse made from India silk."

Ivan turned the mummy slightly and carefully pulled up her blouse to expose her stomach. Despite some sinking of the flesh, they could see she had been cut open and sewn up again: The people who buried their dead on this plateau 2,500 years ago mummified them first. Once they got the corpse back to the lab, they would no doubt discover that her stomach and skull, after being emptied of brain and guts, had been stuffed with wool, herbs, and other area flora.

Ivan maneuvered the blouse up a little further; Miriam bit her lip to keep from telling him to be careful.

"What? You a pervert, Ivanka?" Pasha asked in English. She winked at Miriam.

"Look yourself," he said.

The three stared at the olive-colored skin; at a place just below the breast and rib cage, where the lady would have felt her heartbeat, was another tattoo: the black outline of a bear's paw, with its long claws reaching up to the heart. The artist had made a tiny circle around one claw, making it look as though that claw had pricked the skin.

"It's so beautiful," Pasha said.

Ivan gently pulled the blouse down again.

"Funny thing," Miriam said. "I thought I heard a bear around my cabin last night."

Ivan shook his head. "Nope. No bears around here. But let us show you something we found earlier. Come." He motioned her to his side of the table. "See this hand, her left."

Miriam nodded. Since the woman was locked into position on her side, Miriam had only looked at the palm side of the left hand.

"Come. Look at the back of it."

Miriam crouched down to look at the hand. Two of the knuckles were bare, exposing bone.

"Go further."

Miriam gently drew the sleeve of the blouse down away from the wrist.

"Is that a stain?" Miriam asked. Ivan said nothing. She squinted. A patch on her wrist was black—or brown. Miriam moved closer: It was hair.

"Touch it," Pasha said.

Miriam hesitated, then reached out. It was coarse thick hair.

"It feels like animal hair. I cut a piece and looked under the microscope. I am not an expert but it looks like animal hair."

"Is it glued on?"

He shook his head. "No. It is part of her. We'll find out more once we get her back to the lab."

Miriam rubbed her fingers across the tuft of hair.

"Makes you wonder who she was, eh?" Pasha said.

"Or what she was," Ivan said.

10

Ursula stared at the copies spread out on the work table: line drawings of the front of each of the tattooed Altaian mummies. The Barrows 2 man had a fish and rams on his right leg and a ram and several mythical creatures on his right arm. The tattoos on his chest could not be positively identified because they had deteriorated—along with his chest.

The man at Site 56 found in the late 1980s had what looked like an eagle on his left forearm. On his right hand, a school of fish swam. Below his right knee grew a birch tree. A lion roared on his left thigh. A fox on his chest.

Polosmak's mummy had a being on her shoulder which looked like a reindeer to Ursula but which other archaeologists called a "mythological animal." She also had a deer on her wrist.

The man found frozen to death in a glacier in the Altais had a snow leopard on his chest, a wild sheep below his left knee, a flying insect on his left hand, and a cascade of geese coming off his right shoulder.

So far on their newly discovered mummy, Miriam and company

had found a spider with webbing on her left hand, a swan on her right arm, a bear claw between her breasts, a snake slithering up her right leg, a deer on her right thigh and a red rose on her buttock.

Ursula saw some similarity in the artwork of the tattooing. Barrows 2 and Polosmak's mummy had been tattooed in the highly stylized and exaggerated way of the Scythians, the nomadic warriors who had sliced and diced their way across the Russian steppes on horses, stopping along the way to raise sheep and cattle and bury their dead in kurgans similar to the one Miriam et al had just dug up.

Before the Cascadia University expedition to Siberia, Ursula had known little about the Scythians but had recently started researching them. Some scholars believed the Scythians never traveled as far as the lady's plateau. The Greek historian Herodotus, who died about the same time as the lady, claimed that the Scythians intermarried with the Amazons and rode east, becoming the Sauromations, a tribe who some scholars believed were matrifocal where—among other things—the women fought alongside the men. Historians had not given much credence to Herodotus's tales of fighting women until archaeologists started digging up evidence which indicated the women may have been warriors. Women were often buried with weapons, they had battle wounds on their corpses, and at least one young woman was bowlegged—suggesting, at the very least, that she was a horseback rider.

As archaeologists came up with more artifacts which led them to speculate about warrior women, some published articles theorizing that a race of Amazons had lived in Siberia. Most historians and archaeologists who were knowledgeable about the area said the Greek Amazons—real or not—never traveled as far as Siberia. But no one really knew who these people were who buried their dead in Siberia. It was such a vast stretch of land that many different tribes could have come and gone in the blink of time's eye.

Ursula wondered why everyone got so excited by the thought of women being warriors. Of course women had been warriors and hunters and leaders. The good ol' boy network of archaeologists could not see beyond their own cultural biases. The Russian archaeologists Ursula had worked with accepted the idea of women warriors and matriarchal societies as a matter of course.

"We have always been taught about a time when women were in charge," Ivan told her at dinner one night when he visited Cascadia last year. "It is part of our folklore, as common as the bear is in our children's stories. Why do you think we call it the motherland?"

Ursula wished they would unearth a kurgan and find a nobleman wearing an apron and holding a cooking pot in one hand and a needle and thread in the other. Let the stereotypes fly then. What would the headlines be: Men cooked and sewed, horrors!

"Figure out any similarities?" Bob asked as he came into the workroom.

Ursula looked up and smiled at him. "Barrows 2—that's the Rudenko mummy—and Polosmak's mummy have similar art styles to one another. These three are also more similar to each other than they are to Barrows 2 and Polosmak's. See, the artwork is more realistic."

She fanned out the reproductions of the backs of each mummy.

"All of the mummies have these dots along their spine, except Polosmak's. These could be a form of early acupuncture, perhaps."

Bob nodded.

"Now look at Barrows 2," Ursula said. "They studied his bones and discovered he had arthritis near the areas that were tattooed. His tattoos may have been medicinal as well. On the other mummies, no relationship between the tattoos and disease was detected. Of course we don't know about the lady. There are so many reasons people have gotten tattoos throughout history. Slaves were tattooed, men who weren't slaves were tattooed. Children who had epilepsy were tattooed, children were tattooed to prevent disease, to make them strong, to keep them from drowning. People got tattoos to be rebels or to fit in, to be part of the clan. Some people tattooed their life histories on their bodies, a visual record of their memories.

"Apparently Siberians still create tattoos similar to these dots on the spine," she continued, "to relieve back pain, anthropologists say. I'm interested in the acupuncture angle since these mummies were discovered so close to China. Perhaps early on acupuncture employed more permanent methods. Perhaps all of these tattoos are a form of acupuncture, or some sort of health care."

She sat in a chair and pushed away from the table. As she looked up, she still saw afterimages of the tattoos.

"Where have you been all morning?" she asked. "It is afternoon, right? Some day I'll work in a place where they actually have windows."

Bob smiled and sat on the edge of the table. "The girls wanted to go to the zoo. They've been bugging me forever, so we finally relented. I hate zoos. They loved it. I tried explaining to them that we don't have the right to cage other animals."

Ursula smiled. "Uh-huh. And what did they say?"

"'Oh look, Dad, there's an elephant.'"

Ursula laughed.

"I read once that Barry Lopez said that a bear in a zoo is a mammal but no longer a bear," Bob said. "By putting them in a zoo, taking them out of the wild, they lose their bear-ness."

"Maybe that's what's wrong with people," Ursula said. "We've put ourselves in our own zoo—this civilization." She glanced around the bleak rectangular windowless room. "We're still mammals, but we're no longer human." She looked at Bob. "So how do we become human again?"

Bob stood. "The same way the bear becomes a bear again. We go into the wild." He slapped the table. "But who says there's anything wrong with us? I've got to get my laptop out of the lab; I'll be right back. Have you heard anything about the mtDNA results?"

"Not yet," she said.

Bob went through the lab door. Ursula closed her eyes for a moment and wondered if the helicopter had come for the lady yet. Storms and then mechanical problems had delayed it while the lady lay in her hut, melting and decomposing with each passing day. Miriam's e-mails sounded frantic. Fortunately, they had gotten a sample from the body to be used for DNA testing and sent it to Novosibirsk Institute via land. The sample would be too contaminated from oxidization, bacteria, and fungus to get a nuclear DNA reading—the DNA from the egg and sperm—but they would be able to find some mitochondria DNA—the DNA from the mother's egg. Researchers were building a worldwide database of DNA samples and would hopefully find a distant relative of the lady's. Ursula's DNA was in the database, along with Bob's and anyone else at Cascadia who had volunteered.

Ursula opened her eyes and looked down at the tattoos again. Her grandmother came from Siberia. Perhaps she was related to one—or all—of these mummies.

She picked up the sheet of paper with the reproduction of the red rose they had found on the lady's buttock. None of the other mummies had anything like that on their backsides.

Bob came back into the room carrying his laptop. He took a bag of bones off one of the shelves, set his computer on the table, and sat in a chair.

"Did you see this?" Ursula asked, pointing to the rose.

Bob leaned over to look. "That's unusual."

Ursula nodded. "Someday I'm going to get really wild and

have a rose tattooed onto my ass, just like hers."

Ursula continued to stare at the tattoos.

"I think I can see what the difference is," she said. "These two, Barrows 2 and Polosmak, the Scythian-like tattooing. At first these tattoos seem more wild than the ones on the other three. But they're not. Look at these. They're more realistic or something. I can't find the right word. Except what you said about the bear. These tattoos are more wild. It's a wild spider. Wild snakes, deer, swan."

"And look," Bob said, "even though some are mirror images to each other and they have different animals, they are essentially on the same parts of the body. Chest, left leg, left hand, upper right arm." He pointed to one set of reproductions, then to the next. "Chest, right leg, right hand, upper left arm. Chest, right leg, right hand, left arm. There are quite a few similarities between these three."

Ursula put her hand over the bear claw on the lady's chest.

"You wish you were there, don't you?" Bob asked.

"I wish I weren't so afraid," Ursula whispered.

"Of what?" Bob asked.

"Of everything," Ursula said. She moved her hand off the page. "I hope the helicopter comes soon. Miriam says the local folks have cursed them. I was reading Herodotus last night, about the Scythians. The King of Persia heard about these famous Scythian warriors—a few years or decades before our lady's demise. Anyway, he came after them, but he couldn't get them to fight. He sent them messages saying, 'Fight me! Fight me!' The Scythians said that if they found the graves of their ancestors and dug them up, they'd come after them and fight them. They never did battle. But I was thinking about that story. It's like a curse, too, isn't it? Desecrate our graves and you're done for."

"Isn't it a little late in your career to be worrying about grave robbing? You sound like one of the Russians."

"I am a Russian," Ursula said.

Bob smiled. "You forget: I've met your grandmother. Wouldn't she say you are a Siberian?"

"No, if I could convince her to speak of it at all, she would say I am from the Altai, the place of dreams."

11

Miriam scanned the sky. Clear and blue for as far as she could see. Maybe the helicopter would come today. A warm breeze stroked her face and rippled the lake water. The swans bounced up and down as the waves flowed beneath them. She had plenty of work to do—help Ivan inside the tomb, catalog her findings, write a report, send e-mail.

But she could almost hear the lady decomposing. They should have never taken her above ground without a place set up to regulate her temperature. They should have learned from a hundred years worth of mistakes made by archaeologists with mummies. Tutankhamen's bones had practically turned to ashes as soon as they took him from his tomb—thereby releasing the curse which doomed several expedition members to death.

Not that Miriam believed in curses. She did, however, believe in the laws of nature, and they were going to lose the lady and the knowledge they could gain from studying her if they did not get her into a temperature-controlled environment soon.

Miriam was ready to leave, too. She was tired of her own violent nightmares and weary of listening to the morning recitation of everyone else's dreams.

"I was a tiger hunting deer."

"I think I was the deer."

"I chased down a rabbit and killed it."

"Something was clawing me and when I looked down, the claw was attached to my arm."

She glanced at the sky.

Maybe it would come today.

12

Ursula flipped through Rudenko's *Frozen Tombs of Siberia.* The longer she looked at the tattooing of the three mummies, the more she was convinced they were different from the other two mummies—and the tattoos were different from other Altaian artwork found on clothing, bridles, harnesses, and coffins. None of the animals on the three mummies were twisted—none were pretzel animals—and none were obviously predator and prey. Much of the Altaian representation of animals showed the act of predator catching prey: a tiger catching an elk, a lion jumping on a deer, or a griffin descending from the sky to latch onto any of a number of herbivores.

The animals on the three mummies were just there—floating, walking, or flying on the skin, except for the tattoo on the chest. Each one of those—the bear claw, fox, and snow leopard—seemed to be piercing the skin with claw or fang.

"Ursula." James Paddock, the head of the department, leaned his head into the workroom. "I need to see you in my office."

"Sure."

She got up and followed James through the lab—Bob raised his eyebrows and Ursula shrugged—and down the hallway to his office. He sat at his desk, and she sat across from him, facing the window that looked out at the grassy courtyard where students lounged under several ginkgo trees.

She cleared her throat and smiled at him. Why have a window in your office and then put your back to it?

"What's up?" Ursula asked.

"Well, we got back the mtDNA results on the mummy," he said, flipping through some papers on his desk.

"Great. Do they know what family line she came from?" she asked, meaning was she Turkish, Altaian, Chinese, etc.

"The family line she seems to have come from is yours," he said.

"Pardon me?"

"What do you know about mtDNA?" he asked.

"MtDNA is identical from mother to off-spring pretty much forever," Ursula said. "That's about all I know."

"I don't understand it all, but you know you gave blood, as did we all, to be a part of the database to trace where we come from. Each time an ancient sample is tested, the computer program checks to see if anyone already in the database has similar DNA. Of course there were many with similar mtDNA, but yours came up as *exactly* the same."

Ursula blinked. "I'm confused."

"So are they. You see, the mtDNA does mutate over time, but that mutation is constant. For instance, your mtDNA would be identical to that of the mtDNA from a corpse of your 1,200 year old great great great plus grandmother except for one mutation. Someone related to you who was 2,500 years dead, would have at least two mutations. Now the actual mathematical constant is in dispute. Some say a mutation occurs every 800 years."

"OK," Ursula said, wanting him to get back to how she fit into all of this. "You're saying I'm related to the mummy. That's pretty exciting. But what's the problem?"

"There are *no* mutations," Paddock said. "This mtDNA is *identical* to yours. It could be your own mtDNA we are looking at, or your mother's. Even if this mummy were related to you, she has been dead for 2,500 years old. They've double-checked the dating. Your mtDNA should not match hers exactly. There should be at *least* two mutations."

Ursula stared at him.

"Lucky for Ivan," Paddock said, "they filmed everything and two separate labs have now dated samples of the body and clothing."

"You mean they suspect fraud?"

"Well, this mtDNA finding is very odd," he said. "They had to check. Judging from the results of these lab reports, either you're out of time, or this mummy is. Or this could throw mtDNA testing on its ear. Obviously you are here now and the mummy has been dead for 2,500 years. We would like you to give another blood sample, to be certain. Also, any close relatives. Would your mother be willing to come in?"

"My mother died in Siberia thirty years ago."

Paddock stopped and stared at her. He opened his mouth, then shut it again. Finally he said, his voice slightly off key, "I-I'm sorry. Where in Siberia? It's such a big—"

"In the Altai."

"Is she buried there?"

Ursula shook her head.

Paddock sighed with relief.

Then Ursula said, "They never found her body. She disappeared one day."

"Oh."

"I'll get the test."

"Here's the address," he said, handing her a card. "I'm sure there's a logical explanation for all of this."

Ursula nodded, got up, and left Paddock's office. With her heart racing, she hurried down the hallway.

13

The helicopter was first a dot in the distance, then a buzzard lazily riding the thermals, then a silver creature, all glass and steel, come to take the lady away.

Four expedition members carried the lady, who was pinned down to the board again by the gauze that stretched across her body, into the helicopter first. Miriam and Ivan followed. Pasha and the others would travel in land vehicles after they finished up work for the summer at the kurgan.

Miriam sighed, then grinned at Ivan as the helicopter took off. The plateau rolled away under them, suddenly colorless and flat from the air. She sat back and readied herself for the long trip to Novosibirsk. As they neared the mountains, Miriam glanced at the lady. She felt an urge to reach out and reassure her. After all, this was her first flight—her first time, in all likelihood, away from the Altai.

The helicopter hiccoughed. Miriam looked at Ivan.

"Just mountain air," he said.

The mountains surrounded them. An intense rocky whiteness.

They seemed bigger than anything Miriam had ever seen, more massive than was possible. The helicopter was never going to make it out. It was a foolish venture. They were so tiny. The mountains too big.

Ursula was right to be afraid to fly; she had been the smart one.

Ivan put his hand over Miriam's.

"It is only the spirits of the mountains trying to get you to stay," he said. "It will pass."

She nodded quickly.

Ivan murmured something in Russian, and Miriam thought for certain her atheist friend was praying.

Then suddenly, as if a wall had been lifted—or a door opened— they were out of the mountains.

Miriam patted Ivan's hand and smiled. She leaned back in her seat and breathed deeply. Her heart slowed, and eventually she fell to sleep.

Something lurched. Exploded.

Miriam opened her eyes.

"Please fasten the seat belts," someone from the cockpit said. "Some problems."

Miriam looked out the window. They were a long way up.

The helicopter began to glide to the Earth, back and forth, like a leaf falling from a tree on a windless day. It was going to be all right, Miriam thought. She reached out and touched the lady.

"We're almost on the ground," she said.

The rotor blades slowed.

"Shit," Ivan said in English.

It was the last thing Miriam remembered.

14

Ursula found her grandmother sitting in the semi-darkness of Ursula's old bedroom.

"Grandma?" Ursula walked inside the room and sat on the edge of her bed. Her grandmother was a shadow in the corner. How many nights had she awakened and seen her grandmother sitting just as she was now? As if she were some kind of guardian. Ursula had always felt protected by her grandmother—and slightly stifled by her.

"Grandma?" Ursula asked again.

"Yes, *duscha*."

"I need to talk to you," Ursula said.

Asya sighed and switched on the light next to her.

"What happened to your arm?" Asya asked, looking at the bandage across the crook of her arm.

"Nothing," Ursula said. "I had some blood drawn. They want you to get a blood test, too."

"Why? What's wrong?"

"Nothing. It's for DNA testing, Grandma. I know you don't

like talking about this, but I have to know: What happened to Mom?"

"Why must we always come back to this?"

"Always? We have never talked about it because you never would. Today my boss told me they did some tests on that mummy they found in the Altai. He said she could be my mother; of course, he didn't mean that literally. I mean, the mummy is 2,500 years dead. I know intellectually it can't be her, but I also realize I know nothing about the circumstances of her death."

Asya nodded. "I guess it is time. I have kept too much from you, because of my own fears. There is much I don't understand myself. You know she became interested in cave art when she was a child and I took her to Horsethief Park along the Columbia. That was before they closed the rock drawings to the public. We'd take a picnic basket and I'd sit watching swallows dive off the cliffs and listen to meadow larks, while your mother wandered around talking to the pictures painted on the rock faces." Asya smiled. "We were happy. Later she went to college and stayed in this area since there was a lot of rock art around. Then she went on a trip to Siberia to study cave art there. I was deeply opposed to her going to Siberia, but she went. When she came home, she was pregnant."

"What do you mean? I thought she died in Siberia after I was born."

"Just wait, Ursula. There are many lies to undo. She came back pregnant. She wouldn't tell me who the father was—that much I told you was true. You were born. Your mother continued her work here and all was well for several years. Then she had an opportunity to go on another expedition to the Altai. She had really loved it there—loved the caves. She was going to be gone for the summer at least and wanted to take you. In the end, I convinced her to leave you with me. Reluctantly, she left you behind."

Ursula stared at her grandmother.

"You should have told me she wanted me with her."

Asya looked at her hands. "I never said she didn't."

"Grandma, the implication was always there!"

"She disappeared after she'd been in Siberia two months. They looked for her but she was just gone. The winter storms started after a few more weeks and the expedition had to come home."

"Why all the secrecy?"

Asya cleared her throat. "Where I grew up, it was very rural. We were backward, with lots of superstitions. When you are raised this way, it is sometimes hard to separate truth from superstition. I grew up around the caves your mother studied, or caves like them. We didn't tell outsiders about them. They were mostly for the kams—the shamans—though some believed long ago that even the common people passed through them. The caves scared most of us children. We had heard about Ilya who went into one cave and came out another, twenty years later, without aging at all. Or unfamiliar people would appear in a cave. Or disappear. The kams went to the caves and painted their pictures. It was their way of connecting with the spirits on the other side of the rock. But these were just stories we heard. Like the stories of the People."

"The People?"

"They were sometimes called the Old Ones, or the First Ones. We were taught never to kill them. They looked like us, only more so. Or they looked like the creatures of the wild. You could see their true nature, their wild nature, when they did three things: when they ate, made love, and died. Otherwise, they would seem like us, or like animals you see in the woods." Asya sighed. "These were fairy tales. Or like ghost stories. I didn't really believe them, I suppose. Then one day when I was a teenager, I followed my father and brother when they went out to hunt bear. They found one in a cave—one of the timeless caves—the caves with the drawings, the caves where the kams prayed and the People supposedly lived. The sun did something to me that day I believed. The bear came out of the cave, and as they killed him, I saw he was a man. I held him as he died, and he told me things I still can't remember. Maybe some day.

"I was shaken and sick by what I had seen. I ran. I saw a woman and followed her—and something happened. It was all like a dream. I became totally . . . wild or . . . human. Something. I went into a cave and made love. It was—" She looked at her grand-daughter. "It was beautiful. And I became frightened. Sometimes when we have been locked up forever, freedom is terrifying. The bars were gone and I was afraid. Later when I opened my eyes, stick animals danced on the walls of the cave. I went home and gave birth to your mother nine months later. I called her Ursula, the she-bear."

Grandmother and granddaughter stared at one another.

"I couldn't believe what had happened. It wasn't possible. The villagers called me bear-wife. I had to leave for your mother's sake. I worked in Moscow for a while. Then some relatives in the U.S. sponsored me to come over here."

Ursula did not know what to say.

"When your mother disappeared, I didn't know what had happened. I waited for her to come back for you. But she didn't."

"Why did you hide this from me all these years?" Ursula asked. "If it's all only superstition and stories, why be afraid?"

"I told you," Asya said quietly. "I don't know which parts are story and which parts are true. Here in America none of it seems possible. But this body they found, you say it could be your mother?"

"I don't see how," Ursula said. "The mummy's been dead for a couple of millennia at least. Maybe they got the dating wrong. I don't know. Something is strange. It even rattled my boss a little when I told him my mother died in the Altai."

"Maybe she didn't die," Asya said. "Maybe she went into a

timeless cave—"

"And what? Died 2,500 years earlier? I'm a scientist. Some things are possible. Some things aren't. Will you give them a blood sample?"

Asya shook her head.

"Why?" Ursula asked.

"What if they discover I am one of the People, or you are?"

"So?"

"My father told me stories, old stories, of a time when the People were slaughtered."

"Why? You said they were human, only more so."

Asya shook her head. "No. You don't understand, they were wild, and people always try to kill wild things. If you are one of the People, no one must ever know."

Ursula laughed. "Grandma." She had never seen her grandmother anything other than practical and rational. She was the most non-intuitive person Ursula had ever met. Now she was reciting fairy tales as though they were fact.

"I will tell you this," Asya said, "and then I will speak of it no more because I can see you don't believe me. But I will tell you, I was wrong—in the cave that day. I shouldn't have been afraid. I should have stayed. If someday you can find the wild in you, run with it, *duscha*, not away from it."

15

Miriam opened her eyes and saw white; fat clumps of snow were falling, melting on her face. This meant two things: one, she was outdoors; two, she must be looking up. Where was she? Outside her Michigan home tying up her skates and calling to her sister to hurry up, hurry up, before the snow melted?

She blinked and her eyelashes wiped snowflakes from her vision.

"I'm in Siberia," Miriam said out loud. She slowly sat up, then looked down; her hands bent grass and wildflowers. Sun shined. Yet it snowed.

"Ivan!" Miriam called.

Was this like the poppy field in the Wizard of Oz? Had some witch sent snow to awaken them?

Miriam wiped her eyes again. The helicopter lay sprawled on the ground, probably thirty yards away, its blades bent down, making it look like a droopy-eared metal rabbit. The big door to the helicopter was open, and Ivan and the engineer carried out the pilot. They must have gotten her out first. She looked around until she saw the gauze-covered lady on her stretcher only a few feet from Miriam. Apparently Ivan had his priorities straight.

Miriam tried to push herself up. Pain exploded in her leg. She cried out, then became very still. She was not going to do that again.

"We found a cave not far from here," Ivan called as they went by her carrying the pilot. "We'll be back."

Miriam nodded. The snow was falling fast now. She could not see much beyond the helicopter. The snowstorm slowly doused the sunlight. Who was that by the helicopter watching her? There was that sound. Snuffling. A bear?

"Shhh," she whispered and closed her eyes.

When she opened them again, Ivan was holding a syringe. "We've got to set your leg. I'm afraid you might be going into shock. The radio doesn't work. We're going to have to go for help."

The engineer reached for her leg. Ivan pierced her skin with the needle. Was he giving her a tattoo? Like the lady? Would it be a spider or a bear? A deer or a swan?

Then the men did something to her leg. They called pain into it—placed it there on purpose and then an angel came and took it away. An angel? Or the lady? Miriam tried to open her eyes. To think. Clearly. Precisely.

She dreamed she was skating on thin blue ice. Below her feet, a part of the ice, was the lady, her index finger motioning Miriam to come closer. Down. Down. The ice cracked and splintered.

Miriam opened her eyes and slowly sat up. She was in semi-darkness. An oil lantern flickered next to her. She stared at the light for several moments. The crash had broken her leg but not a glass lamp? Life was too odd. The pilot lay close to her. His eyes were closed, but his breathing seemed deep and regular. She looked down at her leg. It was wrapped in a splint and throbbed in rhythm with her heartbeat. A back pack was within arm's reach.

She wondered where the lady was. Maybe Ivan thought it best to keep her out in the cold. Miriam reached for the lantern and dragged it across the floor toward her. As she turned up the flame, golden light filled the cave—and touched two empty beer bottles. Miriam felt relief. Recent human garbage meant recent humans couldn't be that far off. She got water from the pack, took several gulps, and looked around the cave. As her eyes grew accustomed to the light, she saw paintings on the rock wall. One by one, the drawings appeared out of the darkness. First a ram, then a fish, several deer. A fox. Snow leopard. Raven. And a bear off by itself. She could see that they were only outlines of the various creatures yet they were so realistic—as if the mere suggestion of them, the shadow of their existence, made them more tangible. She could hear the flutter of the raven's wings. Feel the rush of wind as the swan flew by. Smell the musk of the bear. She closed her eyes.

She felt dizzy. The throbbing in her leg moved to her head.

"Help me," she whispered.

She opened her eyes and saw a straight line running from one rock animal to the next. The lines seemed strangely familiar. She blinked and the lines were gone. Now the animals seemed familiar. She looked down at her hand and saw a spider tattooed into her fingers. The spider moved, and she shook it off. She looked at the paintings again. That was it. They looked like the tattoos on the lady.

She closed her eyes again.

Someone lifted her and cradled her in his arms. She opened her eyes and saw a tiny patch of gold shimmering through his fur, just like in the fairy tale.

"So you are a man?"

"Shhh," he growled as he reached down and took the pain from her leg.

16

Ursula dropped her pack by the door and walked into the living room.

"Peter?" she called.

No answer.

On this night, their tiny house seemed emptier than usual.

She sat on the couch and leaned her head back. She was glad Peter wasn't home. She was tired of fighting—tired of being angry. When he had begged her for another chance—well, perhaps begged was the wrong word—when he asked her for another chance and she consented, she thought things would get back to normal, and they had for a while, except sexually. She couldn't get over the idea that his penis had been inside someone else, and because of that, she did not want it inside of her.

It was that simple—and that complicated. She tried not to feel anger when she was with him, tried to recapture that bedazzlement she had first felt when they met. He had seemed so unconventional and smart. Unconventional because he talked easily about sex the way other people talked about food and the weather—smart because he knew so much about so many things. Now he seemed like a know-it-all who didn't. His sexual behavior was no longer erotic, merely juvenile.

But like her grandmother said, Ursula had picked him. It was her bed, now she had to lie in it. Or was that lay in it? Or was it her bed, now she had to make it? She had never been very good with clichés. Actually, maybe tonight, she could try making love with Peter, pretend he was someone else. Currently, she couldn't think of anyone she was sexually attracted to, except possibly Bob, but that was only because he was a nice man and that particular characteristic was arousing to her. Even if Bob would be willing—and she was certain he was not—she would not do that to Bob's wife. Or to anyone else's wife.

She sighed, got up, and went into the kitchen. She reached for the phone to call Peter, but the phone was not there.

She glanced around the room. The knife holder and knives were gone, too. Adrenalin shot through her. She hurried into the living room and switched on the light. The television and VCR were gone, but the stereo remained. The crystal vase Peter's mother had given them as a wedding present was missing from the coffee table. All around the room were little dust-free islands showing her where their possessions had been.

Using the living room phone, Ursula called the police. Then she tried Peter's office and his cell phone. No answer at either place.

Suddenly she realized the burglar could still be in the house.

She glanced at the phone. Should she call her insurance agent first and then run for her life?

She walked to the front door, glanced up the stairs, then went out to stand on the porch.

A few minutes later, the police arrived. She led them inside the house.

"I only looked in the living room and kitchen," she said. "I thought the robbers might still be here."

"I'll check upstairs," the woman said.

The man looked around the living room. "Any sign of forced entry?" he asked.

"I didn't check. I saw all these things missing, and I called you. They must have been fussy burglars. They took the television and not the stereo."

The man nodded. Ursula heard the woman on the stairs.

"Anything besides the TV missing?" the man asked.

"VCR, phone, vase, um—"

The woman came into the room holding a sheet of paper.

"I think this is for you," she said.

Ursula took the paper from the woman. "It was taped to the bedroom mirror," she said.

Ursula looked at it. Peter's handwriting. "I've taken some of my stuff. I'll be back for the rest when you aren't home. In case you don't get it: I'm leaving you. Peter."

Ursula stared at the paper.

She wanted to scream.

He was such a coward.

And a thief. They had bought the television and VCR after they were married.

She looked up at the police officers. They watched her without expression.

"I'm sorry," she finally said. "I guess I've made a mistake. I'm really sorry."

"It's all right," the man said.

"These things happen," the woman said.

Ursula started to say, "I could kill him for embarrassing me this way," but on the off chance she actually did kill him, she didn't want to offer the police any clues.

After she saw the police car drive away, she screamed.

"He wants his things, I'll give him his things." She would

throw everything that was his into the street. And get the locks changed tomorrow.

"You were always a spear carrier in my life anyway!" she shouted. "You almost got lucky tonight, Peter! Now I guess I'm the one who got lucky."

Ursula dropped onto the couch. "How's that for emotion!" she shouted, remembering his remark about her having the emotions of a tight-assed accountant. "Huh!" Speaking of accountants, she wondered if he had cleaned out their joint savings account. "If you did that, I will kill you!"

The phone rang.

"You know, Peter!" she shouted to the empty house. "This is the best conversation we've had in years!"

The phone rang again.

She picked it up. "What?"

"Ursula?" Bob.

"Yes, it's me. What's up?"

"There's been an accident," Bob said. "The helicopter carrying Miriam, Ivan, and the mummy crashed in the foothills of the Altai."

"Oh my god. What's—how's everyone?"

"They're in the hospital," Bob said. "I guess it took nearly a day for them to find help and then another day to get the help to the injured. Miriam's got a broken leg. I guess the pilot's in bad shape. Our tattooed lady seems to have fared OK."

"What can I do?" Ursula asked.

"Nothing right now, but I knew you'd want to know. Paddock wants to see you first thing tomorrow."

"Do you know why?"

"I think he wants you to go to Russia."

Ursula glanced around the room. She had never liked this house much anyway.

"I might be ready to go," Ursula said.

17

Asya sat on her porch and watched night descend. This had never been her favorite time of day. It made her anxious, as if suddenly the door between worlds opened and anything could slip through. Yet lately, she had started to look forward to dusk. Shadows flowed into corners, around trees, and behind corn stalks. Shadows which seemed to shapechange into something else every time she turned away. It all happened on the periphery of her vision—it had always been there at the edges of her life waiting for her to look full upon it.

She was almost ready to look, almost ready to remember what the bearman had told her so many years ago.

She was certain now—more certain than she had ever been and less afraid—that the People were all around.

Soon.

18

Kam stood outside the Novosibirsk Institute. It was a massive dirty-gray stone building—institutional-looking and ugly, as most of the structures were that had been put up during the Soviet era. Even now, at the most beautiful—the most florally creative—time of the year, this city appeared stark and barren. The city was not exactly dead, but it was in a kind of coma. Or a chronic depression. How could people have built places like this on purpose?

A raven called out to her as he flew overhead. Kam reached a hand up and called back to him.

She looked at the Institute. She hoped Ursula would come soon. She did not know how long she could stay in such a place and still remember herself.

"Come soon, little one," Kam whispered. "Soon."

19

Ursula stood in the workroom looking around. She breathed in the smell of dirt and smiled. She was going to miss this place; it was a hell hole but it was her little hell hole.

Bob followed her gaze. "You're coming back," he said.

"If I wasn't afraid of going before, I am now," she said. "Do you know how many shots I had to get? And the travel agent—she told me on no account should I travel Aeroflot. So I'm taking an American carrier all the way to Moscow. Then she says, 'Oops, you have to either take Aeroflot from Moscow to Novosibirsk and risk dying in a plane crash or take a forty-five hour train trip and risk being suffocated by the crush of people or catching a communicable disease or dying of boredom.' Geez."

"So what'd you pick? Train or plane?"

"I decided to crash and burn," Ursula said. "The travel agent told me the Aeroflot planes have machine guns in the cockpits, along with bottles of champagne. Now if she'd said vodka, I would have believed her, but champagne? Come on! Russians can't afford champagne. It'll be all right." She smiled. "I'll only be on a plane for twenty terrifying hours. In addition to all of the shots Dr. Frankenstein gave me, he also slipped me a few Valium. Drugs will get me through."

Bob laughed. "Have you already taken one?"

"No. Why?"

"Because you aren't usually quite this gregarious."

"That's because you never gave me a chance," Ursula said.

"Why are you doing this?"

"Because."

"As long as you have a good reason."

"Miriam's coming home. Someone needs to finish the work she's started. I'll get to look at the tattoos firsthand. Maybe I'll figure out what they mean. Peter's left me. Grandma isn't freaking out like I thought she would."

"I heard they got the results of the second mtDNA results. They're identical to the first results."

"Uh-huh." Ursula picked up her laptop.

"The lady *can't* be your mother."

"I know," Ursula said. "Give me a hug."

They embraced.

"Keep in touch," Bob said when they let each other go.

"I will. If e-mail fails, I'll figure out another way. Maybe smoke signals."

Ursula waved, left the workroom, and walked out of the building. She glanced back once and wondered why she felt like she was seeing everything for the last time.

When Ursula got up early the next morning, her grandmother was making breakfast: pancakes, eggs, bread, potatoes.

"Gee, Grandma, you got enough starch here?"

"You aren't hungry?"

"I'm afraid I'll throw it up." She sat at the table.

"Try to eat. You need your strength."

"I'm going on a plane ride, Grandma. I won't be doing anything more strenuous than vomiting."

Asya sighed. Ursula ate her eggs and potatoes.

"So what about the house?" Asya asked.

"We're selling it," Ursula said, "and splitting what's left. My lawyer will take care of it. Thanks for letting me store my stuff in the garage."

"You can live here as long as you like," Asya said.

Ursula kissed her grandmother's cheek. "You've always been so good to me."

"You got eggs on my face," Asya said, wiping her cheek.

Ursula laughed.

"I put in your briefcase the names of the places where your mother visited."

"Thanks. It's probably futile after all these years, but I would like to try and find out what happened to her. Don't look so scared, Grandma. I'll be back. I'm kind of excited. I'm going home."

"I hope you know I have tried my best. I always loved you, both of you. I don't think your mother ever knew. But I hope I was a better mother with you." She smiled. "You look so much like her."

"I'm coming back."

"I won't hold you here," Asya said. "Go where life takes you."

"I'm not sure I'm ready for where life wants to take me."

20

Ivan stood a little away from the lady and listened to his colleague Nikolai talk about her. They were trying to determine the age of the woman at the time of her death and her race. Because her bones were still in her body—she was a mummy—it was a little more problematic.

"Her face is elongated," Nikolai said. "Her nasal opening and the distance between her eyes are narrow. These characteristics could mean she is Caucasoid. Yet her cheekbones are wide. I believe she is either mixed-raced or Caucasoid. She looks Indo-European."

Ivan nodded.

"Now, about the age. At the center of the chest, the clavicle is fused into one bone. So she is at least twenty-eight. And the sagittal suture—" Nikolai put his hand just above the top of the lady's head and ran it down from front to back. "—it's fused. The coronal suture—" He put his hands at the front of the skull and drew his fingers across the air in front of her forehead, from temple to temple. "—appears to be fused, too. So I say at least 45. She may be a lot older. I could take a bone wafer if you like."

Ivan shook his head. "Not yet." Reading bone wafer results was similar to reading age rings on a tree, but he was not ready to destroy any bone yet.

Nikolai nodded. "We really need better storage facilities for her."

"I know," Ivan said.

Ivan left the room and stood outside the door. He could hardly bear being close to the lady. It was too difficult watching her deteriorate. Her beautiful olive skin was turning darker every day, her tattoos fading. He was trying to get Moscow to do something to help. He was even getting desperate enough to let them take her and give her a chemical bath that would completely halt the decomposition and preserve her permanently as she was now. The preservation process would hinder other testing, but at least she would be saved. He did not have the money to pay for her flight to Moscow. Aeroflot would not take her, so he needed money up front for someone else to fly her. Now they put her in a refrigeration unit that had once held cheese.

No wonder the Native Altaians were unhappy with him. Poor Miriam. She would recover, of course, as would the pilot, but Miriam's summer work was over. He hoped Ursula would be helpful to them. He had met her last year when he visited Cascadia University. She had spoken flawless Russian and had picked out the place where they eventually dug up the lady.

He started walking down the hall to his office. He had instructed Vladimir to begin a facial reconstruction of the lady in the hopes that the final product would entice someone to donate money.

21

Vladimir stared at the skull on his workbench. The lady had undergone a CT scan, and the computer came up with the dimensions for the skull. He did not have the time or money to wait for a styrene foam replica of the skull to be created by a computer-controlled milling machine in England or America, so he made his own latex mold and poured a plaster cast. Next to the plaster skull were round rubber pegs of varying lengths, glue, and chunks of modeling clay.

"All right, lady," Vladimir said. "Speak to me."

He began gluing the pegs to the skull. Each one represented the thickness of the soft tissue. He had determined these thicknesses ahead of time, using the approximation of age, race and the fact that she was female as determining factors. The pegs around her cheekbones and jaws were longer than the ones on her forehead.

He then began chopping up the modeling clay. He hummed to himself as he worked. Like everyone else who had encountered the lady, he was determined to do right by her. He used strips of finger-thin clay to connect the pegs. He started with her forehead, then connected the forehead to the nose, nose to the cheekbones, cheekbones to the chin and mouth.

He stared at the clay road map for a moment. The face was beginning to take shape in his mind now. His memory of the desiccated mummy was beginning to be replaced by a vision of a living woman.

He began filling in the spaces between the clay with more clay. Gradually, a face covered the skull. Vladimir's fingers pushed and stroked the clay, bringing the lady to life. This was quick and dirty facial reconstruction, but in the end, she would look startlingly real. Later, if they had the money, he could make another reconstruction with the exact muscles put in the exact places. Now he set two brown eyes into her sockets and shaped eyelids around them.

He measured the nose, then began sculpting it. Next he shaped her lips. Then her ears.

He held her in his hands and looked at her.

Then he slowed his process and began shaping the clay in more subtle ways, making her more lifelike.

Sometime later, he patted her face with a damp sponge. Then he put a black wig on her head.

He set her on the table and looked at her again.

"Hello, lady," he said. "Welcome to our world."

22

In Chicago, Ursula ran off the airplane, dizzy with anxiety, and headed for a bank of telephones. She could not get back on that plane. She would just call someone to pick her up.

She first called Bob. She got his voice mail. Of course: It was Saturday. He was out with his family. Then Asya. The phone rang and rang. "Come on Grandma." No answer. She hung up the phone and stared at it. She was not going to call Peter. Besides what could any of them do? She was in Chicago.

She turned away from the phones. She felt like she was going to fall down.

"Can I help you, *duscha?*" a man behind her asked in Russian.

She turned around. A stocky muscular man with a red beard and a full head of curly black and gray hair stood near her, smiling. He was dressed in a dark suit, with a vest and red shirt. He looked like a stereotypical rumpled professor, only he was not rumpled, and his blue eyes were the color her grandmother had described of mid-winter ice in Siberia.

"I'm afraid to fly," she answered in Russian.

"Then you have never been a bird," he said, smiling. He put his hand lightly on the middle of her back.

"Neither has an airplane," Ursula said.

"Ahh, but they do dream of it," he said.

"Even as they are crashing down?"

He laughed. "Especially then. May I buy you a cup of coffee?" Now he spoke English, without an accent. "I am Sergei Ivanovich Polyakov."

"I'm Ursula Smith."

"Smith?"

"It was Kuznetsov. My grandmother changed her name when she came to the United States—so she could fit in. Anyway, I don't drink coffee."

Sergei's hand pressed ever-so gently against her back, and she felt steadier.

"Come with me anyway," he said.

She looked at him, and the terminal came into focus. She felt herself coming off the ceiling and fitting back into her toes.

"Are you Russian?" she asked.

He nodded. "My plane leaves in a little less than an hour—going back home." His smile and manner were so pleasant. He was like a big teddy bear. "We may be on the same flight," he said.

They slowly walked to a busy cafeteria. He bought espresso. She got iced tea. They sat near a window that looked out at airplanes and the hot summer day. A white flag attached to one of the buildings snapped soundlessly in the wind.

"You are traveling alone?" he asked.

She glanced at him. Ordinarily, she did not talk to strangers. She wondered briefly if he was a slave trader or a kidnapper.

"Yes, I'm alone. My husband left me. I'm going to Novosibirsk to help work on the mummy they just found in the Altai. The one with tattoos. The woman who was there got into a helicopter crash, and they found out the mummy has my DNA—at least part of it—and my mother disappeared there thirty years ago. Multiply that by about 80, and that's how long ago the mummy died. And now she's rotting away because the institute can't come up with the $3,000 or whatever that is in rubles to take care of her. And—excuse me."

She got up, ran out of the restaurant, went straight into the restroom, and threw up.

When she returned, she apologized. Sweat beaded on her forehead.

"Did you take anything?" Sergei asked.

She nodded. "I keep throwing it up."

"I have been following the story of this woman, the tattooed lady," Sergei said.

"Really?" Ursula said. "I'm studying her tattoos. Trying to figure out what they mean."

He nodded. "I am a scientist, too, of sorts."

"Oh?"

"I'm a doctor," he said. "Have you thought maybe the embroidery is medicinal."

"Embroidery? Oh yes, I've heard it called that."

"For instance," he said, taking her hand in his. He gently moved her sleeve up off her forearm, his fingers lightly touching her skin. If she had been standing, she would have fallen over.

Using two fingers an inch a part, the first an inch from the inside of her wrist, he pressed her skin.

"If you lived long ago and your nausea was persistent," he said, "perhaps they would tattoo these points on your arms." He gazed into her eyes as he talked. She felt mesmerized—and her stomach began calming down. After a minute or so, he pressed the same points on her other arm.

She breathed deeply while he touched her. When he stopped, he gently pulled her sleeves down again. She sighed. She bet he rarely went to bed alone.

"Now, tell me more about your expedition," he said.

She talked until they heard their flight number called. Then they walked to the gate together. She began to panic again as they started down the walkway to the plane.

"It will be all right, Ur-soo-la," Sergei said. "You can always find me, if you need to."

She stepped onto the plane. The flight attendant sent her one way and Sergei the other.

Somewhere over some huge body of water, Ursula began throwing up again and could not stop. She asked for Sergei. A flight attendant took her to first class and allowed her to stay when Sergei said he was a doctor and Ursula needed medical care.

Sergei gave Ursula something—a pill?—and she gratefully fell to sleep.

23

Ivan held open the door for Miriam. Supported by crutches, she came inside. On one end of the table was the facial reconstruction of the mummy, her face turned away from Miriam.

Miriam smiled. "You have always had a flare for the theatrical, Ivanka."

He walked to the end of the table.

"Are you prepared?" he asked.

Miriam laughed. "Get on with it."

He slowly turned the head around until it was facing Miriam. She stared at it.

"Is this some kind of joke?" she finally asked.

Ivan frowned and walked around to stand next to her.

"What? You don't like her?"

"Don't you recognize her?" Miriam asked.

"She does look familiar, but we've been working with her for so long—"

"Do you have a brown wig? With shorter hair?"

Ivan opened a nearby cupboard, took the top off a box, and

pulled out another wig.

"Put it on her," Miriam said.

Ivan gently pulled off the black wig and replaced it with the brown curly one.

Then he stepped back again.

"Now do you see?"

Ivan squinted.

"It's Ursula," Miriam said. "She looks just like Ursula."

24

Ursula would have kissed the ground when they landed in Moscow had she been fully cognizant of her surroundings. Instead, she leaned against Sergei as they walked down the steps to the tarmac. She blinked at the sun and blue sky and thought it did not seem much different from her own sun and sky back home. The air tasted slightly of car fumes. Or was it airplane fuel?

As they walked into the airport to get the luggage, Ursula looked up at Sergei.

"I am usually in complete control," she said. "I'm sorry you're seeing me this way."

"Why don't you stay at my house?" Sergei suggested. "I can have my people take care of your UVIR registration—and all of the other paperwork. I have some influence, and I can makes things go more smoothly."

"Why are you being so nice to me?" she asked. "All I've done since you've met me is cry and throw up."

"It is for selfish reasons," he said. "I'm interested in your work. At what hotel are you registered?"

Ursula pulled her itinerary out of her purse. "The Minsk?"

"Uh! Please, you are one of us, come home with me."

"One of us?"

"Don't you remember? I grew up in Siberia. To us, hospitality is everything."

Ursula nodded. "So my grandmother has said."

"Then it's agreed."

They picked up their luggage, then got in line for customs. The wait seemed interminable until Sergei caught the eye of one of the young custom agents. He escorted them off to the side and gave their luggage cursory examination. At first he seemed distressed by Ursula's laptop, but she groggily assured him that it was for business purposes—and not for blowing anything up. Fortunately, she said the last little bit in English.

Sergei led Ursula by the elbow outside to a waiting black sedan. The driver opened the back door for them and said, "Good day," to Sergei.

Ursula slid across the black leather seats. "How very capitalistic of you, Sergei. I thought you were a doctor."

"I've dabbled in business ventures."

"I guess."

The squat-looking limousine lurched forward.

Ursula closed her eyes and fell to sleep again.

When she awakened, they were stopped in front of a large white stone house, rectangular and plain-looking, except for its size. Vines crawled up the walls and deciduous trees surrounded it.

Sergei helped Ursula out of the car. He took her arm, and they walked up the steps. He opened a huge wooden door, and Ursula heard a crow call out in Russian, "Caw, caw," as she stepped into the foyer.

Sergei shut the door, and Ursula gasped. It was as if she had stepped into a museum—or a church—some place grand and awesome. Beneath her feet was a circle mosaic: blue stones created water, green stones the grass around a lake, gray and blue stones a heron on shore, white stones the two swans at the center of the mosaic, black stones their beautiful eyes looking out at the world. Next to the door was a round stained-glass window, turning sunlight into a rainbow of colors that bled onto the lake mosaic.

Ursula followed Sergei down a wide hallway into a large room with a huge fireplace, now cold and covered with golden filigree, the twisted metal shaped into two rams, head to head. Above, in the dome-shaped ceiling, was more art—this time less Byzantine, more Michelangelo, only God was not giving life to Adam. Instead, scenes of the steppes and mountains moved above them. Wild goats grazed the foothills; a pair of black and white Japanese cranes danced their ecstatic courtship rites in the snow; iridescent blue-green swallowtail butterflies flew above an evergreen forest, like a field of wildflowers suddenly airborne. At the center of it all, a huge dark cinammon-colored bear stood watching.

"Here is the phone so you can call your friend at the institute," Sergei said.

Ursula looked away from the bear and into Sergei's blue eyes. He smiled. "Dial 8, wait for the tone, then dial the city code and phone number. I'll give you some privacy."

Ursula dug Miriam's number out of her purse as Sergei left. Then she dialed the number. Miriam was not there, so she called the institute and spoke with Ivan. She gave him Sergei's name, number, and address. When she hung up, Sergei came back into the room.

"Everything feel safe now?" Sergei asked.

Ursula smiled. "I feel quite askew."

"Some rest and then dinner."

Ursula put her hand on Sergei's elbow and followed him down a mosaic hall to a white marble staircase that flowed down to them, like the overlapping layers of a tiered cake. Stained-glass windows positioned every few feet let in colored light.

Sergei led her up the stairs to a small dark room that contained her luggage, a bed, dresser, and armoire. As soon as she closed the door, Ursula peeled off her clothes, fell onto the canopied bed, and went to sleep.

When she awakened, it was dark outside. She yawned and sat up. She felt almost human again. Someone had turned on a small Tiffany-like lamp on the dresser. Next to the lamp was a basin of warm water and a wash cloth. She splashed her body, dried off, and put on clean clothes.

She opened the door and went into the open hallway. She stood at the railing and looked down at the mosaic floor below. From up here she could see some of the designs more clearly. Directly below her was a snow leopard. She started down the stairs. At the foot of the stairs was a fox. She stepped onto the fox and kept walking. Next, the mosaic circled, then became a snake. Her shoes clicked on the stones. A deer. A birch tree glen. She turned right: a lion. She stopped. To the left of the lion a school of fish. She went straight again. Wild sheep stared up at her. She turned left and looked up. She had found the dining room. Sergei, dressed in purple and gold, stood at the head of a long table. The candlelight touched the crystal goblets with starlight. Sergei smiled. Ursula suddenly felt like she was in a fairy tale.

She looked down at her feet. A spider wove her web. She walked toward Sergei, then stopped in the center of the room and looked down. Pressed into the floor in a circle were blue-green stones. At the center of the circle was a black bear's paw, with one of its claws seeming to pierce whatever lay below it—drawing a single drop of blood set in red stone.

Suddenly she knew why the mosaics had seemed so familiar. They were the same as the tattoos of the three mummies. Only that was impossible. These mosaics were not new, and they had found the lady only a few weeks ago.

Ursula walked over to Sergei. He pulled out a chair for her.

She looked down as the chair legs scraped the stones. Beneath her seat was the bud of a tiny red rose.

She slowly looked up at Sergei.

"Who are you?" she asked.

"Who do you think I am?"

25

Ivan, Miriam, and Nikolai sat in a small stuffy room. The frosted glass windows were open but no air moved in or out.

"This we know," Ivan said, speaking English for Miriam's benefit. "The lady is 5'7", quite tall for that time and particular part of Siberia. Preliminary tests tell us she is probably over 45 but less than 80."

"We'll have a more definitive approximation soon," Nikolai said.

Miriam smiled. "Definitive approximation." Words for an archaeologist to live by.

"She was alive 2,500 years ago, give or take 50 years," Ivan continued. "Judging from the conical headdress and her elaborate burial, she was a VIP, as you say, a shaman, priestess, storyteller. She could have been a Scythian, or a member of any number of tribes in that area."

"Those headdresses are similar to ones brides still wear in Kazakhstan," Miriam said.

"She seems too old to be a bride," Nikolai said.

Miriam rolled her eyes.

"Very preliminary DNA testing matched her to a living human who has identical mtDNA," Ivan said, "so we aren't sure what that means. Quite a coincidence that we should know her, eh? Do you know it was Ursula who actually picked out the site?"

Miriam frowned.

"When I was in Portland," Ivan said, "and we sat looking at the maps. She pointed out that area on the Ukok plateau. I said I thought it had been dug out. She said she felt it in her bones that it would be good. We laughed when she said that."

"I don't remember any of this."

"Ah yes, I see. We were speaking in Russian!"

"Those are incredible coincidences," Miriam said. But what could they be except coincidences?

"To continue," Nikolai said, "the hole in her skull was post-mortem to accommodate the removal of the brain. We cannot tell if she had children or not. The womb was also removed in the mummification process."

"Using a variety of human and animal hair samples for comparisons," Ivan said, "we have determined that the peculiar tuft of hair on her left hand is coarse human hair."

"You seem disappointed," Miriam teased.

Ivan smiled. "Only puzzled."

"Perhaps she had a mild form of hypertrichosis," Miriam said. Nikolai and Ivan stared at her.

"It's a rare congenital condition that causes a thick coating of hair to grow all over the body."

"Yes, I am recalling it," Ivan said. "In the past, some people were mistaken for werewolves because of this condition."

Miriam nodded. She rubbed her throbbing leg.

"I have not heard of a mild case," Ivan said.

"Just a thought," Miriam said.

"We have some good news," Ivan said. "Someone has donated

funds for the lady. She will soon be on her way to Moscow to be preserved for eternity!"

"Who was the donor?" Nikolai asked.

Ivan answered, "Anonymous. He doesn't want his identity to be known."

26

Ursula stood in the ornate candle-lit dining room staring at Sergei. He smiled at her and pulled the tall wooden chair with purple felt cushions out further for her.

"Shall we eat?" Sergei asked.

"I don't mean to be rude," Ursula said, "but I am no longer afraid or drugged and some things seem a little strange."

"Please sit. I will answer all of your questions."

Ursula hesitated, then sat in the proffered chair. Sergei sat kitty-corner from her. They were the only two at the long rectangular table. Steam rose from her soup bowl.

"It is vegetarian," Sergei said. "I remembered you telling me on the plane."

"I don't remember anything from the plane."

"Have some rye bread. Best in the world. The soup is—"

"Shchi," Ursula said. "I know. My grandma makes it."

She stared at the food and was suddenly famished. She could not remember when last she had eaten. She dipped her spoon into the concoction of cabbage, potatoes, onions, carrots, and spices, then took a sip. She closed her eyes and sighed. It was delicious. Next she bit into the soft spongy bread.

"The wine is not bad," Sergei said. "From Georgia."

Ursula gazed around the room again. Scenes from nature decorated the rounded ceiling. Gold edging created a border between the ceiling and the rose-colored wall paper.

"Why do you seem suddenly so suspicious of me?" Sergei asked.

"Why did you speak Russian to me when we first met?"

"Maybe I tried English, French, and German, and you did not respond."

"Why have you been so nice to me?"

"Because you were in need, and I am a doctor."

"All right," Ursula said. "All that is logical. But what about the mosaics? Each animal is one that decorates our mummies in the form of tattoos."

"Truly?" Sergei said, looking down at the floor. "How extraordinary it must seem to you. But remember where you are now. There are paintings and mosaics of animals all over this house—all indigenous to Russia, most from Siberia. I am Siberian, after all, and so are your mummies. It is only natural. For instance, look at these cabbage pies." He pointed to a plate of shiny golden triangular pastries. On top of each one, the baker had carved several commas. "I'm sure you've seen these patterns on your mummies' clothing and coffins. It is part of our heritage."

Someone lifted Ursula's empty soup bowl and slipped away before she could see who it was. Sergei held out a plate of pancakes; she took one bliny and spread butter over it. Then she added a couple cabbage pies to her plate, along with slices of tomatoes.

"This all looks delicious," Ursula said.

"So you trust me again?" Sergei asked.

"I never said I didn't trust you," Ursula said. "I look for patterns. That's part of my work. And my life. I followed certain new patterns in my husband's life and figured out he was having an affair. It's what I do, I guess."

"Your husband must be a very foolish man," Sergei said.

Ursula looked at Sergei. He was beautiful, rich, powerful, and accommodating to her every whim, as if he had been plucked from a Gothic romance. As she watched him, she realized she was right: He was playing a role. He was being careful to act a particular way.

Why?

Ursula ate and ate. In between mouthfuls, she told Sergei about her life. He listened attentively and poured her wine or tea. When she asked him about his life, he said, "I am a doctor. My patients have been my life until recently. I am becoming interested in my homeland. Tell me more about your discovery."

Ursula told him about them lifting off the stones on the grave and finding ice beneath, how they had chopped and dug and melted ice until they reached the coffin.

"I wasn't there," she said, "but Miriam e-mailed us every day, complete with pictures. Finally they opened her coffin. Six-inch bronze nails held the lid on. They melted more ice until they came to the lady."

"The lady?"

"That's what they started calling her. I looked up the word 'lady.' It means 'kneader of bread or clay.' 'Figure' and 'paradise' have the same root."

"Paradise, yes," Sergei nodded.

"And 'transfigure' has the same root. It all fits. She has transfigured. She was once alive and now she has transformed into this mummy, sleeping inside the earth."

She glanced at Sergei. For an instant, she thought tears rimmed his eyes, but he blinked, and they were gone.

"She has these wonderful tattoos. A bear claw, swan, deer, snake, and spider."

"And a wild rose," Sergei said.

Ursula nodded. "How'd you know? Did I tell you that on the plane, too? You've heard all of this before and I just keep babbling." She spread jam on a bliny, then ran her lips across the knife to wipe it clean. She tasted wild strawberry. "This has been a great dinner, but I'm tired."

He reached for her hand and gently squeezed it. Something about his touch tickled every bone in her body. She smiled.

"I will walk you," Sergei said.

"Thank you, sir."

Ursula stood and stretched. She felt completely relaxed. Perhaps she could stay here forever. No more plane trips. She put her arm through Sergei's and together they left the dining room and went down the corridor toward the stairs.

"I think I'm a little drunk," Ursula said. "I don't drink." She laughed. "I don't do drugs either. I guess the last twenty-four hours have been fairly atypical for me. And now here I am in the home of a Russian prince."

"I am no prince, *duscha*."

"My grandmother calls me that, too."

"So I remind you of your grandmother?" He patted her hand. "That was not what I was hoping."

Ursula laughed. "I love my grandmother."

"I *am* older than you," Sergei said. They walked up the stairs.

"But not as old as my grandmother," she said. "Maybe as old as my father. Or his younger brother, if he had one." She looked at him. "You're not my father, are you?"

Sergei laughed. "No!"

"Good. I don't think I should be having these thoughts about my father. Did I say that out loud?"

They were at her bedroom door. Sergei looked at her. She smiled. She did not know how to be drunk or flirtatious. She hoped she did not seem too ridiculous. He smiled at her. His Siberian ice-blue eyes looked at her with such . . . What? Familiarity? Longing?

"Sergei—"

"Get some rest." He kissed her forehead. "I will see you in the morning, as you say."

Ursula nodded, opened the door and went inside. She stripped in the dark, then got under the covers. She listened for Sergei's returning footsteps but heard nothing. He was not coming to her. She smiled. "You've read *Jane Eyre* one too many times, woman," she said, giggling. Then she fell to sleep.

27

Sergei sat very still in a chair facing the wall his and Ursula's rooms shared. He wanted to be in the room with her. Breathing the air she breathed. Touching the things she had touched.

He waited.

Then he quietly got up and walked downstairs to the dining room. He had told the servants to leave everything just as it had been. The candles flickered as he walked around the table. Her fork lay across her plate. Her cup was partially filled with tea.

Sergei picked up her knife and ran his tongue along the same path her lips had taken. He tasted her—and wild strawberries.

He had waited a long time for her. So long that he had often thought he would go mad—*had* gone mad once or twice.

Now that she was here he was transfigured, like the lady. Only he was returning to life. He could feel himself changing. Becoming himself once again.

28

Ursula awakened to golden sunshine spilling into her room. She put on her robe, left the room, and padded around until she found the bathroom.

A massive free-standing bathtub dominated the room. Its lion-clawed legs were golden, as were all of the fixtures. The stones in the mosaic floor shaped themselves into two mammoths spraying water at one another. Ursula laughed at the image, then got into the tub and showered herself with the attached sprayer. After she got dressed, she went downstairs to the room she had first been in yesterday—the one with the bear looking down upon them. Sergei sat on the couch reading the newspaper.

"Hello," she said.

Sergei quickly folded the paper and stood. "Good morning."

"Sit," Ursula said. She came and sat on the couch, next to the newspaper.

"There's coffee and tea, some croissants and pastries," he said, indicating the tray on the coffee table in front of them. "Or I can have them cook something for you." He sat down and moved the newspaper to the table next to the couch.

Ursula poured herself a cup of tea and put a croissant on a plate.

"Did you sleep well?" Sergei asked.

Ursula nodded. "I don't even have a hangover."

Sergei smiled. "We've had some bad news. Your flight was canceled for today, but it is supposed to go out tomorrow. Good news is that your papers are all in order. I left your new flight numbers by the phone should you need them."

"Is it all right with you if I stay another night?"

"I would very much enjoy your company," he said.

"Don't you have to work?"

He shrugged. "I need the vacation."

After tea, Ursula called the Institute and left a message for Ivan about her delayed flight. Then Sergei took Ursula outside. She stood on the steps looking around. She had thought this was an ordinary house when she arrived yesterday, drugged and exhausted. Now she could see the massive walls of the house half-hidden with vines and trees. Birch trees lined the long drive that curved away from the house like a dry streambed.

"We're in Moscow here?" Ursula asked.

"We are in the country," Sergei said. "I have an apartment in the city, but I live here in the summer."

They began walking away from the house, on a lawn that flowed into a meadow that ended at the edge of a deciduous forest.

"I didn't know Russians still lived like this."

"Actually, the state had the land for a long time," he said, "but they needed the money and I wanted the land back."

They walked to a large oak which had split itself into several trunks reaching up into the sky, then split again into branches sprouting leaves that sheltered Sergei and Ursula from the summer sun. They leaned against the tree.

"You are very mysterious for a man of science," Ursula said.

Sergei laughed. "I don't know what that means."

Ursula shrugged. "I work with scientists all of the time. None of them are mysterious. You don't really tell me anything about yourself—though that part is fairly typical of most men I know. That's a gross generalization. I should say that is typical of most *people* I know. We talk about our work, not ourselves. For some reason, I talk to you about both. I've wanted to be here, in Russia, my entire life, but I was afraid of it, too, because my grandmother felt like an exile, and she didn't like talking about her life. Now that I'm here it seems familiar and alien. Do you know what I mean? The phone sounds different. The light switches aren't the same as at home. But the birch trees move in the wind the same. The crow sounds a little off, but the grass looks the same."

Sergei smiled. "Yes, I know what you mean. Is this your first trip out of America?"

"No." Ursula smiled. "But we're talking about me again."

Sergei looked at her. "What can I tell you? Let's see. I love the smell of snow—how it changes. Amongst the birch, snow smells almost damp—like it does here right after a spring shower. But amidst the larches, as you crunch over the snow, watching for tiger or marmot, it smells of ice. You know that smell, like iron? And out in the plains, you can't smell the snow at all—the winds whip away most scents, though you might detect the aroma of smoke from a faraway house. I love the colors of ice—the shades of blue and green. I love the sounds the ice makes in the rivers as they begin to melt—as if everything in the universe is collapsing as I watch the sun changing ice into water in slow motion. I like making love in the summer wheat fields where red poppies mingle with the golden stalks, covering field after field with their blush. I like the sound of my own heart as I run through the woods. I like the feel of the Earth beneath the soles of my feet. I think I can be happy for an eternity if only I can touch the woman I love, but I know that isn't true because I will then long for the next touch, and the next."

They were silent for a few moments, then Ursula said, "Thank you."

"You are most welcome."

They ate lunch on a stone patio overlooking a duck pond. Afterward, Ursula showed Sergei her "maps" of the mummy tattoos. For dinner, she put on the only dress she had brought with her and met Sergei in the dining room again.

Tonight the room sparkled even more than it had the previous evening. Sergei was dressed in a dark suit the color of the sky just at the moment it becomes true night. His eyes were such a light blue, they were almost white.

"You are beautiful," she said.

Sergei smiled.

"Did I say that out loud?"

As they quietly ate rye bread and cabbage soup, Ursula gazed at the painted ceilings. The more she looked at them the more she realized they were not ordinary peaceful bucolic scenes. She was not sure how, but the artist had created a different sense of nature. It reminded her of how she felt when she looked at the lady's tattoos: wild. Looking at these paintings, she had the sense that she could easily die in those woods or on that river or climbing those mountains, but she could just as easily live.

Sergei watched her looking at the paintings.

"I like your house," she finally said. She smiled. "You stare at me a lot."

"I'm sorry. I don't mean—"

"No. It doesn't bother me. You actually seem to see me. I've always been kind of in the background, not shy really, but I've never really wanted to draw attention to myself, so people would often not see me, even when they were with me. You seem to be looking at me."

"Who else would I look at?"

"Yes, who else?"

They said good night at Ursula's door. Sergei kissed her forehead. Ursula reluctantly went into her room and sat on the edge of her bed.

Tomorrow she would fly to Siberia. If they did not crash and burn, she would soon be able to examine the mummy firsthand. Maybe for once in her life, she would be truly focused or dedicated to something or someone.

She listened for Sergei's footsteps. She must be losing her mind. She did not do one night stands. In fact, she had only been with two men in her entire life. Now she wanted this strange gorgeous Russian to knock on her door. Actually, he didn't even have to knock . . .

29

Sergei sat in his chair, staring. He had planned this out for so long—he had calculated it all. He had been so sure he could remain cool and calm. In charge. Yet he could feel the blood pounding in his veins—could almost feel himself spinning out of control. He shook his head and briefly closed his eyes. No, that would not happen again.

He stood and began pacing, his bare feet silent on the rug that now covered the mosaic picture on his floor. He did not know what the right thing to do was. He only knew he ached for her, had to have her head resting against his chest, listening to his heartbeat. Then he would know he was alive.

He opened his door, went into the corridor, and walked to Ursula's room. He knocked.

30

U rsula opened the door.

"Hello," she said.

"I-I wanted to show you something," he said. He walked across the room and pushed open the curtains. Moonlight streamed inside. "Come." He motioned to her. She went to his side and looked out. The moon was nearly full.

"It's beautiful," she whispered. "I've always loved moonlight. I used to dance in it after my grandmother had gone to bed when I was a kid. I even have this vague memory of dancing with my mother in the moonlight."

Sergei took her hand in his and put his arm around her waist.

"Shall we?" he said.

They slowly danced in the shaft of light. Sergei's face was pale, his eyes almost luminescent.

"Sergei, you're shaking," Ursula said. The moonlight faded.

"Am I? I thought that was you."

He leaned down to kiss her lips. She put her arms around his neck and drew him closer. He was trembling.

"Are you all right?" she whispered in his ear.

"It has been such a long while," he said.

"Yes, I know. Me, too. I've never felt this way before."

He smiled. "That is what I wanted to hear."

They undressed each other slowly, then lay on the bed together, entangled in each other's legs as they kissed and stroked the other's skin.

"Is this what you want?" Sergei asked.

Ursula nodded. "Yes! Haven't I dropped enough hints?"

He laughed. Ursula had never heard such a joyful laugh. She kissed his ear and mouth, his chest, and pulled him down on top of her. He pushed himself gently inside of her. All of him fit perfectly along her body. She could feel his belly against hers, his thighs pressed against hers. She felt him. As if she were suddenly wide awake for the first time in her life. He kissed her neck and breathed deeply as they moved together. She smelled his musk, heard her heartbeat and his. She could feel her body hair meshing with his.

"I've waited so long for you," he said. "Yours is the touch I have ached for."

They moved together, faster and faster. Something was changing.

She felt wild.

Sergei bit her shoulder gently, pushing deeper inside of her, and Ursula suddenly knew she had smelled his scent before. Or one like it. In her dreams. She smelled bear. She looked into Sergei's eyes and saw the shadow of something, felt his massive furry body against hers and her body matched his weight and strength with her own. She remembered her grandmother telling her not to be afraid. Not to run from it. She felt a moment of panic, but she ate it and whispered her ecstasy into Sergei's ear.

She awakened to darkness. She lay quietly for a moment, then realized the bed was shaking. She reached for Sergei. He was weeping.

"Sergei," she whispered, turning him toward her. "What's wrong?"

He did not speak. She put her arm under his shoulder and drew him to her. His tears watered her breast. Ursula closed her eyes.

"It's all right, Sergei."

"I can't stay," he whispered, reaching up to kiss her chin.

"Just a little while longer," she said.

She awakened to sunlight. Sergei lay next to her, looking dark gold against her white sheets. He moaned in his sleep and kicked the covers, pulling the sheet down to expose his chest and arms.

Ursula gasped and quickly got off the bed.

On Sergei's chest was a tattoo of a bear's claw. On his left arm was a tattoo of a swan.

Ursula carefully pulled the sheet down further until she could see his left calf. A snake undulated up it.

Sergei turned onto his side. Tattooed dots decorated his spine.

"Oh my god," she whispered. "What is going on?"

31

Ursula quickly dressed, then tried to quietly pack her suit-case; every time she moved, the floor creaked or the dresser drawers stuck.

Then suddenly Sergei sat up and called her name.

She moved away from him.

"Ursula?"

He looked down at his naked body. "Let me explain," he said, getting up and pulling on last night's discarded clothes.

"Explain what?" she asked. "Are you going to try to say that you having the same tattoos as the lady is a coincidence? I'm getting out of here. I thought you were someone special but you're—I don't know what."

"I'm still the same person."

Ursula threw the last of her clothes into the suitcase, then shut and locked it.

"I'm out of here," she said.

"I won't hurt you," he said. "You must know that. Please, let me explain."

"All right, I'm listening," she said, standing by the door, suitcase in hand.

Sergei sat on the bed. "Ask me whatever you like."

"This was all some kind of weird set-up, wasn't it? You meeting me in Chicago and bringing me here."

"I did come to the airport because you had to get back on that airplane," Sergei said. "I was there to help."

"What do you mean I *had* to get on the plane? Why?"

"To come here. Your destiny is here."

Ursula rolled her eyes. "I don't believe in that kind of crap. Who told you I'd be on that plane? Who said I had to come here?"

Sergei stared at her.

"Well?"

"I can't tell you everything," he said. "You have to trust me."

"Trust you! I barely know you."

Sergei got up and went to her. He took the suitcase from her and put it on the floor. Then he led her to the bed. They sat next to each other.

"You do know me," Sergei said. "And I know you. I have loved you for a very long time. I have waited for you for a long time."

"Who told you I'd be on that plane!"

Sergei sighed. "You did."

Ursula stared at him. "I did? What, do I have a split personality? You say I know you and I told you what plane I'd be on? I don't believe you."

"This is what I can tell you," Sergei said. "You had to be on that plane. You have to go to Novosibirsk. You'll meet a woman there who will offer to show you the caves your mother explored. You have to go with her. The lives of many people depend upon it."

"Sergei, you aren't making sense."

"You've heard of the People?"

"My grandmother told me some stories just before I left,"

Ursula said. "I didn't really understand."

"I am one of the People," he said. "It is with the People that your destiny lies."

"Don't start that again."

"Look at me," he said. "I am being truthful. I met you a long time ago. You saved my life more than once. You don't remember because it hasn't happened to you yet."

Ursula stared at him.

He grabbed her hand and pulled her up. "I will prove to you that what I say is the truth."

They left her room and went into his. He released her hand, bent down, and began rolling up the rug.

"Sergei. What are you doing?"

"Look." He pointed to the mosaic that had been covered by the rug.

There, laid out in stone, was her own face.

"How'd you do this? We just met. Have you been stalking me? What is going on?"

"I've been trying to tell you," he said. "This house was built in the second half of the eighteenth century. Nearly all of the mosaics in this house were created back then, including this one. *I* designed them."

Ursula looked at him and laughed. "You're saying you are over 200 years old?"

"I'm trying to explain to you that I knew you before, in the past."

"Now I'm a reincarnation?"

"No. *You.* This body and soul. You. You told me about the tattoos. You told me to meet you in Chicago at the airport on that particular day on that flight. You never told me where you lived in America—I guess because you knew I would look for you."

Ursula slowly sank to the floor and ran her fingers across her stone face.

"This is bizarre," Ursula said. "I don't understand any of it."

Sergei sat next to her and took her hands in his. "You must see in my eyes how much I love you. How could that be if I'd really only known you for two days. I'd have to be a madman."

Ursula laughed and pulled away her hands. "Now you get the picture."

Sergei looked hurt.

"I'm sorry," Ursula said. "But come on, Sergei. I spend two seductive days with you. You cater to my every whim. We make incredible love and then you tell me this story about me in the past telling you to meet me in the future. Is that how it goes?"

"I know it sounds peculiar to you," Sergei said. "I've lived with it for so long that it seems normal.

He stroked her arm, and Ursula leaned against him. Even now, after hearing his story, she wanted him, wanted to be next to him, skin to skin.

"After waiting all these years to see you again," Sergei said, "I have to let you go. You have to go to Novosibirsk and meet this woman."

"Why?"

"If you don't, for one thing, we'll never meet."

"Huh?"

"We only have a few hours before you have to be at the airport."

"Can you come to Novosibirsk with me?" Ursula asked.

"No."

"Why?"

"Because that's not the way it happens."

"Sergei. I'm not a destiny kind of person. We make our own fate and then we trip over other people making their own fates. No, not fate. Life. We make our own lives. I think our fate is pretty much determined by what we're afraid of. I'm afraid to fly so my fate—if you will—is to be miserable flying."

"There is so much you don't know," Sergei said.

Ursula laughed. "Tell me something I don't know. Really. Tell me!" She sighed. She no longer felt afraid, or angry. She had made love to him, with him, and she did not think he was crazy.

"Sergei, I don't understand a word of what you've told me. But I intend to go to Novosibirsk. And if I meet someone who wants to take me to some caves, I'll go."

After breakfast, Sergei and Ursula went outside to the birch trees. Sergei spread a blanket under the trees, and they lay on it together, looking up at the branches.

"We Russians love the birch tree—the *berioza*," Sergei said. "It is the most beautiful tree in the world. The World Tree is a white birch. Just think of that! The central axis of the universe, with roots reaching into the underworld and branches reaching into heaven, is our beloved *berioza*. Hundreds of years ago, we decorated it with ribbons and flowers, we made bark shoes—*lapti*—from it, as well as baskets to use for gathering berries and mushrooms. But the People, *duscha*, the People loved the birch tree. It was our home. There is a Siberian story that the birch foretold the coming of the Europeans. The *taiga* used to be all conifers—all dark, like the Natives. And then the birch appeared, white like the Europeans. It was then the Siberians knew they were doomed. But it is only a story. Birch trees have been here as long as the People have been here."

"And did the People make love under the birch trees?" Ursula asked.

Sergei turned to her and smiled, "Often."

Ursula kissed his neck. "Show me."

32

Ursula tried to sleep during the five hour airplane ride from Moscow to Novosibirsk, but she could not. Even after she swallowed one of the pills Sergei had given her, she was wide awake. And afraid.

In Novosibirsk, Ivan met her at the baggage check in.

For a moment, he stared at her.

"What?" she asked.

"It's really amazing," Ivan said. "The resemblance."

To get into town, they took a kind of airport shuttle—a battered van driven by a crazy man, judging from the way he drove.

"The Ob," Ivan said as the shuttle went across a bridge spanning the river. "One of the largest rivers in Russia."

Ursula glanced around as they drove. Except for the occasional tree, Novosibirsk looked like what she had always thought a city in the Eastern Block would look like: stark, gray, and filled with utilitarian-looking buildings.

Eventually, Ivan tapped the driver on the shoulder, the shuttle stopped, and Ivan and Ursula got out. Ivan pointed to a group of tall, gray, boxy buildings.

"We have an apartment here," Ivan said, "for visitors. Miriam has been staying there."

They walked to one of the buildings and went inside. Ivan knocked on the door on the first floor.

"Come in!" Miriam called.

Ivan opened the door and motioned Ursula inside. Miriam sat on an old sofa that practically filled the small living room.

"Hey, girl," Miriam said. "Pardon me for not getting up." She tapped her cast.

Ursula went over and embraced her colleague.

"I'll leave you two alone," Ivan said. "I will come by in the morning to take you to the Institute, Ursula."

Ursula sat on the couch next to Miriam and let out a sigh as the door closed.

"I've had the most peculiar seventy-two hours," Ursula said. She glanced at Miriam's leg. "But I bet you've got a better story than I do. What's been going on?"

"There's tea on the stove," Miriam said.

"I'm fine," Ursula said. "On this plane ride, I didn't throw up once."

"Well, I've got good news and bad news," Miriam said. "That's why Ivan ran out of here so fast."

"What do you mean?"

"They found an anonymous donor to pay the lady's preservation expenses," Miriam said.

"Great. I assume that's the good news."

Miriam looked over at Ursula. "You've always wanted to visit Novosibirsk, right? You weren't having a great time in Moscow were you?"

Ursula laughed. "Well, actually, I was. Why?"

"They picked up the lady today. She's gone. She's on her way to Moscow."

"What!"

"I'm sorry," Miriam said. "We didn't know it would happen this fast. Nothing ever happens this quickly in this country, yet so much associated with the lady has gone at breakneck speed—like the DNA tests. And now within a day of getting word of the donation, the mummy is spirited away."

"You mean I won't get to see her at all?"

"Who's to say? Maybe they'll do the preservation work quickly and send her back. Though we've already heard from the Native Altaians. They want her reburied."

"But I just flew I don't know how many miles to see her," Ursula said. "Do you know how many shots I got? Do you know how much paperwork I had to do?"

"Yes, and did you notice how quickly all that went for you? It took me months to get mine all squared away."

"That's because I had it all started beforehand," Ursula said. "And you got to see her! I hate to fly. I don't mean I dislike it. I mean I go a little insane when I fly. I mean I lost half my body weight throwing up!"

Ursula stood and tried to pace, but there wasn't room.

"I know it's not your fault," Ursula said.

"How long you staying?"

"Four weeks. I wanted to get out before the snow." She sat on the couch again.

"I'm leaving tomorrow," Miriam said. "You can coordinate with our part of the team."

"That would be Leonard?"

"Your trip won't be a waste. We recovered textiles from the kurgan and her coffin."

Ursula looked at Miriam. "I'm sorry you were hurt."

"I thought of you," Miriam said.

Ursula laughed. "Because your helicopter crashed?"

"Exactly! I figured you were smarter than all of us. It was a strange experience. I was in so much pain—and so drugged—that I started to hallucinate. I was in a cave with rock drawings and I saw a line going from one drawing to the next. It reminded me of those pictures of constellations. They'd show the Bear, for instance, with the lines drawn to each star and the star is high-lighted. Do you know what I mean?"

Ursula nodded.

"The pain got really bad. Then someone picked me up and held me. I know it was only a dream or a hallucination, but it was so real. He was so real. He wasn't human. He was—he was like the bear in that fairy tale of Red Rose and Snow White. They're sisters living with their widowed mother and this bear comes knocking on the door one winter's night. He's cold and sits by the fire and lets the sisters play with him. Then one night he rips his fur and one of the sister's sees a bit of gold underneath the fur. Eventually whoever cursed him dies, and his bear skin falls away, and he's a prince underneath it all and marries one of the sisters. That's who this man—this being—reminded me of, this fairy tale bear prince. He pressed this place on my foot and the pain in my leg went away." Miriam reached down and pressed two fingers into a spot on her foot below the cast. "Even now I can do that and the pain gets better for a while. How can that work if it was only a hallucination? That is what happened, don't you think? I was delirious?"

Ursula thought about what her grandmother and Sergei had told her about the People—and what she had seen and felt making love with Sergei. What had she seen? She had felt ecstasy.

"I'm sure you were hallucinating," Ursula said to reassure her. "My mother studied cave paintings in this area. Maybe I should take a look at your cave."

"I doubt any of us could find it again," Miriam said. "Ivan said there are lots of caves in Altai. He says most of them are still unknown to the general populace because the Natives consider them sacred."

"Timeless," Ursula said.

"What?"

"That's what my grandmother called them. The timeless caves."

In the morning, Ivan came to take her to the Institute. She and Miriam had spent most of the evening talking about the expedition, so Ursula knew what was expected of her.

Ursula and Ivan went into a bright clear day. The apartment buildings seemed like the exoskeletons of long dead industrial monsters. Ursula and Ivan walked several blocks to the bus stop, then waited in a long line to get on the bus. The bus was crowded, so they stood most of the way as they crossed the Ob again. They got off of the bus in front of a gray rectangular building that reminded Ursula of one of the old deserted warehouse buildings down by the docks in Portland.

"This is the place?" Ursula asked.

"This is the place," Ivan said. "Very modern, isn't it?"

"Yes, very modern."

"I have something to show you," Ivan said as they walked up the steps and went inside the building. "Did Miriam say anything about the facial reconstruction of the lady?"

"Just that I'd be surprised," Ursula said. "I got the sense she was tired of the surprises that keep popping up on this expedition."

"You will be surprised."

They walked down a narrow hallway until Ivan unlocked a door and held it open for her.

"This was the lady's last resting place," Ivan said. "I'm afraid the freezer malfunctioned and she was growing fungi."

Ursula glanced at the frosted windows which allowed some natural light into the room. At least they had windows here. She looked at the back of the head on the table.

"Is that it?" she asked. "The facial reconstruction?"

Ivan nodded. He went to the head and slowly turned it around.

Ursula's mouth fell open.

Then she laughed.

"Is this a joke?"

Ivan shook his head. He walked to a wall and knocked on it. Ursula stared at the head—at the woman who looked so much like her. A few moments later, the door opened and two men came inside. Ivan introduced them as Vladimir and Nikolai. Both men watched her.

"Vladimir did the reconstruction," Ivan said.

"You look just like her," Vladimir said. "What does this mean?"

"Her mtDNA is an exact match, too," Nikolai said. "She is a very close relative."

Vladimir walked around Ursula as if she were on display.

"Astonishing," he said.

Then all three men crossed their arms and stared at her.

"This is as baffling to me as it is to you," Ursula said.

"Maybe not," Ivan said. "I just found out who our mysterious donor is. It turns out it's your friend Sergei Ivanovich Polyakov. You stayed with him in Moscow."

She nodded. "He was a nice man I met on the plane. He's a doctor. I got sick, and he took care of me. I told him we didn't have enough money to take care of the lady, so I guess he decided to help us out."

She was not going to tell these three gentlemen that he also claimed to have known her in the past in her future—or in the future in her past.

"Do you recall that you chose the spot where we eventually found the kurgan?"

"Yes, so? I thought it'd be a good place to dig, and I was right.

What's going on?"

"It's a mystery, as you say," Ivan said.

Ursula looked at the lady's head.

"How do you think I feel?" she said. "I look like someone who is dead."

33

Miriam embraced Ursula and Ivan, then sat in the wheel-chair an attendant had waiting for her. She was getting a first class seat because of her cast, but since it was Aeroflot, she was not sure what that really meant. Maybe she'd get her own parachute. She glanced back once as the attendant wheeled her through the gate and outside onto the tarmac. Something about Ursula was different. Miriam couldn't really put her finger on what it was. Maybe it was that she had had a couple of days of great sex with a handsome Russian philanthropist. Miriam smiled and thought she could benefit from a couple of hours with a Russian philanthropist.

Perhaps Ursula wasn't the only one who had changed. Miriam thought Ursula was very brave to have flown all this way even though she was terrified the entire trip. She seemed to be opening up, and Miriam felt like she was closing down. Too many things had happened too quickly; that wasn't normally how archaeology or her life worked. That was one of the reasons she loved her work: It seemed to naturally and slowly unfold. Everything with the lady had been different.

They reached the stairs to the plane. Miriam stood on her walking cast and let the attendant guide her up the steep steps.

She was anxious to be home where things were normal. Steady. Where she could think about her work. Right this moment as she teetered up the stairs, she could not imagine missing Russia. Finding the lady had been awe-inspiring—a once in a lifetime experience—but she was ready to start analyzing of her findings. She was ready to stop thinking about things she did not understand.

Maybe she would come back one day. Find the cave where she had stayed for a day or more with an unconscious pilot and a hallucination of a being who embraced her and took away her pain. Even if it had only been a hallucination—and of course it had been—the feeling of the arms of the being holding her had been wonderful and, when she let herself think about it, frightening. She had not had any control over anything during those two days. Yet she had survived.

She limped onto the plane.

She glanced back and silently said goodbye to the land of the lady and wished Ursula good luck.

34

Ursula spent the night alone in the small sterile apartment inside the tall ugly apartment complex in Novosibirsk, Russia. She had seen no other people in the building, heard no sounds of human inhabitation. Looking outside through the one small barred window, she saw only the glow of some distant streetlight. She lay on a lumpy mattress trying to sleep for hours. The air was still and smelled slightly of diesel. It felt peculiar to be alone, even though she had stayed by herself in her and Peter's house for a couple of weeks before she left for Russia. She was tempted to phone Sergei, but each time she had used the telephone for long distance the reception had been poor; during one call she had been disconnected.

Finally she fell to sleep.

In the morning, she made her way to the Institute via bus. She spent the morning reading Ivan's and Miriam's notes and viewing the video made of the expedition. She paused on the close-ups of the lady more than once, trying to discern some familial resemblance.

After lunch, Ivan showed her items they had recovered from the burial chamber. She gently picked up the small wooden mirror and ran her fingers over the carved outline of a swan. Then she set it down and turned her attention to the tall conical headdress made of felt and hair. Sickle-shaped gold pieces covered most of the cloth. Sewn to the front of it was a felt bear's paw. Tiny bells hung down where the headdress fit over the head. The entire hat was nearly three feet tall.

"This is similar to the *saukele,*" Ursula said. Ivan nodded. Worn by Kazakh brides and passed on from generation to generation, the *saukele* would be covered with pendants, coral, pearls, and other jewels. Kazakh brides wore it until their first child was born. Some scholars believed these headdresses were symbolic of the World Tree.

"Actually the lady's headdress is very close to the Issyk gold man's," Ursula said. The "gold man" had been discovered in south Kazakhstan in 1969. "This could strengthen Jeannine Davis-Kimball's supposition that the gold man was really a gold woman."

"Yes," Ivan said. "We had discussed that. Also, Polosmak's mummy had a similar headdress. She speculated the woman had been a shaman or priestess."

"It's like an apex—you know, like the tall hat the pope wears, only this one is more decorated. The Norse god Frey is often shown wearing an apex. He was Freya's brother and son. She's related to Modir, the Slavic Earth goddess, so maybe there's some connection?" She stared at the headdress. She wanted to put it on. "It's like a witch's hat, too, without the flap."

"I believe the world tree is a more likely symbol," Ivan said.

"How is the World Tree conical?" Ursula asked.

"Perhaps the World Tree is a conifer," Ivan said. "But even deciduous trees, like the birch, are wider near the bottom and then narrow at the top."

"Do you know much about tattooing?"

"What do you mean?"

"You've seen the reports I sent Miriam about the similarities of the placements of the tattoos on the three mummies?"

Ivan nodded.

"Have you heard of any modern day equivalent?" she asked.

"No. People here still tattoo and some tattoo the dots on the spine, yes, but not like the mummies—one on the chest, one on the arm and same side on the leg, one on the opposite hand. No. I wish you could have seen them on the lady. They were really quite remarkable."

"I wish I could have, too," Ursula said. "C'est la mort. Tell me what you've figured out about the blouse."

35

The steel laboratory door shut firmly, and Sergei was left alone in the stainless steel room—alone, except for the covered corpse on the stainless steel table. Sergei stepped a little closer to the body. Beneath the sheet, he could see she was lying on her side. Her right arm lay against her side in the dip of her waist that curved up into her hip.

Sergei felt a lump in his throat. He had to know if it was her. Was she lost to him forever? He thought if he saw the body, he would be able to tell. Then he could go on—no matter what the truth turned out to be.

His hand shook slightly as he reached for the sheet. He had seen death before, many times. He had witnessed people he loved die in gruesome and peaceful ways. Still, his hand shook. He drew the sheet back to the mummy's feet and stared at the naked desiccated body. Most of her face had decayed and bone was visible. He sighed. She did not look familiar—could not look familiar. The flesh had dropped away and left only skin and bones. He reached out and touched the swan tattoo on the mummy's arm.

He quickly withdrew his hand. She was ice cold.

Sergei stepped back.

He could not do this. He could not look for signs that his beloved was dead.

He gently pulled the sheet up over the mummy again.

"Blessings on your sleep," he whispered.

He quickly left the room. He knew she was alive now, and he knew where she was. Destiny be damned. He was going after her.

36

Ursula ate dinner with Ivan and his wife Peytra. Ursula drank too much vodka and ate too many blinkas. She told Ivan she wanted to explore nearby caves with rock paintings; Ivan promised to call around and see what he could find out. The couple offered to let her sleep on the couch, but Ursula insisted on going back to the apartment. Ivan walked her to the bus stop and reminded her where to get off. Ursula waved to him and sat looking off into the darkness as the bus bounced down the street. When they drove over the bridge, Ursula saw the lights of the city twinkling in the Ob. She wondered if another city lived beneath the water. Perhaps a city of the People. She smiled. Since coming to Russia, she had consumed more liquor, taken more drugs, and had more bizarre thoughts than she had had in all of the previous ten years.

The driver reminded her which was her stop. She thanked him and sleepily got off the bus. She stood in almost total darkness and wondered where her apartment building was. There. One or two lights were on. She hurried forward. In the United States, she would be too afraid to walk alone in the dark. For some reason, she wasn't afraid here. Probably foolish ignorance, she thought, comfortable in her vodka-induced warm glow.

When she reached her apartment building, someone suddenly stepped out of the shadows. A woman.

"You startled me," Ursula said.

"Are you Ursula, the she-bear?"

Ursula laughed. "I'm not a bear, but I am Ursula. Who are you?"

"Call me Kam. You wanted to visit the caves your mother studied."

Ursula stared at the woman. "Ivan couldn't have found anyone this quickly. Are you the woman Sergei told me about?"

She nodded.

"Well, I do have work to do at the Institute."

"Yes, but you want to see the caves. Now is the best time, before the snows. You can make the arrangements?"

Kam spoke English without an accent.

"Who are you?" Ursula asked again.

"I am the one who will take you to the timeless caves."

"I will talk to Ivan in the morning," Ursula said.

"The train leaves at 10:00. I will meet you here at 8:30."

"All right."

The woman stepped into the darkness again and was gone.

Ursula stared after her for a moment, then shook her head and went inside the building to her apartment.

She dreamed she was running through a birch forest. Faster and faster. The trees were slender white beings dressed in tiny green leaves reaching for her and urging her forward.

"Ursula!" someone called to her.

She looked down at her hands. Her nails turned into claws, her skin sprouted hair.

"Ursula." A whisper.

She opened her eyes and felt warm breath on her ear.

"Ursula."

Her heart did not race; she was not frightened. She turned to the voice.

"Sergei." She put her arms around him and drew him down on top of her.

"I'm not supposed to be here," he said, kissing her neck.

"I won't tell anyone," she said.

"I couldn't let you go again," he said. "I was afraid—"

"Afraid of what?"

"That I'd never see you again."

"As far as I'm concerned," she said, "you can stay forever."

37

When Ursula awakened, Sergei was sitting in a chair in the corner of the room watching her.

"My grandmother used to watch me while I slept," Ursula said, sitting up and yawning.

"How did that make you feel?" Sergei asked. His eyes were bloodshot. Ursula wondered when last he had slept.

"I felt safe," Ursula said. "And a little confined."

Sergei smiled.

"Do you want to come to the caves with me today?" Ursula asked.

Sergei stood. He was naked except for his shorts. Ursula smiled. She wanted to kiss his rounded belly.

"To the caves?"

"The woman you told me about came here last night," Ursula said. "Kam. She said she'll take me to the caves." As Sergei came closer, Ursula kissed his stomach. "What's wrong? I thought you wanted me to go with her."

Sergei sat next to her on the bed. "It's not what I want, but what must be."

"You're getting all serious on me again," Ursula said.

He looked at her. "You're too skinny and weak. You need to prepare yourself. Do some strength training. Start eating."

Ursula laughed. "What are you talking about? Why do you look so worried?"

"I'm not worried," he said. "This is the normal expression of all Russians: perpetual angst. When are you meeting the kam?"

"The kam? I thought her name was Kam."

Sergei shrugged. "It is one of the names given to shamans."

"She's a shaman? Why is she showing the caves to me then?"

"The caves are sacred to the shamans," Sergei said. "They know the caves best of anyone."

"I'm meeting her at 8:30 to catch a train at 10:00."

"How about taking a helicopter instead? I could charter one."

"How much money do you have?" Ursula asked.

"Enough."

"Would this be the same kind of helicopter that recently crashed, causing injury to my teammate?"

"Yes, they are all former military craft. But they are quite safe. It's either that or hours and hours on a train."

"Well, it's OK with me," she said. "Does this mean you're coming with?"

"Let's see if I can get a helicopter first." Sergei slipped on his clothes. "I'll be back by 8:30." He kissed her, then left the apartment.

Ursula ate toast for breakfast, then called Ivan and told him she'd be gone for a day or two. She packed an overnight bag, stuffing into it anything she thought would keep her warm—she remembered Miriam's snowstorm after her crash. Crash. Ursula shuddered. That wasn't going to happen again.

She went outside at 8:30. Kam stood by the steps.

"Good morning," Ursula said.

Kam nodded. In the bright sunshine, Kam looked older than Ursula had thought, her hair gray, her green eyes tired. She was dressed in layers of brightly decorated—and dirty—clothes.

Sergei came up the walk. Kam looked startled when she saw him.

"Sergei offered to take us by helicopter," Ursula said.

Kam stared at him. "You are not to come with us."

"But I want him to come," Ursula said. "It'll be more fun."

"Fun?" Kam looked away from Sergei and gazed steadily at Ursula. "What makes you think this will be fun? You want to find your mother, don't you?"

"What? I thought we were going to look at caves my mother studied."

"I will take you to the cave where your mother disappeared. I will help you go where she went."

Ursula glanced at Sergei, then looked back at Kam. "How do you know where my mother disappeared?"

"I know."

"Like Sergei knew what flight I was taking out of Chicago?"

"We have similar ways of knowing."

Ursula looked from one to the other. "How do I know you aren't both a couple of fruitcakes?"

Sergei smiled and looked at his shoes.

"You can only go by your own heart," Kam said.

Ursula sighed. She had come this far. She wanted to see what would happen.

"OK. But I want Sergei to come."

Kam nodded. "Actually, this might be good. We were going to find him next. But he must not interfere."

"Interfere with what?"

"I won't go into the caves," Sergei said.

"Why not?" Ursula asked.

"Because he is not supposed to be there," Kam said.

"Who says?" Ursula asked.

They both looked at her.

"*I* told you?" Ursula rolled her eyes. "At what point will this make sense to me?"

Kam squinted at her. "Shall we go?"

Sergei had a car ready to take them to the airport. They were silent in the small limousine, with Ursula sitting between Kam and Sergei.

At the airport, Sergei spoke briefly with someone, and soon Kam and Ursula were following him outside to one of the huge helicopters. Ursula thought she heard they were going to Biysk. As they got inside the cavernous vehicle, Ursula briefly wondered if she had lost her mind. They put on headsets and strapped themselves in. Sergei and Ursula sat next to each other, Kam behind and to the left of them. Ursula clutched Sergei's hand when the engines whirred on. Soon the helicopter was airborne.

Ursula did not throw up during this flight—her first time in a helicopter. She passed most of the two hours flipping through an archaeology journal she had brought with her. She liked the noise of the helicopter. It was so pronounced, different from the white noise of an airplane where she could still hear little things which might signal catastrophe. Whenever Ursula glanced back at the shaman, her eyes were closed. Sergei sat quietly next to Ursula, his shoulder and arm touching hers.

At Biysk—an unremarkable city as far as she could tell—a hired car awaited them. When the driver took her bag, Ursula realized she was the only one with any luggage. Kam sat in front of the jeep with the driver; Sergei and Ursula got in the back. Kam gave directions to the driver, and the car jerked forward.

They left the gray city behind. Soon they passed fewer and fewer cars and trucks. The road narrowed and more and more trees grew alongside until it seemed they were driving through the forest. It reminded Ursula of the Gifford-Pinchot forest on the way to Mount Saint Helens in Washington, only slightly different in a way she could not quite define—the green was darker, or lighter, the smell sharper, more resin than humus odors. The road curved around the trees going up and up and down again. Every once in a while, the trees would clear and Ursula glimpsed alpine valleys and rolling hills. Then the mountains appeared, first as a kind of deep dark blue mist in the distance; then as they grew closer and the clouds shifted and the sun came out, Ursula saw snow. Yet the mountains still appeared almost gentle, not as sharp and angular as the Rockies. These mountains had let the ages and the wind soften them; at least so it seemed from this distance.

"Those are the mountains of the Altai," Sergei said.

They passed no cars, only an occasional donkey-pulled cart or horseback rider. After a long while, Kam directed the driver to stop the car.

They all got out and stretched. The air was cool and moist. The conifers moved with the wind, creating the gentle lulling sound that comes from soft needles stroking soft needles; Ursula heard no other sound besides their feet on the gravel.

"We walk from here," Kam said.

"Should I take my pack?" Ursula asked.

"Only if it has food and water," she answered. "Put on warm clothes if you have them—layers."

Ursula pulled on a sweater and jacket, along with a thicker pair of socks. The driver took a pack from the car and handed it to Sergei. The two of them stepped away from Kam and Ursula for a few moments.

Then Sergei walked to them. "I'm ready."

Kam stepped into the woods. Ursula and Sergei followed. After a few minutes of traveling through the forest, Ursula was tired and remembered what Sergei had said about strength training. They came out of the woods into a field covered in dark pink and light purple flowers and grass, all of it at least two meters high. Kam plunged right into it. Ursula glanced at Sergei; he shrugged. They followed her.

Ursula was grateful when they finally left the meadow until they started climbing a scree-covered hillside. She heard the familiar cry of the pika, a small guinea pig-sized animal who also lived in Washington. Legend had it that wherever pikas went, a Bigfoot followed—because Sasquatch liked to gobble up the little fellows. Ursula wondered if the Altaians had their own version of a Bigfoot.

At the top of the incline, another meadow stretched before them, though this one was covered in lichen and moss. They stopped for a drink and Ursula looked around. Below, valleys and hills undulated. Behind them the tops of the mountains were closer; mist partially covered the glaciers. She stared at the mist and it began to rise—almost dance. Playful. Ursula touched Sergei's arm, and they watched it together. Sunlight polished the glacier. The mist rose higher. Became a cloud. And Ursula was staring at the broad face of a mountain top, so close she felt as though she could reach out and touch it.

She dropped to her knees. The earth felt solid and warm beneath her.

"That is Mount Beluckha," Sergei said. "It is there, or just beyond, some believe, that Shamballa lies. Paradise." The ground trembled beneath Ursula; then she realized it was she who shook—like Sergei had when they first made love. She stared at the mountain. Was this her beloved?

She glanced back at Kam. She watched the mountain, too, transfixed, her face soft and relaxed.

"It is good to be home again," Kam said.

"Yes, it is," Sergei said. "Look."

Ursula followed his gaze. Above them, a large bird circled. Its belly was light-colored, its tail wedge-shaped.

"This is an honor," Sergei said. "That is the lammergeier, the bearded vulture. It is quite rare nowadays."

"It doesn't look like a vulture," Ursula said, shading her eyes.

"That is because it is a shapechanger," Kam said. "When it hatches from its egg, it is first an axe—an axe that can cut anything! If no person takes the axe from the nest within three days, it becomes a puppy. This puppy can protect a person from any wild animal. But if no one takes the puppy from the nest within three days, it becomes a vulture."

"With extra feathers," Sergei said. "It has a beard of feathers, like a goatee. It waits until the carrion is stripped of all flesh, then it flies away with the bones and lets them drop onto the stones, so that they break open."

"Though sometimes," Kam said, "they keep the bones as treasure, like dragons hoarding jewels."

"Or like an archaeologist," Ursula said. "I'm not dead yet!" she called up to the bird. "You can't have my bones!"

They walked into another forest and followed a mountain stream. Then Kam stopped along a rocky ledge.

"I want you to eat," Kam said, "as much as you can. And drink. You'll need your strength. I'll be back soon." Then she walked into the woods.

Sergei and Ursula sat on the sandy ground next to the rocks. They pulled food and drink out of the pack and began eating sandwiches.

"I don't know what these are, but I'm so hungry I could eat a horse," Ursula said.

"You can't stay vegetarian in Siberia for long," Sergei said.

Ursula laughed. An easy wind rocked the conifers.

"For you and Kam knowing one another, you don't say much to each other," Ursula said. "Of course, she doesn't say much period. She's so serious. You both seem so serious."

"I don't know her," Sergei said. "This is the first time I've met her, but she knows I don't want to let you go."

"What do you mean? Go where?"

"There's a cave just around these rocks," Sergei said.

"And?"

"You're a scientist," Sergei said. "You've told me there are things you believe and things you don't. For instance, what do you think of time? Can you accept, as others have, that the passage of time is a construct—a cultural construct?"

"I've heard that," Ursula said, "but I come back to the multiplying gray hairs on my head. If it's a construct, why do we age?"

"Or what about the idea of time being simultaneous? Do you think it's possible that there are places on the planet where time shifts? Like places which are considered haunted, where people see people from the past. Maybe those are places where time overlaps or intersects—or acts like a portal."

"That's an interesting idea," she said, "but if it's true, wouldn't people be running around in different times all of the time?"

"Maybe it's a skill," Sergei said. "Or maybe it was a skill we had and lost. There's so much of our brain we don't use. Maybe a particular chemical or hormone needs to be released in our bodies for us to be able to see the time intersections."

"Have you eaten enough?" Kam asked as she came around the corner.

Ursula nodded.

"Say good-bye to Sergei, then follow me."

"Good-bye? Won't you be here when I come back?"

"Yes, I promise to wait for you, no matter how long it takes."

He kissed her lips, then put his arms around her.

"I'm coming right back," she said, gently pushing him away.

She followed Kam around the outcropping to the front of the cave. A treeless plain dropped down into a valley in the near distance. Mountains hunkered down behind mist.

"You were lucky to see Mount Beluckha today," Kam said. "I think the mountain only shows her face about eighty-six days a year. You've been welcomed home."

Kam ducked into the dark cave opening. Ursula followed. It smelled slightly fecund, like decomposing leaves. Kam had already lit a lantern that sat in the middle of the cavern, spreading red light throughout. Several painted horses raced across the rock.

Ursula walked to the horses and put her hand on the rock.

"My mother was here?"

Kam picked up the lantern. "There's more." She left Ursula in darkness as she walked away. Ursula hurried to catch the receding light. They went down several narrow passageways, finally stopping in a large damp cavern. The light did not quite reach the ceiling. The rock was various shades of pastels, and drawings of animals took up nearly all the space on the rock. Ursula walked around the cave, touching bison and elk, marmots and spiders, salmon, owls, reindeer, goats, sheep, swans, leopards, eagles.

"Sit," Kam said, pointing to the center of the room.

Ursula did as she was told, suddenly feeling like a five year old late for class.

"Are you ready to do what you must do?" Kam asked. The light painted her fiery red.

"Well, I think so."

"I can help you go where you need to go," Kam said. "Take off your shirt. Although you are one of the People, you are not aware of who you are. I must embroider a spot on your spine. This will open you up."

"Embroider? With needles? Like acupuncture?" She pulled off her jacket, sweater and shirt.

Kam went around behind her.

"It is not unlike acupuncture," Kam said, "but it will leave a mark, like tattooing."

"You're not going to use dirty needles or anything are you?"

"You must trust me," Kam said gently, her voice almost in her ear. "This is all something you asked for."

"I should tell you I don't believe in that. You know that New Age crap where people say that you asked for your parents or you asked for an illness or an accident. That's all bullshit."

"No, Ulla, *you* asked for it. You will see. I'll numb this a little, but it will hurt." Kam lifted the back of Ursula's camisole. Ursula felt a sharp prick.

"Ouch!" she cried. "That hurt more than a little."

"Don't move. I need to press the needle in."

Ursula suddenly felt dizzy.

"What are you doing?" Ursula asked. What had she been thinking, coming out here in the middle of Siberia with two strangers?

"Ursula!" Sergei's voice.

"I told him he couldn't come in here," Kam said. "Don't move. I'll be right back."

Ursula glanced back, but Kam was shadow.

"I feel strange," Ursula whispered.

What had she let this woman do to her?

Maybe if she stood.

She looked at the rock paintings. They glowed and wavered like phosphorescent fish beneath a slow-moving river. Or like stars in the sky. Hadn't Miriam said something about that?

"Hello!" someone called.

Ursula looked around. Where had that voice come from.

"Hello?" Who was calling out?

The bison. It came from the bison. Yes, they were watching her. She went over to them and put her fingers in their eyes.

"I'm here," she said. "What do you want from me?"

38

“You cannot come in.” Kam stood in the dark cavern, blocking Sergei’s entrance into the passageway that led to Ursula. “You know you would not be able to resist preventing her from going.”

“No. That’s not it. I heard her cry out.”

“Don’t you remember your own embroidery?” Kam asked. “She must go and you mustn’t interfere.”

“I—I waited for so many years. It is only with her that I feel like myself. It is only with her that I feel like one of the People.”

“You cannot stalk her, Sergei. You cannot feed off of her like you are some kind of vampire.”

“You don’t understand. I am only this that you see before you. This man. Unless we are together. When she saved me, she also broke me.”

“I know someone who can help you. An old enemy of yours. But first, I must finish with Ursula.”

“Wait!” Ursula’s cry came from inside the cavern.

Kam hurried back to where she had left Ursula. Sergei followed.

Kam looked around the cave and saw only Sergei.

Sergei slowly sank to the floor. Kam picked up the lantern.

"She's gone," Kam said, looking around at the cave paintings. "And I don't know where or when she went."

Part Two

WILDER

K

39

Ursula's world tilted. The bison called out to her. She took her fingers from their eyes and reached around her back and pulled out a needle. She held it up to her face. It looked like a porcupine quill.

"Are you mad? You'll freeze for sure."

The world balanced itself. Ursula turned around. Natural light somehow flowed into the cave, and a raggedy-looking man stood several feet from her. His coat was a patchwork of furs, his hat black and pointed like a furry boy scout cap.

"Do you know how cold it is?" he asked in English, his accent Scottish. His eyes were black, his moustache dark brown, his skin pale. "Granted it's warmer in this cave than out there, but it's still cold."

Ursula looked at the center of the cavern where her jacket and sweater should be. They and the lantern were gone.

"Kam!" she called. "Sergei!"

The man stared at her. "There is no one here. I will ask you again. Are you mad, girl?"

"No, I-I don't know what happened."

He took off his coat and put it over her shoulders. She wrapped the furs around herself.

"Did you see anyone on your way in?" Ursula asked.

"No, I didn't see anyone here either until you stepped out of the shadows. Are you hurt?"

He was dressed all in black, with a scarf around his neck and stuffed into his overcoat. He took off the scarf and handed it to her. "Put it around your head."

Ursula did as he said.

"I must get you out of here before someone else finds you. It wasn't too long ago that women were sold in Siberia. Hasn't anyone told you this is no place to be?"

Ursula glanced at the cave walls. All the rock pictures were gone except for the bison. The man touched her now-furry elbow.

They walked out of the cave—no passageway, no first cave. It was an entirely different cave. They walked into a white world and a blast of winter colder than anything Ursula had ever experienced. She gasped and stepped back into the overhang of the cave.

The surrounding woods were gone. A snow-covered hill sloped down to a bare birch growing along a frozen river.

Ursula put her hand on the rock.

"What happened?" she asked. "Where am I?"

"Have you had a seizure of some sort?" the man asked.

"I—" Ursula ran back into the cave. "Kam!" she screamed. "Sergei!" She ran to the bison, who were no longer phosphorescent, and put her fingers in their eyes. Nothing happened.

The man watched her. She threw off her coat. He averted his eyes.

"Here!" she said, holding up the needle. "You have to put this in my back. There should be a black dot on my back." She started pulling up her camisole.

"I will not!" the man said.

"But I'm not supposed to be here!" Ursula cried. "I was in Siberia with friends. It was summer. I came looking for my mother, Ursula Kuznetsov."

"You are in Siberia, but it is definitely not summer. Here." He bent over and picked up his coat. "Put this on. We will sort it out. I have heard from the Natives about these caves. People coming and going. My name is Jonathan McDougall."

"I-I'm Ursula. Ursula Smith."

"Like your mother?" he said.

"You speak Russian?" Ursula asked. Was he good at languages then? Maybe he was one of the People.

"Not well. My mother was Russian, but I do remember Kuznetsov is the Russian equivalent of Smith. Come."

Ursula let him take her outdoors again. Now a wind blew and slapped her face. Jonathan took her above the cave where a sled pulled by several ordinary-looking dogs stood. The dogs jumped up and began barking as soon as they saw Jonathan.

"Get in," Jonathan instructed.

Ursula stepped into the back of the crescent moon-shaped craft. Jonathan sat in front of her, took the reins and called to the dogs; the sled jerked forward, taking them easily across the hard snow.

Ursula watched the white landscape and wondered if this was all some kind of hallucination induced by whatever Kam had put into her back. If that were true, perhaps she should stay in the cave. As the sled went faster, she ducked her head down into Jonathan's coat. She couldn't have stayed in the cave. She would have frozen to death within the hour. No, she would go with Jonathan and find a telephone.

They reached the river. Instead of stopping, the dogs carried them onto the ice, bouncing the sled once—hard—over the bank. Jonathan turned the dogs, and they headed down the river. The wind got colder and colder. Ursula felt sleepy. After a time, they began passing other sleds—some of them not drawn by dogs but moved by wind in their sails. Then, up on the ridge above the river, Ursula saw what looked like a fort, with watchtowers topped with cupolas like something out of the Arabian nights.

The dogs crossed the river and quickly pulled the sled up the incline toward the palisades.

Ursula started to shiver. John glanced back at her.

"We're almost there," he shouted.

They went by several streets with rows of wooden houses along them, then past the palisades into a small town. In the near distance, Ursula saw several cupolas with crosses atop them. People in horse- or dog-drawn sleighs passed them in both directions. Dogs barked. No cars. No neon lights. Mostly small rectangular houses.

The sled bumped over the uneven ground. They took a side street and stopped in front of a house at the end of it; the house—off by itself and gray from weather—had settled crookedly into the frozen ground.

Jonathan helped Ursula out of the sled. "Go inside. I'll be right in. Quickly. Before you freeze."

Ursula stumbled into the wooden structure. She stood against the closed door for a few moments, trying to adjust to the darkness. She spotted embers in a huge stone fireplace and hurried across the room to it. Shaking, she stood practically inside the hearth, her hands over the cauldron that hung in the middle of the fireplace.

The room had two windows made of thick distorted glass. A bench and table were situated near the fireplace. Behind them was a kind of kitchen with cupboards and a narrow countertop that was not much more than a piece of wood. On the other side of the room were shelves of books and jars and a table laden with vials and more jars. It all looked like a scientific laboratory from a couple of centuries ago. In the midst of the work area against the wall was a wood stove.

The door opened and closed, and Jonathan stepped inside. He strode to the hearth, moved the cauldron to the side, and tossed several logs onto the fire. Then he went into the other room. A few minutes later he returned with a pile of clothes.

"My sister left these," he said, holding them out to her. "You can change in the other room." He nodded toward the darkness from which he had just emerged.

Ursula took the clothes and went into the small dark bedroom. She closed the door and took off the fur coat.

She sighed and saw her breath.

Quickly, she put on a white shift with long wide sleeves. Over it, she pulled on a light blue sleeveless ankle-length tunic. She remembered it was called a sarafan as she fastened up the pretty ball-like closures that went up the front of it. She reached into the front pockets in her slacks and found only her travel itinerary.

"I bet this stop isn't listed," she said, slipping the paper back into her pocket. She left on her slacks and shoes beneath the sarafan. This should keep her warm—at least until she figured out where she was so she could leave.

She returned to the main room which was now cozy with heat. Jonathan tended the fire in the wood stove.

"Thanks," she said. "Where's your sister?"

"Dead," Jonathan said, standing up straight. "Two winters ago broke her heart. Last winter broke the rest of her. Now what are we to do with you? You'll have to become part of my family or someone else will claim you. If you'll excuse the indelicacy, but you must understand your peril: White men in this region will do about anything to bed a white woman. So you can be my cousin, Ursula, who is a foolish adventurer but who is nonetheless under my protection."

"I don't need protection. I need a telephone and then I'll be out of here."

"A telephone. I'm afraid I don't know what that is. Can you tell me anything more about how you got to the cave?"

"I—someone was giving me a tattoo. Everything became strange. I got up, touched a cave drawing, then I heard your voice."

"Tattooing? Interesting. I've been exploring the caves to try and find a correlation between the cave drawings and tattoos on the local people."

Ursula looked at him. "Really? Do the locals have elaborate tattooing?" Had she stumbled upon a village of the People?

"Actually, most of them have dots tattooed onto their backs. I've seen an occasional bird or sheep. I know some of the ancient graves in this area held tattooed people. I've been interested because I've noticed in my alchemy texts that in some of the drawings of people, they appear to be tattooed. And I met a China man alchemist some time ago, and he had several elaborate tattoos of mystical creatures on his body."

Ursula nodded. Others had tried to match rock art with tattooing before, but a link had never been established.

"Wait. Did you say *alchemy*? Where am I? Who are you?"

"You're in Kytan. A nondescript garrison town between Tomsk and Irysk, where Russians live within the palisades and the Natives live closer to the river, where everyone is taxed—only the Natives are taxed twice—and where the occasional exile is sent. I would be one of those exiles."

"An exile? They don't do that in Russia any more," Ursula said.

Jonathan laughed. "Please inform the Empress, will you?"

"Empress? Who are you talking about?" Ursula was suddenly tired. She sat on the bench and faced the flames voraciously gorging on wood until they flared several feet high and the wood began its transmutation into ash.

"Empress Ann. Peter the Great's niece. Have you had a loss

of memory?"

Ursula shook her head, then pinched herself. It hurt.

This was either a hallucination or . . . what?

"What year is this?" Ursula asked.

"1735."

Sergei had asked her what she thought about time. "What if there were places where time intersects?"

Ursula blinked. They had brought her to that cave to fulfill some preordained destiny.

Only Kam had told her to stay still.

And she had gotten up and answered the call of the bison.

They had meant her to go someplace sometime—but not this time and place. Except Jonathan had mentioned tattoos and ancient graves. Perhaps she was supposed to be here? She rubbed her face. *Supposed to be here?* She was starting to talk like Kam and Sergei.

"I have to figure out a way back," Ursula said.

"Back where? You can't be in that cave. You'll freeze. And you really can't go any place else until spring. Have you family? Money?"

"You're a Scot," Ursula said. "How can a Russian empress exile you?"

"She is an empress. She can do whatever she likes. My mother was Russian. The empress feels she has a claim on me. She says she exiled me because I am an alchemist, but in truth it was because I declined her advances and I couldn't produce gold for her." Jonathan smiled at Ursula. "You are welcome to stay with me. I'd love having some family."

"But I'm not your family," Ursula said.

"You have a perfect Scottish brogue."

"I hadn't noticed, but I am good with languages."

"Then you can be my assistant as well as my cousin. I cannot read Arabic very well and some of the texts are in Arabic."

"You're an alchemist?" Ursula said. "Then I have to tell you: You can't make gold out of mercury, or whatever it is you're doing. Gold out of lead? It won't work. They are chemically different and transmutation will not occur, no matter how much you wish it to."

He smiled. "You're wrong. Transmutation does occur. But I'm not interested in the gold you speak about or in the gold the empress wanted—or the gold the superintendent is now trying to force me to create. I am interested in our true nature. I am interested in the transmutation of people into human beings. To find the divine in nature. That is my gold."

40

Night was upon them suddenly. Ursula was exhausted. Jonathan fed her stew from the huge cauldron and brewed tea after pulling a small chunk of herbs from something shaped like a brick. After supper, Jonathan made her a bed on the bench near the fire.

Ursula dreamed a grizzly slashed her.

She opened her eyes to morning and the face of a wrinkled woman peering over her.

The woman said something like, "Who be ye?" only she said it in Russian.

Ursula blinked.

"She's my long lost cousin Ursula," Jonathan said.

The woman stood straight and looked at Jonathan who sat on his bench leaning over several open books.

"Ursula? What kind of name is that for a Scot? And how'd she get here? I haven't heard of any travelers."

Ursula sat up. The older woman took off her hat and cloak and began moving about the kitchen, mumbling to herself.

"This is Olga," Jonathan said in Russian. "She cleans house and cooks for me. If you must know, Olga, Ursula's party got waylaid by bandits. I happened upon her by chance yesterday in one of the caves I regularly explore. The bandits took all of Ursula's things."

Olga turned and looked at Ursula.

"Poor dear! Do you have enough clothes, then?"

"She's my sister's size. It'll work out. Thank you."

Ursula went to the back of the house and used the water closet.

Then Olga fed them some kind of porridge and bread along with the strongest tea Ursula had ever tasted. When she started coughing after one swallow, Olga came by and whacked her a good one on her back.

"Need another slap?" Olga asked.

Ursula held up a hand and tried to swallow her cough. "No! No! I'm fine," she said hoarsely.

Jonathan smiled over his tea cup. "Olga is under the impression that food and drink must have spirit and body—it's a very alchemical way of thinking. Because of the spirits she adds to the food she had me completely drunk for the first few months I lived here."

"Bah!" Olga said. "You better watch yourself, Cousin Ulla. He stinks up this place with his foul odors. Mixing this and that. You'll be lucky if you don't both get blown clear to St. Petersburg."

"I've never exploded anything."

"But she's right about the stuff you use," Ursula said. "Mercury is poison. They think Isaac Newton accidentally poisoned himself with mercury during his alchemical studies. And arsenic is poisonous."

"Arsenic," Olga said, looking up from the counter she was wiping down. "You have arsenic?"

"No!" Jonathan glared at Ursula. "And even if I did, I take care with all my ingredients."

"Hah!" Olga said. "You're lucky my people are of the Black Earth or I could turn you in as a witch."

Jonathan looked at Ursula. "Have no fear. The Russian Orthodox Church cares little about witches. If they did, they'd have carried off Olga herself. She runs around naked in nature worshiping Mokosh as often as she can."

Olga threw back her head and laughed.

"Yes, that is what I do every single day!" She went back to the kitchen, chuckling as she continued cleaning.

"Thank you for bringing me into your home, Jonathan," Ursula said quietly to him. "I will assist you in any way I can while I try to figure out how to get back to my home. You said Natives told you about the caves. Do you think I could talk with them? Is there a shaman I might speak with?"

"I'll see what I can do," Jonathan said. "I should warn you that there are some powerful people unhappy with me."

"More powerful than the Empress?"

"As they say here in Siberia about matters of religion and politics: God is far above and the czar is far away. But the superintendent of the garrison has demanded I produce gold for him. If I don't, he will evict me and otherwise make my life miserable."

"You've already been exiled—"

"But he can make my exile less comfortable than it is now. Like you, I do not believe the alchemical methods I am conversant with can produce gold. Yet we do know that some alchemists did make gold."

"What do you mean you *know* it? Have you seen it happen? And if you did, have you performed a chemical analysis of the materials?"

"No, I haven't seen it. But the ancient Egyptian alchemists are very highly regarded. If I could have you translate some of the texts, maybe I would discover something new."

"Of course, I'll read whatever you like, but I don't hold out much hope—"

Suddenly the door burst open, sending in a blast of cold. Standing in the doorway, with the glare of the outside snow creating a halo around them, were two men, their bodies covered in so much fur that for an instant they looked like some kind of mutated animals. Ursula waited for their growls—or roars.

Instead, the door slammed shut and the men tossed off their coats, revealing shiny green and red uniforms beneath the fur. Braids of gold decorated their sleeves, collars, and the front and back of their uniforms. Their black boots shined in the firelight.

Ursula glanced over at Jonathan. He now stood. Olga had disappeared. The man in front—the one with a little more white and gold in his uniform and dark curly hair sticking out from beneath his fur hat—stepped near to the fire. He took off his gloves and slapped one against the other. For an instant, he reminded Ursula of a black-booted Nazi.

"What is your excuse this week, Scot?" the man asked in Russian.

"I have told you I haven't the skill to make gold," Jonathan said.

"Then acquire it. I have offered to procure for you whatever you need." He looked at Ursula. "Who is this?"

"Superintendent Sidorov, this is my cousin Ursula Kuznetsov."

The superintendent bowed his head slightly.

"I have heard nothing about this visit. You know she must register with my office."

"I was on my way to do that," Jonathan said. "She was waylaid by bandits, and I wanted her to recover her strength."

"I shall send someone after them at once. Were they Kalamuks?"

"They weren't from here," Ursula said. "They were members

of my own expedition. I think they grew weary of me. Please, they are long departed."

"As you wish," Sidorov said.

"You speak better Russian than your cousin," the man by the door said.

Ursula looked for the first time at the other man. His hair was brown and straight, his eyes light-colored, maybe green. He smiled at her.

"This is Lieutenant Mikhail Petrovich Nikovotov," Sidorov said.

Nikovotov held out his hand, and Ursula shook it. He stared into her eyes as he held her hand, just as Sergei had when they first met. Did he know her?

"My cousin is good with languages," Jonathan said. "She will help translate some texts. Perhaps from those I will obtain the knowledge I need to help you."

Nikovotov continued to stare at Ursula.

Sidorov nodded. "I will give you more time then, Scot. But my patience is limited."

"Oh really," Jonathan said in English.

"Miss Kuznetsov, welcome to our little community," Sidorov said. "I'm certain my wife Anna Ivanovna will want to meet you. We will invite you and your cousin to dinner soon." He glanced at her dress. "Did the bandits get your clothes, too?" When Ursula nodded, he said, "You are about my wife's size. She can loan you a dress for the occasion. We must make do with what we have out here. Now I must take my leave."

Both men bowed slightly, then put on their coats and went into the day. Olga stepped out of the dark and shut the door, cursing under her breath.

Jonathan sat again, sighing deeply.

"He was much easier on me today," Jonathan said. "I suppose he didn't want to get too angry in your presence—at least this time."

"What will you do?" Ursula asked.

"I'll try to make gold."

41

Jonathan brought Ursula texts written in Arabic and Greek; some were bound in books, others were loose pieces of paper. She read them out loud while Jonathan nodded and took notes.

Most of it made no sense to Ursula. Some quoted Maria, the Jewess—the Mother of Alchemy, Jonathan called her. "One becomes two," she wrote, "two becomes three, out of the third comes the one as the fourth."

"I am the walrus," Ursula said.

"It says *that*? That's new."

"No, no," Ursula said. "It was only my lame observation that this stuff is rather obscure. Why don't they just say what they mean?"

"For some, they were guarding state secrets. For others, they felt only the initiated should have access. Others were protecting themselves. The pope outlawed alchemy."

She read about Hermes Trismegistus's emerald tablet: "What is below is like that which is above and what is above is like that which is below. Just as all things proceed from One alone by

151

meditation on One alone, so they are born from this one thing by adaptation. Its father is the sun, its mother the moon, the wind has borne it in its body, its nurse is the earth. Thus the little world is created according to the prototype of the great world."

Ursula looked at Jonathan. "You expect to make gold from these instructions?"

He shook his head. "I've heard all this before. Keep going."

Ursula read. Gradually, she realized the authors seemed to believe that—like everything Earthly—gold was imbued with the divine. They believed it was alive and it grew like grass or a tree which needed warmth and water. Like human beings, all of nature wanted to improve; lesser metals could—and had the natural chemical tendency to—transmute into more valuable minerals, like gold.

Jonathan and Ursula stopped to eat borscht, blinis, cheese, some kind of smoked fish, and potatoes—or something like potatoes.

"I'm not good at puzzles of this sort," Ursula said.

"That doesn't matter," Jonathan said. "Having you read the texts is enough. Just you being a part of it is grand. The feminine principle is needed for alchemical work, just as the masculine principle is required. White and red. Semen and menstrual blood."

Ursula shook her head. "I don't believe in masculine/feminine stuff. I think it's a social construct and doesn't represent truth, per se. In one culture women act one way and men another, but then in another culture women act a different way, according to what is acceptable behavior in that culture."

"You think there are no differences between men and women?"

"Of course there are differences. But I don't think we can declare one set of behaviors as feminine and another as masculine."

"I'll go along with that. So let us say that behavior has nothing to do with it. Let us look at our physicality. Alchemy is elemental. Earth, air, fire, water, and something deeper than even those:

prima materia. Prime matter. We are earth, air, fire, and water, and *prima materia.*"

"Actually we are made up of ninety percent water, some protein, other organic compounds, and some minerals."

Jonathan opened his mouth, started to say something, stopped, then said, "Close enough. In my work, you now act as my *soror mystica*—my mystical sister. You become my familiar—or I yours. We are a part of each other. This is what we must remember to be transmuted."

"What has this to do with gold? And you mentioned tattooing. I've not seen anything about that."

"In alchemy, making gold represents the joining of opposites. Sulfur and quicksilver."

"And which am I, as your *soror mystica*, I mean?"

Jonathan laughed. "You ask many questions!"

"I'm just trying to understand."

"This is the story of alchemy, at least how I understand it. All of it can be related to the chemical process and the chemical process can be related to the human process."

"OK."

"Think of humans as containers, like in the laboratory. To begin the alchemical process we have to go deep into ourselves, to dive for the *prima materia*—go deeper than chaos, to that which is physical and mysterious. Grasp the handful of Earth, that Hidden Stone, that passive raw material that is our soul. We get rid of that which keeps us from committing to our work and our life. We're looking for the Secret Fire—that fire we create in ourselves. Alchemy begins in darkness.

"We keep going deeper, descending. This is *nigredo*, the blackening. We burn away our mind. We mortify. Dissolve the intellect, the mind. The *prima materia* and First Agent are combined and pulverized. Earth and fire.

"Boy and girl come together—Sol and Luna. They make love

in water. *Coniunctio*. The lusty, uninhibited joining of opposites. This opens the body, and we catch a glimpse of what could be our lives."

Ursula thought of her grandmother making love with her grandfather on the floor of that cave.

"The body opens. We return to the hurt we've experienced. Mercury is born from this connection. Then *nigredo* begins. Sol and Luna are polarized. Rage breaks them down. Their original forms are destroyed. They die. All rots. This is when our minds are gone."

"And then you have gold?"

Jonathan laughed. "After a time of blackness, of drying out, ash forms and from this Mercury is born again. Solid to liquid to ash, but now the soul has been released from the mind."

"Do Sol and Luna get back together? They've got this Mercury kid to raise."

"Wait," Jonathan said. "Now the soul is bared. Constriction is released. There is expansion—like the full moon. Upward movement. This is *solutio*—when the heart opens. Lots of tears and water as the heat grows stronger. Now you have the strength of love. Sol and Luna make love again and are reborn in love. Our soul is now unweighed by the intellect and is the fire in our bodies. With coagulation, Sol sinks into the Earth. This stage strengthens the body, it is grounding. Fire sinking to the Earth. Now with this free soul, grounded body, and open heart, *rubedo* begins—the realization that everything comes from the One and returns to the One by the One, for the One. Unity occurs between Sol and Luna. They arise golden. True wholeness."

"And you can relate all of these activities to chemistry?" Ursula asked.

"Yes. Although finding the *prima materia*—the primal material—has been, for me, the most problematic." He stood and went to his lab. "This is my equipment." He touched one of several pale green pear-shaped objects with a kind of cap with a spout. "This is an alembic. Vapor rises from the bottom and condenses in the dome and channels into the spout."

"It's a still," Ursula said.

Jonathan nodded. "Of sorts, yes."

Ursula flipped carefully through an open book on the table. On one page was a picture of four women, each standing on a sphere with a triangle on it. The picture was titled "Four stages of the alchemical process."

The first woman had her hands on her hips and balanced a pear-shaped flask on her head; inside the flask appeared to be a hairy monster. The triangle on her sphere was upside down with a line through it. The next woman had her right hand on her hip and the left hand down with her fingers pointing to the ground. Inside the flask on her head was a bloated person on a chair. The triangle pointed down and had a dot at its center. The third woman had both hands on her hips. Inside the flask was a bird with outstretched wings—a Phoenix perhaps? Her triangle pointed up and had a horizontal line running through the center of it. The fourth woman had her hands on her hips. Inside the flask was a lion's head. The triangle was upright with a dot at its center.

"Figuring out these symbols looks more difficult than trying to figure out tattoos," Ursula said.

Jonathan turned several pages until he came to two drawings side by side.

"Look," he said.

Ursula peered closely at the drawings. One was of a woman in a white dress inside the flask. From the top of the flask a white rose bloomed. Rosa Alba. The woman was partially immersed in a white liquid though she didn't appear to be wet. In the next picture a man in red was inside a flask, partially immersed in red liquid which did not leave him drenched either. From this flask a red rose emerged. Rose Rubeo. Both flasks were in nature, surrounded by flowers, trees, and hills.

"Look at their hands," he said, handing her a magnifying glass.

She held it over the pictures. On the right hand of the woman was a blemish—or a picture? A tattoo? On the man's left hand was a similar mark. It almost looked like a spider with webbing.

"From this picture you've ascertained tattooing is relevant to alchemy? Do you know what it means?"

"No. I've also talked with the Chinese alchemist I told you about," Jonathan said. "I asked him about his tattoos. He was quite mysterious. All he would say is that they helped him transform. Perhaps the tattoos somehow imprinted into his body how to be a better alchemist—or a better human being. I'm not sure yet."

"All of these pictures are quite puzzling."

Jonathan shrugged. "I've been doing it for so long that they've started to make sense." He flipped the pages of the book back to the four women on the spheres. "For instance, this picture. The triangle pointing down with the line through it represents earth. The beast is the earth. Then the triangle pointing down represents water. The bloated man is also water. The triangle pointing up with a line running through it is air—thus the bird."

"Let me guess. The fourth triangular pointing up is fire and the lion represents fire. It's all elemental, my dear Watson."

"Yes, it is elemental. That's the point. Who's Watson?"

"Don't worry about it," Ursula said. "While I'm here, I'll help you, but I need your help, too. I want to know anything you know about tattooing, or the caves. Also, I'm going to start strength training. I need to work on my endurance." She looked around the room and saw a jar of beans on the counter. She went over and picked it up. "I can use stuff like this as weights. It's not pumping iron, but it'll do. And I should start doing stuff outside, to get used to the cold. Slowly. For instance, when you get water, I can help."

"Olga does that. She goes to the common well. She'll be glad for the help. I've studied some of the caves around here. I might be able to help you with that."

Ursula nodded and slowly moved her forearm up and down as she held the beans. "Maybe together we will figure out how to make gold and how to get me home. I'm starting to believe anything is possible."

42

Ursula lay on the bench near the fire trying to sleep. On the first night, it had been so easy—exhaustion had dropped her directly into slumber. Now she listened to Jonathan's snores twining with the wind outside, creating a low moan inside and out. The place smelled slightly of cabbage, wood smoke, and something indefinable. Her muscles throbbed slightly—too much strength training—and her mind raced. Would something about alchemy teach her the meaning of the tattoos? She believed the caves and the tattoos had something to do with the People, and they were why she was here. She wished she had asked Sergei and Kam more questions—or had listened better to them and to her grandmother when they spoke of the People.

Sergei, Asya, and Kam all seemed so far away now.

In the morning after breakfast, Ursula volunteered to go with Olga to fetch water from the community well. Jonathan studied his books while Olga supervised Ursula getting dressed for the outdoors.

"How far are we going?" Ursula asked as she pulled boots over pants that were over several pairs of stockings. Olga wound a scarf around Ursula's neck and made her put on one of Jonathan's fur hats.

"Jonathan's sister Jane, bless her heart, never dressed warm enough. Here's her coat. Make sure all the clasps are fastened."

Olga put on her own coat, hat, and mittens.

"I've never had this many clothes on in my life," Ursula said. Her only exposed skin was a narrow slit that revealed her eyes.

"Good. Then you are ready for winter in Siberia!" Olga said, handing her a couple of empty water jugs. Olga gathered several more under her arms, and they went outside.

Ursula closed her eyes from the shock of the bright sun. After a few moments, she was able to see again. Snow had fallen overnight and sparkled cleanly in the morning light.

Olga pulled a sled out of a shack against the house. Ursula noticed another building a few feet from the house.

"What's that?"

"The banya," she said. "Do you not know about this? Jonathan did not tell you?" She shrugged. "He isn't quite Siberian enough, hasn't the Siberian soul. Everyone has a banya—it is the place where the spirits reside. And where you can sweat and wash yourself. Nothing better. You should take yourself out there."

Olga set the jugs on the sled, along with several large metal containers, then took the reins and began pulling the sled.

"I'll do it," Ursula said.

Olga gladly handed over the reins.

"Where are the dogs?" Ursula asked.

"Dogs? Oh, when Jonathan found you. Probably borrowed them. We all share what we have."

They walked down the snow-covered street, passing houses that looked sturdy and warm, some appearing to be made more of snow than wood. Dogs bayed. Crows flew above Ursula and

Olga.

"Ignore them," Olga said. "They think I killed their mother, but I have never killed a crow in my life. I don't eat wild bird. At least not often."

They went down another street without passing anyone else. Olga unexpectedly stopped at a small building and went inside. Ursula followed. The cold seemed sharper out of the sun, damper. Olga leaned down and slid a board away to reveal a hole in the ground. She dropped the bucket in. A few seconds later, Ursula heard the splash as the bucket hit water. Then they pulled the bucket up and poured the water into the jugs.

"Try not to spill it or this building becomes a lake of ice."

"I'm surprised you can get water at all," Ursula said.

"It has never frozen," Olga said. "My entire life I've lived here and beyond. It has never frozen. We are good to the water spirits and they are good to us."

After they finished filling the containers, Olga whispered a prayer and slid the cover back into place. They loaded the water jugs onto the sled and went outside. Ursula pulled the vehicle across the bumpy road. The water sloshed, then began splashing out of the containers.

"We won't have anything left by the time we get back," Olga said, stopping Ursula. She held out her hands for the straps. Ursula gave them to her.

"Watch."

Olga put one strap over each of her shoulders, then began pulling the sled forward. It slid easily across the ice. The jars remained still. Olga didn't look down or back. She walked steadily forward.

"How can you do that?"

"My feet are firmly on the ground. Yours are not." She waved a hand in the air above her head. "That is where you are. And the Scot. His sister, too. Our feet are on this Earth. We have always known, the Black Earth people and those like us, that we are spinning in the ether of the universe, and we must ride the surface of the earth, like the seals ride the waves of the ocean."

"Go with the flow, Olga. Is that what you're saying?"

Olga glanced at Ursula. "I say you should keep your soles on the Earth, otherwise you'll fall off."

They went around the corner, and Ursula thought she saw someone in the shadow of a doorway, watching them.

"Who's that?" she whispered to Olga.

Olga glanced at the house. "I see no one."

Ursula looked again. Nothing was in the doorway, not even a shadow.

At Jonathan's house, they unloaded the jars on the threshold of the closed door, then Olga put away the sled. Ursula picked up what jugs she could and went into the house. The blast of heat nearly took her breath away and the semi-darkness temporarily blinded her. She stumbled toward the kitchen and put the jugs in the cupboard. As she stepped out of Olga's way and began shedding her hat, mittens, and coat, she suddenly noticed Lieutenant Nikovotov standing next to an uncomfortable-looking Jonathan.

"Good morning," Ursula said.

"Good day to you," Nikovotov said in German. "I have come to invite you and your cousin to a party at Superintendent Sidorov's in two days time."

Ursula glanced at Jonathan. "I don't know what to say. The Superintendent is most kind, I'm sure but—"

Nikovotov smiled. "Your German is flawless," he said in English. "Did you not know that if your cousin could speak German he probably would not be here now? The Empress loves all things German. The Superintendent's wife will send over several dresses. You may choose which one you prefer. Olga here can alter the dress for you should none fit."

As Olga noisily put away the water, she grunted assent.

"I wouldn't want to trouble anyone," Ursula said. "I'm not really a party gal."

Nikovotov smiled. "Madame Sidirovna would be very disappointed. May I tell her to expect you? We can send a sleigh to bring you."

Ursula looked at Jonathan. He shrugged. That's helpful, she wanted to say.

"All right," she said. She wondered why the Lieutenant was so anxious for her to attend this dinner.

"I look forward to seeing you there," Nikovotov said. He took her hand and brought it up to his lips and kissed it. "Until then."

He was gone before his kiss had dried on her hand.

"Couldn't you have come up with some kind of excuse!" Ursula said to Jonathan.

"I prefer to make the Superintendent happy, at least for now. He's not invited me anywhere since my sister died and then only once. You'll have to be careful. Nikovotov is a snake charmer."

Olga hissed.

Jonathan looked at her. "My pardon. I didn't mean to insult the snake."

Ursula laughed.

"Are they that bad?"

"Sidorov is downright cruel. He enjoys torturing Natives and exiles."

"Why?"

"Because he can," Jonathan said. "It's a form of entertainment, I suppose."

"So that's what people did for fun before cable."

"And Nikovotov," Jonathan continued, "has bedded—or attempted to bed—nearly every woman in Kytan."

"They say there is something peculiar about that one," Olga

said. "My sister works for him. He lives in one of the big houses on the hill. She says he keeps odd hours and seldom has anyone in."

"Yes, that does sound very odd," Ursula said, rolling her eyes.

"It's lonely enough being out here without being alone," Olga said. "You should go. The food will be wonderful. The Superintendent has the best smoked salmon. I have heard he even sometimes has eggs and fruit."

Jonathan rubbed his hands together.

Ursula smiled. Then she suddenly realized she had eaten dried fish for breakfast. Yesterday she had had dried and smoked fish and some other kind of meat at supper. Without a thought, she had eaten meat, after nearly fifteen years as a vegetarian. She was surprised she had not gotten sick—or at least had a twinge of conscience.

Sergei had told her one could not stay vegetarian for long in Siberia. She had ended her decade and a half long fast of meat in less than a day.

So much for commitment.

43

Ursula translated alchemy texts for Jonathan and helped Olga with her chores, offering to do anything that would help her develop her strength and stamina. She remembered reading once that the Eskimo were not physically better equipped to deal with the cold than anyone else. They were just acclimated to it. Each time Ursula went into the frigid air, it got easier. She ate more food at each meal than she used to eat at three. She pumped jars of beans and did push-ups and sit-ups. After a while, Olga and Jonathan stopped remarking on her odd behavior and either ignored her calisthenics or gave her advice for surviving the cold. Olga said the key was food, and plenty of water—hot water if one could manage it. Jonathan said it was layers of clothing that could be taken off or loosened—and steadiness.

"Don't run and then sit," he said. "Just walk. Otherwise you'll sweat too much and as the sweat cools from your body you'll lose your body's heat."

"If you're in a snowstorm," Olga said, "dig yourself into a snowbank unless you can find a cave. If you're on a mountain in a lightning storm, don't stand up to pray. My cousin did that and he was struck dead. Don't run under an overhang either; the lightning can find you there. Roll into a ball on the open ground—this lets the storm know how grateful you are not to be struck. And if you're in a fog in snow, hunker down and sing. Sometimes this entices the fog to let you live."

Jonathan talked to Ursula about alchemy when they sat alone at night by the hearth.

"Last spring when I was out exploring I met another China man. His grandfather had been an alchemist. They used the principle of alchemy to try to achieve immortality. His grandfather regularly drank gold to live longer. Plus the alchemists performed certain exercises. Something to do with the energy force in the body he called *chi*. If *chi* was flowing properly then there was no disease.

"People where I live do *chi* exercises: *tai chi*, *chi gong*, things like that. But they still die." Ursula stood and performed several *tai chi* movements. "I went to classes in college, outside before my real classes."

"That looks similar to the movements the China man showed me."

"I never noticed much difference," Ursula said. "It's one of the million things that so many of us try so that we can look better, be healthier, and live longer. None of it works."

She shook off her last posture and sat again. She felt a tingle of energy throughout her body.

Jonathan smiled. "You're very cynical, Ulla, for someone who has traveled through the caves."

Ursula laughed. "I'm not cynical. I'm hopeful. I'd like to feel better, look better, and live longer. But mostly I'd like to feel as though I have a purpose—to be committed. To feel whole. Where I come from people seem to always be trying to fill up every second with some kind of activity. They want connection and community, yet people irritate them. In my country, we consume more than any other country on the planet—we have this huge vacuum in our lives, and we try to fill it by doing or buying things. And it doesn't work."

"Of course not. Before I was exiled, I spent countless days trying to make certain I came to the attention of the Empress. If she noticed me, I would be an important person! Then she turned her eyes upon me, and I thought I would feel blessed or bigger than life. But when I refused to give her what she wanted, she turned on me, sent me into exile, where I have been, for the most part, quite content to be nobody and quietly study. Sometimes I feel as though we are all demanding notice from God—or whatever name you put to that being—and when it finally notices us and asks something from us, we refuse to give it. You say you are looking for a purpose. Maybe you already know it and have turned away from it, so now you are in exile. I have spoken with shamans from this region and many tell me they first refuse the call and then they are very sick until they agree to become shamans."

"Have you a calling?" Ursula asked.

"I want to demonstrate that the Divine is evident in all of Nature. Spirit and body are not separate."

"I wish you good luck."

"And you, have you been called and not answered?"

"A friend told me my destiny lies with the People," Ursula said. "And I told him I didn't believe in destiny. Yet here I am."

"Who are the People?"

"I'm not really sure," Ursula said. "I think I'll know when I find them."

A day before the dinner party, someone dropped off three dresses for Ursula.

"It's too tight," Ursula said when she put on the first one— a satin rose-colored dress with white lace. She could scarcely breathe. "And you can see my breasts. It's the middle of winter. I feel like I'm wearing a giant silk dinner bell."

Olga laughed. "This is the style."

Ursula wiggled out of that one and into a light green dress of a similar design. This one was not as tight but it showed even more of her bosom. She knew she would spend the whole evening waiting for her breasts to pop out. The third, a dusty-blue dress, gave her some breathing room and nearly covered her breasts. Olga found a pair of Jane's shoes that almost matched.

"I'll hem it a bit," Olga said, sticking pins into the cloth. "Now take it off."

"This really isn't me," Ursula said, stepping out of the dress. "I've never been to a formal dinner party in my life. I can't dance. They'll figure out I'm not from around here."

"Everyone knows that," Olga said, as she picked up the dress.

"They'll figure out—" Ursula stopped and glanced at Olga.

"That you're not the Scot's cousin?" Olga shrugged. "Who cares? They don't really want to know anything about you. They want someone new to try to impress."

"How'd you know Jonathan and I aren't related?" Ursula asked as she got dressed again.

Olga shrugged. "Don't worry. I won't tell any souls. Not even the banya spirits. Though, of course, they already know. You haven't been to the banya yet, have you? Go out there now. Don't forget to pray to the spirits."

Ursula thought it was a lot of work to get bundled up to walk a few feet to get undressed again, but she put on her outdoor clothes and went out the back door. It was nearly dark, and the streets were quiet.

Ursula put her mittened hand on the bath house door and re-membered Olga's admonishment to pray to the spirits.

"Please, spirits of this place. Let me in." She shook her head. "I am an idiot." She went inside the building and breathed deeply the moist warm air. She quickly lit a candle and glanced around. She was in a kind of foyer, partitioned off from another room; inside that room stood a wood stove. Several pails were positioned at various places near the benches.

Ursula quickly disrobed, lit a candle and went into the other room. The air was hot. She moaned and closed her eyes. "This is wonderful. Thank you, banya spirits!" She picked up a bucket and poured the warm water over her head.

"Yes," she moaned. "This is the life."

She went to the stove—it had two openings: one for the wood, one for stones. She took several logs from the wood box and dropped them into the stove. Then she scooped water from the bucket with a metal cup and poured the water on the red hot rocks. Steam filled the room. She walked to the benches and lay down on one.

All was silent. Not a sound from inside—except for the snapping of the wood as it burned. Perfect silence.

She held her breath.

Suddenly, the candle flickered and went out.

Someone else was breathing.

"Hello?" Ursula called. "Is someone there?" No, it couldn't be. She would have seen the door open.

Yet . . .

She held her breath again.

She heard the deep breath of some being. In and out. Slowly. The sound seemed to fill the bath.

Goose bumps broke out all over Ursula's body.

"Hello!" Ursula called.

Was it the wind through the eaves? Through the crack in the door?

She held her breath again.

It wasn't the wind.

Outside something scratched the wall nearest to Ursula. She jumped.

"This is not amusing," she said loudly in Russian. In English, she added, "I'm American, you know, which means I'm loaded for bear. I've got a semi-automatic, a 6'7" husband meaner than a tiger PMSing, and two Rottweilers. Don't mess with me."

Silence.

Then scratching and breathing.

Something was at the door.

The wood latch shook.

Ursula got up and grabbed a towel from the pile. She passed it quickly over her body; then, humming so she couldn't hear the breathing, she put on her clothes again. She fumbled for something to light the candle.

Something scratched.

Breathed.

Ursula pulled on her shoes and tiptoed across the creaking boards. She reached for the door.

It flew open.

Ursula screamed.

Olga raised up the lantern.

"What are you yelling about?" Olga asked.

"Something's out there trying to get in," Ursula said.

Olga shut the door again. Ursula could hear her stomping around in the snow outside of the building.

After a minute or more, Olga opened the door and stepped inside.

"I saw nothing," Olga said, "but it is that time of the day when the crack between worlds widens."

"What are you doing here?"

"The Scot said I could soak my old bones." Olga set down the lantern. Its light filled the small building. Nothing untoward lurked in the shadows. "And I wanted to make sure you got clean. That hair of yours is a sorry sight. Never seen anything that short on a white girl. Now take off those clothes."

44

The following day, the day of the party, Jonathan was more nervous than Ursula. He sat in the banya for what seemed like hours. Then he changed clothes several times and paced the main room.

Outside, the sky turned white. Snow powdered everything, quietly, slowly, on the windless day. As Ursula came back from the well, she had trouble seeing—the perspectives were all wrong. That snow-covered pile of wood seemed to be off in the distance until she nearly tripped over it. Then she turned down the wrong street. She stopped and glanced around. Everything was white— almost foggy. She broke out in a sweat.

"Don't panic," she whispered. "You're in Siberia. These people will help you."

She looked around again and saw something moving ahead of her. A man? Jonathan?

She went forward, pulling the sled steadily behind her.

"It'll be all right," she whispered. "It'll be all right."

She followed the lurching amorphous shape ahead of her.

She could feel her sweat evaporating. Her temperature would soon plummet and she would end up dead in a snowbank.

Then she turned a corner and saw Jonathan's house.

Whomever she had been following was gone. The air began to clear. By the time she got to the house, the snow had stopped. Ursula silently thanked her savior, then began unloading the jars.

She took a quick bath in the banya, then put on her new dress. Olga told her not to worry about her hair—a servant at the Superintendent's house would fix it. Jonathan came out in a dark waistcoat and vest and light colored breeches with gold trimming.

"They like gold," Jonathan said. "Ahhh, you look beautiful, Ulla."

"Thank you," Ursula said. "I feel foolish."

"Think of it as an opportunity to get away from Olga's cooking."

"Hah!" Olga said. "I know when I'm not wanted. I'm off to my own family."

As Olga put on her coat and hat, they heard the bells of a sleigh.

"Enjoy your evening," Olga said. She opened the door and stepped into the night.

Ursula glimpsed the sleigh before the door shut again. She and Jonathan put on their coats and hats.

"Into the lion's den," Jonathan said as he opened the door.

They went outside. Snow had started to fall again. The driver sat up front, holding the reins of two dark horses with thick winter coats dusted with snow. Jonathan and Ursula climbed into the back of the sleigh—after Ursula tripped trying to get into the sleigh and hold up her dress at the same time.

Jonathan spread a blanket across their laps. The driver slapped the reins and the horses stepped forward. A lantern next to the driver bobbed slightly as the horses trotted. The sleigh bells rang, the runners slid easily through the snow, and Ursula smiled as they hurried through the town, past the dimly lit windows of each house. The cold was damp, the falling snow heavy, and Ursula wondered how the horses or driver could see where they were going. She didn't care. She squeezed Jonathan's arm and smiled at him.

"This is fun!" she said.

He nodded and patted her hand.

Quickly, the sleigh wound up the hill, through the trees, to eventually stop in front of a large house covered in night. The driver helped Jonathan and Ursula out of the sleigh. They went up the steps and into the house. Ursula heard the sleigh bells shake as the horses pulled away again.

She and Jonathan stood momentarily in a well-lit foyer while taking off their coats, scarves, and boots which servants immediately whisked away. Ursula tried to focus on her surroundings but only saw paintings of what seemed to be religious scenes as the butler—or whatever he was—directed them out of the foyer.

"This way, Miss," a woman said, indicating the stairs; she wouldn't go up them until Ursula followed her. Off the foyer, the butler opened two wooden doors, and Ursula caught a glimpse of a roaring fire before the doors shut as Jonathan went inside.

Ursula went up the stairs and down a short dark hallway until the woman stopped her and opened a door. Inside was a small brightly-lit room with pale blue walls—similar to the color of her gown—with gold edging. A small sofa and a chair in front of a dressing table and mirror were the only furniture.

"I will fix your hair," the woman said.

"All right." Ursula sat in front of the mirror. "Thank you."

"Do you want some powder for your face or a wig?" the woman asked.

Ursula smiled at her in the mirror. "Do I look that terrible?"

The woman looked distressed. "No! No. I was only asking."

Ursula wondered if she was a paid servant, or a serf, which

was not much better than being a slave. The woman looked tired and hungry.

The woman brushed and combed and twisted Ursula's short hair until it was almost curly and slightly fluffy. Then Ursula walked downstairs with the woman to the room where Jonathan had gone.

Inside, two fires burned and the heat was almost banya-like. The ceiling was high. Paintings and gold trim covered the walls. Oil lamps made the room bright. The men stood when she entered. All wore glittery waistcoats. The women stayed seated, except for one beautiful blonde who stepped forward with her hands outstretched.

"Welcome, welcome to our home," the woman said. "I am Anna. We are very informal here." She squeezed Ursula's hands and smiled. Her eyes were light blue.

"But not too informal." The Superintendent stepped forward wearing his uniform. Every piece of metal on it gleamed and reflected the light back at Ursula. "We are careful not to be the Russians Adam Olearius wrote about in his scandalous book."

"Oh?" Ursula said.

"*The Travels of Olearius in Seventeenth Century Russia*," Anna said. "The Superintendent has never forgiven him. It seems, according to Olearius, we are all drunken lazy louts who have no manners or industry."

Nikovotov stepped closer to them and smiled at Ursula. "Olearius came before we made the Swedes our prisoners-of-war. They brought culture—music, dancing, language, art—to Siberia."

"Yes, we are grateful," Anna said. "Now let me introduce you to our civilized friends!"

Anna led Ursula around the room and introduced her to the red-haired gentleman Walter Syme and his dark-haired wife Charlotte Syme. Sasha Desnizkoi clicked his heels together when Anna brought Ursula to him. He held his glass high.

"Most of us *are* drunks," he said. "But we don't say 'fuck your mother.'"

"Sasha, please," Anna said. "Olearius claimed that was the first phrase out of a Russian's mouth—almost at birth. They don't know the name of God, he said, but they say 'fuck your mother' to their parents.'"

Ursula laughed. That phrase seemed absurd coming out of Anna's pretty mouth.

"We are an intimate group tonight," Anna said. "I hope you don't mind."

"Of course not." Ursula looked over at Jonathan. He smiled wanly and took a gulp of his drink.

The Superintendent handed Ursula a glass. She took it but did not drink from it.

"A toast," the Superintendent said. "To the newest member of our community. May the roads be clear and her stay long."

They all raised their glasses. Ursula did the same. She took a sip. Several more toasts were made. Jonathan came alongside Ursula.

"Do you know what a cannibal is?" he whispered.

Ursula nodded.

"Remember, they eat their own kind."

"Food awaits," Anna said, taking Jonathan's arm.

Nikovotov held his arm out for Ursula, and she took it. His other hand curled around her fingers on his arm. She was startled by his touch. She looked up at him; he smiled and whispered in English, "You have nothing to fear."

At that moment, she was suddenly afraid. Goose bumps rose on her arms. Anna glanced back as Ursula shuddered.

"Oh," Anna said, "I guess someone just walked over your grave."

45

The dining room was large, warm, and lit by candles. Plates of food covered the table. People passed food around and took for themselves what they wanted. Ursula sat next to Jonathan and Walter, across from Nikovotov. She had never seen so much silverware, glasses, and plates assembled at one table. She watched the others and did as they did. She ate various parts of birds and other meat, along with dishes she did not recognize. She washed it all down with liquor.

The men briefly spoke of war, lamenting peasant rebellions up north and giving opinions on this or that campaign. Ursula didn't really listen. Then Charlotte said, "I like your hair. I haven't seen a style like that."

"I travel a great deal," Ursula said. "Short makes it easier."

"And you can pass for a boy," Anna said, "and be out of harm's way."

"I never thought of that," Ursula said.

"I doubt she could ever pass as a man," Nikovotov said. "She is too lovely."

"She doesn't look like someone who enjoys false flattery," the Superintendent said.

Ursula glanced at the Superintendent. Did he just say she was ugly? She frowned.

"We heard you were waylaid by bandits," Charlotte said. "I'd love to hear about your adventure."

"I'm sure it was most harrowing and she doesn't wish to relive it," Anna said.

"Then a Cossack story from Nikovotov," Walter said.

"Yes!" Anna said. "Please, Niko dear."

"Of course," Nikovotov said. "I will tell you about the great Cossack hero Stenka Razin. My ancestors ran with the Don Cossack Stenka. He has been called the Russian Robin Hood. He was somewhat of a pirate—disgusted with the cruelties of the tsar, he stole from the rich and rallied the peasants and serfs with cries of 'live free and smash the rich.'"

"Let's not hear those slogans again!" Walter said.

"When it suited him, he worked for the tsar and the landowners, too. He was not a stupid man. It is said he had one great love in his life." Nikovotov glanced at Ursula. "He was a pirate for a time in the Caspian and there he captured a Persian princess. Stories have been told of her beauty. Stenka fell helplessly in love with her. He made her his mistress. But the time came when he had to return to Russia. Cossacks did not allow women on expeditions, so Stenka had to leave his beloved behind. On the night before they were to leave, the Cossacks feasted and made love on the banks of the Volga, the Mother of Russian Rivers. Suddenly Stenka picked up his beloved and carried her to the river's edge and threw her into the tumultuous waters, crying, 'You have given me so much and I have given you nothing, Volga-mother. Now I offer you the thing dearest to me.'"

Charlotte gasped. "How romantic!"

Ursula felt slightly woozy. She had to stop drinking.

"How is that romantic?" Ursula asked.

"Well—" Charlotte started.

"Stenka later angered the tsar and he was tortured for days," Nikovotov said, "then drawn and quartered while still alive. The tsar made certain his end was not pleasant."

"Here, here," Sasha said.

Jonathan laughed.

"A toast," the Superintendent said, raising his glass, "to dead rebels everywhere. May they remain dead."

Ursula continued eating.

"You won't join us, Ursula?" Superintendent Sidorov asked.

Ursula chewed and swallowed. "I prefer not to toast to anyone's death, though this Stenka sounds like a nasty guy."

Everyone laughed and drank their toast. Ursula didn't know what she had said that they found amusing.

"Tell me, Superintendent," Walter said. "I have heard there have been animal attacks on the citizens of our little burg."

Anna looked at her husband. "Animal attacks?"

"Two people have been attacked," the Superintendent said. "I didn't wish to worry you."

"I have heard they are not so sure they were animal attacks," Sasha said.

"What do you mean?" Jonathan asked.

"The victims claim the creature was clothed," Sasha said.

"What are you saying?" Walter asked.

"Werewolves," Sasha said. "They are saying they were attacked by werewolves."

"Hah!" Walter said. "That's nonsense."

Nikovotov looked at Walter. "You are English. Though you have lived in our country these many years, you cannot understand what this land breeds."

"But werewolves?" Charlotte asked.

"It *is* nonsense," Sidorov agreed. "Yet the scratches and bruises are unusual. It was dark out—two separate nights. One victim a woman, the other a man. Both claimed the creature walked upright."

"Perhaps a Domovoi has left his house and got a bit aggressive," Anna said, smiling.

"A Domovoi?" Jonathan asked.

"The Grandfather of the house," Anna said. "You would call him a spirit, or a god. He is shaped like a human, with a great deal of hair. Usually he does not leave his home unless he is neglected."

"Or the Rozhenitsye," Sasha said. "They are always seen at this time of year." He looked at Jonathan. "They are the Mothers, the fates, sometimes beautiful young women, sometimes beautiful old crones, three, seven, or nine of them. They are dressed in white with gold and silver in their hair, and they carry candles to light the way. You must never look at them or you'll be paralyzed."

"Have you considered that they may have been attacked by the Dvorovoi?" Anna asked. "It can be a very dangerous spirit."

"Or the Bannik, Ovinnik, Polevik," the Superintendent said with disgust. "Fairy tales for the feeble-minded." He bottom-uped his glass. "Some animal or crazy man attacked two people. That is all."

"They heard it beforehand," Walter said. "Isn't that right? They heard breathing or something similar before the attack."

Ursula looked at him.

"Is this true?" Charlotte asked.

"Apparently," Sidorov said.

"In this age of science, do people actually believe werewolves exist?" Jonathan asked.

"Of course they exist," Anna said. "They are a sign that the devil has infiltrated our town. We must be on the look out."

"Why the devil?" Ursula asked.

"When man lets loose his animal nature," Anna said, "that is devil's work."

"But if it's his nature and God created nature, how can it be the devil's work?" Ursula asked. "If people can change into other animals, wouldn't that be wondrous, not evil?"

"God, of course, creates everything and puts evil in our path to see if we are worthy," Anna said. "One becomes a werewolf by prancing around in a circle in the woods and pledging himself to the devil. One becomes human again by facing God at the altar and having the animal beaten out of him."

"I've heard that never works," Sasha said. "No matter how brutally they are beaten, they do not renounce the beast, and they die as werewolves."

"Probably because they never were werewolves to begin with," Jonathan said.

"I recall the story of a Livonia werewolf," Sasha said, "about forty years ago. An old peasant was accused of being a werewolf. He refused to repent. He actually admitted to being a werewolf, but he said he was defending the harvest against devils and sorcerers. He and the other werewolves, he said, were the dogs of God. He was sentenced to ten lashes and was set free to be a werewolf again."

Several of the diners laughed.

"Now," Sidorov said. "How about some cards?"

They all got up leisurely, most with glass in hand, and went into the other room. Ursula felt light-headed. She definitely had to stop drinking.

Sidorov, Anna, Charlotte, and Walter sat at a table together and began playing cards. Jonathan and Sasha stood near the fire talking.

Nikovotov touched Ursula's elbow.

"Let me show you the view from upstairs," he said.

"It's night time," Ursula said.

"Nevertheless."

He led her out of the room, into the chilly hall and up the stairs. A single lamp created little light. Ursula felt sleepy and too drunk to be with a man who would no doubt try to seduce her.

They walked in darkness until Nikovotov opened a door. They went inside the room and over to the tall windows and looked out. A light from somewhere below illuminated the falling snow. No tracks remained on the ground from earlier. Everywhere Ursula looked, she saw snow or darkness.

"It's not much of a view," she said.

Nikovotov put his hands on her shoulders.

"It was an excuse to get you alone." He turned her around. Ursula realized she was in a bedroom, a warm bedroom. Had Nikovotov planned this?

"Since I first saw you," he said, "I have felt about you the way Stenka felt about his Persian mistress."

Ursula looked up at him. She could see only the outline of his face. "OK, am I supposed to be flattered? And by which part of that story. The part where he kidnaps and rapes her? Or the part where he murders her?"

Nikovotov dropped his hands and stared at her. Then he laughed and stepped back.

"You are quite right, of course," he said. He sat on the bed. "It's an obscene story and you're the first to remark upon it."

"You mean it worked on all the other ladies?"

"Yes! Every single one!"

Ursula laughed. "Ah well. You can't win them all." She sat on the bed next to him. "Besides, I'm half drunk. It wouldn't be much fun."

"I'm a very good lover," Nikovotov said.

"I've no doubt you believe you are," Ursula said.

He laughed again.

Ursula got up. "Let's rejoin the others. I'm ready for dessert." She started for the door.

Nikovotov grabbed her hand. "Stay," he whispered.

She turned and looked at his shadow. "You may be a very nice man, but I know nothing about you."

"But I know you."

Ursula pulled away her hand.

"The last man who said that to me—" She stopped. "Do you mean we've met before?"

Nikovotov stood. "No, of course not. I mean that when I look into your eyes I recognize you. I see myself in you. We are alike."

"This sounds like another attempt at seduction, Nikovotov."

"Call me Niko. Of course I would like nothing more than to be with you. But what I see—what I know about you—is that we both honor our instincts—our animal nature."

"I don't know what you mean," Ursula said. "Don't be subtle with me. I don't pick up on that kind of thing—at least not in my personal life."

"I'm saying these attacks began when you got into town."

Ursula stared at him. "What? You think I'm responsible? You think I'm crazy? Or a werewolf? I can account for my whereabouts the entire time I've been in Kytan!"

"Don't be alarmed," Nikovotov said. "It wasn't an accusation."

"Then what was it?"

"Why are you afraid of me?"

"I'm not," she said. "We were having a pleasant conversation until you suggested I was a werewolf."

He laughed. "That wasn't what I meant. I'm sorry I offended you. What can I do to make amends?"

"Stick to trying to seduce me." She felt dizzy again. "I'm joking. What you could do is get Sidorov off my cousin's back. Jonathan cannot turn lead into gold. No one can."

"Sidorov enjoys his little cruelties," Nikovotov said. "And he isn't too bright."

"And what about you?"

"I'm not too bright either," Nikovotov said, "but I don't relish cruelty. However, I will protect myself. I have learned over the years to protect myself."

"Of course," Ursula said. "Could you at least convince Sidorov that alchemy is most successful during May and April, and even then, the process takes weeks?"

"I'll see what I can do." He took her hand again. "You will be spending the night you know. The snow is too thick for the horses. Everyone will bed down with everyone. Charlotte and the Superintendent. Walter and his drink. Anna and her bible, Sasha and Jonathan."

"Charlotte and the Superintendent?" Ursula said.

Nikovotov laughed. "You are amusing. If you change your mind, this is my room for the night and you will be right next door." He leaned down and kissed her. She remembered standing in the darkness with Sergei, falling into him, being with him. Nikovotov tasted of liquor, yet when he pulled away from her, she was almost sorry. Siberian nights were made for making love.

They went downstairs again and joined the others for dessert and an aperitif. The dessert was a kind of chocolate cake with fruit filling. The room wobbled as Ursula ate the chocolate. Everything seemed foggy and giggly. She smiled and put her hand out to steady herself. She glanced around the room and saw something—someone eating cake—only the someone was not quite human—or animal—wrapped in a gilded costume, so stunningly beautiful she wanted to cry. She blinked and looked down at her own furry white hand holding cake, her own gown was gilded. She looked up again. It was a mirror.

She was the beast.

She screamed and dropped her cake. The room spun.

There was another—another being—one of the People—

reaching out to comfort her. She closed her eyes.

"Shhhh," the other whispered.

She awakened to spinning darkness.

"Here's a bucket, miss," someone said.

She grabbed the proffered pail and threw up.

The room settled.

"Eat this bread," the woman said. "It'll help."

Ursula leaned back on the pillows and stuffed pieces of bread into her mouth.

"I don't drink," Ursula murmured.

"Yes, miss."

She sighed deeply. Someone had removed her gown.

"Do you want light?" the woman asked. "Drink this."

Ursula gulped water and immediately felt sick again.

Nikovotov appeared, carrying a candle. Ursula turned from the light.

"Leave us," Nikovotov said to the woman. "I will care for her."

The woman nodded.

"Go away, Niko. I'm going to throw up again."

"Here." He set the candle down next to the bed, then reached under the covers and pressed just beneath her rib cage. After a minute or so, he asked, "Is that better?"

"Yes."

He sat on the bed. "Give me your head." Ursula leaned closer. "Put your head in my hands." She did as he asked, and he gently massaged the bottom of her skull while cradling her head. When he was finished, she lay back on the pillows.

"I'm going to be sick," she said.

"Put your hands where mine were on your ribs."

"Shouldn't I throw it all up? Get it out?"

"It'll foul up your *chi*." He put his fingers on her ribcage again. Her stomach settled.

"What do you know of *chi*?"

"I studied in China for a while."

"A man for all seasons," Ursula said. "Did I disgrace myself grandly?"

"No. You passed out. What happened?"

"I drank too much."

"And? What did you see?"

"I saw . . . I saw that I shouldn't drink. Please, let me sleep."

"Do you want me to stay?"

"Only if you don't turn into someone else."

"Go to sleep. You'll feel better in the morning." He kissed her forehead.

"You don't seem like the Florence Nightingale type." She closed her eyes and heard a chair creak as Nikovotov sat in it.

"Who is Florence Nightingale?"

"It doesn't matter," she murmured. "If you only—"

"Shhh."

She awakened to darkness and the sound of someone laughing; then she heard a scream.

"Gee, is there a madwoman in the attic?" she whispered as she slipped down farther under her blankets.

Still later in the night, she awoke and slowly got out of bed and went to the window. Her head was clear, the nausea gone. She looked outside. The storm had stopped, and the night was snow light, as if it were just before dawn, but Ursula knew that morning was hours away. Snow hung from the branches of the trees. Everything looked still and silent, ethereal and earthy at the same time. She longed to be outside in it, running, or lying in it, making snow angels. A rabbit ran across the open area in front of the house. It stopped and looked up at her. She stepped back out of view. Then she shook her head and looked out again. Something gray ran into the woods. A wolf? The snow slipped off a conifer branch as the creature ran beneath it. A crow flew past the window and glanced inside.

"Weird," she whispered.

Several of the trees shook and a bear emerged out into the clearing. Was it a bear? It stood on its hind legs. Was it silver? Black? Red. It opened its mouth and roared her name. On the last syllable, the creature dissolved into snow.

Ursula backed up. She pinched herself; it hurt.

She backed into someone and turned around.

Nikovotov.

"They know you're here," he whispered.

"Who?"

"The People," he said. "You needn't worry. You're safe. I know who you are, but I won't tell. You told me all kinds of things tonight."

"I shouldn't drink."

He took her hand and helped her into bed.

"Sleep with peace," he said.

She closed her eyes and slept.

In the morning, Ursula awakened strangely refreshed. She ate food a servant brought her, then climbed back into her gown and went downstairs. Fortunately, the mistress of the house still slept and everyone else had gone home or off to work. Ursula sent her regards and thanks to Anna via a servant; then she and Jonathan bundled up and went home in the sleigh. As they slid through the firs covered in fresh snow, Ursula remembered seeing herself in the mirror as . . . as what? Then another like her. And later from the window, what had she seen? A bear calling her name?

The strangest part was that the voice seemed familiar, but she could not quite place it.

No, the strangest part was that she knew she had not been dreaming. Everything she had experienced last night had been very real.

46

Ursula took off the gown and put on one of Jane's simple dresses as soon as she got home. Then she went into the banya and stripped down again. She threw more logs into the fire, then poured a bucket of water over her head.

Olga came in holding several small branches tied together at one end.

"You drank too much," she said.

Ursula nodded. Olga threw water on the rocks, and steam filled the room. Ursula breathed deeply. Olga began hitting her gently on the back with the twigs.

"It's birch," Olga said. "It will cleanse you."

Ursula did not protest. She needed cleansing. "I drink too much here," Ursula said. "I don't know why."

"You're frightened. That's why."

Ursula nodded. "You have no idea."

"Maybe some. How was your party?"

"Very strange."

"And Nikovotov?" Olga whacked her a good one.

"Ouch. I think I'm sufficiently cleansed. Why do you ask about Nikovotov in particular?" Ursula looked at her.

Olga set the birch twigs on the bench and made a face. "Something about the way he looked at you."

"Uh-huh. I have the feeling you know everything that goes on in this town."

She made a noise, then said, "No, not all."

Ursula laughed. "We ate good. Then Nikovotov tried to seduce me. And failed. I drank too much, looked in the mirror, and saw this beast." She glanced at Olga; the older woman nodded.

Ursula looked at Olga. "That's your only reaction? How come you never ask anything about me?"

"It's not my concern."

"Remember the other day when I heard something outside the banya?"

"Yes."

"Last night they mentioned two people have been attacked by some kind of animal—and they both remembered hearing it breathe, like I did."

"I heard of these attacks. There was another last night—on the hill."

"On the hill? Where we were?"

Olga nodded.

"At the party someone said something about werewolves and the devil."

Olga sighed. "Of course."

"Of course werewolves or of course the devil?"

"They cart out the devil every time something beastly enters their lives. I think you've sweated enough."

Olga picked up a bucket of cold water. Ursula stood, and Olga dumped the near freezing water over her head. Ursula screamed and laughed, then dried herself and got dressed.

Together the women returned to the house. Olga fed Ursula

and Jonathan broth.

"What is this, Olga?" Jonathan asked. "Fish eye soup? More witch's brew?"

"You are the drunks. This will help you dry out. Some roots and herbs, sheep's piss."

Jonathan and Ursula stopped eating and looked at each other. Olga laughed, put on her coat, and left.

"I'm certain she's joking," Jonathan said. He stared at the broth. "I think."

Ursula smiled. "Did you have a good time last night?"

"It was very pleasant," Jonathan said. "To my surprise. And you?"

"A laugh riot."

"Pardon me?"

"Nothing. Do you have any translating for me today?"

"No. I am going right to sleep. I advise you to do the same."

After Jonathan went to bed, Ursula cleaned up the house and stoked the fires. She felt restless. Something had happened last night that she could not explain.

She laughed out loud. As if she could explain how she had gotten from summer to winter nearly 300 hundred years into the past.

She put on her outdoor clothes and went into a nearly blinding light. Wishing she had sunglasses, she began walking away from the house and street toward the open snow. Her feet kept falling through the snow, and she knew she would be exhausted in minutes. She returned to the house and looked inside the shed and brought out snowshoes. She put them on, adjusted the straps, and glanced around until she found sticks to stand in for poles. Then she started across the snow. After a few starts and stops, she got used to the snowshoes. She left the town behind and crossed the snowy plain until it ended and she stood on a ledge looking down at the river. Sailing sleighs rode the frozen waves, pushed along by an easterly wind. Several dog sleighs joined the procession. It was a beautiful sight.

Ursula turned and headed for a nearby wood, the darkness alluring on this glittery winter day. Soon she stood within the quiet forest. She walked deeper into it until trees were all she could see. Black, green, and white.

She breathed deeply. Had she ever in her life—before coming to Siberia—ever tasted such clean air? Ever tasted such quiet?

Someone breathed with her.

She turned around.

Some distance away—half visible between the lines of the tree trunks—a man stood. Ursula squinted. A familiar shape.

"Sergei," she whispered.

She raised her hand and waved.

"Sergei!"

The man turned and ran away from her. Ursula tried to run in the snowshoes and slipped on the snow that had been transmuted into ice, melted by the sun, then frozen by cold darkness. She landed on her belly, the wind knocked out of her.

Someone touched her shoulder.

"Sergei?" She turned her head to look up.

Nikovotov looked down at her. "Who?" He took her arm and helped her up.

Ursula brushed herself off.

"I thought I saw someone I know."

Nikovotov glanced around the woods.

"I see no one." He looked at her. "You should not be out alone."

"You're out alone," Ursula said as they started walking back the way she had come.

Nikovotov laughed. "I am bigger than you are."

"And you've got a sword," Ursula said. "I'll give you that. I've been working out—building up my strength."

"Whoever is attacking people is very strong," Nikovotov said. "He attacks men and women, day or night. He is stronger than you."

They emerged from the woods. A black horse stood waiting for Nikovotov. The horse shook his head when he saw Nikovotov; his bridle rattled, making a sound almost like bells ringing.

"He just waits?" Ursula asked.

"He just waits," Nikovotov answered. He rubbed the horse's nose. The horse pushed against his hand. "Ursula, this is Night."

"He is beautiful," Ursula said. She stepped closer, pulled off her mitten, and let the animal smell her hand. She put her mitten on again and stroked Night's forehead.

"You've been around horses before?"

Ursula nodded. "When I was a girl, I was horse crazy, and I rode some—bareback. After a while I discovered boys and pretty much lost interest in horses."

"The people of the Steppes have long ridden horses," Nikovotov said. "The people who are buried in this region were often buried with their horses."

"Jonathan mentioned something about ancient graves."

Nikovotov nodded. "Most of the tombs have been robbed, but I have collected some pieces, should you care to see them one day."

"I would! Most definitely."

Nikovotov climbed onto the horse. "Give me your hand."

Ursula took off her snowshoes and gave them to Nikovotov who shoved them into his saddle pack. Then she held out her hand. He pulled her up onto the saddle sideways, in front of him.

"I guess you've been working out, too," Ursula said.

He laughed. "Promise me you'll be more careful when going out."

"I am always careful."

Night leaped forward. Ursula wondered how he could run across the snow with such agility and grace. The cold whipped the small exposed part of Ursula's face. She turned her head to Nikovotov's chest to keep warm, then relaxed against him as Night galloped along. She knew at any second she could slip from Nikovotov's grasp, but she felt he would not allow it. He was one of those people who could will accidents away. He did not bend to the chaos of the Universe. He exerted control. For these moments, as she felt the powerful animal move beneath her and Nikovotov next to her, she relaxed. She had nothing to figure out, nothing to accomplish.

Too soon, the horse stopped. She opened her eyes. They were at Jonathan's house.

She looked up at Nikovotov.

"Shall I send a conveyance to bring you up to the house tomorrow morning to show you some treasures from the tombs?"

"All right." She held onto his arm and slipped easily off the horse and to the ground. Nikovotov bowed, and Ursula patted the horse's neck. She glanced down and saw spots of blood falling on the ice just beneath the horse's fetlocks.

"He's bleeding," Ursula said.

Nikovotov jumped down and lifted Night's left hoof.

"Ice cuts," Nikovotov said, letting the leg fall again. "He gets them this time of year from his hooves breaking through the ice crust on the snow and then coming up again. I've tried to keep him indoors on days like this, but he'll kick his stall to pieces. I understand. I feel the same way. The man who takes care of my horses says Night needs some shamanizing. His wife is a shaman. I think he's trying to extort more money from me."

"Yes, I'm sure he's become quite rich taking care of your horses."

Night snorted. Nikovotov stared at her. "You say the oddest things. I will see you on the morrow."

He mounted Night and galloped away.

Jonathan was awake, poring over his books, when Ursula came in. She took off her outdoor clothes, then went to the hearth to warm herself.

"Jonathan," Ursula said, "do you know many people in town?"

"A fair amount."

"Do you know a Sergei Polyakov?"

He looked over at her. "I don't recall a man by that name. Why?"

Ursula shrugged. "I thought I just saw him."

47

In the morning after breakfast, a covered sleigh arrived at Jonathan's doorway. Olga and Jonathan watched Ursula as she slipped on her coat and things.

"He won't hurt me," Ursula said. "Don't look so distressed."

"You're going alone to his house," Jonathan said.

"Is that a crime here?"

"No. It's just odd."

"I'm an archaeologist. He's going to show me old stuff!"

"My sister Urga is there," Olga said. "Call on her if anything appears odd. Tell her I said good morning. Promise me."

"Yes, I'll say good morning," Ursula said. "And Jonathan, I promise I'll keep my clothes on."

Olga laughed, then made a noise. "You think we take our clothes off to have sex? It's winter in Siberia! Have some sense, girl!"

"OK. Then I promise to keep my dress down."

She waved and left the house.

The driver dropped Ursula off in front of one of the smaller houses in the hill district. An older woman who looked like she could be Olga's twin brought her inside the house and helped Ursula off with her things as they stood in the small dark foyer.

"Are you Urga?" Ursula asked.

The woman nodded.

"I'm Ursula. Your sister Olga asked me to wish you a good morning."

"Oh!" Urga smiled as she helped Ursula off with her coat. "So it is you!"

"I think she's afraid Lieutenant Nikovotov will eat me alive."

Urga grinned. "Yes, well, everyone who comes here has left unbitten."

Ursula laughed. Urga, weighed down with Ursula's things, walked to a door, knocked, then opened it.

"Miss Ursula," Urga said.

Ursula went inside a dark room, lit only by the fire in the hearth and the light coming from a single tall window. Books filled recessed shelves, along with various vases and other art pieces.

Nikovotov stepped out of one of the shadowy corners, today wearing casual clothes instead of his uniform. He looked softer, almost ruffled, though he did not have a hair out of place.

Nikovotov took her hand and kissed it. "Good morning. Thank you for coming. I thought you might be talked out of it."

Ursula smiled. "Concern was expressed."

"Tea?"

Ursula shook her head. "I'm anxious to look at your Scythian treasures."

"You hold with Herodotus then, that these burials are Scythian?"

"There were so many tribes that it's difficult to say," Ursula said, "but the art we've seen from the tombs in this area has definite Scythian characteristics."

Nikovotov took a candelabra from the mantel and lit it, then carried it to a table in the middle of the room. Gold gleamed as he set it on the shiny wooden table, highlighting the pieces on it. Ursula gasped. Nikovotov smiled.

"May I?" Ursula asked, reaching for a golden comb.

"Of course."

Ursula carefully picked up the comb. All of it was gold: the teeth, the five lions crouched between the teeth, and the three golden warriors. "This is probably fifth or fourth century BCE," Ursula said. "Probably Greek made for the Scythians. See, the warrior's dagger and that sword are of Scythian origin, yet that helmet on this warrior is Corinthian and that helmet is Macedonian." She set the comb on the table again and leaned down to gaze at a sword sheath. "Wood cased in gold. Sixth century, I'd guess." Fantastical creatures walked down the sheath—each had a lion's tail and feet, a griffin's head, and fish-shaped wings. Every other one held drawn bows.

She picked up a gold belt buckle of a winged lion-griffin attacking a horse. "These are beautiful," Ursula said. "Superb workmanship." She set it down again.

In the middle of the table was a large gold plaque, which she guessed had been originally used to decorate a chieftain's shield. Ursula carefully picked it up and took it over to the window. It was a bear's paw, shaped exactly like the tattoo on the lady's chest—exactly like Sergei's tattoo.

"Ah, this is familiar?" Nikovotov came up behind her.

Ursula nodded. "I've seen a mosaic and a tattoo exactly like this."

"It came from a tomb not far from here. Along with a carpet I have. We believe it was a woman's grave. She had no horses sacrificed with her but her tomb was quite elaborate. The carpet is upstairs."

Ursula replaced the bear paw, then went with Nikovotov out of the room, into the hall, and up to the second floor. Inside a small room, was a large wooden case with a glass top. Ursula was struck by how modern the case appeared. Nikovotov opened the curtains on two tall windows and light streamed in and spotlighted the carpet inside the case. It was deep red and yellow knotted woolen pile, with bands of animals going around it. The outermost band showed stylized horses and their mounts. The next band depicted various wild animals. Then suddenly the style changed. The next band had depictions of swans, snakes, fish, foxes, and leopards which were more realistic than the other animals, similar in style to the lady's tattoos. In the next band, the animals were again depicted realistically except each had a human characteristic. The fox had a human face, the swan had human feet, the fish human eyes. At the center of the carpet was an upright bear—only it was not quite a bear—more like the reflection she had seen of herself in the mirror. It was human. And it was bear.

"I've seen this before," Ursula said.

Nikovotov laughed. "If you live long enough in Siberia you'll see lots of bear."

"Is that what you see when you look at it?" Ursula asked.

Nikovotov looked at her. "Of course. What else?"

Ursula felt slightly nauseated. She started to step back when suddenly she noticed two tiny flasks at the feet of the bear. She leaned over to get a closer look. Inside one was a white human holding a white rose; inside the other was a red human holding a red rose.

"Rosa Alba and Rosa Rubedo," Ursula whispered. They looked very much like the illustrations of the tattooed people in Jonathan's books.

Nikovotov leaned down next to her. "Isn't that interesting? I've never noticed it before."

"I've seen those symbols in alchemy texts," Ursula said. "This is quite strange. And it was in one of the frozen tombs?"

"Yes. Are you well? You look quite pale."

Ursula stepped away from the display case and sat in a nearby chair.

"I'm fine. Your carpet is magnificent. Thank you for showing me."

"Let us go downstairs for tea then."

Ursula drank tea and ate cookies and scones while holding Scythian gold in her free hand.

"I feel quite decadent," Ursula said, "to be handling these priceless pieces. Does the Superintendent know of these? I know he's obsessed with gold."

"I share these with only a select group of people," Nikovotov said. "The Superintendent does not have a true appreciation of history or art."

Ursula smiled. "Do you know—are there people in this area with tattoos that are like the bear's paw?"

Nikovotov set his cup down. "I have not heard of any. I know some of the Natives tattoo—they call it embroidery."

"Do you have any tattoos?" Ursula asked.

Nikovotov laughed. "No. I don't believe in defiling nature's creation. But I'll be glad to make myself available for your examination."

Ursula laughed. "I bet you would. You mentioned your horse's manager is married to a shaman. Do you think she'd see me?"

"Why?"

Ursula shrugged. "So she could read my aura, cleanse my vibes, do my chart."

Nikovotov raised his eyebrows

"Sorry. I've never met a real shaman," Ursula lied.

"Actually, she has agreed to meet a group of us in two days—the same people you met at the party. You are welcome to join us. Bring Jonathan if you'd like."

"Great," Ursula said. "I think I should go home now. You have been very hospitable. Thank you."

"You are always welcome," Nikovotov said as they stood.

"Now you can return to the bosom of your family, and everyone can see I didn't gobble you up."

"At least not this time."

Jonathan jumped up when Ursula came into his house again.

"Ulla!" he cried. "I had a visit from one of the Superintendent's men. He has given me leave until the spring to begin the alchemical process! Whatever you did, it worked." He put his arms around her and embraced her tightly. "You are a good cousin."

Ursula laughed as she took off her outdoor wear. "I'm not your cousin."

"Details, woman, details. This gives me some breathing room. Olga has left us a banquet. Let's feast. Tell me all about Lieutenant Nikovotov. Did you keep your clothes on?"

Ursula laughed. "Every stitch."

48

Ursula awakened before breakfast the next morning to get water. She threw wood into the fireplace and stove, then put on her outdoor clothes and went into the early morning that was still gray with night. The air was damp and so cold it hurt her lungs to breathe it in. She wrapped her scarf around her mouth and neck one more time, took hold of the sled, and walked down the road. Hoar frost had formed in the night and now covered everything—the windows, sleighs, eyebrows of people who passed her this morning. The streets were busier than usual, and everyone was in a hurry. As she crossed the street to continue down the Y toward the well, she realized she saw fear on the faces of the villagers. She glanced back at the river but could not see it; fog had rolled over it and snatched it from sight.

She remembered Olga's admonishments about fog and hurried down the road to the well. Two women were ahead of her in the well house. No one spoke as the bucket splashed into the water or as the woman hauled it up and poured the water into the jars. She dropped the bucket down again.

"It's not a good day," the woman in front of Ursula said. "The fog will be bad."

"The sun will burn it off," the other woman said. She poured part of her second bucket of water into her jars, then handed the bucket to the other woman and left.

"It's a curse," the woman said as she poured water. Her hands shook and she sloshed some water onto the floor. Instant ice. "The fog and the werewolf."

"Do you need help?" Ursula asked.

"No."

Someone outside screamed.

Both women looked at one another. The other woman dropped the bucket, grabbed her sled, and went outside. Ursula followed.

The day had changed completely. Fog covered everything, thick and icy. Ursula could see no houses, no streets, nothing but fog and the well house next to her. The other woman disappeared into the fog.

Another scream.

Ursula started forward, slipped, and fell. She carefully pushed herself up and went inside the well house. She slipped again but did not fall. She checked her clothing—at least nothing got wet. Her heart pounded, and she tried to breathe deeply to calm herself, but it was too cold. She squatted down. She had to get calm. So what if she couldn't get back home because of the fog? Some mad killer would get her before then anyway. No, she thought, they didn't have psychos in this century.

She laughed. This was not the time for ignorant nostalgia. She had to get somewhere warm before too much time passed.

Someone was coming. She heard footsteps. No, not footsteps. Snuffling. Breathing.

She quietly picked up a jar from her sled and pressed herself against the wall. The noise seemed to get louder and louder, until it was pounding in her head. She closed her eyes—no, that was her own heart. Yet it sounded so similar.

The door opened and the other woman came inside, her eyes wild, her mouth uncovered.

"It got another one! Almost killed him. Did you hear the scream? Like a baby being pulled apart." She looked at Ursula as though she wanted to strike her. "It's you. It all started since you came. You've brought a curse to us."

Ursula started to protest, but the woman left again. She didn't know her, yet the woman knew Ursula. They all did. So Nikovotov wasn't the only one who linked her arrival with the attacks.

Maybe they were right.

The snuffling had stopped. Or the breathing. All was quiet.

She took the jars off the sled, then pulled it outside.

"Hello!" she called out. Her voice sounded strange, the sound dead. She had never seen or felt anything as alien as this fog seemed.

"It's only condensation," Ursula whispered.

She started forward, slipped, and fell.

"This won't work."

She glanced around. Several sticks rested against the well house. She reached for two of them. Then she got on the sled. Using the sticks and her feet, she steered herself down the road. She couldn't see anything but the icy road so she concentrated on following the path other sleds had taken, assuming that would take her some place. Occasionally someone emerged from the fog—like some suddenly carnate ghost who disappeared immediately into the fog again, so quickly that Ursula barely had time to be startled.

After a time, she began hearing someone call her name. She steered the sled toward the sound until she reached Jonathan's house.

"Thank you, thank you, thank you!" she whispered as she got

up and put the sled away. She staggered into the house, exhausted and sweating. She pulled off her coat and things and hurried to the hearth. Jonathan stood at the stove stirring something in a pot.

"Thanks for calling out for me, Jonathan," Ursula said. "I could have been out there all day."

Jonathan looked at her. "What are you talking about. I never called for you. Why would I?"

"Olga must have then," Ursula said, rubbing her hands. "There's a terrible fog."

Jonathan went to the door and peered out. He closed the door again. "You were in that? You're lucky to be home. Olga's not here, by the way, probably because of the fog."

"Then who called out?"

Jonathan shrugged. "It wasn't me."

Ursula sat on the bench near the fire.

"I'm sorry but I left the water behind," Ursula said. "I was really scared."

"And yet you got back here."

"It was so icy, I couldn't walk. I got on the sled and slowly made my way back."

"You are able to act even when afraid," Jonathan said. "I admire that."

"I was cold," Ursula said, "plus, some maniac is running around. I heard screams, and this woman said someone else had been attacked. She also said this is all my fault."

Jonathan came and sat next to her. "You? Why?"

"She said these attacks started when I got to town," Ursula said. "I didn't know anyone knew I was here."

"Everyone knows everything," Jonathan said. He patted her hand. "You coming to this town doesn't have anything to do with anything."

"Nikovotov even mentioned it. I *am* out of time. I mean maybe I'm not supposed to be here. Maybe everything is out of balance.

I feel like I should be doing more to get home or figure out what I'm doing here."

"Tomorrow you'll go see Nikovotov's shaman. Perhaps she'll have something to say."

49

The fog settled over Kytan and held on all day and through the night. It seemed to seep into Jonathan's house, even though Jonathan did not notice. Ursula stayed near the fire listening for the sound of breathing outside the door. Olga never came. When night fell, Ursula did not get to sleep for many hours.

The next morning, Olga burst into the house, singing and banging pots.

"Nice to see you, too," Ursula murmured as she pulled the blanket over her head.

"Mokosh has blown the fog away," Olga said. "We are free again."

"Dancing naked under the trees did it, eh, Olga?" Jonathan asked as he came into the room.

"I told you there's only one thing to do in a fog. Make yourself small and pray."

After breakfast, they heard the sound of sleigh bells.

"Going to the shaman?" Olga asked as Jonathan and Ursula put on their coats.

"Yes," Ursula said. "Nikovotov arranged it—the wife of his horse trainer, I think."

"Yes, I know her," Olga said. "She is my cousin. Tell her I said good morning. Promise me."

"Yes, of course," Ursula said. "But I thought she was Native."

Olga made a noise. "I am not Russian, what do you think? I am born of this land. I am a child of the Black Earth. Mokosh's kin."

"OK. OK. I will greet your cousin."

"Here." Olga handed her a tiny bag. "These are her favorite candies. Butter honey. Give her these. You yourself."

"Me, myself, and I. Got it. Bye!"

They went into the gray morning. It was much brighter out than it had been yesterday. The air was dryer. A crow flew overhead. Things were normal again.

The driver got down and opened the door of the sleigh carriage. Inside were Walter and Charlotte Syme, Sasha Desnizkoi, and Anna Sidorov. Ursula got into the carriage and sat next to Anna. Jonathan sat by Sasha. The door shut. A few moments later, the carriage slid forward.

"Nice to see you again," Anna said, taking Ursula's hand.

"Isn't this exciting?" Charlotte said. "We're going to see a real sorcerer."

"I think they call themselves shamans, my dear," Walter said.

"Or kams," Sasha said.

"Do you know what question you'll pose to her?" Charlotte asked Ursula.

Ursula shook her head. "I hadn't thought about it." She hoped she could get her alone and ask about the caves.

"I shall ask if my husband is faithful," Charlotte said, smiling at Walter.

"Why not ask your husband?" Anna asked.

Ursula remembered Nikovotov said Charlotte was having sex with Sidorov and Walter went to bed alone. Apparently, Charlotte enjoyed games.

"I don't think she is a fortune teller, Charlotte," Anna said.

"Niko said we can ask whatever we like," Charlotte said, looking down at her red gloves. "So I shall do just that."

Ursula glanced at Jonathan. He gave an almost imperceptible shrug. There were undercurrents to this conversation that Ursula did not understand.

"Lieutenant Nikovotov has great influence with you?" Sasha asked.

Anna looked out the window. "We hold Lieutenant Nikovotov in high regard. His words are always truthful."

"Where is the Lieutenant?" Ursula asked.

"He and the Superintendent will meet us there," Anna said. "They have been busy trying to capture that mad man. They may be late and have to leave early."

"Any news?" Walter asked.

"Two more were injured the other day during the fog," Anna said. "That's all I know."

"I've heard the attacks grow more savage with each victim," Sasha said.

"It is fortunate no one has died," Walter said. "Or been otherwise violated."

"Please, let's not spoil our outing," Anna said.

Ursula looked outside. They passed out of the palisades and started down. She glimpsed sail sleighs on the river.

"We live in a glorious world," Anna said. "I never tire of looking at the sleighs and sails on the frozen river. It is like something out of a fairy tale." She smiled. "I quite love it here."

The sleigh eventually stopped. Soon they all stood amidst several small, tidy-looking houses. Nikovotov's horse Night chewed on hay beneath an overhang at one of the houses. Anna led the way to the door of the house. It opened before her hand touched it. A small man stood on the threshold smiling.

"You are welcome," he said, his Russian accented.

They went into the small house. Fire burned in the hearth. At one end of the room was a sort of bed about eighteen inches high, six feet across, covered with mats. The walls were made of wood and moss, with a layer of the moss between each beam and the next. A square had been cut for the window. Ursula stepped closer and saw the window was made of ice.

"Two, sometimes three pieces, are good for the whole of winter," Nikovotov said. He touched her elbow. "Good day, Ulla. It is good to see you."

"And you," Ursula said.

A woman Ursula did not know stirred the contents of a pot hanging in the hearth. The man encouraged everyone to sit on the bed. Charlotte giggled and sat. Walter stood near her. Anna sat between Jonathan and Sasha.

The place smelled of earth.

Nikovotov motioned Ursula to a small bench near the bed. The woman at the hearth began smoking a pipe. Then she turned and walked across the room. When she went by the window, Ursula glimpsed her features. She looked just like Olga.

"This is Yaga," Nikovotov said.

"Where's the Superintendent?" Anna asked.

"He has been detained," Nikovotov said.

"You'd think they'd offer us tea," Charlotte said in a stage whisper.

"One brings presents *to* the shaman," Nikovotov said.

Sasha pulled a box from his coat. "A tea bar," he said as he gave the box to the woman's husband.

Nikovotov nodded approvingly.

Anna pulled a lace handkerchief out of somewhere and handed it to Walter. "My gift."

Ursula started to stand. Nikovotov put his hand on hers. "I already gave her a gift in your name."

"That is generous, but I have something for her."

The woman walked back toward the hearth, paying no heed to any of them. Ursula went up to her and said, "Olga asked me to say good morning to you, and she sent you honey butter candies. She asked me to give them to you personally."

The woman took the bag and looked into Ursula's face.

"Good morning to you, Ulla," the woman said. "Now we can begin."

Yaga brought out a piece of wood with bits of colored cloth hanging from it. Something appeared to have been carved into it, but Ursula could not really tell what—a human head perhaps? A bear's head? A dog's?

"It's her *shaytan*." Nikovotov whispered.

Yaga set the shaytan in a corner near to her. Then she brought out a drum that had cloth, pieces of brass, and iron rings attached to it. Closing her eyes, Yaga began hitting the drum. She and her husband sang. The words were slurred and Ursula could not make out what language they spoke. The singing and drumming went on for about fifteen minutes. Then they stopped. The man took Yaga's drum from her, and she sat cross-legged on the floor.

"You may ask questions now," her husband said.

The party goers looked at one another. Walter cleared his throat.

Ursula glanced at Nikovotov. He smiled.

Finally Anna said, "Will winter end early this year?"

"Those are matters of nature," the woman said in Russian. "But I can tell you the magpie has smelled green ice in the mountains."

Ursula raised her eyebrows. What did that mean?

Anna nodded as if satisfied.

Sasha asked. "Will they catch whoever is attacking people?"

"I do not know the future," Yaga said.

"Oh dear," Charlotte said.

"She is a healer," Nikovotov said. "Not a fortune teller. Ask something personal."

Charlotte glanced at Anna, who shook her head.

"I would like to know if my husband is faithful to me," Charlotte said

Ursula rolled her eyes. What a peculiar woman she was; unless, of course, Nikovotov had lied and Charlotte and the Superintendent hadn't had sex. Why had that not occurred to her? For some reason, she believed Nikovotov implicitly.

"Your husband is as faithful to you as you are to him," Yaga said.

Walter patted her hand. "See there."

Charlotte looked suddenly pale.

Ursula turned her face into Nikovotov's shoulder to hide her smile.

"I should like to know if my long lonely exile is almost over," Jonathan said.

"It is over," Yaga said.

Jonathan glanced at Sasha, then looked back at Yaga.

"I mean my exile here in Siberia."

"It is finished," Yaga said.

The room was silent again except for the crackling of the fire.

Yaga looked at Ursula. "And you?" she asked in a language Ursula had not heard before.

"I would like to know why I'm here and how I can get home again," she answered in the woman's language.

"What are they saying?" Charlotte asked.

"You are here to help one of your own. It is his skin you must press against yours, his skin you must pierce with knowledge. He is lost. You are home. When you have healed the man, return to the cave and it will continue."

"Niko, can't she speak so that we may understand her?" Anna asked.

The woman stood and went to the fire, her back to them.

"It is over," the husband said.

"Thank you," Ursula said.

"What did she say to you?" Charlotte asked.

"You understood her?" Anna asked.

"I am good with languages," Ursula said.

"Come," Nikovotov said, gripping her elbow. "We must go."

The group filed outside into the cold again.

"That was rather—" Walter started.

"She's a charlatan for certain," Charlotte said.

"She is quite genuine," Nikovotov said, "with genuine people."

Charlotte closed her mouth; Walter took her hand and helped her into the sleigh.

Nikovotov leaned down slightly to whisper in Ursula's ear. "I must see you. Soon."

Ursula looked up at him. His eyes were shiny with excitement.

"Of course," Ursula said.

"I must go to work now, but may I come over when I am finished?" He gripped her hand. Behind them, Night stomped a hoof and neighed.

"As long as it's a reasonable hour," Ursula said.

He nodded, then helped her into the sleigh. After they were all inside—except for Nikovotov—the driver flicked the reins, and they were on their way again.

"Will you and Jonathan come up to the house to eat?" Anna asked.

"That's very generous," Ursula said, "but we've got work to do."

"Work?" Charlotte asked. "What kind of work? And what did that smelly old woman say to you, anyway?"

"Charlotte, that's a beautiful pin," Sasha said leaning forward.

"Yes, I was going to remark on that as well," Jonathan said.

"Oh, well, thank you."

Sasha and Jonathan kept Charlotte distracted until they arrived at Jonathan's house. Then Ursula and Jonathan said their good-byes and quickly disembarked and were inside the house before the sleigh was gone.

"I like Sasha," Ursula said as they took off their coats. "He understands subtlety."

Olga stood over the stove, stirring something in one of her pots. "You didn't stay long."

Jonathan and Ursula stood by the hearth to warm themselves.

"We all got answers to our questions," Jonathan said.

"Yes, Olga, she said Jonathan's exile is over."

"Whatever on Earth that means!" he said.

"If Yaga said it, it is so," Olga said.

"She looks just like you," Ursula said. "How many sisters do you have?"

"She is not my sister," Olga said as she brought them each a cup of tea. "And you, Ulla, did you get any answers?"

"Oblique ones," Ursula said.

"She talked to Ursula in her native tongue and Ursula talked back to her."

"As I've said before, I'm very good with languages."

Olga looked at her. "Heed what Yaga says but be careful. All is not what it seems."

"How very cryptic, Olga," Ursula said. "If you know something, I wish you'd just come out and say it. I'm really lost here. Neither of you understands how far I've come."

"Or how far you'll go," Olga said, returning to the stove. "We know."

Ursula rolled her eyes. "I wonder when I'm going to wake up from this."

50

Before night set in, Nikovotov's driver knocked on Jonathan's door. He asked if Ursula could please come with him. She dressed for the outdoors, then stepped outside and into the waiting dog sled. After the driver tucked two blankets around Ursula; he whistled to the dogs, and they slid forward. Soon they left the palisades and were heading for the frozen river.

"Where are we going?" Ursula called.

The driver ignored her. The dogs pulled them across the ice and up to the other side of the river. The world was cold, white, gray, and silent. Any sign of human civilization soon disappeared from sight. Ursula wondered whether the driver had decided on his own to kidnap her. She sighed. Nothing she could do about it now.

The dogs sprang up and into a sparse wood of larch trees. Soon after, the driver reined in the dogs and whistled them to a stop.

"He's in there," the driver said, pointing to the darkness in an outcropping of red rocks.

Ursula got out. The driver slapped the reins and the dogs lunged away. Ursula stood in the fading light of the woods, listening to her own heart beat. She had just been dropped off out in the middle of the wilderness during a Siberian winter.

Nikovotov had better be inside that darkness or she was in trouble.

Ursula walked to the rocks and stepped into the black. Once inside, she saw light shaking from some source further in. She walked toward the light until the corridor widened and opened into a cave washed golden with candle light. On the floor was a fur blanket and an open wooden box filled with food. On the cavern wall was one painting: a bear paw. Next to the bear paw, Nikovotov stood. He wore a white shirt, tight beige pants, black boots, and a purple cape. His curly black hair nearly touched his shoulders.

He looked like the perfect Russian aristocrat, only more handsome than Ursula had ever imagined anyone with blue blood could look.

Ursula suddenly realized the cave was warm. Nikovotov walked over to her as she unclasped her coat. He lifted it from her shoulders and laid it carefully on the blanket.

"How?" Ursula asked.

"It is a timeless cave," he said, "the temperature stays fairly constant. Please sit. We will eat, and I will explain."

He smiled and reached his hand out to her. She took it; together they sat on the blanket.

"It is beautiful in here," Ursula said. "Peaceful."

"Yes, it is in these caves that we can feel the heartbeat of the Mother Earth. It is here we can feel the heartbeat of the People who have gone before us. You, Ursula, you are one of the People."

"So I have been told," Ursula said, "but I don't know what that means."

"It is said that long ago humans, animals, trees, clouds, mountains all understood and loved one another. From that love and understanding came the People. For a long while, there were many clans. The Crow People. Fox People. Deer People. Bear People. But time and humans being what they are, only the Bear People were left. Or so it was said. They became the only People."

"Are they bears or humans?" Ursula asked.

"That is a different question," Nikovotov said. "When a frog is a tadpole, is it still a frog? When a butterfly is a worm is it still a butterfly? Or when a worm becomes a butterfly is it still a worm?"

"Are you saying it's a similar biological process?" Ursula asked.

Nikovotov shrugged. "I only know the stories of our beginnings. I do not know the mechanisms. One cannot ask a fish how it swims or a swan how it flies."

"But one can ask a human how we walk, talk, breathe, because we've studied these things. Niko, my grandmother told me about the People. Sergei told me about the People. I am a scientist. I don't believe in werewolves. Or were-bears."

"But you have seen for yourself," Nikovotov said. "At the party, you saw yourself in the mirror while you were eating. The People can hide who they are except when they are eating, making love, or dying. Then those who are truly perceptive can see the People as they really are. You saw yourself as you truly are. And you saw another."

"Yes, another." Ursula stared at him. "You just said 'our' beginnings. It was you I saw the other night?"

"Yes. I am one of the People. I thought I was the only one left—until I met you. I suspected but did not know for absolute certain until today. I am the one Yaga told you about. I am one of your own you are here to help."

"You understood her?"

"I am good with languages, too. All of the People are."

"You can't be the only one," Ursula said. "I know that in the future the People are alive. I've met at least one."

Nikovotov took her hand in his and brought it up to his lips. "Perhaps he is a descendant of ours."

"I hope not," Ursula said.

She wondered why Nikovotov did not ask her how she knew about the future.

"It is my skin," Nikovotov whispered, "that you must press against yours."

Ursula shivered and looked into his eyes. His face was full of passion. It would be easy to fall into his arms. Sergei and Kam had told her her destiny was with the People. Now here sat one of the People.

"I thought the People had tattoos," Ursula said. "You told me you had none."

"I don't," he said. "Those who are tattooed are not true People. They are unnatural."

He unclasped his cape and it dropped off. Then he pulled his shirt over his head.

His body was unmarred.

And beautiful.

"This is your destiny," Nikovotov said. "You can save your people by being with me."

Ursula's heart pounded in her ears. If she stayed with Nikovotov, she would know what her life would be. Perhaps it would all make sense finally.

"I don't believe in destiny," Ursula said. "I will not have someone or something making my decisions for me—no matter how much easier that may seem."

"Then you decide. Be with me. Stay with me. We can reclaim our lives as a part of the People. We can search for others. Or stay here. Choose."

Ursula looked around the cave. She had so many questions.

"Make love with me," Nikovotov said, "and you will know who I am. You will know who you are."

Ursula smiled. "That is a pretty good line, Niko. My cousin warned me about you."

"He knows nothing. No other woman can compare. We are the same, you and I."

"I need to think," Ursula said.

"No. You need to feel the wildness. You need to be part of nature again."

"Niko, please. You don't know all the things that have happened to me in the last few weeks. You wouldn't believe me if I told you." She looked at him. "Well, perhaps you would. I understand what you've told me is important and I am tempted. I am drawn to you. I have been from the beginning. Give me some time to absorb all of this."

"Of course. I have waited a long time to be with one of my own. I can wait a little while longer. Now, shall we eat?"

Nikovotov drew the box of food closer to them. He did not put on his shirt. She wanted to touch him. She closed her eyes and breathed deeply.

"Eat," Nikovotov said.

Ursula opened her eyes. Nikovotov held a piece of white cake in front of her. She opened her mouth and bit into the cake. Nikovotov took a bite, too. They chewed silently. Then Nikovotov leaned over and kissed her softly on the lips.

"Sweet," Ursula whispered.

"Me? Hardly."

"The cake, Niko, the cake."

Ursula regretted her decision not to stay the night making love with Nikovotov as soon as they stepped outside into the cold black night. The lamp Nikovotov held barely illuminated a foot in front of them. He whistled and dogs came out of nowhere, pulling a sled behind them. She and Nikovotov got in and the dogs leaped into the darkness.

"Trust me," Nikovotov called as the cold whistled around them.

Ursula wrapped herself in a blanket, then held onto the sides of the sled. There was little else she could do except trust.

Besides, she knew Nikovotov would protect her. She could spend the rest of her life with him and be confident he would keep all harm from her. That fact alone drew her to him. She wasn't sure that was very adult of her—perhaps she missed her grandmother's protective care. Or she missed the parental protection she never had. Or maybe it was all some kind of comforting illusion—to think someone else could keep the chaos at bay. Maybe that was why people wanted to believe in a god. They thought they could pray to someone for relief from suffering—or they could blame someone for their suffering.

Finally the lights of the palisades came into view. The dogs began barking in anticipation of home. They slid across the river, went up the banks, and in through the palisades.

When they stopped in front of Jonathan's house, Nikovotov pulled away the blankets and helped her out of the sled.

"I will see you again?" Nikovotov said.

"Of course," Ursula said. "Good night."

Ursula hurried into the warm house. The hearth fire was high, but no other lights burned. She took off her outside clothes quietly in case Jonathan was asleep.

Something growled.

Ursula stood absolutely still.

Something inside the house growled.

Goose bumps rose on Ursula's arms.

"Jonathan?" she whispered.

A whimper. A snuffling sound.

Another growl.

Ursula stepped forward.

"Jonathan?" she called loudly.

Another growl.

She walked quietly toward the blackness of Jonathan's room.

All was silent.

Then Jonathan stepped out of the hallway.

"There you are," he said. "I've something to show you." He lit a candle from a taper.

"Jonathan, I heard something—"

"Come."

She followed him into the dark bedroom.

Something breathed on the bed.

"I believe I've found our werewolf." He held the candle closer to the bed.

Someone writhed on top of the covers. Dirty and disheveled, his once brightly-colored clothes were ripped and faded.

"He begged me to put him out of his misery," Jonathan said. "I found him groveling in the snow near the banya. He was howling—or growling. So I brought him inside, before someone else found him."

The man whimpered and growled.

"Why did you bring him here if you think if he's violent."

"Because he kept calling your name."

"Mine?"

Ursula took the candle from Jonathan and leaned closer to the man. His face was bearded, his hair dark and wavy, his skin dirty.

"I don't know this man," Ursula said.

The man's eyes opened. They were the color of blue Siberian ice. He grabbed her wrist. A tattoo of a spider and a web laced his fingers.

"Ursula," the man said, then closed his eyes and released her arm.

"Sergei," Ursula whispered.

51

Ursula started to reach out to Sergei when suddenly he changed. For an instant, he appeared to be more beast than man. She blinked, and he was a wretched-looking Sergei again.

She glanced at Jonathan.

"Yes. I saw it, too," Jonathan said. "Let us allow him rest. I'll tie his wrists."

"Jonathan!"

"He keeps trying to hurt himself. It's for his own protection."

"Sergei," Ursula whispered, "I'll be right out here."

Ursula went into the other room and sat at the benches in front of Jonathan's alchemy tables. A few moments later, Jonathan emerged from the bedroom and joined her.

"You know him then," Jonathan said.

"He's the man I asked you about," Ursula said. "Sergei Ivanovich Polyakov. I thought I saw him in the woods the other day. He is so different he is nearly unrecognizable. What did he say to you?"

"He was fairly incoherent," Jonathan said. "He said he couldn't control something and he had to find you."

"He's found me."

"Could he be the one behind the attacks?" Jonathan asked.

"I don't know."

"I think he's been sent to us," Jonathan said.

"What do you mean?"

"I explained to you that my goal as an alchemist was to discover the true nature of human beings. And Sergei seems to be on the edge of being a beast or a man. He is in the *nigredo* stage of alchemy. He is breaking down. He is losing his mind. Remember what I said about us all being flasks—containers. We can help Sergei become gold—become a true human being."

Jonathan picked up one of his alchemical texts and flipped through several pages. Then he stopped and pushed the book in Ursula's direction. It was the illustration of the four women standing on triangles with flasks over their heads. Jonathan pointed to the first flask with a hairy beast inside.

"This is Sergei," Jonathan said.

"There is a modicum of resemblance," Ursula agreed.

"That's Earth. *Nigredo*. Next is the bloated man. Water. Purification. The white stone. Then the Phoenix. Rising up. Free of constriction. Air. And finally, the lion. The sun. Gold. Fire." His eyes shone. "Yes, Sergei is a gift from the universe." He closed the book. "This will be wonderful, Ursula."

They took turns staying awake to watch over their guest.

Jonathan whispered Ursula awake as Olga came into the house.

"I think I heard spring coming," Olga said. "She is closer than she was a month ago."

Jonathan straightened as Ursula sat up.

"What an astute observation, Olga," Jonathan said.

Olga narrowed her eyes. "You shouldn't take the cycles of nature for granted. Who knows what will happen?"

"Speaking of surprises. Olga, we have a guest. No doubt he will be hungry."

Jonathan went into the bedroom.

"He?" Olga said. "Who?"

"Ursula," Jonathan called, "he is awake."

Ursula hurried into the bedroom. The bedraggled Sergei sat at the edge of the bed rubbing his wrists.

"Sergei?"

He looked up at her.

"It's Ursula."

He stared at her.

"Ulla," he said. He reached a shaking hand out to her. Ursula took it and sat next to him on the bed. "Something has happened."

"We'll have lots of time, Sergei," Ursula said. "You need to eat and get some rest."

"And clean up." Olga stood in the doorway. "You smell worse than—"

"Olga." Jonathan stepped in. "We'll take care of this. I've got the banya all set."

"I'm a little weak," Sergei said.

"I will help you," Ursula said.

Sergei smiled. "You've gotten skinny again since last I saw you. I doubt you could help a flea. Besides, I'd rather you didn't see me quite so beleaguered."

"I will help," Jonathan said. He held his arm out and Sergei grabbed it and slowly stood. Ursula watched as they walked away. Sergei looked like a very old man.

Ursula changed her clothes, then ate breakfast while waiting for the men. She was grateful Olga did not ask any more questions. Finally Jonathan emerged from the back of the house. When he stepped to the side, Sergei stood before Ursula. His skin glowed red, his blue eyes sparkled, his hair was clean and wet, his face shaven. He was a young man, twenty or twenty-five years old, younger than the Sergei Ursula had met in the airport terminal at Chicago a few weeks earlier.

"Now that is a transformation," Olga said. "Sit. Eat. Now."

Ursula watched Sergei eat. He stared at her, too, smiling as he chewed. How could Sergei have gotten younger?

"The last time I saw you was the morning before you went to rescue Casta from the warriors," Sergei said. "You sent me away. You told me to return to the Wu, but I never found my way back, and I never found the rest of our people."

"Uh—the last time I saw you was in a cave during the spring, not in this century. You were older. You lived in a house in Moscow with beautiful mosaics of certain tattoos. Your tattoos."

"And yours?"

"I don't have any tattoos," Ursula said.

"I don't have a house in Moscow. I don't even know where that is."

Olga and Jonathan stared at them.

"Are you certain he's the Sergei you knew?" Jonathan asked.

"In addition to the spider, he has a bear paw tattoo on his chest, on his right arm is the tattoo of a swan. A snake is on his right calf and a deer is on his left thigh."

Jonathan glanced at Sergei and then back at Ursula. "You got everything right. Are you certain she's your Ulla?"

"She has a mole above her right buttock. A freckle on her left breast. A scar on her left thumb."

"So far so good," Ursula said.

"I wouldn't know," Jonathan said.

"She also has the same tattoos as I have, except she has a rose tattoo on her butt. She can make love and ride a horse better than anyone I know."

"I don't have any tattoos," Ursula said, "and I haven't ridden a horse since I was a girl."

"But you are my Ulla. I know your body, your soul. No lack of tattooing or skinny body is going to change that. I know who you are."

"And I you," Ursula said. "We've just come through the caves at different times, I guess. Jonathan said you've been ill."

"As I told you, I got lost. So I found a timeless cave, but when I left the cave again, I was in a different place. I wandered alone until I found another place. I got ill. I don't remember a lot about that time. A man found me in the cave and he and his wife brought me back to health. I was in and out of myself. When I was well enough to leave, I discovered that I could not control myself. I was no longer truly one of the People—I kept becoming and unbecoming. I can only describe it as feeling off-balanced and sick. And if others saw me, I terrified them. I continued looking for you."

"I saw you in the woods the other day. Why didn't you stop?"

"I don't know. My thinking has been altered, too; I feel as though I am disintegrating." He put his head in his hands for a moment, then looked up again. "I have gone to the caves and found no relief. I run in the woods and find no People. Only shadows of. Only creatures whose language I no longer understand."

"I've been told that in this time and place, no People survive. Well, almost no People."

"Who are the People?" Jonathan asked.

"The ancient ones," Olga said. "Those who can take the shape of human or beast."

Jonathan looked at Olga. "Those are only stories."

Olga shrugged. "So you say."

"We both saw what we saw last night," Ursula said. "And I've witnessed more than one peculiar event since coming here."

"You doubt the People?" Sergei said. "You who helped us remember we were the People? You who fought to save us?"

"I know this is strange, Sergei," Ursula said. "When you—the future you—tried to explain it to me, I didn't understand it either. I haven't been to your time yet. I haven't fought to save anyone."

"But you must. Without you, we wouldn't have remembered who we are. I don't know what would have happened." He shook his head. "I don't know what's happening now. Do you know? Can you help me?"

Suddenly Sergei pushed away from the table and ran out the back of the house. She could hear him vomiting. A few moments later, he stumbled back into Jonathan's room. Ursula got up and went to him. He lay huddled on the bed, shivering.

"Sergei," Ursula said, sitting on the edge of the bed. "How can I help?"

"I wish you didn't have to see me this way," he said, keeping his back to her. "I hope this has not happened to all those who were tattooed."

"You mean some kind of poisoning?" Ursula asked. "What was used? What materials?"

"Just crushed rock, shell, plant dye. The Wu gave it to us and they have used these same materials forever."

"Maybe the needles were contaminated."

"No," Sergei said.

Sergei's form seemed to waver before her. For an instant he was the beast. Then the man again.

"Do you do that on purpose? Change your form? Is it a type of hypnotism?"

Sergei turned to look at her. "Did I transform?"

"For a moment. Or it looked like it, but it didn't look solid, almost like a blurry television picture."

"Television?"

"Never mind. I saw something similar when I looked in the mirror once, but it seemed as though I really was this beast, this bear-like beast, beautiful, magical and powerful all at once. Dressed in an evening gown—quite incongruous. But your change doesn't look real. Perhaps what the People employ is a kind of mass hypnosis."

"I don't know what hypnotism is either. Now I truly recognize you—much of what you said before often didn't make sense to me either."

Ursula laughed.

Sergei briefly closed his eyes. "I feel as though the lines of communication—as you used to say—are being closed down. I am losing the connection."

"I wonder why."

"He is Earth," Jonathan said. "Now it is time for the whitening, for the purification."

Sergei pushed himself into a sitting position. "What?"

"He thinks he can cure you with alchemy," Ursula said.

"Alchemy? You spoke a little about that. You said that's what the People are—that our bodies are gold."

"Yes," Jonathan said. "We need to help your body find its way to gold again. Let's be off to the banya then. Lots of sweat and water."

Jonathan helped Sergei up.

"Sergei, have you hurt anyone since you've been ill?" Ursula asked.

"Hurt anyone?" He leaned on Jonathan. "No. Why?"

"It doesn't matter," Ursula said. "Take care of him, Jonathan."

"I'll do my best."

Ursula went into the other room.

"You and he were lovers," Olga said.

"Yes, but I don't know if he knows it."

Olga raised her eyebrows.

"It's too complicated," Ursula said. "I have to get him help."

"What did Yaga say?" Olga asked.

"I'd almost forgotten," Ursula said. "She said I have to find one of my own and press my skin against his. I had to pierce his skin. Then be on my way. I thought she meant Nikovotov."

Olga made a noise.

"Why don't you like him? You seem to admire the People. How do you know he isn't one?"

"This I will say: Have you ever seen a wild animal who has been taken out of the wild and tamed? He forgets what made him wild. He only knows he longs for it and after a while, that longing and lost memory can drive him mad."

"I wish people would stop speaking to me in riddles."

Olga made a sound of disgust and turned away from her.

"What? I like Nikovotov. He seems like he has everything under control. He wants me but doesn't seem desperate. He doesn't expect me to save the world."

"None of us is expected to save the world but all of us must save the world."

"Olga! You're doing it again. I'm saying I think life would be nice with Nikovotov. Easy."

"Don't you want to go home?" Olga asked.

"Maybe this is home. I don't know."

"I know that man Sergei needs your help. You can save him. *You.*"

"Olga, I don't even know how to save myself, let alone someone else."

"Well, then, maybe it is time for you to figure out how."

52

Sergei slept peacefully after his sauna. Ursula watched him for a time, standing over him, trying to picture him as he had been in her arms—strong and loving. Now he seemed small. Physically. She wanted to hold him and take away his illness.

She had no idea what to do.

Jonathan brought her out into the other room to eat. She chewed her food and tasted nothing.

"He was so good to me," Ursula said. "I was sick and frightened when we first met and he helped me feel so much better."

"He spoke again about waking up in the cave and feeling ill," Jonathan said. "He vaguely remembers someone—or something—being there."

"Before or after he got ill?"

"He doesn't remember, at least not yet."

"He told me, before, that I had saved his life. I wonder if this was when I did. I've got to figure it out. It's something to do with the tattoos—I'm sure of it."

"Or maybe he just needs you," Jonathan said.

"I know he was in love with me—I mean in the future. But here, he seems so distant. He won't look me in the eyes."

"I think he saw something before you two parted," Jonathan said. "In that time or place or whatever. He saw something happen to you and he felt like he couldn't stop it. He mentioned something about it in the banya." He squeezed her hand. "During this stage of alchemy, the whitening—*solutio*—it is a time of feeling. Or purity. Of love. It is a time for the masculine to dissolve into the feminine. The sun is eclipsed by the Moon. Full Moon."

"Jonathan, speak English."

"Open your heart to him. Make love to him."

"Just like that?"

"You've done it before."

"So? He wasn't changing into a beast then."

"He wasn't?"

"OK. Maybe he was, but I didn't understand what was going on."

"And now you do?" Jonathan asked.

Ursula smiled grimly.

The next day, Jonathan stayed at Sasha's, and Olga never came. Ursula heated Olga's soup and ladled some into a cup for Sergei. He sipped it and stared into the fire.

Ursula sat next to him.

Sergei shivered.

"Are you cold?"

"N-no," he stammered and tipped off the bench and onto the floor. For an instant, he was the beast. Ursula stepped away. The image seemed to solidify. He reached for her. She wanted to run.

Then he was Sergei again.

He screamed.

Ursula dropped to the floor. "Sergei." He began weeping. She cradled his head in her lap. "Sergei," she whispered. "It'll be all right. I'll figure out how to keep the beast at bay."

"No," he wept. "It is not the beast I wish to be rid of."

"The man then?"

"No. The silence. The disconnection."

"One can get used to it. I have never felt connected—"

Sergei pushed himself up. "You don't know what you're talking about."

"I know."

He wiped his eyes. "Someone was in the cave with me. I think he did something to me." He felt the back of his knee, then showed it to her. She saw a tiny black dot. "This is new to my body."

"You think someone wanted to make you sick? Why?"

Sergei shrugged. He slowly stood. "I-I think I'll rest now."

"All right. We'll talk later."

Ursula watched Sergei slowly walk into Jonathan's room. Then she cleaned their dishes and went to the banya. She lay on the bench and sighed deeply. She fell into, out of, and back into sleep.

She opened her eyes to see Sergei standing over her. She sat up. The banya had started to cool. She got up and threw several logs into the stove.

"I awakened and you were gone. I had to see if you were all right."

"I'm fine," Ursula said. She poured a bucket of water over her head, then toweled off.

"You are so beautiful," Sergei said, "even without any meat on your bones."

Ursula smiled. "I'm trying. I'm eating and working out."

"I'll leave you alone to your bath."

"Stay," Ursula said. "I should leave. You don't seem embarrassed. Have you seen me naked before?"

He smiled. "Many times. And why should someone's naked body cause me embarrassment?"

"Of course you're right. You look a little better. Soak. I'll meet you back in the house."

He nodded.

Ursula grabbed her clothes, put them on, and went into the house. She sat in front of the fire until Sergei returned. He smiled at her, and she saw the man who had loved her in Moscow. He was not so different, only ill now, and she had been holding herself at a distance from him. She got up and went and put her arms around him. He returned her embrace.

"I'm so glad to see you again," Ursula said.

"And I you." He kissed her neck. "I—I thought you were dead. The last I saw you you were trying to talk to the enemy and I saw you—"

Ursula pulled gently away and looked into his warm icy-blue eyes. "What, Sergei, what did you see?"

"I saw you killed. I saw you fall. I tried to get back to you, but they wouldn't let me. They said you had ordered them to make sure I continued to the mountain, to Belovdia. I thought I'd never see you again, even though you told me I would."

They embraced. Ursula led Sergei into Jonathan's bedroom.

"Lie down," Ursula said. "Let me do all the work."

"I don't know, Ulla."

"It'll be fine," she said. "This is all part of the cure."

Sergei smiled, slowly took off his clothes, then lay on the bed. Ursula took off her clothes and lay down beside him. She gently stroked his tattoos. She kissed his mouth, neck, chest, thighs, then straddled him and fit him inside of her. She could barely see him in the semi-darkness. His eyes glowed. Suddenly it seemed as though she were a part of his cells—and he a part of hers. She felt his strength returning, felt him transforming beneath her fingers, just as she transformed beneath his.

It was as though a conduit suddenly opened between her and the wild, except *she* was the wild. Had always been. She was not herself. Every part of her was exploding.

Or coming together.

Thought ended.

She and Sergei were all body and feeling.

They cried out together—roared or growled or laughed—and she was Sergei, the snow, ice, winter, the crows. Bear.

She was Ursula, She-Bear. It was Sergei's skin she needed to press herself against, his skin she needed to pierce. She would heal him. One way. Or another.

53

Sergei stayed well as long as Ursula touched him or made love to him. But Ursula could see he was deteriorating. Sometimes when he slept he cried and shivered.

Jonathan assured Ursula that tears were part of the alchemical treatment.

"That's what you said about me making love with him," Ursula said. "It has not healed him."

"Has it healed you?"

"I don't need healing," Ursula said. "I've just lost my way, and I don't mean that metaphorically."

"But your heart. Has it healed?"

"My heart was never broken," Ursula said.

"Your heart is closed."

"No!" Ursula said. They sat in front of the fire, awakened early by Sergei's cries. "I love my grandmother. I care for you and Olga, my friend Bob back home, Miriam. And I love Sergei."

"But you don't feel passion for him?"

"Yes, I do," Ursula said. "I've never felt physically about

anyone the way I feel about him. It scares me to think about loving anyone so much. Those I love go away—my mother, my husband."

"Husband?"

"Yes, though I suppose I never loved him with every bone in my body. I never got lost in him."

Jonathan smiled. "So to you being in love is equated with being lost. I understand. One does have to let go to love another fully, I suppose."

"How philosophical, cousin."

"Next on Sergei's alchemical journey is the phoenix, air—coagulation or yellowing."

"What does that mean?"

"He must sink to the Earth again. He must really inhabit his body—and get some sun."

"Is that all?" Ursula asked.

"Do you fully inhabit your body?"

"No one else's."

"I mean are you free of shame? Do you experience bodily sensations or run from them?"

"I believe Sergei is quite in touch with his body," Ursula said.

"Or is he in touch with yours?" Jonathan asked. "When he awakens and if the sun is shining, I shall take him outside for a few minutes and then to the banya. That will earth him. I registered him, by the by. I thought that might keep the Superintendent and Lieutenant away. He's my long lost cousin Sergei."

Ursula laughed. "You've quite an eclectic family. I'd almost forgotten about Nikovotov."

"I'm quite sure he hasn't forgotten you."

Later that day, while Olga was hauling water and Sergei and Jonathan were sunbathing, Lieutenant Nikovotov knocked once on Jonathan's door, then came inside.

"Hello, my dear," Nikovotov said. "I was concerned when I didn't hear from you."

"I know. I'm sorry. I—" Ursula could not very well tell him she had forgotten about him. "I'm sorry. It was rude of me."

"I heard the Scot has acquired another cousin?" He shook off his coat.

Ursula nodded and stirred the fire in the hearth.

"May I meet him?" He pulled off his gloves.

"He and Jonathan are out," Ursula said. "Shall I make tea?"

He shook his head. "I can't stay."

They were silent. Their previous intimacy had vanished: perhaps because Ursula had made her choice—though she had not thought about it until this moment—and her choice about her life did not include Nikovotov.

This meant Nikovotov would continue to be alone. Without the People.

She suddenly wanted to put her arms around him and tell him he was not alone. Sergei was one of the People; perhaps he knew of others.

"He is a suspect in the attacks," Nikovotov said.

"Who?"

"Sergei Ivanovich Polyakov."

Ursula laughed. "That's absurd. He's desperately ill. He couldn't hurt a fly. Besides, he arrived well after the attacks had started."

"He was spotted before. Since he has been under this roof, the attacks have stopped."

"Niko," she said, trying to relax her voice, trying to be friends again. "He is having problems with—"

"He is a tattooed one," Nikovotov said. "I know."

Ursula looked at him, surprised. "But I asked you if you had seen any tattoos."

"I saw no reason for you to be contaminated by one of

them."

"One of them? He is one of the People!"

Nikovotov shook his head. "No. They are an abomination."

"You don't know him, Niko," Ursula said. "He's a good kind man."

Nikovotov's eyes narrowed as he and Ursula stared at one another.

Then he said quietly, "I thought you understood what you meant to me. I can see now that I was mistaken." He looked away from her and walked to the door. "I warn you: Anna has heard of this. She will no doubt insist on seeing if he is possessed by the devil."

"You can't believe that."

He glanced at her. "It doesn't matter what I believe. She is the wife of the commandant, and you are merely the cousin of a sodomite, as far as she is concerned. Good day."

"Nikovotov—"

He was gone. Ursula felt a knot in her stomach. She remembered how Anna said they got the werewolf out of a man: They beat him until the devil released his hold or the man died.

She suddenly wished she were back in Portland where no one believed in werewolves. She remembered sitting on the bench on campus when the woman with the rose tattoo had asked, "Are you one of us?" Ursula had been eating. Had the woman seen her true nature? Was she really one of the People? How could that be? Wouldn't she know if she regularly turned into—into what? Into something else. None of it seemed real or solid—despite the fact that she was sitting in Siberia more than 250 years before she had been born.

Jonathan and Sergei returned within the hour. Sergei went straight to bed.

"He's getting worse," Ursula said to Jonathan as he studied his alchemy texts.

"I know. He needs to rise up. He needs air. To be free of restriction. Alchemically speaking."

"Jonathan, I don't think he is an incarnate metaphor for your alchemy work. He's a man in pain."

"Because he isn't fully human," Jonathan said. "Alchemy can help him realize who is—"

"No. He says he doesn't need to get rid of the beast. He needs connection—communication."

"Yes! Of course. Air. Speech is air. Communication is air!"

"We need to find out why he's sick," Ursula said. "He thinks someone poisoned him."

"Why? Who?"

"I don't know," she said, "but Nikovotov was here. He says Anna is on her way to cast out the devil."

"If she sees him change, all will be lost."

"We'll keep him covered," Ursula said, "and the room dark and only let her stay a few moments."

"That might help."

"I need to see Yaga," Ursula said. "Maybe she can heal him."

"When Olga comes, we'll go together."

Jonathan borrowed a neighbor's sled and dogs and he and Ursula left Sergei in Olga's care. On this sunny day, the air did not feel quite so cold and Ursula wondered if Olga was right and spring was just around the frozen corner. They slid past the palisades and down to the tiny houses built close to the river, stopping in front of Yaga's.

Jonathan put the dogs under the overhang while Ursula knocked on the door. When she got no response, she slowly opened it and called out in Yaga's language, "Baba Yaga! Baba Yaga. It's Ursula. May I come in?"

"You may," came the answer.

Ursula went into the dark house. For a moment she could see

only the fire in the hearth. After a few moments, the shadow near the fire resolved itself into Yaga.

"You have found the one you must help?" Yaga asked. She looked so much like Olga.

"Yes, but he is very ill. I don't know what to do and I'm afraid the authorities will hurt him. They think he's responsible for the assaults."

Yaga nodded. "Have you pierced his skin?"

Ursula shook her head.

"You must. The one who sickened him can make him well but be wary of treachery."

"Can't you heal him?"

"No," Yaga said. "It is out of my hands but if you need an embroiderer, I can do it, as can my cousin Olga."

"Thank you," Ursula said.

She went outdoors again.

"What I wouldn't give for a telephone," she said as Jonathan pulled the dogs and sled out from the overhang.

That night, Ursula lay next to Sergei's trembling body. Sweat poured off of him. Once he whispered, "I'm disintegrating." Another time he cried, "It's night! It's night!"

In the morning, Ursula awakened to the sound of pounding on the front door. She covered Sergei with blankets he had kicked off.

"Good morning, Jonathan." Anna's voice.

"Good morning," Jonathan said. "Come in! Come in! To what do we owe this honor?"

Ursula ran her fingers through her hair, straightened her dress, and went into the main room.

"He is finally resting," Ursula said, pretending she did not know Anna was there. Then she looked over at Anna, her attendant, and Jonathan. "Oh, Anna. How good to see you. Olga was making us breakfast." She glanced at Olga who gave her a nearly imperceptible nod. "Would you care to join us?"

"How very kind," she said, "but I have come on behalf of the Superintendent and the Church to meet your cousin. He is quite ill, I understand, and we must ascertain that he is not a threat to the village."

"The Superintendent has sent *you*?" Jonathan asked. "My cousin is ill, perhaps contagious."

Anna looked at Jonathan, then Ursula. "God protects me." Her eyes were cold. "Please bring him to me."

"He is too ill to get out of bed," Ursula said.

"But I was told he was outside yesterday. Another woman was attacked and nearly killed yesterday."

"We were out near the banya," Jonathan said. "We stayed close to the house and he leaned on me the entire time."

"Nevertheless. Perhaps he tricked you—"

"What are you implying?" Ursula asked. "I thought you came to find out about his health. Now you're accusing him of what?"

"I am concerned with his spiritual health." Anna's face softened. "I can go to him. I shall endeavor not to disturb him."

Ursula started toward the bedroom.

"A candle please," Anna said.

Jonathan and Ursula looked at each other; then Jonathan picked up a lit candle and said, "I shall light your way, madam."

The three of them walked into the bedroom. Sergei slept with his back to them.

Anna said, "Hold the light nearer please."

Jonathan stepped marginally closer. Anna took the candle from him.

"The light bothers him," Ursula said. "Please."

"I must see." Anna brought the light closer. Sergei suddenly turned over. Startled awake, he cried out. His face was distorted, half-human, half-beast. Or was it only fear that twisted his features?

Anna dropped the candle, and the light went out. Jonathan quickly put his arm across her shoulders, turned her around, and took her into the other room. Ursula sat on the bed and put her hand on Sergei's arm.

"It's all right, she said. "Go back to sleep."

"No," Sergei said. "I remember. It was a man in gold who talked to the night."

"OK. Shhh. I'll be right back."

Ursula left the bedroom.

"You saw what I saw," Anna was saying. "I will bring the priest—"

"I saw a sick man frightened out of his rest," Ursula said.

"I saw the beast," Anna said, her voice hard. "It has to be exorcised. I will have the priest confirm my suspicions, then we shall pick the holy place where this poor man can be set free."

"I won't allow you to torture him!"

Anna looked at her. "He is already being tortured. Can't you see that? We will help him. Good day."

She left.

"They'll kill him," Ursula said.

"Maybe not," Jonathan said.

Ursula shook her head. Suddenly she realized what Sergei had said: "a man in gold who talked to the night." Nikovotov's uniform was braided in gold, and he talked to his horse Night. Of course! She should have suspected sooner.

Sergei stumbled into the room.

"Sergei, try to remember. Was the man's name Mikhail Nikovotov? Did he have a black horse named Night?"

Sergei sat on the bench near the table. Olga brought him a bowl of soup.

"I never knew his name," Sergei said. "I had forgotten it all, but I met him in one of the caves. He was one of us. He said he knew where to tattoo me so that I could travel the caves directly back to my people. But after he tattooed me, I got sick and forgot about him. He wore gold and rode a horse, yes, a black horse named Night."

Ursula put her hand on his shoulder and squeezed it. "Eat up. Jonathan, Olga, I need your help. You've got to take Sergei away from here as soon as you can. There's a cave Niko took me to—he'd never think I'd go there—so take him there."

"Which one?" Olga asked.

"How can I tell you to get there? It has a bear claw inside of it."

Olga nodded. "It is one few know about, but I know how to get there."

"Good. We need to bring some food, clothing. Olga, take along your embroidery equipment. Yaga said you can tattoo."

"Of course. Where are you going?"

"To Nikovotov. Yaga said only the one who made Sergei sick could help him."

"No," Sergei said. "If he harmed me, why wouldn't he hurt you?"

"Because he thinks you're an abomination and I'm his true love. Please, trust me. I'll need a sled and a driver. Can you get me one? Someone who is loyal to you rather than to Nikovotov."

"No one is loyal to me—except Olga."

"I can get you what you need," Olga said. "I'll be back within the half hour."

While Olga was gone, Sergei finished eating. He seemed to have a tiny burst of energy and went to the banya to bathe. Jonathan and Ursula packed bags of food, clothes, and blankets. Then they quickly ate soup and bread.

"What are you going to say to him?" Jonathan asked. "How do you know he won't keep you with him?"

"I don't," Ursula said. "I'll appeal to his good side."

Jonathan laughed. "What world do you come from?" He emptied his soup bowl and got up. "I'll get the dogs and a sled."

"Have Olga take you on a circuitous route to the cave," Ursula said, "in case you're watched."

"Around here, one is always watched."

"Jonathan," Ursula said, putting her hand on his arm, "I don't want you to get into trouble."

He patted her hand. "I will be fine. I haven't told you but I went to the Superintendent's office. My exile *is* over. I can leave any time. They 'forgot' to tell me. The Superintendent was furious that I'd found out. I told him I'd stay for a while longer. I was stalling for time until I could figure a way out."

"You should have told me," Ursula said.

"You have Sergei to worry about," Jonathan said. "He is from your past. He has ties. I am—"

Ursula put her arms around him. "You are my cousin. I can never repay you for all you've done." She kissed his cheek. "I'll see you soon."

He put on his coat and hat and went outside. Sergei came out of the banya looking almost healthy. Ursula put her arm around his waist.

"I've got a plan," she said.

"You always do," he said.

"I think I can help you, but I don't know. The trip alone could be dangerous."

Olga came inside, followed by Jonathan.

"I have a sleigh and driver ready outside for you, Ursula," Olga said.

Ursula nodded. She kissed Sergei on the lips. "It's going to be all right. I promise. I've seen you in the future, and you weren't sick."

She put on her outdoor clothes, glanced at the three of them watching her, and then she went into the freezing sunny weather. The driver—a young man she didn't know—stepped away from his dogs.

"Hello," he said. "I am Olga's son. She calls me Doubra. You may, too."

"Good. I'm Ursula. Can you take me to Lieutenant Nikovotov's house?"

He nodded. Ursula got into the small wooden sleigh. Doubra followed her, then whistled the dogs forward.

54

Several minutes later, they pulled up in front of Nikovotov's house.

"I won't be long, I hope," Ursula said as she got out of the sleigh. She walked up to the front door and banged on it. Urga opened it. She looked so much like Olga that Ursula was startled.

"You! Come. He's here."

Ursula went inside.

"Make him give you what you want," Urga whispered as she opened the door to the big room. Nikovotov sat in a straight-backed chair and turned the golden bear claw in his hands. He did not stand when she entered. Urga closed the door behind Ursula. The room was hot and stuffy.

"I know it was you," Ursula said.

Nikovotov set the claw on the table next to him. He motioned her to a chair. She sat across from him.

"It has been such a long time," Nikovotov said. "I was not raised with the People. I was raised by farmers. I know little of the ways of my own people. I never stood on the shores of the Volga after spring thaw and fished for salmon. I never tasted the raw blood of the river. I never sank my teeth or claws into prey. I never hunted. Isn't that the difference between humans and the People? We hunt for our food with our own bodies. We don't separate ourselves from death and violence. Then I met you. I knew you were for me. I felt my blood boil with the beast and I'd see these small helpless people and something changed in me, roared in me, and I had to strike out at them. I'd always stop—I didn't kill them—I just—I just exerted my superiority."

Ursula's mouth went dry. She tried to swallow. Finally she said, her voice cracking, "You must stop."

"I will," he said, "when you decide to stay with me."

"I will do that," Ursula said, "if you will help me first. You've deliberately misled the authorities into believing Sergei is a were-wolf. Anna's planning an exorcism!"

"I have no control over that."

"Sergei remembered it was you who made him sick by giving him a tattoo."

Nikovotov looked at her. His body stiffened. "Is that what you meant when you said you knew it was me?"

"It doesn't matter."

"I won't apologize. It is my duty to search out the tattooed ones and stop them."

"You mean you killed them?"

He shook his head. "I am not a murderer."

"But what you've done to Sergei has kept him from transform-ing—connecting—kept him from being himself."

Nikovotov looked out the window. "I have heard it said that the People who have left the wild lose what makes them who they are. Sometimes I feel I have never known what it is to truly be one of the People."

"What did you do to Sergei?"

"It's an old folk remedy to stop demonic possession. The farmers taught me."

"He isn't demonically possessed!"

"You are getting lost in facts," he said.

"Do you have an antidote?"

He looked at her again. "No."

"You do. You can help him. If you can, I'll send him on his way, and I will remain here with you. We can have the life you want."

Silence throbbed between them.

"I will have to embroider it for you."

She shook her head. "I have a tattooist. I will stay with Sergei until he is well. If he doesn't get well, you will be exposed in this community. All your secrets will come out. If he gets well, I will return to you."

"I could give you something to kill him. To make him sicker."

"If you did that, I could never be with you. Besides, you said you weren't a murderer."

Nikovotov slowly stood and crossed the room to a bureau of drawers. He opened a small drawer, took out something, and folded his fingers around it.

He turned toward Ursula. She stood and walked to him. They faced one another.

Ursula held out her hand.

Nikovotov placed a tiny square box on her palm.

"This will cure his sickness," Nikovotov said.

"What is it?" Ursula asked.

"I don't know," he said. "I got both formulas from the people who raised me. This one was in case the other did not rid the person of the demon but only made him ill."

"Where do I tattoo him?"

"I don't think it matters, but I was told to do it alongside the spine."

"Thank you," Ursula said.

"You'll be back?" Nikovotov asked.

She looked into his eyes. "That's up to you. Can I trust you?"

"Of course. I will see you soon then."

Ursula turned away and walked out of the room. Nikovotov followed her to the door.

"It will never be like it was, will it?" he asked as she started to go outside.

"Like it was? We haven't known each other long enough for us to have it be like it was, but I promise you, if Sergei is healed by this, I will commit myself to you."

"Then I will see you again shortly."

Ursula hurried outside to her waiting sleigh. She got in next to Doubra and suddenly realized she could not give him directions to the cave. She glanced back at the house. How could she be so stupid? The dogs started barking. She looked at Doubra.

"Will I take you to the cave now?" Doubra asked.

"Yes! You know where to go? Yes, take me, please."

Doubra whistled, and the sleigh jerked forward. Ursula tucked a blanket around her. She pushed the tiny box inside her glove, then put her hands beneath the blanket. As the dogs pulled them along the snowy road past a conifer wood toward the palisades, Ursula closed her eyes and hoped she was doing the right thing.

After a time, the dogs pulled them up into an outcropping of rocks. None of it looked familiar to Ursula. Doubra stopped the sleigh and Ursula got out and went inside the cave. She followed a serpentine path in the darkness to the lighted part of the cave where Olga, Jonathan, and Sergei waited. The walls were lavender and pink-colored, the light rosy gold. The air was warm—a sign that they were inside a timeless cave, she realized. Perhaps all of this was becoming ordinary to her, or at least familiar.

Sergei sat cross-legged on a blanket on the floor of the cave. He smiled at her, but his face was ashen, his eyes watery. Olga and Jonathan sat near Sergei and rose when she entered.

"What did you learn?" Jonathan asked.

"It was Nikovotov," Ursula said. *"He's* been attacking people."

"What?" Jonathan said.

Olga nodded. "I am not surprised."

"If Sergei doesn't get better," Ursula said, "you have my permission to tell the authorities—tell everyone what he's done. And that he is one of the People."

"What?" Now Olga seemed shocked. "How could one of the People attack villagers. No, they are not like that!"

"There are bad apples in every barrel," Ursula said.

Olga and Jonathan looked at her.

"Hey, I don't mean to be glib," she said. "I don't understand all of this! I'm flying by the seat of my pants." She held out the tiny wooden box. "This is supposed to help Sergei."

Olga took the box and opened it. "It's red." She dipped her little finger in, picked up several grains, then put her finger in her mouth. After a few moments, she said, "It is not poison. Some spices, Earth, shell. Where shall I embroider it?"

"Nikovotov said to do it on the spine."

Olga nodded. "All right. Sergei. Lie down. This won't hurt."

"Yes, it will," Sergei said, smiling wanly. He lay on his stomach. Olga pulled Sergei's shirt up enough to expose a patch of skin. Ursula sat near Sergei's head.

"How are you feeling?" Ursula asked.

"Strange," Sergei said. "Since this has all started—getting sick, finding you—I feel in limbo. Or as if it's all a dream."

Jonathan sat near Olga. She washed Sergei's skin with a damp cloth, then pulled out some kind of needle and held it over a candle flame Jonathan brought to her. Ursula raised her eyebrow; she hadn't realized eighteenth century Siberia knew about sterilizing needles.

"I have felt that same way, Sergei," Ursula said. "As if I'm being directed and I have no control. All of my life I wanted a sense of purpose, but now I feel as though purpose has found me, and I can't say no." She smoothed her hand over Sergei's hair. "It'll be all right now, Sergei. You'll feel better."

He flinched slightly as Olga pushed the needle into his skin. Ursula looked around the cave until she saw a rock painting. She got up and walked to it. It was a red rose and a white rose, their thorny stems intertwined. She had never seen anything like it in any of the rock painting literature. Yet it did look familiar. *Jonathan's alchemical texts.*

She glanced at Jonathan. He got up and came to stand next to her.

"Olga says this rock painting is very old. Maybe not as old as some of the others but many hundreds of years."

"The style seems more modern," Ursula said. "I mean more contemporary to this time."

"It is the alchemical yin and yang," Jonathan said. "*Albedo* and *rubedo*, left and right, masculine and feminine. See how the stems still have thorns but they aren't pricking the others."

"I asked you to meet me at the Bear Claw cave. Olga, this must have been your doing."

Olga didn't look away from her work. "Nikovotov does not know about this cave. I thought this would be better. I told Doubra." She shrugged. "Simple."

"Yes, all of this is so simple," Ursula said.

She returned to Sergei's side and held his hand while Olga tattooed him. After a while, Sergei's body relaxed.

"Sergei?" Ursula whispered.

He breathed deeply with sleep.

"He's fine," Olga said. "Leave him be."

Ursula watched and tried to imagine what her life would be like with Nikovotov. Safe. Exciting? Or would she become a part of his collection? Just the person he came home to. That was what had happened with her and Peter. He had blossomed into the world, and she had shrunk further away from it. Life had seemed simpler when she was not actively participating in it.

"How did you convince Nikovotov to help Sergei?" Jonathan asked.

Olga glanced up, then looked down again.

"It doesn't matter," Ursula said.

"You promised yourself, didn't you?" Olga said.

"It was all I had to bargain with," Ursula said. "I couldn't let Sergei continue to suffer."

"People always suffer," Olga said, shrugging. "How is trading someone's suffering for your own better?"

"I didn't say it was," Ursula said. "Days ago—or was it weeks, I've lost track of time—I was actually thinking of staying with Nikovotov. Freely, of my own accord."

Olga shook her head. "You think it is your duty to sacrifice yourself. It is how women have come to think of themselves— there is no greater glory than to sacrifice. Look how they celebrate those men and women who have died in war for their countries. It is only to raise more citizens who will think it is the greatest glory to die fighting for one's country." Olga patted Sergei's skin with a cloth, then wiped her needle and put it away. "In the beginning of the People, there were no nations—no governments to die for."

"People have always killed one another," Jonathan said.

Olga snorted. "You believe that because you have been taught that it is so, and it is so because you have been taught to believe that it is so."

"Olga's right," Ursula said. "Not every civilization on the planet has been violent. Archaeologists have found evidence that peaceful cultures flourished for thousands of years."

"But no longer?" Jonathan said. "That's the thing: Humans eventually revert to their natural tendencies to be violent."

Ursula laughed. "Why is it that because peaceful civilizations last thousands of years but eventually fall they are considered failures? Or unsuccessful experiments. Remember Rome fell and the Romans were not peaceful. Why aren't they considered failures? Besides, Jonathan, I thought you were trying to ascertain true human nature with alchemy. Sounds to me as though you've already decided we are violent."

"Can you say we're not?"

"I agree with Olga. We've been programmed to be violent. We are a war culture worshiping death by war and fearing natural death."

"Programmed?" Jonathan asked.

"We've been indoctrinated," Ursula said. "So it could be that our responses are violent because that's all we know."

"But isn't sacrifice the opposite of violence?"

"No," Olga said. "To lay yourself on the altar is part of it all! Ursula decided her life was less valuable than Sergei's."

"I really hadn't thought of that, Olga," Ursula said.

"The true meaning of sacrifice is to make something holy or sacred," Olga said.

Ursula looked at her. "Who are you, old woman?"

Olga smiled. "So how would you giving up your life to Nikovotov be a holy act?"

Ursula looked over at Sergei. "I suppose it wouldn't be." She thought of her mother. She had been angry with her mother for years because she thought she should have sacrificed her work and dreams to be with Ursula. She'd been angry because her grandmother had sacrificed her life to take care of her grandchild.

Perhaps each of them had chosen to make their lives sacred.

"We all make sacrifices," Ursula said.

"Yes, and they are only true sacred acts when we recognize

who we are and know that we shouldn't jump into the fire at every turn. There are other ways."

"Is Sergei all right?" Ursula asked.

Olga shrugged and pulled down Sergei's shirt. "Let us all sleep on it."

The three of them ate quietly. Then they lay alongside one another, one on each side of Sergei, and pulled a fur blanket over themselves. The dimmed lantern light made a small circle around the lamp. Ursula stared at the cave walls for a long while. They undulated with color and subdued light. The roses blossomed, withered, blossomed, withered. Blossomed.

Ursula smiled. She felt enveloped by the warmth of Jonathan's and Sergei's bodies and the walls of the cave. It was like a womb, she supposed. She felt held, protected, and on the verge of . . .

On the verge of what?

Realizing who she was?

On the edge of adventure. Life. Whatever one called it. She wanted to giggle. Things were so odd.

"Go to sleep, child," Olga said. "Time does not stop in the timeless caves."

"How ironic," Ursula said.

Jonathan snickered.

"Sleep, children."

"Yes, Baba," Jonathan said.

Ursula dreamed she visited her grandmother.

"Asya," Ursula whispers. "You're dead?"

Asya nods.

"I need something of yours," Ursula says. "A keepsake. A ring. Something to help me out in the world."

Asya hands her a box filled with beautiful folds of material. One of the pieces is flecked with gold. She has never seen such beautiful cloth.

She is perplexed but realizes her grandmother has given her a meaningful gift.

It is time to go. She wants to kiss her grandmother good-bye but is afraid because Asya is dead.

She kisses her and says good-bye.

Ursula came out of her dream slowly, keeping her eyes closed. She whispered, "I have the material. I can do it, whatever it is." She swallowed hard. Grandmother Asya was dead, she was certain. Tears streamed down her cheeks. Now she was truly alone in the world.

Someone kissed her mouth.

She opened her eyes. Sergei sat next to her. Jonathan and Olga stood away from them, eating.

"Are you all right?" Sergei asked.

Ursula roughly wiped her tears away. "I'm fine. How are you?" she asked, sitting up.

Sergei smiled. His skin color was back to normal, his eyes were bright and clear. He reached for her hand and squeezed it—his strength was returning.

"I am much better," he said. "The shifting has stopped. The loneliness is gone. I don't feel as connected as I was before, but I don't feel insane. Or sick."

He leaned over and kissed her. "Thank you, my love."

Jonathan and Olga came and sat near them.

"Ursula," Sergei said, "we hope you do not intend to keep your promise to Nikovotov." His voice was strong again, like the Sergei she had known in Moscow.

"I-I don't quite know what to do," Ursula said. "If I don't do as I promised, he will cause a lot of problems."

"Not if we don't go back," Jonathan said.

"But where would we go?" Ursula said. "We're in the middle of nowhere."

"In the middle of everywhere," Olga corrected.

"And Olga has family—"

"I will return. Niko cannot harm me."

"I am no longer an exile," Jonathan said, "and Sasha agreed to meet me at Tomsk. He and Doubra are getting together my things even as we speak."

Ursula looked at Sergei. "And where would we go?"

Sergei glanced at Olga and Jonathan, then took her hand.

"I cannot go with you," he said.

"Why?"

He stared at her.

"Not this again," Ursula said.

He laughed. "You told me we would meet again in this cave, and I could not go with you."

"What will you do?" she asked.

"I will go on with my life without you."

Ursula pressed her fingers against his spider tattoo.

"Am I to go home?"

"You can go whenever you like," Sergei said. "This cave will take you back to before I first met you."

"And all the mysteries will be solved?" Ursula asked.

"Or we can find the cave which will take you back to your time," Sergei said. "It is up to you."

"Or I can stay here now with you," Ursula said.

"Niko will look for you," Jonathan said, "if you stay here."

"You already know what I choose, don't you?" Ursula asked Sergei.

He smiled slyly.

Ursula closed her eyes. "I started this to find my mother, to solve the mystery of the tattooed lady. I guess I might as well continue on."

Sergei nodded. "This is as it was."

Olga got up and brought her a pack. "Take off Jane's clothes and put on your own. They will be more suitable."

"Except I had no shirt."

"I brought you one of mine," Jonathan said.

Ursula stood, unfastened her snaps, and took off her tunic and shift. She pulled on her slacks, socks, and walking shoes.

"Hold on," Olga said. "First we must tattoo your back."

She nodded. "I need to talk to Sergei for a minute."

Jonathan and Olga stepped away from them. Sergei and Ursula walked to the entwined roses.

"Sergei, I want to tell you that we will be together again."

"I know. You've already given me your itinerary—the dates and flight numbers—though I don't know what that really means. I have memorized it all. Someday I will see you in a place called Chicago. And I will have to pretend that we are strangers." He put his arms around her waist and drew her close. "You said it may be a very long time before I see you again."

Ursula kissed his lips. "But will I see you again soon?"

"Very soon."

They embraced. Sergei held her tightly; she knew this would have to last him for many years.

When they released one another, Ursula said, "Sergei, have a good life. I mean, be happy. Fall in love. Have children. Don't spend your life waiting for me."

"We're ready," Sergei said. "Do you know what to do, Ulla?"

"No!" Ursula said.

"Sit down," Olga said.

Ursula did as she was told. Olga pulled down the back of Ursula's camisole.

"Put the dot opposite the other?" Olga asked.

"I don't know," Ursula said.

"I wasn't talking to you."

Ursula glanced over her shoulder.

"Yes," Sergei said.

Ursula felt a cloth across her back, then a prick, and the point of the needle going deeper and deeper.

She felt like she was going to throw-up.

Sergei came around in front of her, squatted and held her hand. "You all right?"

Ursula looked at him and nodded. "Does it have to go so deep?"

"Hurt usually does," Olga said.

Ursula rolled her eyes. "How proverbial of you, Olga."

Ursula felt dizzy.

From what seemed like a long way off, Jonathan said, "I'm going to miss you, cousin."

"Will I see Jonathan and Olga again?" Ursula asked.

"I don't know," Sergei said. "You never said."

"Don't worry about us," Olga said. "We have our own lives!"

Olga tapped the needle once.

The room shifted.

Ursula felt Olga pull out the needle. She sighed with relief. Someone helped her put on her shirt, tunic, coat, hat, mittens.

Ursula stood. The ground beneath her moved, as though it were a wave of water instead of earth and stone. She put out her hand to steady herself. Slowly she turned to face the wall. The red and white roses glowed, called to her.

She looked back at Olga, Jonathan, and Sergei; they were mere shadows, ghosts, already fading from her reality. "Good-bye, my love." She turned to the cave painting.

One of the rose thorns dripped red, another dripped white. Milk and blood?

She reached out to the flowers and plucked a single white petal.

The room spun, and Ursula fell to the ground.

Part Three

WILDERNESS

55

Someone shouted.

Ursula pushed herself up. The dizziness was gone, the cave dark and empty.

More cries.

Ursula hurried out of the cave and into chaos.

Was it day or night?

The air shook with—what?

Smoke. It was smoke choking out the day.

"Ahhhh!" Something raced by her so close she fell to the ground.

She could smell the black earth—and the smoke.

She stood again. The smoke whirled clear for a moment and she saw—in a split second—a black horse charging toward her—about to run her down. A black horse with a red sash across its chest and gold as a face plate. The horse stopped less than a foot from her—rearing and screaming. Ursula put up her hands to protect herself from flailing hooves.

The horse's rider screamed something at her. Ursula could not understand her words at first; then the rider held out her hand and shouted, "Fool, get up or die!"

Ursula reached up.

She heard hooves. Suddenly someone had her around her waist and threw her up behind the rider.

"Hold on!" the woman shouted. Ursula put her arms around the woman's waist, then glanced at the man who had helped her up. His horse reared. He was bearded—his chest covered in gold—and he was laughing. His eyes were the color of blue Siberian ice. *Sergei.*

The woman screamed a fearsome spine-chilling cry, and they raced out of the smoke into a bright blue day. On either side of them, horses thundered across a plain that seemed to go on forever on all sides. Behind them, the steppe burned. Ursula could not see the cave and wondered how it could have even existed here.

The horse ran on.

Sergei passed them. The woman laughed and leaned forward. Her horse went faster.

After a while, the horse slowed to a trot, then a walk. Ursula looked around. They were amidst a huge army of horses and riders. All were dressed similarly—red pointed hats with flaps over the ears, light colored shirts with long puffy sleeves beneath brightly-colored tunics, tight dark pants partially covered by knee-high boots. Some of the warriors—including Ursula's savior—sported gold breastplates. All had various weapons on their belts.

"What scrawny thing is that you've found, Opyea!" someone called.

Ursula's rider laughed. "She appeared out of nothing! I figure we can feed her to the wolves to keep them from our fires."

"Ha! One bite and she'd be gone!" Sergei's voice.

Ursula looked back. He grinned at her, but she saw no recognition in his eyes.

The horses walked through the tall wavy grass as though they were gently plowing a green sea. Ursula watched the grass as she hung onto Opyea's waist; the horse rocked her gently. She closed her eyes.

Ursula awakened to Opyea slapping her hands.

"Come on, girl. Get off!"

Ursula let go of Opyea's waist. The woman jumped down from the horse, Ursula slid off. Behind them lay the plains. Before them was a tent town of sorts: yurt-like tents and covered wagons that looked like gypsy carts.

Opyea patted her horse's neck and looked at Ursula.

"Who are you, scrawny girl? Whose side are you on?"

"My name is Ursula," she said. "If your enemies are on the other side of that fire line, then obviously I am on this side, your side."

Opyea roared a laugh. Ursula smiled. Opyea must have been a lion in another life.

"You speak our language like one of us, though your name is foreign. Come, my attendant was killed in battle today. You may take her place."

"Killed in battle? I'm not a warrior. I can hardly even ride a horse."

Opyea stared at her. All around, people called out to one another, embraced, walked their horses, handed over their horses, went into tents and wagons.

"What can you do?" Opyea asked.

"I'm good at languages," Ursula said.

"We don't like foreigners."

"I'm good at details."

Opyea handed Ursula her horse's reins. "You can walk a horse, can't you? Water her. Follow the other horses, then take off her bridle and saddle, cool her down, then hobble her and let her go."

"Hobble her?" Ursula said.

"You heard me. Bring the saddle and bridle back to me. I'll be where the noise is."

Opyea turned and walked toward the tent town.

Ursula stood for a moment with the reins in her hands. She looked at Opyea's chestnut horse, and the horse looked at her.

"Go with the flow, girl," Ursula said, and she and the horse stepped forward and followed the line of other horses and attendants as the prairie sloped down to a creek shaded by birch trees. The horse led Ursula through the riparian grasses to the water. Some of the men and women took off their clothes, dropped them on the banks, then washed themselves in the stream. When the chestnut finished drinking, she and Ursula walked up the slope again. Ursula watched one of the attendants tie a rope around their horse's front legs.

"Here." Ursula turned around. Sergei stood holding a piece of rope out to her.

"Can you tie a knot?" he asked. He looked so vibrant, strong, healthy. The man she had just left in the Rose Cave had been a ghost compared with him.

"Of course I can tie a knot. I'm not an idiot," Ursula said.

Sergei laughed. "Opyea would kill you if Chatra ran off." He squatted and tied the ends of a rope around the horse's front legs as the animal grazed.

"That seems cruel," Ursula said, trying to watch his hands make knots. "I thought you said there were wolves here. How can she run?"

His task finished, Sergei stood and nodded toward a woman standing not far from them, bow and arrow in hand. "Her arrow is faster than any wolf. Now Chatra is safe and so are you." He pulled the leather, wood, and bone bridle off the horse and handed it to Ursula. "Those are the scalps of Opyea's previous attendants."

Ursula glanced at what appeared to be pieces of dried skin with hair on them hanging from the bridle.

"Not really." She looked up, but Sergei was walking away.

Ursula looked at the bridle again. The wooden cheek pieces were shaped like lion heads. The leather knots, wood decorations, and antler tines helped hold it all together, along with the two-piece cast copper bit. She slipped it over her shoulder and fumbled with the belly and breast straps as the horse grazed, then pulled the saddle off and examined it. The saddle cover was soft, thin, made from dyed blue felt. Ursula carefully took off the cover to look at the saddle. It was made of two cushions, joined and sewn from two pieces of leather—top and bottom—with two small pieces on the front and back forming a kind of arch. She held the saddle closer. Sinew thread. Probably stuffed with deer hair and sedge cloth. The arches were trimmed with red woolen cloth that was decorated with animal heads. Three leather straps sewn across the cushions held them together and they, too, were embellished with lion and horse heads. The saddle blanket was the same shape as the saddle, made of thick white felt, and sewn under and onto the saddle.

"Pazyryk," she whispered.

Were these people related to the tattooed lady? She glanced at the naked men and women in the creek. None of their bodies bore the marks of an embroiderer. She breathed deeply. What other archaeologist got to live with the ancient people she had studied? She grinned.

She took off her scarf and wiped down Chatra with it. Then she shouldered the horse's gear and started back to the tent town. The sun was descending, and the steppes turned violet while the sky took on the color of forest-fire red.

She walked by warriors wiping blood from their daggers and swords, drinking, and cheering one another. She followed the noise until she got to a crowd gathered near an open fire.

A burly man with red hair and beard held a cup in the air. "We have done well. Kovo will not have us this day! The graves of our grandmothers and grandfathers are safe. We have all survived to die another day! We thank Tabitia and the spirits of the fire who always protect us!"

Several people threw their drinks into the fire and the fire spat at them.

The crowd cheered.

The man suddenly looked at Ursula.

"Who is this foreigner?" he demanded.

Opyea stepped forward.

"I found her on the fire line. I have taken her as attendant, with your permission, Cylas."

"Come here," Cylas said brusquely.

Ursula made her way through the crowd until she stood face to face with Cylas. He was about her height and he was all muscle.

"Make your statement," Cylas said.

Ursula did not know what to say.

"Well!" he bellowed, his face inches from hers. "Shall we burn you as prisoner, blind you as slave, or scalp you as enemy?"

"My people are from the Altai," Ursula said.

Cylas stepped away from her.

"Where?" Opyea asked.

"From the Pastures of Heaven," Ursula said. "West of the Sacred Sea, looking south to the Beloved Mountain."

"So. One of us!" Cylas said. "Your dress is peculiar but you speak well. Follow our customs, and you may remain with us. What can you do?"

"She knows languages," Opyea said.

"Has she killed in battle?" Cylas asked.

Ursula wanted to declare herself a pacifist but sensed she was not with similarly-minded folks.

"I know every language," Ursula blurted out.

"That is quite a boast," Cylas said.

A black and gray crow flew overhead, crying hoarsely, "Karr-karr."

"And what does she say?" Cylas asked, pointing to the crow.

"I don't know," Ursula said.

"Then you don't know every language," he said. "Opyea, see to it that she learns to fight and ride."

"I will," Opyea said.

Then the drinking, singing, and swearing started again. Ursula moved away from the group. Someone clapped her on the back, nearly knocking her over. She turned around. Opyea grinned.

"You are fortunate," Opyea said.

"Apparently," Ursula said. "I had heard you blind your slaves, but I was hoping that wasn't true."

Opyea kept her hand on Ursula's shoulder and maneuvered her through the crowd of men and women, toward one of the tents. As they got closer, Ursula could see the tent was probably made of felt and bark. It flowed outward like a circus tent—or a yurt. Around this tent, several children ran. Two women sat near what looked like a small metal stove. A pot of food boiled atop it.

"A stove?" Ursula asked. "I didn't know you had stoves."

Opyea moved her past the women who looked up at her and smiled. She and Opyea stepped over the small wall of stones which created the base of the tent, then ducked into the dark opening.

"So this is more or less a permanent structure?" Ursula said.

Opyea released Ursula's shoulders, took the gear from her and hung it in a shadowy corner.

"You ask strange questions."

Ursula stood still, blinking until her eyes adjusted to the darkness. Then she looked around. Felt draped the tent walls; each section of the felt had the same scene on it: a woman on a throne—probably the goddess Tabitia—with a blossoming branch in her hand and a horse and its rider before her. A plain carpet covered the floor of the tent. Ursula recognized several oil lamps made from small blocks of sandstone. Fur and leather bags and pouches lay in a pile near the door: some red, some white with bright blue fur, others brown or cream-colored. All were decorated with animal shapes and patterns. Cauldrons and drinking vessels of wood and clay sat on low shelves, alongside small collapsible wooden tables with oval dish-shaped tops—a kind of TV-dinner tray with shorter legs. She wanted to touch every thing: smell it, taste it. She had seen so many similar items from the tombs of the Siberians.

She laughed.

"Are you mad?" Opyea asked.

Ursula smiled. Jonathan had asked the same thing when he first met her.

"Can I ask you some questions?" Ursula asked.

"Let's eat first. Come, help me with this."

Ursula went to Opyea's side and unfastened her armor which was made of oval-shaped gold plaques. She held it up while Opyea ducked out of it.

"Hang it by my saddle," Opyea said.

Ursula hooked the armor to the wall with leather fasteners. Opyea took off her weapons belt and handed it to Ursula who laid it on the low table next to the bow and arrows.

"Come." Opyea grabbed two mats from the floor and tossed one to Ursula.

They went outside. The day was light again as the setting sun cleared the clouds before going below the horizon. Many more people now gathered nearby.

The older woman stood as Opyea came out.

"Our clan thanks you, Opyea, for defending our pastures and keeping the enemy far from the graves of our ancestors."

Everyone cheered.

"Thank you, my mother Myrus. We live to die another day!" Another cheer. "I have picked up a stray. She goes by the name

Ulla, the Woman Who Talks. I will see if she can do us good. If not, we shall stew her!"

Ursula looked at Opyea. Everyone but Ursula laughed.

Opyea slapped her on the back. "Our foremothers were called the Oeorpata—the mankillers—before they married the men of the pastures, but we have never *eaten* anyone!"

The crowd roared; once again, Ursula thought of lions.

Opyea dropped her mat to the ground, then sat on it. Someone opened a collapsible dish/table in front of her. Myrus scooped food from the pot onto her plate and handed her a spoon. Opyea dipped the spoon into the mixture, then took a bite.

"Superb!" she said. "Let us eat!"

Ursula put her mat just outside the circle. All around them, other groups of people settled down to eat. The sun pulled daylight away until the flames of an occasional campfire was the only illumination.

Ursula did not know what she ate or drank but it was delicious. When the crowd around Opyea thinned Ursula sat beside her.

"Thanks for bringing me here," Ursula said. "It's like a dream come true—a dream I didn't even know I had."

Opyea nodded in the darkness. "It is more rewarding to save a life than to end one."

"I didn't know warriors were allowed to think such things."

Opyea laughed. "I am free to think. No one has say over my thoughts! Except perhaps Tabitia."

"Are those scalps of your enemies on your horse's halter?"

"Maybe yes. Maybe no." Opyea took a sip from her oval-shaped cup. "The thing is for the enemy to believe that you would do anything: kill, maim, scalp, burn, torture."

"You're saying you don't do those things?"

"No." She handed Ursula her cup. It felt like bone. "That is what is left of someone who was not afraid and who did not run."

"A skull?"

"Yes. A skull of a great warrior who was foolish enough to try to kill me."

Ursula handed the cup back to Opyea.

"Tomorrow we must start your training," Opyea said.

"I don't want to learn to kill."

"Your desires don't matter. To be of use to our clan and our tribe, you must know how to survive. Kovo will come after us another day and everyone must know how to defend themselves."

"Don't we have to leave this place? Won't your enemies—this Kovo—follow you here?"

"No. We believe they wish us to stay east. We are east. They have grown weary of following us. It is ended for now." Opyea slapped her thighs and stood. "Before I grow too tired I must find myself a man," she said loudly. She looked at Ursula. "You will find—once you have proven yourself—that our men are the finest anywhere, just as our women are. The women must learn to fight and the men must learn to serve women."

"Serve women? Serve us food?"

Opyea laughed and slapped Ursula's back.

"Ouch!"

"I like you, Woman Who Talks. Yes, they serve us food, and they can stay hard all night. Not a short-termer among them. Good night. Sleep close to the tent—less likely that the wolves or tigers will get you then."

Ursula sat on her mat for a long while listening to the night noises: insects rubbing elbows, the occasional scream of a raptor finding is prey, the sounds of children settling down to sleep, and lovers moving together. She listened until she grew drowsy but could not immediately fall to sleep because of the chill in the air. She huddled under her coat.

She dreamed of Mount Belovdia. Snow fell like feathers.

When Ursula awakened, she took off a blanket someone had

thrown over her and slowly sat up. Opyea sat by the stove braiding her hair. Today she wore a short red caftan and tight black pants with felt boots over them. Gold appliques of twisting deer with huge stylized horns decorated the front of her caftan.

Myrus, who wore a long blue caftan and let her gray hair loose, nodded to Ursula.

"Serve yourself, Woman Who Talks," Myrus said, handing her a dish/table.

Ursula slapped whatever was in the pan onto her plate. Myrus poured what looked like yogurt over it. Ursula ate hungrily. "It's very good," she said with her mouth full. "What is it?"

Myrus glanced at Opyea.

"Mutton."

"Oh. I used to be a vegetarian."

"Hmph!" Opyea said. "No wonder you are so skinny."

"Where are the sheep?" Ursula asked. "I didn't see them."

"They are out," Myrus said, "with the shepherds."

"Do you run cattle, too?"

"Our tribe has cattle, sheep, and horses," Myrus said.

Opyea nodded.

"Is Cylas your king?" Ursula asked.

"He is the chief," Opyea said, "of the tribe. I am clan head. Why do you ask so many questions?"

"I'm curious about how things work. I've heard so much about your people."

Opyea cocked an eyebrow. "Your people? Aren't we your people?"

"I'm from further—" she looked around. She had no clue as to where she was. "I'm from further east and south—from the mountains."

"Yes. We are from the mountains. So long ago. I've never been actually."

"I have," Myrus said. "Once my father took us back. It was

more beautiful than anything I could have imagined. And the people there, they still understood the language of the Old Ones."

"The Old Ones?"

"Our ancestors," Opyea said. "We are all descendants of the Old Ones, those who walked and flew before we were born. We were all once part of the People. Our clans still honor this connection which is lost but not forgotten."

"What is your clan?" Ursula asked.

Opyea stood and turned around. On the back of her caftan was a gold applique of a bear's claw.

"We are Bear Clan," Opyea said.

Ursula nodded. She should have known.

"So am I," Ursula said.

"I knew I saw the glint of bear in your eyes!" Opyea cried.

"Welcome," Myrus said.

56

After breakfast, Opyea and Ursula went to the river to find Chatra. She grazed near a smaller unhobbled horse.

Opyea made sweet talk with her horse as she unhobbled her and put a bit-less bridle on her head.

"This little horse is called Runner," Opyea said, nodding to the other horse. "You will learn on him."

"He's called Runner because he's fast?"

She shook her head. "Because he's always running from a fight." She patted his hindquarters. "He's lucky we haven't eaten him, but we've taken his balls and he's gentled. He'll do fine for you."

Just then, Sergei rode up on his black horse. He looked glorious under the bright blue sky with his long hair pulled back into a ponytail. Today he wore no hat, only a blue tunic over a puffy-sleeved shirt with tight blue pants that left nothing to the imagination. When he dismounted his horse, Ursula couldn't help but smile.

Opyea hit her arm. "Pay attention."

"Ouch. I wish you'd quit hitting me."

Opyea rolled her eyes. "Here's Runner's bridle. Can you put it on him?"

Sergei came and stood next to Opyea, his arms folded across his chest. Ursula went up to the smaller horse.

"Hey, Runner. Come here."

The horse continued grazing, his ears twitching.

Ursula squatted and put the bridle on the ground. She started to pull it on, but the horse's head snapped up and knocked Ursula on her butt.

Sergei laughed. Ursula's face reddened. Runner stood passively. Ursula got up, put the bridle over his nose and up over his ears.

"Good. Now leave the reins hanging to the ground. He'll stay. Watch me put on Chatra's saddle."

Opyea lay the saddle across the mare's back. She made sure the blanket was straight, then took the cinch and pulled it up through the loop, tightened it, and slipped the end of it through and under the loop again.

"Now you."

Ursula put her saddle gently on Runner's back. He continued to graze. She smoothed out the blanket beneath it. She reached for the belly strap, pulled it tight, then looped and knotted it.

She stepped back. Not bad, she thought.

"He held his breath," Sergei said.

"What?"

"He's a tricky horse," Opyea said. She grabbed the saddle and it slipped around and down to Runner's belly.

"Scopasis, show her how to do it right," Opyea said.

Scopasis?

Sergei pushed the saddle up, loosened the cinch, put his knee against the horse's belly, then pushed while pulling the cinch tight. Afterward, he held out his hands to give Ursula a leg up on the left side of Runner. Ursula hesitated.

"We don't have forever, woman!" Opyea said.

Ursula grabbed the arch of the saddle, put her left foot on Sergei's hands, and swung her other leg up over the horse. Sergei handed her the reins.

Opyea got on Chatra.

"Now keep your seat with your thighs. Don't press too hard though—if you press your left thigh against his side, he'll turn right, right thigh left. Same with the reins. He's very well trained—except for that running from battle thing. All right, walk him."

Ursula pressed both of her legs against Runner's sides. He started forward. Ursula kept her balance. She smiled at Sergei; he returned her smile.

"Now turn him left. Left! Use the right rein. OK. Good. Now go with the flow of the horse."

They walked around in circles for a while. Then Sergei got on his mount, and they headed out onto the plains. Ursula held tightly to the saddle when they trotted—praying to all the spirits and beings of the universe to keep her from falling and splitting her head open. Then they started galloping. She wanted to scream; instead she hung on.

Opyea cried out joyfully. Sergei ran circles around Ursula. She lay down close to Runner's neck and suddenly she wasn't bouncing, she was moving with the rhythm of the horse. She was still terrified, but she was riding a galloping horse and it felt great.

After a time, they slowed and walked the horses.

"Not bad," Opyea said. "But you aren't a true horse rider until you can hang on and shoot an arrow at the same time."

"I think that would take a lifetime to learn," Ursula said.

"Then let's start," Opyea said.

They came to a small larch wood. Opyea and Sergei jumped from their horses. Ursula sat on Runner and wondered how to get down without a saddle horn or stirrups.

"Slide or jump, Woman Who Talks. Come on."

Ursula brought her right leg up behind her, turned her body to face the saddle—hung on to it—then slid to the ground. Slow but effective. She dropped Runner's reins to the ground, just as Sergei and Opyea had done, then followed them down to the woods.

Sergei took a wooden arrow from the leather quiver slung over his left shoulder. With his other hand, he held a bow out to her. She took it and turned it lightly on her fingertips. She had never seen a Scythian or Altaian bow—she was fairly certain none had been recovered before. It was small, with the wooden bow curving in at the center, making it look like a giant exaggerated upper lip—or a sloppy M. The string was probably sinew. Rams and lions decorated the bow—each caught in motion, twisting and turning. Classic Scytho-Siberian style.

"Ulla! Attention!" Opyea scolded.

Ursula looked up. Sergei handed her a wooden arrow with a barbed head. She stroked the feathery end.

"Shoot the tree," Opyea said.

"That tree never did anything to me."

Opyea stared at her. Sergei turned his face to hide a smile.

"I've never used one of these," Ursula said.

"You've never ridden a horse or released an arrow to fly through the air? Woman, how did you eat?"

"It's a long story," Ursula said. "And I have ridden a horse before."

Ursula held the bow in her left arm, then lay an arrow across it, fitted the nocked end onto the string, pulled it back, then held the bow and arrow up. She closed her left eye, aimed, and released the arrow.

She dropped her arm to watch the arrow fall yards away from the target and into the grass.

Opyea rolled her eyes.

"Keep both eyes open. Watch the target—not the arrow. Keep

your position until the arrow hits the target." Opyea pushed Ursula, and she nearly fell over. "Balance, Woman Who Talks. Balance!"

"I wish you would stop hitting and pushing me around!"

"If you were balanced, I wouldn't be able to push you. Look, Ulla, I don't enjoy killing anyone whose name I know. I picked you up. Now you must earn your keep or die."

Everything suddenly got still. Ursula stared into the other woman's blue eyes.

"I understand," Ursula said.

"Good." Opyea looked at Sergei. "I will check on the herders. Keep her out of trouble."

Opyea jumped on Chatra and raced away. Ursula watched until they became only a black pinprick on the vast green-gold plain. Overhead, a buzzard circled. A blue bird sat on a larch branch and squawked at them.

Ursula followed the path her arrow had taken and found it in the grass. Then she came back to stand next to Sergei. She lay the arrow across the bow, nocked the arrow, pulled the string back, and raised both. She looked at the target, released the arrow, waited until it fell in the grass, then relaxed.

"She would not let them kill you," Sergei called as she went to fetch the arrow. "Not without reason. The worst that could happen is that you'd be kicked out."

"To live on my own?" Ursula said as she walked back to him. "I'd last long. I can't die. I've got things to do." She handed him the bow. "Show me how to do it right."

Sergei shot his first arrow so quickly Ursula could not discern anything about his method. Next shot, he slowed. He looked at the target first, then raised the bow and released the arrow. It sailed through the air—up—then down into the dead tree, going almost all the way through the wood to the other side.

"That's beautiful," Ursula said. "You look beautiful doing

it."

Sergei laughed. "You are so easy with me."

Ursula smiled. "It's because I know you from another time and place. Only you had another name."

"Another time? Like dreamtime? I have dreamed of a foreign woman. I never saw her face—only the markings on her body."

Ursula gazed at Sergei. He looked so young—as yet undamaged by all that would happen to him.

"I have no markings on my body," Ursula said.

"Then I suppose it wasn't you."

Ursula shrugged. "Who knows what will happen tomorrow." She smiled. "If a few body markings make me the woman of your dreams, I'm ready." She flashed him a grin, then ran to retrieve the arrow.

Sergei laughed. "You sure can talk. We'll get you a bow with different tension tomorrow. This one was made for me."

Ursula brought the arrow back, and Sergei gave her the bow. She looked at her feet and tried to find her balance. First she stood with her feet parallel, shoulder-length apart.

"Now push me," Ursula said. "Gently."

Sergei pushed her chest. She fell back.

She moved her left foot back, at a forty-five angle. "Push me."

Sergei did as he was asked. Ursula kept her balance much easier this time. Was this what Olga had been trying to tell her when she said she didn't have both feet firmly on this world?

She lay the arrow across the bow, nocked it, and pulled the string back, raised it up, sighted, then released the arrow. Ursula watched the target until she saw the arrow fly over it.

"Good distance," Sergei said. "That's better."

She continued to practice, emptying the quiver first, then combing the woods for the arrows. Her distance remained good, but her aim was always off. Eventually they took a break.

Sergei leaned against a pale yellow rock. Beyond him, the rock seemed to move ever so slightly, as if it were breathing. Ursula blinked. It was not rock. It was a she-lion, just like the kind she would have expected to see in an African jungle. And she was getting ready to spring on Sergei.

Ursula yelled, "Get away! He's mine!" as she jumped up and pushed Sergei away. The lion flew over them both and disappeared into the feathery grasses.

Sergei stared at Ursula.

"How did you do that?" Sergei asked.

"Do what?" Her heart pounded in her ears. "I guess I scared her."

Sergei laughed. "Lions don't scare. If she couldn't get me, she should have gotten you. You roared! What did you say to her?"

"I didn't roar! I think I said get away."

Sergei shook his head. "You said it in her language. You roared just like a lion, Woman Who Can Talk."

Ursula looked out at the prairie. No sign of the she-lion. Had she really talked to her?

"You saved my life," Sergei said.

Ursula turned to him. "It's not the first time." She grinned. "Probably won't be the last."

Sergei smiled. "It's so strange." He reached out and took something out of her hair. "It is as if we have known each other forever."

Ursula smiled. "Not quite that long."

At camp, Sergei offered to take care of the horses. Exhausted, Ursula let him. She returned to Myrus's tent. The older woman was directing preparations for the next meal but ducked into the tent and brought out a mat for Ursula who took it around the tent, away from the others. Seconds after she lay down on it, she fell to sleep.

"Wake up, She Who Roars!" Opyea cried.

Ursula jumped to her feet before she was awake.

"What!"

"Cylas wishes to see you," Opyea said. She held the back of Ursula's neck with her hand and steered her away from the Bear Clan tent.

The sun was setting. Ursula had slept away the afternoon. They wove their way through the tents and wagons until they came to a tent bigger than all the rest. Sergei waited for them. He nodded a greeting, then stepped through the opening into the tent. Opyea and Ursula followed.

Several oil lamps illuminated the inside of the tent. Cream-colored carpets decorated with woven pictures of various animals in twisted poses and the goddess receiving gifts hung from the tent "walls." Several people—including Cylas—sat on floor cushions. Next to Cylas was a woman with long wavy red hair and blue eyes, wearing a long shiny-blue caftan, with white pants or tights beneath it.

Cylas said, "Ah! There she is. Sit. Join us."

The others moved so Ursula, Opyea, and Sergei could sit. One of the men passed food-filled dish trays to each of them. They ate in silence for a few minutes. Ursula could not keep her eyes off the woman. She was beautiful and seemed to emanate something—power? Confidence?

"So you spoke to the lion," Cylas said. "You do know many languages."

"I don't recall talking to the lion," Ursula said. "I was trying to scare her away."

Cylas smiled and glanced at the red-haired woman.

"You weren't afraid?" the woman asked.

"I didn't have time to be."

"Opyea says you can sit a horse," Cylas said. "Your shooting skills are another matter. You aren't much of a warrior."

"No, I'm not."

"Yet you saved Scopasis's life," the woman said. "For that, I am grateful."

Ursula glanced at Sergei.

"You have proved your value," the woman said. "You will be allowed to stay with us. You will be of the most use where wild animals or foreigners are. So you shall accompany those of the warrior class when they are protecting the herds or going to war."

"But I—"

Cylas looked sharply at her, and she closed her mouth.

"You will continue improving your horse riding skills," Cylas said. "Since you saved Scopasis's life, he will become your attendant."

"At least for the time being," the woman said. "My son is young and no doubt needs to improve his lovemaking skills before he marries."

"But Opyea saved my life. Aren't I her attendant?"

"Yes. So?" Cylas stuffed more food into his mouth.

"Where is your home?" the woman asked.

Ursula hesitated, then said, "My ancestors are buried near the Beloved mountain. My grandfather was one of the People. The Bear People. My mother disappeared while studying the caves near the mountain. I have been searching for her."

The woman nodded. "I am Veras. My son calls you Ulla, She Who Roars. It is now your right—because his life is part yours now—to name him. What shall you call him?"

"Sergei. I'd call him Sergei."

"That is an unfamiliar name," the woman said. "What does it mean?"

Ursula glanced at Sergei. What did it mean? She had no clue. He Who Is Loved? No. They were not exactly a kissy huggy bunch. He Who Is Tattooed. No. He didn't have any tattoos. She thought of all the time periods she had seen him.

"Sergei, He Who Is Long-Lived."

"Then so it will be," the woman said.

Soon after, Opyea and Ursula stood and went into the night. Billions of stars lit the sky.

"Well, you did a good thing," Opyea said. "Come. Sleep inside tonight. I feel a chill in the air."

As they walked toward the Bear Clan tent, Ursula said, "Who was that woman?"

"Veras? She's priestess, my own true love, and she's married to Cylas. Scopasis—Sergei—is their son. If she has given you the nod, your life is protected. You have a home." Opyea slapped her on the back.

"What about Sergei being my attendant and what she said about love-making?"

Opyea laughed. "He's a fine looking man. Be glad. She's given you the gift of her son. If he takes after his mother, he will be a magnificent lover."

Ursula slept amidst the clan—somewhere between Opyea's younger brother Nels and cousin Banth. She listened to everyone's breathing, smelled the rich odor of bodies and food, incense and spices. Her mat was hard, her blanket scratchy, yet she fell to sleep almost instantly, glad to be close to so many of her clan.

In the morning, Ursula tried to help Myrus with breakfast. The older woman firmly pushed her away.

"Food must not be prepared by those of the warrior status," she said.

"I am not a warrior."

"But that is your place now. Go on."

Opyea called to her from inside the tent. Ursula went back inside.

"It's time to dress you," Opyea said. "Take off your clothes."

Ursula did as she was told, leaving on her camisole and underwear. Opyea handed her a blue tunic with a belt, black trousers, and boots. The tunic had long puffy sleeves and gold disk appliques on the front and a gold bear's paw on the back. Ursula slipped it over her head, then pulled on the thin trousers which were almost like tights. The boots were soft, made of felt. The bottoms of the boots were covered in leather.

Opyea nodded as Ursula tied the belt. "Now you look like one of us."

"Here." She handed Ursula a dagger in its leather case. The handle of the dagger was decorated with swans. "Slide your belt through here." Opyea indicated a slit in the leather case. "Then your weapon is always at the ready."

Ursula started to protest, then shut her mouth, untied her belt, and put the dagger on the belt.

"Thank you," Ursula said.

"Good. Today we ride."

Ursula went to get Opyea's horse. Sergei already had Runner and Chatra saddled and ready for her.

"Good morning," Ursula said.

Sergei smiled almost shyly. "Hello."

"Thanks but you don't have to do my work, too."

Sergei shrugged.

"This is silly." Ursula took the reins from him, and they began walking the three horses across the plain toward the village. In the distance, a herd of wild sheep grazed. Several looked up at them. Their horns curved away from their heads like two halves of a heart—just like the ram tattoos on one of the Pazyryk mummies.

"You did save my life," Sergei said. "And you are older. I would like to make love with you."

Ursula laughed. Sergei frowned.

"Sorry," Ursula said. "Making love with you would be fun. I know. We've done it before. But you know what I'd like from you? I want you to show me how you live—so I can survive on my own if I had to."

He glanced at her. "We don't survive on our own. We survive together. Besides, every child knows such things."

"I don't. I told you I come from a different time. We learn different ways to survive."

Sergei nodded. "I will teach you."

Ursula rode with Opyea, Sergei, and several others back to the fire line. Runner grew skittish as they neared the burned ground. For hours they rode but found no sign of Kovo or his warriors.

When they returned to camp, they ate heartily. Drummers and dancers came out during the meal. Costumed men and women moved like belly dancers—their bodies undulating sensuously to the music.

Sergei sat next to Ursula as the drummers and harpists made music for the dancers.

"Is there meaning to this dance?" Ursula asked him.

"They are creating the universe," Sergei said. "Everything is made from sacred forms and when we recreate those forms with our bodies we harmonize with the rest of the universe. Would you like to try?"

"In front of everyone? No!"

Sergei grabbed her hand and led her away from the crowd, into the dusk where they could still hear the music.

"Stand with your feet apart and find your balance. Knees slightly bent. Now keep your torso centered and still and move your hips in a circle. Arms out."

Ursula rolled her eyes. This felt just like learning to shoot a bow and arrow.

"Don't stick your butt out." He put his hand on her tail bone and gently pushed it in. Then he made a circle with his hips; Ursula followed his lead. "Good. Now hold your hips still and make a circle with your torso."

Ursula tried. Sergei smiled. "It takes practice."

"Yep. I'm on my way to Carnegie Hall."

"Now try this. You're making two circles looping on to each other."

She watched his hips circle to the right, then left. She put her hands on his hips and closed her eyes. "Do it again."

It was the figure eight.

She tried it.

She laughed. "It feels nice."

They danced together for several minutes, finally coming close enough to kiss—which they did. Then Sergei took her hand in his and led her away from the village, out into the prairie. The sky was rose and orange-colored. He pulled off his caftan and laid it on the grass. Ursula untied her tunic and let the belt and blade drop to the ground. Then she pulled off her tunic and her pants.

Sergei and Ursula lay together on the ground.

"Have you ever made love before?" Ursula asked.

"Of course. I am not a boy!"

He gently slipped her camisole over her head and kissed her breasts. Soon they were naked. He slipped easily into her. His skin pressed next to hers felt so familiar and exciting. She climaxed and he continued to move until they came together, then fell apart, hot and sweaty.

He was a good lover—a great lover—but the wildness she had experienced in Moscow was missing from him. She had seen or felt nothing of the wild—the Bear—in him this time.

Sergei moved close to her. "Who are you?"

"What do you mean?" she whispered.

"While we were making love, you changed. Or something. You were you and something else. Like a bear. Or another being. I can't explain it."

Ursula put her arm under his shoulders and drew him near.

"Who did I just make love with?" he asked.

"Just me. Ursula, She Who Roars, Granddaughter of Asya, daughter of Ursula, part of the Bear Clan, of the People."

57

For Ursula, the days took on a kind of blissful routine. In the mornings, she usually trailed after Opyea, checking the "borders" or guarding the herds. The herders all wanted Ursula to stay with her and "talk to the animals," so Opyea often left her behind with them for part of the day.

On rare occasions, a predator did stalk the small sheep near where Ursula and Sergei sat astride their horses. Ursula would call out to the animal, telling the wolf or lion that the sheep were hers. For reasons Ursula did not understand, the predators usually left the sheep alone.

"You not only roar," Sergei said, "you bark and growl."

She even scared away a polecat once. The small weasel-like animal showed up one day and made the sheep nervous, so Ursula asked him to leave. He looked at her, spat, then sauntered away.

During the afternoons, if they were free, Sergei taught Ursula about life with his people. He tried to help improve her archery skills. He also showed her how to repair saddles and bridles, dig for grubs and roots, cool down a horse, and fix a frayed mat or blanket.

Weeks went by. Ursula loved the life. She liked the chill in the morning that made her move closer to whomever she slept near. She liked splashing in the creek or at the swimming holes. She loved the smell of grass—first sweet, now a dry dusty smell as the summer wore on. The sounds changed, too, as the days passed. The sweeping gentle brushing noise—like fir boughs against fir boughs—now had a drier sound, like autumn leaves on deciduous trees. She loved pestering Myrus to show her how to sew and wash clothes—even though those were the honored duties of the hearth class, not the warrior class.

She did not enjoy the hunt, although she participated several times. They always stopped at Veras's hut and asked for a blessing. She would step into the day that was blue with sky and gold with grass—her hair fiery red—and pray to the animals to give up some of their own to feed the clans.

Once after the kill, Ursula tried to watch them skin one of the strange-nosed little deer creatures they had killed; she threw up. They all laughed at her but left her to herself.

Some nights she and Opyea ate with Veras and Cylas and their clan. Afterward, Veras would make Opyea sit still while she braided and unbraided her hair and whispered in her ear. Opyea would lean backward so that she was pressed ever-so-gently against Veras's breasts. Cylas would glance at them and smile as if he were watching a scene from a movie and continue playing some game with his youngest daughter, Elio.

One night Veras called Ursula over to her and they sat alone together.

"My son has told me about you," Veras said. "When he makes love to you, he makes love with a wild one. Sometimes when you eat, he can also see your true self. I have glimpsed it myself but have said nothing. Some of our people would not understand."

"I don't understand."

She nodded. "We have been away from our homeland for too long. Some day I would like us to return to the mountains. I have heard that the People still live in peace there and are undisturbed. I believe it is there that we could find our place. There are too many of us who think our only value is as warriors, as wanderers. We wander because we have forgotten where home is. Someday we will return. Opyea has promised. And you will care for my son."

"Of course."

One morning, while Ursula was saddling Chatra, Opyea told her, "We're going to be gone for a few days. We've lost touch with some herders up north so we'll go check on them. Ask a hearther if she would pack some food for us. You, me, Sergei, Nels, and Sheera. Leave the horses to me."

Ursula nodded and hurried back to the village to the Bear Clan tent.

"Myrus," she called as she stepped inside. "We have to take a trip up north, five of us. Opyea asks if a hearther would honor us by packing some food for our journey."

Myrus looked at her. "Is there trouble?"

"We're going to look for some missing herders."

Myrus still stared at her. "Nothing more?"

"No. Why?"

"I heard Kovo has asked for a peace alliance."

"That's good, isn't it?"

Myrus turned away from her. "I will make ready for your trip, She Who Roars."

"Thank you. Can I help?"

Myrus glanced at her.

"Yeah, all right," Ursula said. "I'm leaving."

An hour later, after they saddled their horses and added a few extra bags of food and pouches of water, they stood outside Veras's tent. She wore a long bright blue caftan that almost looked like a kimono without the obi. On the back of it were two beautiful white swans.

"I still think we can postpone this trip until after you meet with Kovo, Cylas," Opyea said. "He's a fanatic. I don't trust him."

"It is three days hence," Cylas said, "at the herder's tent where the prairie meets the forest in the west. You can detour there on your way back."

Veras went to Opyea and kissed her on the lips. "It is my fault, Pi," Veras said. "I dreamed you all should go."

"Then let it be," Opyea said. "We ask for your blessings."

"They are given. I spent the morning in meditation and ceremony. The elemental spirits will guide and protect you. Tabitia guides you always."

Sergei kissed his mother and embraced his father.

"I can stay," Sergei said. "Ursula would release me to be at your side during negotiations."

"No. You must go, too," Veras said.

"Come, Sergei," Opyea said. "We shall see our families soon enough again."

The five of them got on their horses and galloped away from the village. They soon slowed the horses and walked them for hours across unending prairie. Hours turned into days.

On the third day, Opyea and Sergei walked alongside their horses looking for footprints or any other traces of the missing herders. The land dipped and rolled and sprouted trees. Opyea took them east for a time, then south again. Late morning they smelled a fire. Soon after they trotted into a camp. A small tent stood under a tree. Someone sat near the fire.

"Dolg!" Opyea shouted as they jumped from their horses. "Where is everyone?"

Dolg looked wan. "They are rounding up the herd. We were

ambushed a week ago. Tath and Cera were killed and part of the herd was stolen. I've been trying to heal from a knife wound. I need a hearther, or a priestess."

"I apprenticed with a hearther," Sheera said. "I'll look at your wounds."

"Were they bandits or did they carry colors?" Opyea asked.

"I think they were Kovo's warriors," Dolg said. "But it was night and they let three of us live, so maybe not."

Sheera began poking around Dolg's side. Opyea looked at Sergei.

"I don't like this. Sheera, you patch him up and get them back, even if you have to leave the herd. The rest of us will eat and head out again."

"What's wrong?" Ursula asked.

"Two of our people are dead," Opyea sad. "I pray to Tabitia that is all that has happened."

They ate quickly. Ursula felt sick to her stomach and didn't know why. Soon they were on their horses—now four of them—traveling southwest. They could not gallop their horses or they would run them into the ground, yet home was at least two days away.

They traveled until dark and awakened before dawn, ate quickly, and rode out again. No one talked. Ursula felt as though they were suspended between now and some possible horrible future. None of them slept well the next night, and they started early again. Ursula did not recognize the territory and guessed they were headed for the meeting place Cylas had mentioned.

"Be aware," Opyea said.

Nels, Opyea, and Sergei had their bows at the ready.

Across the prairie on the horizon, a dark line appeared. They were nearing the place where prairie and forest met. Another line ascended into the sky. Smoke.

"Nels and Sergei," Opyea said. "Go around back through the

trees."

Sergei and Nels galloped away. Opyea and Ursula's horses trotted forward.

"Try to aim and shoot," Opyea called to her. "And if you can't do that, take out your dagger and slash."

They smelled disaster before they saw it: the acrid odor of burning hair and flesh. Suddenly Opyea galloped forward. There were no waiting troops. No horses. A charcoal fire smoldered in one larch tree. Darkness lay beyond the trees—and scorched earth where the encampment had been.

Then Ursula saw them. The dead. Sprawled on the ground— looking so distorted in death that they did not appear quite human. Her horse whinnied.

Opyea dismounted and handed Chatra's reins to Ursula. "Take them to the stream beyond the trees. Then hobble them both. Horses run from blood."

Ursula slowly got off Runner and held tightly to their reins. She stared at the dead. How could 2,500 year old mummies look more human? Opyea shouted and waved her hands and several buzzards flew up and away.

Nels and Sergei came out of the trees. Ursula walked by them and into the woods. She listened for the sound of water and followed it. The horses settled down as they got farther from the camp. Ursula breathed deeply.

The ground sloped, the trees opened, and a tiny stream ran through the woods. While the horses drank, Ursula easily hobbled them, then pulled off their saddles and bridles. Neither were sweating, so she left them and reluctantly walked back to the camp.

She emerged into the light. Opyea, Nels, and Sergei walked amongst the dead. At least two dozen murdered. A vat of red wine—or some kind of liquid—still stood next to where the tent had been; three crows staggered near the vat as if drunk or stunned.

"The clan heads," Opyea said. She began walking amongst the dead. Ursula followed. "Look, she didn't even have time to draw out her dagger."

"They were drunk and asleep," Sergei said.

Nels began throwing up.

Opyea recited the names of the dead out loud. Ursula wondered how she recognized any of them. Their faces were bashed-in or mutilated.

"How could they do this?" Ursula asked.

"We have done no less to them," Opyea said.

"You mutilate them like this?"

Opyea said, "What did you think? Death isn't an easy thing." She sighed. "The horses are exhausted. We can't go back until they've rested."

"There are too many dead," Nels said. "What will we do?"

"Hope not everyone was killed," Opyea said. "We will gather the dead together to keep the vultures off until the hearthers and priestesses can come."

Sergei knelt on the ground next to one of the bodies. Ursula came closer. The dead man lay face down. On his tunic were two swans.

"Cylas," Opyea whispered.

Sergei put his hand on his father's head. "Thank you for my life."

They spent the rest of the day bringing the dead together and lining them up, side by side. The bodies had apparently gone into rigor and come out again and were difficult to carry. Tears streamed down Ursula's face as they worked.

When the job was done, the four of them were covered in blood. One by one, they went to the creek, washed, and changed their clothes. Ursula stood naked in the middle of the stream shaking for a long while until a magpie flew into a nearby larch.

"The mountains await you," the magpie said. "The People will celebrate your return."

Ursula stared at the bird. Now she was Dr. Doolittle?

She stepped out of the water and began pulling on her clothes. She glanced up where the bird had been. Was that a man sitting there grinning at her, his hands claws?

She blinked.

"I don't like this," she said.

The bird flew away.

"I meant I didn't like—" Ursula called, then stopped. What an inadequate statement: She did not like slaughter, death, and destruction. How original of her.

She returned to the others. They had built a fire upwind and away from the dead. Nels stood near the line of bodies, aiming his bow and arrow at the circling vultures.

"Some people consider the vultures sacred emissaries of the underworld and offer their dead to them," Ursula said as she sat on the ground next to Sergei.

"That is not our way," Sergei said. "These are all clan heads and their attendants. They deserve honorable burials."

Ursula looked over at Nels. His arrow whistled through the air, just missing a descending vulture.

Ursula got up and went to Nels and shouted at the vulture. "These are our dead! We cannot allow you to have them. If you leave them, we promise to reward you."

The vultures circled once more, then flew down and settled on the gray trunk of the highest larch.

Nels stared at her.

"What did you say?" Nels asked.

"You didn't hear me?" Ursula asked.

"It sounded like screeching."

Sergei and Opyea stood and came to her.

"I promised we would reward them if they left the bodies

alone," Ursula said.

"I will take care of it," Sergei said. He went to the fire, picked up his bow, then walked away across the prairie.

Nels, Opyea, and Ursula sat near the fire and ate. Ursula was not hungry, but she forced herself. Sometime later, the vultures took off from the larch and flew in Sergei's direction.

When Sergei returned, Opyea said, "The horses are rested and watered. We'll leave now. I'd like to have someone stay with the dead, but we may need every person at camp."

"I will stay," Ursula said. "I'm not a warrior."

Opyea shook her head. "No. Let's find out what awaits us."

They rode hard half the night until they came to the village. In the light of a half moon, they could see little, but the place smelled of blood and smoke, and no one challenged them as they drew near. They got off their horses and walked toward a fire. As Ursula looked around, she could not tell if any caravan or tent remained.

At the fire, twenty or thirty people huddled. Only a few looked up.

"It is Opyea of the Bear Clan."

"Opyea!" Myrus jumped up from the group and embraced her daughter and son Nels. "Thank the goddess you were spared. We'd heard all the clan leaders were killed."

"What has happened here?" Opyea asked.

"What has happened," one of the men said, "is that the warrior class failed us. While the leaders got drunk and were slaughtered in their stupor, the rest of Kovo's warriors rode fast here. Burned the wagons, tore down the tents, raided our stores, and killed nearly everyone they could find."

"Kovo was looking for someone," Myrus said. "Finally they left. We've sent riders to our clan brothers and sisters. We need hearthers. Most were killed. We have so many to bury. Have you been to the camp where the trees meet the plains?"

"We have," Opyea said. "All are dead, including Cylas."

The group moaned as one.

"Where is Veras?" Opyea asked.

"I will take you to her," Myrus said.

Nels dropped down by the fire and took a proffered plate of food. In the darkness, Ursula grasped Sergei's hand. They walked in the darkness to what looked like a small tepee. Myrus opened the flap. A tiny lamp illuminated Veras who lay on a mat, her hair pulled away from her pale face. Someone tended her side. Blood soaked the dressing.

The tent was too small for all of them, so Myrus and Ursula stayed outside. Myrus put her arm across Ursula's shoulders as they sat on the ground together in the darkness.

"You are wounded," Opyea said to Veras. "Will you recover?"

"So they tell me," Veras said. "But we are finished. More than half of us were murdered. Scopasis, your sister has gone for help. She has been very brave. Have you seen Cylas?"

"I have," Sergei said.

"Was he given an appropriate funeral?"

"No, Mother. But we will see to it."

"Good. We have to leave. Kovo will return. There is no longer room for us on these plains." She sighed. "I must rest. Opyea, stay with me."

Sergei came out of the tent, hurried past Myrus and Ursula and soon became part of the darkness.

Myrus whispered to Ursula, "I wonder if anything will ever be the same again."

58

Ursula slept sitting up, dreaming of a talking magpie. She opened her eyes to a sky pink with dawn. She heard thunder but the sky was clear.

Horses.

Ursula stood. Horses and riders roared into camp just as Ursula saw the devastation of the camp for the first time in the light of day. Scorched earth remained where wagons had stood. Nearly every tent had been destroyed.

Opyea emerged from Veras's tent and hurried toward the mass of riders. Dust filled the air.

"Fala!" Opyea cried. "You have come!"

The woman Fala jumped from her horse and embraced Opyea.

"We will take you to the land of the ancestors and bury our dead."

"We are honored," Opyea said.

The horses and riders continued to pour into camp from the prairie. All who had been wounded and silent, dead and dying, now appeared alive—as if a carnival had come to town and nothing that happened before had been real.

"Ulla," Ursula heard Veras's whisper above the horse thunder.

Ursula opened the flap and went into the tent.

"Veras," Ursula said, sitting next to her. The tent smelled of blood.

Veras looked at Ursula and smiled. Her blue eyes were clear and warm.

"This way does not work," Veras said. "We have forgotten how we used to live."

Ursula squeezed her hand and wondered if every age always believed the ones before it were better.

"You must listen," Veras said.

"I am," Ursula said.

"You can't wait for someone to tell you what to do," Veras said. "You must be your own leader. Your own chief. Someone will not always tell you what your choices are. The freedom is having the choices; that is also the agony. But this time, I will tell you what to do. I am dying."

"No—"

"In their grief, they will want to take revenge. You mustn't let them. The others must go east, until you can figure out how to protect them from Kovo."

"Me?"

"You must follow the magpie. I want you to take some of the others and find the People. You will find the answers in the mountains. Go to Belovdia. I want you to save what is left of us. Can you promise me this?"

"I will try."

"You have heard the story of our mountain?" Veras asked.

"Not all of it."

"It is said we come from the Gold Mountain, from our Belovdia.

We lived on the Beloved for thousands of years. We were nearly immortal and we lived in complete harmony with everyone. Our neighbors and ancestors the bear, unicorn, deer, tiger, the wind, snow, trees—because we were all those things, too. Then some of us wandered off the mountain in search of spring flowers. When we tried to return, the landscape had changed, and we could not make our way back. We not only lost our sense of direction when we left the mountain but we no longer understood the speech of our neighbors. We tried to return for hundreds of years, but could not. Finally one day, a magpie woman came and told us in our language that one day a woman who could understand the speech of the animals would come amongst us and guide us home again. Until that time, we were doomed to wander."

"And you think I'm that woman?"

Veras squeezed her hand. "Yes."

"You don't have the grip of a dying woman!" Ursula said.

Veras laughed. "Maybe you're right. Now let me rest, just in case I do live."

Ursula kissed the woman's hand and left the tent. How had Veras known about the magpie?

How was any of this possible?

For the next several days, Ursula helped where she was needed. Some of the bodies were mummified, then wrapped, and placed in a wagon-like vehicle. The other bodies were anointed, wrapped and put into other wagons. When Cylas was brought back to camp, the people wailed and cried for hours; some pulled out their hair and cut themselves. Ursula watched it all and wept, wondering what had happened to the prairie-life she had come to love. She rarely saw Sergei or Opyea. The camp was filled with more strangers than friends.

One morning, they struck camp. What was salvageable was gathered up in only a few hours. Opyea laid Veras in a cart pulled by two horses. Behind her came the dead. The prairie was dark with horses and riders. En masse, they moved northeast. Ursula felt strangely alone amongst all of these people. Opyea rode alongside Veras. Sergei was lost in the crowd.

Time stood still, or dragged on forever. Ursula could not concentrate on anything—not the blue sky or the gold grass turning into forests of spruce, fir, or larch and then prairie again. Herds of horses, cattle, and sheep occasionally joined them. At some places, people left the procession with their dead. Nights Ursula slept alone, when she actually slept. One night just before dawn, Ursula heard Opyea's long plaintive wail and she knew Veras had died.

The next day, the mourners pulled Veras's adorned body around the campsite in a cart. A tall richly decorated cone-shaped hat lay next to Veras—a hat similar-looking to the one Miriam had found in the tattooed lady's tomb. Once again, the people wailed, and some cut their arms until they bled; some hacked off pieces of their hair with a dagger. Ursula wept, too, and felt strangely removed from it all. She was once again an observer.

One day the nomads slipped down through a sparse wood, then up to a high grassy plateau. In the distant south and east, snow-covered mountains undulated. The funereal procession was over. The carts, wagons, and horses stopped, and hearthers quickly erected tents while the warriors and their attendants took care of the horses. Ursula got off Runner, grabbed his reins and hurried to Opyea and took Chatra's reins. Opyea looked at her blankly.

"Can I do anything?" Ursula asked.

Opyea blinked. "We must gather with the new clan heads. Discuss our strategy." She looked around. "I cannot remember when I was last here."

"Where?"

"This is where many of our ancestors are buried." She nodded toward the mountains. "That is our ancestral home."

"Then we are where Veras wanted us to be," Ursula said.

Opyea got very still as the chaos of setting up an instant town swirled around them.

"You speak her name," Opyea said. "You are a stranger."

Ursula felt her voice catch in her throat. "How is it that I am now a stranger? I may not be a warrior, but I am *not* a stranger. I am Bear Clan." She turned and walked away.

She had to find Sergei. She had hardly seen him for days. Peculiar to be intimate one moment and strangers the next. But then she was merely a dilettante. These people were living their lives. What was she doing?

She walked away from the town and across the plateau toward one of the grass-covered mounds she knew to be a kurgan, a Siberian tomb. Was this the same plateau where Miriam had thawed out the ice-lady? In the near distance, men and women worked. As she came closer, she realized they were finishing the insides of several tombs, pounding the larch beams into the earth to become walls for the kurgan. The air smelled of damp earth.

Beyond the tomb diggers, a red outcropping of rocks grew. A lone figure stood near the rocks looking out across the fog-covered mountains: Sergei.

She stared at his distant back. She wanted to go to him, but she hesitated. She had felt lost and alone ever since that terrible day when they found the dead warriors. She felt disconnected from everything and everyone.

Perhaps if she reached out to Sergei, he would feel a connection to her and she to him.

But she couldn't do it.

Why?

She rubbed her face and closed her eyes. She saw once again the mutilated bodies of her comrades.

Part of her had died that day. Maybe it was the part of her that connected her to the people around her.

She turned and walked back to the tent village.

The next morning, they began the funeral procession. Horse-drawn wagons carried the dead to the open graves. The clans stood in a circle around each grave as the priestess Preva performed the ceremony. After she again anointed the dead, they were lowered into the kurgan where their larch coffins awaited. Beside them, a plate of mutton rested so that they would not grow hungry in the afterworld. Mirrors, brushes, daggers, and axes were put in the coffins with the dead. Preva called out to the elemental spirits and to Tabitia to bless the dead. The mourners wailed. Inside the kurgan, diggers pounded nails into the coffins. Above, Preva blessed the horses that had been led to the edge of the grave. Then a man with a battle-axe raised it up and drove it quickly into the forehead of one horse. Without a sound, the horse's legs buckled beneath it and it fell to the ground.

Ursula winced and felt sick. She could hardly keep her balance. She looked away as the executioner raised his axe again. How could she have forgotten they buried their horses with them? She stepped away from the crowd and the slaughtered horses. Catching her breath, she looked across the prairie. A marmot stood partway out of her dirt home, watching Ursula.

"You will leave this place," the marmot said, rubbing her paws together.

Ursula almost laughed.

"Winter calls," the marmot said. "Find the mountain."

The clouds had temporarily lifted from the mountains in the distance.

"The mountain isn't lost," Ursula said.

"But you are," the marmot said.

"Apparently I have lost my mind because I'm talking to a rodent."

"Ahhh. You're an elitist."

"I'm a realist."

"Then you are interested in what is real and true."

"Yes, and this conversation is an example of anthropomorphism. I don't believe a marmot would have a philosophical discussion on reality or care anything about me and my world."

"It is my world, too," the marmot said.

Ursula felt sick again. She closed her eyes for a moment. When she opened them, the marmot was gone, and she was lying on the ground vomiting into the golden grasses.

Someone helped her up and carried her away from the open graves. She tried to protest. She wanted to be there when they buried Cylas and Veras, but she kept vomiting. She closed her eyes and woke up once or twice beneath a felt blanket with Myrus rubbing oils on her forehead and feet.

Ursula awakened to the sound of voices outside the tent. Dizzy, she threw off the blanket and tried to stand—and could not. She sat still for a moment. A small oil lamp rested in the middle of the room. Behind it, a giant brown bear sat. He licked his paws.

"Will this be another session with me as Dr. Doolittle?" Ursula asked.

The Bear looked up over his paws at her. His eyes were nutmeg-colored.

"Is that who you are? She Who Does Little?"

Ursula laughed. "You want me to do more?"

"I want you to know yourself," the Bear said.

"Why should you care?"

He stared at her. "Anger. Good. You need that."

"Why should you care?" she asked again.

"Because I am your ancestor. Everything I do is for me and for you. Every cell of mine is filled with love for you and yours."

"I have no yours," Ursula said. "I am alone."

The Bear growled. "Ulla, you must awaken to who you are."

"I am awake."

Ursula opened her eyes. She sat up and looked around. A tiny oil lamp stood in the middle of the tent. Outside, voices rose in argument.

"We must go back and fight!" someone cried.

"In the spring we will gather our forces from behind every blade of grass on the steppes!"

"We must travel further away."

"We cannot. Kovo's warriors await to murder us in our sleep. What does he want from us?"

Ursula breathed deeply and got up and went out in the cold night. She walked toward the fire. Fala was standing.

"Fala, I ask to speak," Ursula said. "I have words from Veras."

"Who are you to have words from Veras?" Fala demanded.

"I am Ulla, She Who Growls, of the Bear Clan."

"Who vouches for you?"

Ursula swallowed and looked out into the crowd. She could barely see anything but darkness.

"No one," Ursula said. "I vouch for myself."

"She is of us," Opyea called.

The priestess Preva stepped into the light. "Veras told me in a dream that the one who speaks to the animals would bring us a message from her. Are you the one?"

Opyea moved forward in the crowd. "She is the one. Speak to them, Ulla."

"Veras said that you should not seek revenge. She wanted me to take a group to Belovdia and seek answers there while the rest of the tribe traveled east to be with your flocks. It is in the mountains that we will find the answers about how to save ourselves. We are to seek out the People."

Preva stepped closer to Ursula. "Do you understand the speech of the animals?"

Ursula clenched her jaw. She remembered the Dream Bear's words: "Ulla, you must awaken to who you are."

"Yes, I understand the speech of the animals."

"Then we must all go to the mountain!" someone called.

Preva slowly shook her head. "No. We will do as Veras requested. We will send a group to Our Beloved. You will go, Ursula, and find out how to save us from Kovo. You will return to us in the spring before he does."

Fala said, "You must leave early before winter sets in."

The drumming began and dancers soon joined the circle of light, moving their bodies into the sacred shapes—becoming the shapes.

Ursula stepped back into the darkness. The beat intensified—faster, louder—and everyone danced. Opyea grabbed Ursula's hand and pulled her back into the circle to be part of the dance. She closed her eyes and moved. She felt the ground beneath her feet and the cold air on her head. She moved her elbows to the beat and was her elbows, moved her hands. Her hips. Her knees. Her body tingled with the dance.

Was the dance.

For an instant—an explosive mind-shattering moment—Ursula was awake to herself.

She opened her eyes and she was on the edge of the circle of dancers, facing south. The moon was out, the light reflecting off the glossy glacier on the face of the distant mountain.

Ursula smiled at the Beloved and twirled back into the circle.

In the gray light of early morning, they readied for the journey. The hearthers prepared food, clothing, and shelter. The warriors looked after the horses and weaponry. Preva prayed over it all and asked the elements for blessings.

As Ursula brushed down Runner, Sergei came up to her.

"Hello, Sergei," Ursula said, patting Runner. The horse nuzzled her.

"Hello," he said shyly. He cleared his throat. "I don't want to go."

Ursula nodded. "It's your choice."

He shook his head. "It was my mother's choice. I will go to honor her."

"Sergei, I'm so sorry for all of your losses. I wish I could help."

"How could you help? There is nothing anyone can do. It is our life to wander and die."

Ursula looked at his eyes. "You will find joy again, Sergei. I promise. I lost my parents when I was only a child. After a while it does not hurt quite as much." She wanted to clap her hand over her mouth. Could her advice be more banal?

Sergei nodded, then turned and walked away.

Along with Opyea, Myrus, Nels, Ursula, Elio, and Sergei, seventeen others joined the group. Some were hearthers, others warriors. The rest of the nomads came to see them off.

Ursula mounted Runner and looked around at the colorful tents, the carts and wagons, horses, sheep, and smoky fires. It reminded her of old photographs she had seen of gypsy caravans. She watched the men and women of the tribe embrace one another, slap each other on the back, kiss, smile. She had witnessed this same scene over and over in her own world, had imagined it when she looked at the bones and threads of those she had studied. Loved ones connecting and letting go. Living. The stream of life. The curve of it. The spiral. And she had always been above it and apart from it.

Suddenly someone pushed Ursula's right leg up into the air. She lost her balance and fell backward. She started to brace herself for the moment of impact, then decided to relax, and she fell into Fala's and Opyea's arms.

They laughed and pushed her into the crowd before she could get her balance. Someone hugged her. Someone else slapped her on the back. Another hug. Tossed from one person to the next, until rejuvenated and laughing she stood on her own again, staggering slightly.

Sergei put his hand on her back.

"They will hold you in their arms and hearts for eternity," Sergei said.

Fala shook Ursula's hand. "May you be comforted and find your way home."

"I hope so, too," Ursula said. She got on Runner and looked at Opyea who then clicked Chatra forward.

The journey had begun.

59

For days, they traveled toward the mountain which often disappeared from view—depending upon where the group was. The journeyers were joyful, singing, racing each other, telling stories, sleeping close together during the cold nights. To Ursula, it seemed as if the mourning ended as soon as the journey began.

They tried to find other nomads in the villages they passed through. One night they stayed with horse breeders and Ursula got sick on *koumiss*—fermented mare's milk. Another day they spent in the forest gathering cedar nuts with villagers who told them their own stories of Belovdia. They believed immortals lived in beautiful houses on the mountain and that if any human caught sight of one, she would turn to stone.

"Are you descendants of these immortals?" Opyea asked them.

"No," the storyteller said, "we are descendants of the wolf."

Sometimes the mountain appeared close enough to touch. They could see the milky streams fed from visible glaciers and the almost fluorescent green lichens like lights on the rocky gray sides of the mountain. Other times the mountain was hidden by forests of yellow birches or larches. The world was gold, russet, and crimson with autumn. Ursula was excited by it all—the horse moving beneath her, the crisp cold air, the laughter of her people. She watched squirrels hurrying through the woods, their fur changing from brown and black-gray to ash-gray. The hares who were starting to turn white became easier targets for the hunters, and Ursula's group frequently dined on rabbit.

In nearly every village—each nothing more than a few tents, with an occasional log building—the people had stories about the mountain, but no one seemed to really know how to find the immortals, gods, or spirits who supposedly resided atop the mountain.

"You follow the north glacier to the left and the elemental spirits will take you further." "No. It's the east glacier and if you meet an elemental, you will die." "You can go beyond the lip of the middle of that glacier only if you have never killed anyone." "You can only find the trail if you are one of the immortals."

They traded away their wagons and carts for supplies; wheels would not do well on mountain sides.

Soon they encountered fewer people, and the mountain filled their view. In the distance, they heard the great mountain sheep smashing their heads together as they competed for mates. The ground got rockier and steeper. In the mornings, frost covered everything. The group began traveling in near silence, hushed by the scenery and the sense that something watched them.

"What are the animals telling you?" Opyea asked one morning as they sat around the fire. Low clouds covered the foothills they camped on and the mountain above. The clouds even touched the tops of the larch forest that nearly surrounded the nomads. The white butt of a roe deer flashed like a light in the woods and caught Ursula's eye. She watched the creature bounce away into the darkness.

"The animals have said nothing," Ursula said.

Opyea rolled her eyes. "That is helpful."

Nels laughed.

"We'll have to keep going until the mountain stops us," Ursula said.

Elio leaned against Sergei and said quietly, "I have never climbed a mountain."

"None of us has," Opyea said.

Ursula did not correct her. She had driven up Mount Hood and Mount Rainier, then walked the trails, but she could not lay claim to mountain climbing.

"Has anyone had any strange dreams?" Prine asked.

Their voices sounded tinny in the fog. A bird called out.

"What is it you've dreamed?" Sergei asked.

"I dreamed I was following a snow leopard," he said. "I could see her prints in the snow along with the path her tail made. Finally I caught up with her on a snow-covered ridge that looked over a chasm. She turned to look at me and she was Elio."

Everyone glanced at Elio. She moved closer to her brother; Sergei held her hand.

"She was a snow leopard and Elio at the same time," Prine said. "She told me, 'You must learn to fly.' Then she leaped into the chasm."

Opyea nodded. "The mountain is guiding us."

The clouds burned off early, and the day got unexpectedly warm. They rode leisurely through golden grain fields surrounded by yellow birch trees mixed with the darker larches. They dismounted their horses and picked berries.

Then they rode through a dense larch forest. Ursula heard water falling but seldom saw a river. The mountain was hidden from view. Occasionally, they glimpsed the walls of the canyon they were traversing. Ursula kept glancing over her shoulders, thinking someone followed.

They left the woods behind for a time and walked the horses up a scree-filled ravine. A light snow fell. Overhead circled the biggest eagle Ursula had ever seen.

"I've heard those eagles can carry away full-grown wolves," Opyea said to Ursula. "So watch yourself."

"I told you you need to get some fat on your bones," Sergei said.

Ursula smiled. Runner stumbled, then kept walking placidly. Some of the other horses were skittish. Ursula patted Runner's neck. He kept plodding along as if he knew right where they were going. If he did, he was the only one. They had been in the foothills and now in the mountain for days and Ursula had no clue as to where they should be headed. They kept going in the direction of the mountain's north face. As a light snow began to fall, Ursula thought of all the news reports she had listened to over the years of climbers lost on Mount Hood, Mount Rainier, or Mount Adams.

"This is foolish," Ursula whispered as she walked alongside Runner. "We could all die."

At the top of the ravine, they bedded down for the night at the edge of a copse of trees and against a nearly straight wall of gray rock that went up into the clouds. After they put up the tents and hobbled the horses, Ursula sat near the fire staring into the dark woods. Night birds called out to others of their kind—back and forth in the trees and rocks, obviously annoyed at the intruders. A woodpecker drummed on a trunk somewhere within the woods. The trees and branches creaked as the wind blew through their tops.

In the distance, a wolf began to howl.

Inside the woods, green eyes glowed. Stared at them.

Ursula nudged Prine. "What is that?" she asked pointing.

Prine squinted. "I don't see anything."

The eyes blinked.

Ursula heard a peculiar snuffling above the sound of the crack-ling fire and low-voices of her comrades.

She had heard that sound before when she had been in the banya.

"Did you hear that?"

Prine looked at her. "Ulla, I hear lots of things." He laughed.

Ursula stood, left the circle, and walked toward the green eyes. Night had nearly diluted all of the day out of the woods. Ursula stepped inside.

A dark figure turned and loped away from her.

"Wait," she called. "I need help. I don't know what I'm do-ing."

She ran after the green eyes, her hands out in front of her so that she would not run into any trees.

She ran until the trees opened slightly. The dark figure disap-peared. And Ursula was standing on a trail.

She looked down, then up. "Thank you!" she called.

She grinned. Sometimes life worked out.

She looked around for something to mark the spot and found round stones that she piled one on top of the other. She turned to go back into the woods as Sergei stepped onto the trail.

"You've found a way?" Sergei asked.

"I've found a trail," she said, shrugging.

"Is that a cave?" he asked, looking behind her.

Ursula turned around. Shrubs nearly covered what appeared to be an entrance to a cave.

"It's probably occupied," Ursula said.

"One way to find out."

Before Ursula could say anything, Sergei pushed the shrubs aside. Dagger drawn, he ducked inside.

A moment later, he returned. "All clear. It's hardly even a cave." He took her hand and pulled her into the darkness.

They could barely stand, and the walls of the cave only went back a few feet. This was no timeless cave. No paintings. No warmth.

They sat in the entrance. The cave smelled of dried leaves.

"We haven't been alone for a long time," Sergei said.

Ursula leaned her head against his shoulder.

"It's been strange. Since the day we met."

He nodded.

"No," Ursula said. "I mean from the very beginning. You met me in an airport in Chicago. I've got the itinerary. I'll give it to you later so you can meet me some day. I was so afraid of flying I could barely see straight."

"Flying?" Sergei said. "So Prine's dream was right."

"It's a different kind of flying, I think." She paused. "We don't really know anything about each other."

"I know you have great heart! You've tried to learn so much."

"*Tried* to learn?"

Sergei laughed. "We're all good at different things. If anyone ever asks, I'll tell them you're the best rider I've ever seen!"

Ursula laughed. "A boastful liar, then. Is that what you'd like said about you? That you're a great horse rider."

"It's what I know." He turned to her. "I became a warrior because that's what I was good at. But I was always more my mother's son. I wanted to be her apprentice. She could understand much more of the world than I could. Just as you can. You tried to learn what you don't know. I only know what I know."

Ursula smiled. Sergei kissed her lips.

"You are different from us. When I am with you, I touch that which is still untamed."

"And I feel like I am still part of humanity when I'm with you. I don't know why." She looked at his face. Maybe no one ever really knew why one person made them weak in the knees and another made them want to run for the hills. Maybe it was what was comfortable and easy. She had not been comfortable with Peter. She had always felt like a bystander, even when they made love. With Sergei, life was not comfortable or easy and he was a part of her life.

They laid their jackets on the floor of the cave, then shed their clothes and pressed themselves against one another, Ursula felt the jackets beneath them, smelled the woods, heard the wolf, and sensed Sergei all around her and in her, looking at her, seeing her, being with her. She growled and roared and laughed and reached for the stars until the ground grew cold. Then they pulled on their clothes and hurried through the dark back to camp.

Ursula dreamed a bear tore her to pieces.

She sat up in the dark and heard something moving around outside the tent. She breathed deeply, trying to quiet her still racing heart. Sergei slept on one side of her, Elio on the other, Nels at her feet.

Someone outside yelled.

Clattering of pots or dishes.

More yelling.

Ursula and the others stumbled out of the tent.

Opyea waved a small lit oil lamp in front of her—trying to stave off an attack by a brown bear rearing up on its hind legs.

Opyea's left arm hung limp.

Everyone started shouting and banging on things. The bear roared and lunged for Opyea.

Ursula screamed, "Old Man, we mean you no harm! Please leave us be. We'll gift you with honey!"

The bear looked at her, opened his mouth, and roared again. This time, he was coming for Ursula.

"Old Man! Leave us alone! What have we done!"

The bear did not answer except to raise a paw to swipe at her. Sergei pulled her down and away. She knew in another few minutes, many of them would be dead.

Then she saw the green eyes at the edge of camp. A figure nearly indistinct from the dark.

Green Eyes whispered.

The bear stopped and howled.

Green Eyes whispered again.

The bear staggered, growled and turned away and went back into the woods.

"What happened?" someone cried. "Why'd he stop?"

"Didn't you see the figure in the woods?" Ursula asked. "With green eyes? It called the bear away."

"I saw no one," Sergei said.

Opyea moaned and sank to the ground.

Prine kicked the dying fire and dropped wood and moss onto it until it roared. Myrus tended to Opyea's wounds.

"Stepas," Opyea moaned. "Stepas is hurt. She's by my tent."

Sergei and Ursula hurried to the prone figure none of them had noticed. They turned her over. A gash darkened her face. Sergei put his cheek close to her mouth. Ursula held her wrist, searched for a pulse—and found none. She felt her neck. Nothing.

Traiger joined them.

"The bear has taken her," Traiger said.

"You mean she's dead," Ursula said. "What happened?" Why hadn't the bear understood her? She had dragged these people up here on some wild goose chase to find what?

Ursula shivered. All around, things sighed and moaned, howled and breathed.

"He could come back," Ursula said, standing.

"Make some torches!" Opyea shouted. "Maybe a line of fire will keep him away until morning."

"Why would he attack?" Ursula asked.

"Why wouldn't he?" Opyea answered.

No one slept any more that night. The torches lit up the camp site and made everything outside the line of light even darker, more foreboding. Myrus and Traiger dressed and wrapped Stepas's body.

At dawn, the group dug a shallow grave.

"May she roam free in the vast plains beyond," Opyea said.

They covered Stepas with stones. Ursula kept glancing around, listening for the sounds of the bear.

They quickly broke camp. The sky was clear, the day cold.

Ursula led the way through the woods until they reached the trail. They traveled up for a time, then through more trees and another ravine. Around midday, they reached a lake.

The surface of the lake was as still and clear as a mirror; in it, inverted, lay a perfect reflection of the Beloved mountain. Ursula looked up from the reflection to the sheer north face. The sight of the jagged snowy mountain brought tears to her eyes. She remembered this site from before, when she had walked a similar trail with Kam and Sergei. Was there a timeless cave nearby?

Sergei came up behind her.

"Are you well?"

She nodded. "I have been here before. With you. I feel as though I'm coming full circle, or spiraling back."

"It is a beautiful place," Sergei said. "I am glad to know that I will be here again."

"When I was here before, I felt as though I'd come home," Ursula said. She glanced at Sergei. "Do you feel the same?"

Sergei stared out at the mountain.

"I can feel it breathe," Ursula said. "Or pulsate. Something."

"It feels like—it feels strange. Off-balance."

"The plains are where our ancestors are buried," Opyea said. "On this mountain, I fear we are treading on hallowed ground not meant for us."

Ursula looked around at the other nomads. They all appeared uncomfortable. She saw beauty; they saw strangeness. They had just buried a compatriot—another loss in a long series of losses.

"I know this is difficult," Ursula said, "but I believe this is what should happen." She looked at her feet and rolled her eyes. What was she saying? She had no idea what she was doing.

"We'll rest here," Opyea said. "And eat."

Myrus and Traiger began making a fire. Several ducks splashed away from them, then flew up into the mountain sky. The horses pulled on the occasional bits of grass growing up through the loose snow.

"Something seems off," Sergei said.

"What do you mean?" Ursula asked.

"The air is strange," Sergei said. He shook his head. "I don't know."

"Where to now, She Who Roars?" Opyea asked. "We're on the mountain. Do we keep walking to the top?"

"Let's eat," Ursula said. "Then we'll figure it out."

"Hmph!"

During lunch, without warning, a fog descended.

Myrus looked up from the stew.

"What is it?" Ursula asked.

The mountain had disappeared from view; the lake was now gray. All was still.

Opyea cursed under her breath.

"We've all lost our senses up here!" she said. "On the plains or in the forests we could tell if a fog was a day off, a storm two days! I could smell the deer in rut! Where is this place?"

"It's a different place," Ursula said. "It has different smells. Different weather."

Fat snowflakes fell from the sky, slowly at first. Then a breeze pushed cold air off the lake.

Almost as one, the group started looking for shelter. Ursula and Sergei climbed the ridge on the south side of the lake and looked down. Wind whipped snow up from the ravine below. No shelter that way.

Ursula and Sergei went back to the lake. The fog and snow were creating white-out conditions. The air was damp and cold. Ursula wiped her face. Moisture. They were getting wet. Her heart lurched.

Opyea shouted orders Ursula could not hear. Myrus ran toward them and held out the end of a rope.

"Tie it around your waist," she shouted.

"That seems dangerous!" Ursula said.

Myrus shook her head and shouted, "We'll lose each other if we don't. Traiger found a place near those rocks that is out of the wind." Myrus pointed into the white.

Sergei wove the rope around his waist, then handed it to Ursula who did the same. Myrus tied the rope around her own waist.

The wind howled and snow stuck to everything. Sergei started forward, and Ursula and Myrus followed. They walked up the slope on the east side of the lake. Ursula slipped more than once and nearly pulled Myrus and Sergei down on top of her. After several minutes, they reached the rocks and the rest of their group. Trees broke the wind on two sides. They were protected from the wind but not the cold and snow.

Several of them went amongst the trees and came back with branches, moss, and cones to burn. They quickly erected three tents and went inside—except for the hearthers who were attempting to make hot food to help warm them.

Once in the tent, Ursula leaned against Sergei to get warm. He wiped his face and looked at her.

"We've got to get dry," he said.

Prine pulled a blanket from one of the saddlebags and passed it around. They all wiped down as best they could. Traiger came inside, carrying a pot of boiling soup. His eyebrows and eyelashes were covered in hoarfrost.

Ursula's heart sank. Hoar frost was not a good sign. She pulled her hat down on her head and pushed herself outside. Myrus glanced up at her and frowned. Opyea was attempting to build a lean-to over the fire.

"What are you doing?" Opyea called.

Ursula stepped away from the sheltering rocks and into the swirling snow and wind. When she could not see anything or anyone, she screamed, "We're here! I brought everyone here as Veras asked! Now we need help. We're going to die. Please!"

She could hardly breathe because the air was so damp and cold.

Suddenly, the dark figure from the woods stood only a few feet from her. Still, she could barely see it. Its features shifted as she stared. Snow and wind distorted all. Did the figure wear clothes or fur?

"Find the crack," the figure said. "A woman awaits."

"No riddles!" Ursula screamed. "Help me!"

The wind blew a sheet of snow between them. Ursula ran toward the figure, reached her hands up to pound the figure's chest—and her fists hit stone.

She stepped back as the wind and cold snatched away her breath.

The figure was merely a trick of light and snow? Only stone?

"No!" she screamed.

She leaned against the stone—out of the wind—and caught her breath. The gray stone went up and up into fog and mist. Her gloved fingers touched the stone, found their way to a tiny crack and dug in. Ursula closed her eyes and leaned back. She knew they would die if they stayed here.

Her fingers moved in the crack. *In the crack.*

Find a crack. A woman awaits.

Ursula pulled her fingers out and turned around. That crack was too small for anyone to await within.

She kept one hand on the stone and followed it around behind the snow-covered tents, and past them out of the wind break and into the full blast of the wind. She kept her head down and her hand on the stone. She slipped on the icy ground twice. She was about to turn back when she came to a crack in the stone—a crack barely wide enough for a horse to travel through. She stepped into it.

The wind disappeared. She walked forward—watching her feet so that she would not suddenly fall into a chasm. She felt the weight of the stone cliffs on either side of her.

After a couple of minutes, she looked up. A snow-covered figure stood a few feet from her.

The figure said something in a language Ursula had not heard before and did not understand right away. The figure, whose entire body was covered in furs, repeated herself several times until Ursula heard, "We have shelter. Follow me."

"I have to get the others," Ursula said. "Will you wait?"

"That is why I am here."

Ursula turned in the crack and hurried back to the opening. The wind nearly knocked her down as she stepped out into the storm. Keeping her hand on the stone, she made her way back to camp. She crawled into her tent.

"Where have you been?" Sergei asked.

"I found shelter," she said. "Take what's essential and leave the rest."

"How far?" Opyea asked. She looked pale, and Ursula feared that the bear attack had sapped her strength.

"I'm not sure," Ursula said. "There is someone waiting to take us. Not far, I'd guess."

Opyea nodded. "Let's get going!"

Although most everything was crusted in icy snow, the nomads broke down camp in fifteen minutes. Snow clung to everything— the horses' manes, everyone's eyelashes, hair.

"You know where we're going, Woman Who Roars," Opyea said when they were ready. "Lead the way."

"Tell everyone to keep close to the rock," Ursula shouted.

"I'll take up the rear," Sergei said.

"Be careful!" Ursula called to him.

They went forward until they reached the crack; then Ursula turned into it. She glanced behind her. Elio pulled her horse and Runner into the crevice. Beyond her, Ursula could barely discern the next person. She breathed deeply and kept walking until she saw the woman waiting for them. The woman nodded, turned her back to Ursula, and began walking. Opyea came up beside Ursula.

"Where is this woman who leads us to shelter?" Opyea asked.

Ursula pointed.

Opyea squinted. "I see no one."

"She's a horse's length ahead of us."

Opyea looked at Ursula. "I hope it isn't mountain sickness that's gotten you."

Ursula watched the woman walk. "She's as plain as day, Opyea!"

After a while, the crack opened up and they stepped out of the rock onto some kind of trail. Snow and fog hid nearly all from view. Ursula's legs trembled with exhaustion. She sipped water from the bag she kept close to her chest. The woman she followed never slowed, never faltered on the rocky trail that went up and down and around.

Darkness fell in an instant.

The woman disappeared from view. Ursula's stomach lurched. What if she had been following an illusion?

The wind grew fiercer. Ursula did not know who she followed or if anyone followed her.

She saw a light in the distance. When she came to an archway made of rocks, she hesitated for a moment, then stepped through.

The howling wind ceased. The snow no longer fell, though it lay in drifts around her. Tiny lights lit a pathway to a dark edifice.

Ursula turned around and waited to make certain everyone had made it through. When Sergei came up beside her, she knew they were all safe.

She looked down the lit path and saw the woman again, her hands folded in front of her. Ursula hurried to her.

"Welcome," the woman said. "I am Tei. Leave your horses. We will care for them. Come into our house and we will care for you. You must promise that they will not harm anything within—no matter what they see or what jeopardy they perceive themselves to be in."

Ursula glanced back at her group covered in snow and darkness.

"First you're asking them to be separated from their horses," Ursula said. "That's a big one. But asking them not to kill or defend themselves. It's all they know."

"No harm will come to them if they agree to this one rule," Tei said.

Ursula nodded. She hoped the nomads were so exhausted they would agree to anything.

Ursula walked to her friends and said, "They will care for the horses. When we go inside, we must promise to do no harm, no matter what we see."

"Lay down our weapons?" Opyea asked.

"In a manner of speaking, yes," Ursula said.

"Who were you talking to?" Elio asked.

"So you saw her?"

"I saw no one," Nels said. "You talked to the air!"

"I saw a shadow of something," Sergei said.

"Her name is Tei. Will you agree before we freeze to death?"

"We agree," Opyea said.

Reluctantly, they left their horses and followed Ursula down the path and into the dimly-lit structure.

Once indoors, they continued walking until they came to a large room. Tei disappeared. Ursula could see no heat source, but the room was warm. A single lantern stood in the far end of the room near a pile of mats and blankets. The nomads shook off their wet clothes, then each grabbed a mat and blanket. Myrus passed around what was left of the food. In silence, they ate and drank, then fell into an exhausted sleep.

Ursula listened to the mountain breathe as she tried to sleep. Once she opened her eyes and thought she saw a bear in the corner watching her. Her heart jumped. She remembered her grandmother sitting in her room, protecting her from the bear she knew would some day come for her granddaughter. Ursula closed her eyes again and spooned up against Sergei. Perhaps tonight the bear would finally catch up with her.

"I am Ursula, She-Bear," Ursula murmured. "You cannot harm me."

60

Sun streamed into the room through a narrow window at the top of the room and washed Ursula's face. She opened her eyes and did not know where she was.

Then she sat up. The others still slept. She tilted her face toward the sun, then pressed her fingers against the warm floor. Paintings covered the stone walls: lush, bright, colorful pictures of nature. Near Ursula, a painting of a huge deciduous tree grew from floor to ceiling. Opposite the tree, swans floated on stone, deer ran, wolves howled. Painted snow covered another wall and a lone snow-leopard looked out at her.

Ursula got up, took off her socks, and walked around. The building—if that was what it was—felt enormous. She walked along a wide hallway, glancing into other rooms as she went. All were large, cave-like yet expansive, with walls covered in scenes from nature. She wondered who had created this structure so high on the mountain. Other ancient peoples had built on other remote mountaintops, but she had never seen anything quite like this. She stepped into one of the rooms. Painted onto the stone was a realistic looking waterfall. She could almost feel the mist on her face. Could almost hear the water falling over rock.

She closed her eyes. Such a soothing sound.

Wait.

She could hear it.

She stepped further into the room and saw an opening at the back of it. She walked to it, then went down steps that curved around into warmer air. She stepped off of them and was in a huge cavern where steaming water fell over several boulders into a large pool. A tiny lantern spread light only a short distance, so Ursula could not see how far back the cavern or the hot springs went.

She went back up the steps, left the room, and continued down the hall. Had someone chiseled this building into the mountainside? How was it lit? Why wasn't it pitch dark? She touched the walls. She could not see any chisel marks.

She heard a sigh.

She looked around.

No one.

Another sigh.

She put her hand on the rock again.

A sigh.

Ursula closed her eyes.

"She is the mother. She breathes for us."

Ursula opened her eyes. Tei stood in front of her, smiling, her straight black hair pulled back away from her obsidian black eyes. Above her eyebrows was a row of dark blue dots, curving down near her nose and up again at the eyebrows—the tattoo looked like a stylized seagull seen from a distance.

"Where is this place?" Ursula asked.

"It is where the mountain lives. It is where the People asked us to wait for you. They knew you would need our help."

"We do need help," Ursula said.

They continued down the hall until it opened into a large room, empty except for a single reed floor mat. Painted on its stone walls in gold were the same pictures Ursula had seen as tattoos on the Lady and on Sergei in the future. The swan, bear paw, spider, snake, deer . . . and a red rose and white rose.

Tei and Ursula sat on the mat facing one another.

"Did you build this place?" Ursula asked.

Tei shook her head. "No. It is said the Immortals built it—those great alchemists who learned to extend life. We believe the mountain herself created it."

"Who is we?"

Tei smiled. "We are the Wu."

Ursula nodded. "I have read about you: Chinese women who had their own language. Priestesses or shamans?"

She nodded. "We have struggled to create and preserve our language and our ways with nature. But we are not only Chinese and are not only women." She smiled. "We hid in these mountains for many years. We could not live amongst the others. How can one be with those who do not wake up every morning and kiss the ground? One day, the mountain showed us this place. After a time, the People came to us. We serve them, and they protect us."

"Why can't the others see you?" Ursula asked.

Tei smiled. "Perhaps it is because we have lived amongst the People for so long. The others will be hungry. We will talk more later."

Ursula nodded. She knew when she was being dismissed. She got up and went back the way she had come. She smelled food and followed the aromas into a room with a long low table inside it. Bowls of steaming food covered the table.

"I knew I could sniff out food," Nels said behind her.

Ursula stepped aside. The others followed Nels into the room. Sergei kissed her on the mouth.

Opyea asked, "Did you change my dressing while I slept?"

"No."

"Well no one else will admit to it either. It feels much better. I guess you didn't imagine that woman you followed here last night."

"Guess not."

They sat on the floor around the wooden table. Ursula was not certain what she ate, but it was exquisitely flavored with spices she did not recognize. She looked around the room at the painted rock—scenes of mountains and rolling hills—and thought this must be what paradise was like.

Suddenly Nels jumped to his feet and felt around his shoulder where his bow and arrows usually were.

"Two lions just walked by!" he cried.

Opyea stood and held out a calming hand. She and Ursula went to the entrance and looked both ways down the hall.

Ursula saw Tei and another woman.

"I see nothing," Opyea said.

"I'll be back," Ursula said. She hurried to Tei's side.

"This is Daoa," Tei said, indicating the woman beside her.

"Hello," Ursula said. "Someone just saw two lions."

The women smiled. Ursula walked with them to the sanctuary—the room with the gold rock paintings.

"Please sit," Tei said, motioning to the mat. Ursula knelt down. Then the Wu stepped away from her. After a few moments, Ursula realized a shadow sat in the corner. The shadow rose and moved slowly to her.

The shadow became a beautiful old woman, her long hair gray, her face brown and wrinkled, her eyes green. The woman sat across from Ursula. The other two women left the room.

"I am Sula," the woman said. "I have waited a long time for you."

"I am Ursula," she said. The woman looked vaguely familiar.

"We welcome you," Sula said.

"Thank you for your hospitality." Ursula cleared her throat. "My people are in trouble. Their priestess asked me to lead them here, to this mountain. It was here, she said, that we would find help." Ursula stared at the woman. "Are you the help I sought? Can you save these people?"

"Me?" The woman shook her head. "No. But you can."

Ursula suddenly noticed a fawn sleeping in the corner. She blinked and realized it was a small child.

Ursula looked at Sula. "*I* can save them? How?"

Sula smiled.

They sat in silence for a few minutes.

"Don't you have any words of wisdom to help guide me?" Ursula asked.

"The language of the Universe is not words."

Ursula sighed.

Sula smiled. "You want to save your people. You will have to figure out how. Use all that you've learned, all that you've *felt*. And be in your body, your neck, shoulders, arms, hands, heart, lungs, stomach, womb, legs and feet."

"If you know the answer," Ursula said, "if you know how I can help the nomads, can't you please just tell me?"

"Who said I knew the answer?"

The nomads ate, slept, made love, told stories. Ursula watched and felt separate from them again—from it all. They settled into the place or it into them. Leopards uncurled to become running women. White hares twitched noses and were laughing children. The Wu walked amongst them, often silent, sometimes drifting in and out of rooms as if they were ghosts, unaware of the nomads. After a time—inexplicably—the nomads could see the Wu and began interacting with them as if they had known them always.

Opyea stayed outdoors a great deal of the time, trying to hunt. She came back tired and cold.

"The People gift us with meat," Daoa told her. "You have no need to hunt."

"I have a need to be useful," Opyea said. "Winter isn't even half over."

"How do you pass other winters?" Daoa asked.

"Fucking and fighting!" Opyea said.

Ursula laughed.

"You must do what you must do," Daoa said.

"You made us promise to harm none," Opyea said.

"Then that leaves fucking, I suppose," Daoa said.

Opyea roared with laughter.

Ursula practiced standing her ground. When she walked, she tried to feel her soles against the Earth, her clothes against her skin, the air in her lungs. Sometimes she chased a weasel or hare. She listened for the People. One afternoon she started to follow snow prints into the woods.

Opyea came up behind her and said, "Isn't it grand up here on this Beloved Mountain? I feel as though I am myself again. Veras used to tell me we were more than warriors but I didn't understand what she meant. Now I taste the breath of the mountain in the four winds. I feel the fire from the winter sun. I trudge through the frozen water and remember how it will sound and smell in spring, and at night I am cradled by the Earth. It is transforming."

Ursula laughed.

"What?" Opyea demanded.

"Nothing. I'm enjoying our talk."

"Talk. I haven't time for that." She strode away.

"See you!" Ursula called. She shook her head, then looked down at the prints again.

She followed them into the woods. The day grayed.

Suddenly she looked up and saw a woman gazing down at the valley. She wore a white bear's skin. No, *she* was the bear skin.

She turned her face to Ursula—her face that was human and bear. Ursula gasped. She wanted to bow down, to kiss the bearwoman's feet. To turn her life over to her. She had never seen anything so beautiful.

"I will worship you forever," Ursula whispered.

"No," the Bearwoman said. "Worship the ground you walk upon."

"Is that what you do? Is that how you are able to be in the world?"

"I am this world," the Bearwoman said. "And I worship the ground I walk upon. Do you know who you are?"

"I am Ulla of the Bear Clan," Ursula said.

The Bearwoman stepped closer. Ursula held her breath. The Bearwoman stood only feet from Ursula. She glowed white and smelled of musk.

"I know you," Ursula said.

"I am Sula," Bearwoman said, holding out her hand to Ursula.

Yes, Sula. *She was one of the People.* Ursula took Sula's hand. One of Sula's claws grazed Ursula's arm. She saw her blood. Bearwoman Sula leaned over and licked the drops away.

Ursula's heart pounded in her chest. Everything became very clear—sharp and in focus. She looked around. The People surrounded her. The woods filled with music. Or was it only all their hearts beating together?

"Do you wish to remember?" Sula asked.

"I do."

They walked through the woods together. Ursula felt every snowflake under her feet, the softness of the hand holding hers. Wolves, foxes, birds, trees, clouds followed them. They stopped in front of a cave.

"This is where we come from," Sula said. "Forever. This is where the mother birthed us. Where time has always stood still."

They walked into the cave. Much of the walls were covered with paintings of white and deep-red roses. The red roses were so dark they were nearly black, and the white roses were so white they were almost light. Paintings of animals rode the stone all around the flowers, along with different geometric shapes and lines.

"Have you People been here all along?" Ursula asked.

She felt slightly off balanced.

Sula nodded. "We have always been with you. Your parents were People—you need no key to become who you are. The nomads are descendants of the People, but they need help."

"They need a key to become who they really are? *Who* are they?"

"They are descendants of the People."

"You mean they could become shapechangers? I could become a shapechanger?"

"You already are," Sula said. "You are a shapeshifter. You have seen yourself as the other. You have experienced the wild. Can you recall when? The when is important."

"Can't you tell me how?" She felt almost rude asking such a mundane question.

"There are no rules, Ursula," Sula said. "No ten commandments on how to behave. This is not a thought experiment. Learn to be in your body; then you will discover who you truly are and the answers will come to you."

"Discover *who I am*?"

"Yes. Who you are is the who you were before someone told you you were a good girl because you stood still or were quiet and didn't speak your heart. Who you are is the who you were before someone told you to act like a lady which meant not to squirm, not to move, not to cry when you needed to mourn or sing when you were joyful. Who you are is the who you were before someone told you you weren't tall enough, short enough, skinny or pretty enough. Before anyone told you you were not right."

Ursula looked into Sula's eyes—her familiar eyes. "Sula," she said quietly, "there has never been a time before all those things were said or conveyed to me and everyone else I know. The She who was Before does not exist."

"She exists in your body," Sula said. "Move with her, sing with her. Be her. Become yourself—be *full* of your*self*."

Ursula looked at the roses on the cave walls. She reached out and touched the stone. Warm.

The nomads needed a key. It had to have something to do with the tattoos.

Were the tattoos a form of permanent acupuncture? Opening the energy meridians of the body so that they could easily access some latent abilities they had forgotten?

Or was it what was in the ink? Sergei had been made deathly ill by one kind of ink and cured by another. And what of Jonathan's idea of transformation. Alchemy. Lead to gold. Finding one's true nature.

"It's all elemental," she whispered, thinking of the alchemical women holding up their jars: earth, air, fire, and water.

She stared at the shapes of the pictures all around her. Sergei had said when they danced, they danced the sacred shapes of the universe and thus flowed with the universe.

The curves of the bear claw, the swan, snake, ram. The belly dancing shapes. Spirals, infinity shapes, esses. *A spiral was only a line who had made up its mind*. Ursula smiled.

She looked away from the rock art.

Sula was gone. Ursula went outside. They were all gone. Almost. She could still hear their whispers.

Everything was transforming. Transmutating. *Alchemy*.

"It's all alchemy," she whispered. Jonathan was right: Nature was Divine.

She suddenly remembered what Opyea had said about feeling transformed on this mountain—in touch with the air, fire, water, and earth. *Transformed by the elements*. Could that be what the tattoos meant? Ursula closed her eyes. Sergei in the future and the lady mummy had shared the same tattoos: a swan on the right arm. That could represent water. A spider on the left hand: maybe air or fire? A snake on the right leg: earth. A deer on the left leg: fire? The bear on their heart could be their clan symbol? Their soul animal? The animal they shapeshifted into?

The man at Site 56 had an eagle on his left arm: air, just like Sergei and the lady. Right hand: fish—water. Below his right knee had been a tree. That would represent earth. A lion on his left thigh was no doubt fire. The man in the glacier had a flying insect on his left hand: air. Geese on his right shoulder: water.

"This is it!" Ursula cried.

The left arm had a tattoo representing air, the left leg fire, the right arm water, the right leg earth. That was the key.

No, it was more like a combination lock. The order of the tattooing was important.

If it was about alchemy, perhaps the women on the spheres could give her a clue. The first one held a flask with a hairy beast inside: earth, Jonathan had said. A bloated person sat inside the second woman's flask: water. A bird rose up in the third flask: air. And a lion was caught inside the fourth flask: fire. So the tattooing would go in a clockwise direction around the body: right leg, right arm, left arm, left leg. Then the soul print on their chest.

"Yes!" Ursula cried. She started back toward the compound. She suddenly felt full of herself.

61

Ursula hurried into the sanctuary where Sula stood, as if waiting for her. As Ursula gazed at her, she saw woman and bear. The sight was awesome and made her knees shake.

"It's the tattoos," Ursula said. "They represent the elements and if embroidered in the proper order they will allow the nomads to access certain parts of their bodies or minds so that they can shapeshift. I don't pretend to know how that is possible."

Sula nodded. "We never figure out all of the mysteries in our lives."

Daoa and Tei came into the room. Daoa held a small pot out to Ursula.

"This is what we use for our tattoos," Tei said.

Daoa turned around and dropped her robe to reveal her bare skin. Along her spine were blue dots, like the two on Ursula's spine.

"These help us to walk through the timeless caves," Daoa said. "It is something we have always done. We share with you this ink. It was given to us by the People. It is only clay, horn, and mountain dust that has been breathed on by the People, scorched over the fire, mixed with water, then buried in the Earth for a time. It is sacred to us. We wish you health, prosperity, and vitality. And we are prepared to assist you."

"Thank you," Ursula said. "Now I need to explain all of this to the others."

Ursula led the way into the main room where the nomads were gathered. All looked up when she entered. Opyea and Sergei stood and came to her. She took Sergei's hand, squeezed it, then released it and smiled.

"Veras asked me to bring you to this mountain," Ursula said. "She thought we would find answers here. She wanted us to find the People."

"I saw one of the People this morning," Elio said. "She was a fox. Then a woman. It was like looking into the face of the sun and not having to blink."

"Yes," Ursula said, "that's exactly what it is like."

"I followed a sheep to a bluff and found an old man sitting there," Nels said. "I asked if he was praying and he said yes. What is the name of that which you worship, I asked and he said, 'I worship the ground I sit upon.'"

"I watched a wolfman hunt down a deer, kill it, and lay it on the threshold of this building," Opyea said. "He prayed before, during and after. They are great hunters. And we are their descendants."

"We are more than that." Ursula looked around the room at these people she had come to love. "We are the People. We have just forgotten it."

Opyea laughed. "I have heard that I roar like a lion but I have never actually changed into one."

Ursula smiled. "I've figured out how we can remember ourselves. You'll have to trust me, but I know that if you get tattoos you will become your true selves. Then Kovo can't hurt you. He won't even be able to find you. But it will mean leaving behind what you know, what is familiar. It means embracing the wild."

The nomads watched her silently.

After a moment, Opyea slapped Ursula on the back. "We've gotten too tame of late. Let us take a plunge into the wilderness."

"We will follow you anywhere," Sergei said.

Ursula shook her head. "No, not anywhere! But for now, you can get five tattoos. The Wu will help with the embroidery. You'll need to choose something from the wild that speaks to you, of the air, fire, water, earth, and your spirit or soul. For instance, you could have a tattoo of a fish to represent water or a bird to represent air."

"Let us begin, then," Opyea said.

Dyads of Wu came into the room, carrying tiny pots of tattoo powder. Someone began drumming. Music filled the room. Sergei kissed Ursula, then walked away from her.

Ursula looked at Sula as the nomads sat or lay down in preparation for their embroidery. "I don't need the tattooing?" Ursula asked.

Sula said, "You don't need the tattooing. Just feel yourself in yourself." Sula moved away into the semi-darkness of the room.

Ursula felt the music in the soles of her feet. She began moving to the sounds of the drum and the murmurs of her comrades. She glanced at the darkened walls and saw no paintings. Only darkness. Light flickered near each group of people as the Wu and other embroiderers bent over each body.

Ursula closed her eyes and danced. Danced the sacred shapes. Breathed in the breath of her people.

Her people. A sob shuddered through her body.

"Momma," she whispered.

Ursula danced. Her belly shook. She laughed and opened her

eyes.

Then everything looked sharper. Felt clearer. She could feel the stone on her feet, the warm air surrounding her. She felt herself in herself. Her skin. Her eyes. Her heart. The roaring inside was the roar of herself. She felt. That was it. That was all. She felt. She was feeling.

A bear paw appeared on the stone wall—its outline fluorescent. Then a red rose. A white one. Their stems interwoven. Her grandmother's house. Mount Hood.

Ursula danced.

Those who weren't being tattooed danced with her.

More pictures appeared.

Trees. Rocks. Birds. Animals. People.

The room throbbed and the paintings pulsed with light.

Ursula laughed. The mountain was the invisible artist. Was the Earth embroidering her own skin with scenes from life? Sacred symbols.

The nomads danced.

Ursula stared at the rock.

The mountain *and* the nomads and Ursula were creating the paintings. Wasn't that what art was? Communing with nature? Going with the internal external Universal flow?

That was the answer.

The language of the Universe was not words.

All of Ursula's life she had wanted to be connected, to be a part of something, to feel as though she was communicating with someone. Something. All of her life she had missed the messages that had surrounded her. The visible messages. Visible communication. *Nature*. Of course she had always been a part of the world.

Ursula felt her blood pulse through her veins. Her vision throbbed. The room smelled of rock. Of the People. The beat of the drums. She felt her cells changing.

She was Ursula, She Who Roars, Growls, Makes Love, Eats, Sleeps, Yells, Fails, Falls Down, Gets Up, Dances, Sings, Loves, Hates, Feels. She Who Has Talked to the Animals. And the Earth.

She danced. Twisted. Touched her forehead and drew blood. Roared.

I am here on this Earth now. I belong. I belong. She could feel the wildness—the vital force—of all the People, of the mountain, the nomads, the air, the clouds. It was as though their molecules were hers—part of her body. A living vibrating connection of life.

This was what it was to be truly human.

To be one of the People.

Everything cracked into place. She breathed deeply.

And shifted into Bear. She looked at her arms. White. White Bear. Like the beautiful reflection she had seen in the mirror at Nikovotov's house.

I am She-Bear.

She danced around the room.

I am Ursula, BearDancer.

Ursula roared. Heard roars and songs and growls all around her. She laughed. All was shattered. Changed. Now was time for madness. Or absolute sanity.

She rushed out into the night that was now day. She smelled melting ice. Felt snow on the pads of her feet. Saw a snowbird circling. Her body throbbed. She felt—heard—sensed the others with her, each on their own journey with her.

Smelled salmon.

Ran. Pushed the Earth beneath her feet. Moved the Earth. Galloped with the Earth. Her mouth watered. A crow yelled at her. She stopped at the shore of the river. The ice was the color of Sergei's eyes. Ursula smelled. Saw. Sensed fish. She plunged her powerful white paw clear through the ice and snatched a salmon up into her claws. "Sacred animal I asked for your life—to make you part of mine." She tore the fish open with her paw. She could barely see as the blood thirst overtook her. She ate the fish in two gulps. The river was in her blood. *Was her blood.* The fish was in her blood. *Was her blood.* Part river, part fish.

She roared.

And smelled Sergei before she saw him. Heard his growl.

Then he was next to her, a reddish brown bearman with Siberian ice-blue eyes. His beauty made her shiver.

She bared her teeth. The bearman shifted into bear.

Then they fell upon each other, opening to the other. Ursula felt Sergei in every part of her. She knew only that she wanted him, again and again. Didn't know it—felt it. Until they fell apart, exhausted, and panting.

Then they shifted into bearman and bearwoman. This was what Ursula had missed in Sergei: the bear, the beast, the wild, the real untamed human.

At the same time, Ursula felt every other part of the world inside of her.

Ursula and Sergei returned to the others. One by one, they had re-membered who they were.

Most of the nomads became Bear, a few Leopard, Fox, Wolf, Swan, Eagle. They went outdoors with the People and learned by watching them how to camouflage themselves so they would not be seen by the domesticated humans. They now understood the language of the Wu—and all other languages. Bear-men and women made love, growling and roaring at one another. Wolves howled at the moon.

They learned and became more comfortable in their bodies, as their true selves.

They waited for spring when they could go down the mountain and take themselves, their true selves, out into the world.

62

The days grew clear, sunny, and cold. The light changed, became whiter, or sharper. Something undefinable. Ursula ran through the woods and smelled earth beneath the snow that was beginning to melt beyond the foothills below.

She knew it was time to leave at the same moment the other nomads knew.

"I wish to come with you," Sula told Ursula. "You are infants just out of the womb."

Ursula was glad to have her mentor accompany them.

The nomads packed their horses, who did not seem to care who or what the nomads had become, and said good-bye to the Wu. The sun shined down on them as they trudged through the snow and under the arch.

Ursula looked back once and could not see the complex.

Sula led them off the mountain. Now as they traveled down the sides of the Beloved, the nomads—the New People—walked, shape-shifted, prayed. Everywhere they looked they saw life. Near the bottom of the mountain as they moved out into hills and valleys, the snow became melt. Nuthatches and blue titmice chattered at them. Snowflowers began to appear on thawed patches of ground—white blossoms framing pale yellow insides, like clouds incubating tiny new suns.

One night they slept near one of the lakes—one of the eyes of the Earth, Sula called it. They sang and danced and howled at the moon. Ursula watched her friends and thought of what her life had been like a year ago: in a miserable marriage with no voice of her own and a job for which she felt no passion. Now she was surrounded by friends, committed to saving her people, transforming and shapeshifting her entire life. Sula smiled at her from across the fire. Sergei kissed Ursula's neck. They ran into the woods together, as bears, and Ursula growled gleefully as she felt the forest floor on the balls of her feet, smelled the resin, breathed it all deeply into her lungs, into her being, then rolled over and opened herself up to Sergei, to the world. This was ecstasy, she felt. This was life.

The mountain rose behind them. The sound of running water and melting snow seemed to come from all around. In the distance, as chunks of ice bumped against chunks of ice, a river groaned, as if giving birth. Deer and marals dug up tubers and chewed on new greens.

They made camp on a grassy plateau, much like the Pastures of Heaven. To the south, the Beloved mountain rose. Beneath their feet, the ground began to thaw and grasses started to grow. The air was cold and crisp. Swans flew above them. The nomads called to the swans, and the swans answered.

Opyea found a cave, and they set up their tents outside of it.

After lunch, Opyea stood and said, "We've come far, friends. We have seen many of our comrades die but now we have returned to our Belovdia. We remember who we are."

The nomads cheered. Ursula looked at their faces under the spring sun. The world smelled of water, earth, flowers. And her friends faces' shone with health—and connection. She knew they felt what she did—she felt their blood, their breath, in her body. They felt her in theirs.

"She came to us out of the smoke," Sergei said, standing next to Opyea.

Ursula looked up at him.

"She learned to stand and to ride and to be with us," Sergei said. "She spoke to the animals and the Earth and taught us by example to become ourselves. Ulla, She Who Talks, She Who Roars, She Who Dances, She Who Connects, we have all agreed it is you who earths us, and you who helped us soar, or roar, depending." Everyone laughed. "We ask that you be our priestess, that you continue to guide and protect us." Sergei nodded to his sister. She ducked into a tent, then emerged carrying something wrapped in a blanket.

"We ask you to accept this," Sergei said. "Be the priestess of us, the New People."

Elio carefully pulled off the blanket. Beneath it was a tall cone-shaped headdress. The sun hit the golden sickle-shaped plaques and reflected the light back at Ursula. A felt bear's paw decorated the front. Tiny bells hung over the bottom of the hat.

Ursula knew this headdress. She had seen it 2,500 years in the future—she had touched it. It was the lady's headdress. She stood and went to Sergei's side.

So her mother was not the tattooed lady: *She was.*

This was who she was. The lady.

She smiled. "I have no wisdom. I know so little, but if you trust me, I accept this honor."

The nomads cheered.

Above, a vulture flew.

Sergei and Elio fitted the headdress over Ursula's head. It was at least half as tall as she was. They stepped away from her, and she stood with the hat on. It was heavy and made her slightly dizzy.

"In times past, this sacred headdress allowed the priestess to hear and see the People," Sergei said. "Or so it was said. You don't need the headdress for that—none of us does any longer, but we wanted you to know that you are one of us."

"You honor me," Ursula said. "And I wish to honor you. I am one of the People, but I want to show you that I am one of you, too. I wish to be embroidered. Then for all of time, everyone will know we were kin."

Ursula took off the headdress and handed it to Elio. The drummers began making music. Ursula went inside the cave. It was warm—a timeless cave.

She sat on the floor, near the outdoors so she could see all.

"Are you certain of this?" Sula asked.

Ursula nodded.

Two embroiderers sat on either side of her. She told them what pictures she wanted.

Still Sula stood over her.

"This is who I am, Sula," she said. "You see?"

The embroiderers began.

They created a swan who shared skin with a deer; a spider made her fingers part of her web; a bear's claw pricked her heart.

Outside the timeless cave, the others drummed and sang. Dancers undulated and shook, each moving in such a way that Ursula did not know what she saw, no matter how often she blinked. Was that an eagle or a girl? A fox or a man? A leopard or a woman?

Sergei touched the small of her back.

"You don't have to do this," he whispered. "You are already one of the People." He kissed the sweat from the back of her neck. Then he was one of the dancers, twirling the night into existence.

She felt the needle go into her skin, deeper and deeper. She wanted to roar.

The coriander-colored dirt tickled the soles of her feet.

She gasped as the needle came out again.

After a time, the embroiderer whispered, "We are finished."

Outside, the drums sounded like horse hooves.

"One more," she whispered, pressing her hand against her buttocks. "Right here. A wild rose. A tiny red wild rose."

The dancers whirled faster. Everything pulsed.

"It's a message for someone back home."

That night, Nels stumbled into camp, bloody and beaten.

The nomads ran to his side.

"They've got Casta. We were just below when Kovo and his warriors appeared. They captured us. None of us could shapeshift."

Sula said, "Fear can inhibit the shapechange because you're all so new at it."

"Kovo's warriors beat me," Nels said. "Then let me go with this warning: He will kill Casta unless we turn over our leader to him."

Opyea snorted. "We will rescue Casta at first light. Kovo cannot intimidate us."

"He intimidates me," Ursula said. "He's killed hundreds of our people."

"If we can't rescue Casta," Opyea said, "I will give myself up. But tomorrow we will try to rescue him."

Rescue Casta. Ursula remembered Sergei in the future telling her that she had sent him away the morning before the rescue and from a distance ridge, he had seen her die.

That meant tomorrow she was destined to die.

"Sergei has to leave now," Ursula said.

Everyone looked at her.

"It is time. He must return to the Wu and learn how to use the timeless caves," she said, making up a reason.

"I won't leave now!" Sergei said.

"Come," Opyea said. "Let them speak alone. We will make plans for tomorrow."

"What are you doing?" Sergei asked when the others had moved away.

"I know what will happen tomorrow," Ursula said. "You told me and I know you have to get away now because you must find me in the future. You will go to the mountain, then you'll live in Russia, build a mosaic house, become a doctor, and find me in Chicago." She pulled a piece of paper from one of her pouches. "This is my itinerary 2500 years in the future. You think you can remember to meet me in Chicago?"

"I don't understand," Sergei said.

Ursula kissed him, then said, "The nomads will be saved if you do this. Please."

"You will meet me when it's over?" Sergei asked.

"I will meet you in the future," Ursula said. "I promise."

Sergei and Ursula slept in each other's arm for only a short while. Ursula wondered why she was following a fate she did not understand. They could leave now, run, and maybe she would be saved. She did not have to become the tattooed lady. She did not have to die tomorrow. But then Sergei would never have met her in Chicago and she would never have experienced the last few months. Olga had said she had been indoctrinated to believe that sacrificing herself was necessary and noble. Was that what was happening now? Was she accepting her death, her fate, because she believed that was the only way to save those she loved?

Near dawn, Sergei said good-bye. Ursula held him tightly and kissed his lips. He looked into her eyes.

"I will love you always," he said.

"And I you," she said.

They released one another, and Sergei got on his horse.

"Don't come back," Ursula said. "No matter what you see.

You must trust me."

When Sergei was gone, the remaining nomads traveled to the ridge beneath which, Nels told them, Kovo was camped. The nomads looked out at the warriors' tents scattered about the plateau. Horses grazed. Fires burned. They obviously did not fear the nomads.

"That's Kovo's tent," Nels said, pointing to a tent below them.

Opyea nodded. "I'll try to get Casta back through negotiation. If not, we'll shapeshift and see what happens."

"That's the plan?" Ursula asked.

Opyea shrugged and grinned. "That's the plan."

Ursula groaned.

Opyea climbed down the ridge. A guard immediately challenged her.

"I wish to speak with Kovo," Opyea said.

The guard pushed her forward.

"I am Opyea of the Bear Clan. I have come to retrieve my brother."

Casta stumbled out of the tent. He looked unharmed.

A man followed him out.

"That is Kovo," Nels told Ursula, as they stood hidden on the ridge above the camp.

Kovo turned to face Opyea, and Ursula saw him.

Her knees buckled, and she sank to the ground.

"Nikovotov," she whispered.

"Who?" Prine asked.

He was somewhat older than when she had last seen him and bearded, but he was definitely Nikovotov.

"Why do you hunt my people?" Opyea asked, pointing at Nikovotov.

Nikovotov smiled. "Don't raise your hands to me. My warriors have orders to kill anyone who gets near me."

Opyea stared at him.

"I don't hunt all of your people," Nikovotov said. "I look only for one."

Ursula's heart jumped into her throat.

"One who broke a promise to return to me."

Ursula's eyes widened. She moaned. He had murdered the clan heads because of *her*? She wanted to race after Sergei and stop him from ever meeting her in Chicago. All of those deaths because of *her*? Nikovotov had told her he was not a murderer. She wanted to scream. Fury made her heart beat faster, louder.

"I see from your tattoos that you are one of the false People, too," Nikovotov said. "I will hunt you all down and kill you."

"Why?" Opyea asked.

"Where is she who leads you? Where is Ursula?"

Sula came and stood in front of Ursula.

"Ursula," she said. "I think I can diffuse this situation. If you go down there, you'll get hurt; you're too angry. Trust me. This is how it should happen."

Ursula stared at Sula. Her face transformed as Ursula watched her. Shapeshifting. Transmutating. She was getting younger.

"Now I know why you seemed so familiar," Ursula said. "You're Kam."

"I am who you have searched for," Sula said. "And now I must do what I must."

"No," Ursula said. "I can stop this all right now."

Sula pulled off her mittens. A spider and web tattooed her left hand.

"What's going on?" Ursula asked.

"If Ursula shows herself," Nikovotov was saying to Opyea, "I will give up my vendetta against your people."

"Ursula, you mustn't hurt him," Sula said.

"Who?" Ursula asked.

"Nikovotov," Sula said.

"I'd worry more about him hurting me," Ursula snapped.

If Nikovotov wanted her—if she could save the nomads this way—she would do it. Ursula started forward. Prine and Traiger grabbed an arm each; one of them put his hand over her mouth.

Sula looked at her. "Good-bye, Ulla." Sula went over the ridge and down the slope. Ursula struggled to get away.

Sula stepped in front of Opyea and Casta and faced Nikovotov.

"I am Ursula," Sula said.

Startled, Nikovotov stepped back. "You have grown older," Nikovotov said. "But I see it is you."

"You have grown younger," Sula said, "but I see it is you."

Ursula stopped struggling and stared.

Sula was Kam who was . . . UrSula.

"I am who you searched for," Sula had said.

Nikovotov thought Sula was Ursula because they looked like twins. *Because Sula was her mother.*

Ursula tried to twist away, but she couldn't shapeshift.

No, this wasn't the way it was supposed to be!

"How could you kill all of those people?" Sula asked.

"You didn't keep your promise," Nikovotov said.

"I loved you," Sula said.

Ursula tried to scream. She had never loved him.

Nikovotov looked startled. "You did not love me."

"I will." Sula raised her hand up to his face, then suddenly stopped and reached for her own throat.

Nikovotov screamed, "No! She wasn't going to hurt me!"

Ursula finally felt the bear. Shapeshifted. She tore loose from Traiger and Prine and leaped down the ridge, just as Sula's legs collapsed beneath her, and she fell to the ground, a dagger in her throat. Ursula roared and pounced on Nikovotov. She could crush him. Kill him. Rip out his heart. He stared up at her, and she wondered why he did not shapechange.

"Sula!" Opyea cried.

Ursula became woman and rolled off Nikovotov.

Opyea pulled the knife from Sula's throat. She was not breathing.

Ursula screamed and cradled her mother's head on her lap. Sula began transforming: bearwoman, woman, bear, then woman again, a tuft of bear remaining on her hand in the form of hair. Ursula rocked her. "No! It was supposed to be me!"

Up in the hills, she knew Sergei had witnessed what he thought was her murder.

"I told them to protect me against the shifters," Nikovotov said. "I never meant her." He stared at Ursula. "I mean you—I. Who is she?"

"My mother," Ursula cried. She carefully laid her mother's head on the ground and stood. "She just saved my life—and yours. I don't know why she saved yours. She was one of the People. And you killed her."

"But she's tattooed," Nikovotov said.

"As am I," Ursula said. "What about you? What has happened to you that you could murder hundreds on a vendetta? Were you ever really one of the People! You're like a domesticated dog gone wild. Is that it? You've forgotten who you are, Niko." She ripped open his clothes at his chest. He held up an arm to warn off his warriors. "She saved your life, Niko. Now I'm going to help you remember who you are. Wake up!" Ursula dug her bear claws into him, piercing his chest. He flinched. Blood trickled from the wounds. Ursula stared at him and pushed her claws in deeper. She growled. She wanted to kill him. Wanted to taste his blood. She roared. Felt a connection with him. Connected him with all the other People.

Then she pulled out her claw. Cut the connection.

Nikovotov staggered and almost fell.

"Now you know what it feels like to be one of us," Ursula said.

"And to lose us. Leave us in peace or you will become known throughout history as he who destroyed the People."

The other nomads came off the ridge. They gently picked up Sula and carried her away. Ursula followed. She turned back once. Nikovotov was on his knees.

At camp, Myrus and Traiger wrapped Sula carefully, and they tied her to her horse. Then they began another journey. Ursula sang to her mother and shared childhood memories. They traveled all day and night and another day. The horses rested. Then they kept going until they reached the Pastures of Heaven where the tribes awaited.

Fala greeted them. "Our scouts returned a while ago saying Kovo's warriors have dispersed, and he has disappeared. We heard one of ours died so we came here to await you. Your mother will be buried with honors."

"Thank you," Ursula said. "She was our real teacher, you know. My guide. Don't kill any horses for her burial. It wouldn't be right."

Fala glanced at Opyea.

"No, it wouldn't right," Opyea said. "None of us wishes that."

They built the underground tomb and mummified Sula. Ursula silently oversaw the preparations. She asked permission of the New People to bury the headdress with Sula. They agreed, so she asked the coffinmakers to shape the coffin longer than Sula's height. When Myrus finished the embalming, Ursula helped them dress Sula. She fingered each tattoo that was exactly like her own. Down to the red rose tattoo.

"Who did her embroidery?" Ursula asked.

"I did the spider on her hand," Myrus said, "but everything else was already there."

Ursula nodded. "We're like twins, twenty-five years apart now, with the same tattoos."

Myrus shook her head as she gently pulled up Sula's stockings. "No. You don't have a red rose tattoo."

"What?"

Myrus handed her Sula's mirror. Ursula pulled down her trousers, twisted herself around and looked at the reflection of her right buttock in the mirror.

"It's white," Ursula said. "A white rose. I asked for red."

Myrus shrugged. "Sula told them to make yours white and not to tell you."

"So that I could not be the tattooed lady," Ursula said. She gently helped pull the trousers onto her mother. She sighed. She still did not understand.

When it was time, they carried Sula down into the kurgan and laid her in the larch coffin, on her side, as if she were sleeping. Ursula placed the headdress next to her, along with her mirror and pouch. Myrus set a bowl of mutton stew on a small table. While Preva prayed above them, four workmen drove one long metal spike each into the top of the coffin to nail it shut.

"Good-bye, Mom," Ursula said.

She climbed out of the kurgan and looked around. Clouds covered the mountain. The nomads prayed and sang.

When the ceremony was over, Opyea put her arm around Ursula's shoulder.

"Come. I have something to show you," she said.

Part Four

WILD

63

Siberia, a year before Ursula's birth

Sula heard moans coming from the cave. She stopped and looked around. She was in the middle of Siberia where any manner of wild creature could attack her—in the middle of her mother's dreaded Siberian homeland where Sula had promised she would be especially careful, which meant she should not go into any cave where wild animals might lurk. Except she was an archaeologist studying rock art and most rock art occurred inside caves.

Besides, someone could be hurt.

She switched on her flashlight and called out as she walked up the slope to the cave.

She shouted at the entrance, then stepped inside, waving a light around.

A bear lay on its side, moaning.

She held her breath and started to back out. Wait. It was a man in a bearskin.

355

She sighed with relief and walked to the man and leaned over.

He was a bearman, and he was dying.

She had heard stories of bearmen. Had dreamed all of her life that she was a bear. She was not surprised now to find one of the People in her arms.

She helped him drink water. Later soup. He watched her with beautiful lonely bearman eyes. She caught salmon from the stream and gave it to him uncooked.

She stroked his fur and sang to him as he slept.

"You look like someone I knew," he said one day. "Her name was Ursula."

"That is my name," she said, astounded. "I go by Sula. Who are you?"

"They called me Nikovotov." He squinted at her. "One day you will save my life and your daughter's."

"I have no daughter."

He stared at her. "You will." He turned away. "I am an old man, let me die."

"No." She loved him and could not let him die.

One day as they sat at the entrance to the cave together and she spooned honey into his mouth, he said, "Your daughter told me to learn who I was. I have tried for many years and failed."

"You have been alone?"

He nodded.

"And you've grown old. I thought the People were immortal."

"No," Nikovotov said. "Just long-lived."

"You're lonely," Sula said.

Nikovotov smiled. "You are kind to me."

"I am Bear Clan, too," she said. "My mother told me that my father was one of the People. My mother made love to him once and it frightened her to be so real and connected. She left here and never came back. It is a frightening thing to know oneself. Perhaps you are afraid."

Nikovotov nodded. "And ashamed. I don't remember how to be wild, and I'm too mean to be human."

Sula laughed. "Too mean to be human? Hah! Humans glorify mean and cruel."

"Your daughter had a theory about that: Humans get that way because they've been out of the wild too long, like bears in zoos not knowing how to be bears. Or deer in the Grand Canyon starving to death because they've been fed junk food all of their lives and can't eat their natural diet any more. That is what she told me one night in a drunken delirium. I still don't understand half of it."

"My daughter is a drunk?"

Nikovotov laughed. "You bring me great joy."

Sula smiled. She put her hand over the scars on his chest. "When you are well enough, I want you to make love with me."

Nikovotov took the honey and spoon from Sula and set it on the ground. "I am well enough now." He touched her cheek. "So this is what it is like to love and be loved."

Sula nodded. "I want you to be my child's father."

Nikovotov looked at her eyes, then tenderly kissed her. "Ursula would not like that."

"Ursula has no say in it."

"You should go home and be with your family," Nikovotov told her. "Let the baby be born with your mother by your side."

"I want to be here with you."

Nikovotov smiled and kissed her stomach.

"Go. I will wait for you," he said.

64

*1999, minutes after Ursula disappeared
in her first timeless cave*

Sergei stumbled away from the cave. He had been waiting for hundreds of years to see Ursula. Now she was gone. He sat on the ground and put his head in his hands. He was not certain he could survive her absence again. He could not spend forever aching for what he had lost so long ago.

Someone put a hand on his shoulder. He looked up. The man was bearded and older than when he last saw him, but Sergei recognized him.

"Nikovotov," he said.

"Hello, friend." Nikovotov sat next to him.

"I was never your friend," Sergei said.

"I didn't expect to see you," Nikovotov said.

"Nor I you. What are you doing here?"

"I'm supposed to be here," Nikovotov said. "I had to stay out of sight so Ursula wouldn't see me yet. But I'm glad to see you."

"I thought someone would have killed you by now."

"For more reasons than you know," Nikovotov said, "but I can catch you up on my history later. I've come bearing gifts. I understand that you still are ill. I apologize. I didn't know. I was evil to hurt you. I'm sorry."

Sergei looked at him. "Is this a joke?"

Nikovotov shook his head. "I was disconnected, too. I didn't know how to get back. Sula helped me."

"Sula? Our Sula from so long ago on the mountain?"

Nikovotov nodded. "Yes. She was the one you saw die all that time ago, when you thought you saw Ursula." He looked at his hands. "She is Ursula's mother. When she returned to Siberia, we went up Belovdia together and lived with the Wu for many years, until it was time to come down for Ursula. Sula came first. The Wu heard you were still suffering. They gave me some special tattoo powder for you. They suggested you get a tattoo of a red rose."

Kam came out of the cave. Nikovotov stood and embraced her.

"Sergei, this is Sula."

Sergei stood and blinked. "Kam. Of course. It's been so many years, and you were older. You were on a mountain waiting for us."

"It hasn't happened to me yet," Sula said.

"Why are you with him?" Sergei asked. "He tried to kill me."

"He won't hurt you now," Sula said. "He is Ursula's father."

Sergei stared at them. "What?"

"We can talk about all that later." Sula pointed to the cave. "The Wu believe you can be healed. You want to be whole when you see Ursula again, don't you?"

"Will I see her again?"

"I don't know the future."

Sergei laughed bitterly. "*Now* you don't know the future!"

Sergei walked away from them and went into the cave. He looked around. Minutes before, Ursula had been here. Moments before that, he had touched her. These last few days with her had been the first time since Nikovotov had pierced his skin that he had felt a connection to the wild, a connection with himself. Now Sula and Nikovotov told him if he got a rose tattoo he might finally be healed. Was it possible?

He tried to remember what he had felt so many years ago on Belovdia. He had been ready for life.

He did not think he could recall the feeling.

But he could feel the heartbeat of the Earth through the soles of his feet. He began dancing anyway, awkwardly at first, then humming, singing. He felt his body creak and ache and crack.

After a time he tired, so he sat and prayed and cried. Grew silent. Remembered joy. Felt it in his body.

And the cave began drawing scenes from his life. Learning to hunt. Digging for grubs. Running through the tall grass. Making love with Ursula. Dancing, laughing. The slaughter of his people. Transforming into bear. Feeling the pulse of the world. Seeing Ursula die. Losing the connection. And all the waiting since.

The paintings stopped, faded, until all that remained was a single red rose.

He smiled.

Sula/Kam came into the cave.

"All right, I'll get a tattoo of a red rose," Sergei said. "Just like the one Ursula asked for. In the same spot."

Sula nodded. From inside her tunic, she pulled out a narrow, nearly flat, embroidery box.

Sergei lay down and fell to sleep, just as he had each time they had tattooed him. He dreamed Ursula sat in a cave with Opyea. Opyea was making blue dot tattoos along her spine. Soon Ursula would cavewalk—walk through time—maybe come back to him.

When he opened his eyes, he was alone in the cave. The walls undulated with light and color. He could now hear the heartbeat of the cave. Feel his blood pulsing. Sense the People all around.

He growled joyfully. He was connected once again. He was healed.

And he had Nikovotov to thank for it.

65

Ursula and Opyea walked across the prairie to an outcropping of rock. Facing the north side of the mountain was a cave. Opyea led her inside, down a narrow corridor to a large chamber. A small oil lamp burned.

"Sula said to bring you here after," Opyea said.

"After what?"

Opyea looked at her. "After her funeral."

Ursula shook her head. "It's all wrong. She shouldn't be dead."

"She wanted you to see this cave."

Ursula glanced around. Several bear pictographs ran together on one wall.

"We do better together," Opyea said. "That's what Sula said. She also said that you could rejoin Sergei using this cave, if you wanted. You need a blue spot tattoo along your spine. The Wu showed her, and she showed me."

"Does that mean I'd have to leave you all?"

Opyea shrugged. "I don't know."

Ursula sat on the floor. "Yes, I would like to be with Sergei," she said sadly.

Opyea sat next to her and pulled out a needle and some ink. Ursula loosened her shirt so Opyea could reach her spine. She closed her eyes and breathed deeply as Opyea pushed the needle in.

Maybe this time, she would find peace.

Ursula closed her eyes as Opyea pushed the needle in again and out again.

"Good-bye, priestess Ur-soo-la," Opyea said.

When Ursula opened her eyes again, Opyea was gone.

She was in a different cave but a familiar one. She had been here before. Yes, this was her first cave. She was back to where she had started. She sighed deeply. And she was completely alone. Where were the People? Her mother was dead and buried. Her grandmother was most likely dead, too. Niko had murdered hundreds because of her. She couldn't move. No amount of strength training could give her the energy she needed to stand up, to keep going. It was all too hard.

Then Sergei came striding into the cave—older, Moscow Sergei. Ursula's stomach lurched. He was so beautiful. His eyes sparkled. He looked alive and healthy.

He smiled. She jumped up and flung her arms around him. Sergei held her tightly. She gasped with joy.

"My love, my love," he whispered. "Are you all right?"

"I'm fine." She pulled away. "Look at you. You're better. Something."

"I am connected with the People again. Nikovotov helped me."

Ursula frowned. "What?"

Sergei kissed her. "They're waiting."

"Who?"

"Your mother and—and Nikovotov."

"Mom?"

Ursula ran outside. Sula stood close by the entrance, smiling. Waiting for her? She opened her arms. Ursula ran into them. "Mother." She cried.

Sula stroked Ursula's hair. "It's all right. I know it's all confusing."

"I just buried you," Ursula said. She saw Nikovotov over her mother's shoulder. "It was because of him." She pulled away from Sula. "Why is he here?"

"Do you remember you pierced my heart?" Nikovotov asked. "Of course you do. It was only days ago to you, but it's been a lifetime for me. You made me want to get better. Later your mother nursed me back to health."

Ursula shook her head. She felt jet-lagged—or time-lagged.

"Ursula," Sula said. "Nikovotov is your father."

Ursula backed away until she felt Sergei's hand on her back. "But he tried to seduce me!"

"I didn't know then that you were my daughter," he said. "I hadn't met your mother yet."

"You killed all of those people because you were angry with me," Ursula said. "You tracked me through time. You would have killed me."

"I have tried to make amends for my earlier crimes," Nikovotov said.

"How?" She looked at her mother. "It was because of him that you died!"

"Let me talk to my daughter alone," Sula said.

Sergei and Nikovotov stepped away from the women.

"Listen to me, Ursula. Niko is not the man he was. He has changed, body and soul. He is a good man now. He has loved me and we have been together for many years."

"Why did you leave grandma and me? Why didn't you come back?" Ursula asked. "It was because of him, wasn't it?"

Sula looked into her eyes. "I had every intention of coming back. I wanted to find Nikovotov, then come back to you. We went up the mountain to live with the Wu, to learn to be one of the People, to discover my own ancestry. They were the ones, by the way, who told me it was time to come off the mountain and find you. It's not a good excuse but . . . time just went by." She put her hand on Ursula's arm. "Niko has told me what he knows of my death. Now I want to hear it from you."

Ursula looked away. Sergei and Nikovotov walked through the woods together. Had Sergei forgiven him?

"You pretended you were me," Ursula said, "so that Nikovotov wouldn't kill me, or whatever he was going to do."

"He wouldn't have killed you," Sula said.

"You didn't know him then," Ursula said.

"He's told me what he did," she said. "I know he killed others. I don't believe he would have killed you."

"You got the same tattoos as mine," Ursula said, "and when the embroiderers were tattooing me, you secretly told them to put a white rose on my ass instead of a red rose, so that historically I could not be the frozen lady, the tattooed lady of the Pastures of Heaven. You got the red rose tattoo instead so that you would be the tattooed lady. But you don't have to do it, Mom. I tried to stop you, and I don't want you to do it for me. Don't reach for Nikovotov. Don't try to touch him. Maybe it'll be all right."

Sula smiled. "I'm not worried. I've been on this journey for a long time."

Ursula put her arms around Sula. "Don't die for me, Momma."

"Tell me everything I need to know about your life and mine."

Later, Ursula lay in Sergei's arms.

"This is going to take some getting used to," Ursula whispered.

"I hated Nikovotov so much." Ursula leaned on her elbow and looked at Sergei. "So you got a red rose tattoo to go with my white one. Yin and Yang? Rosa Alba and Rosa Rubedo?

"Maybe love and love?"

Ursula kissed his lips. "You're so sentimental."

"Where do you want to go?" Sergei asked. "Back home to America? Moscow? Up the Beloved mountain with your mom and dad? Back to the nomads?"

"I want to go where I can be the most alive."

"We could probably find some People here in Siberia today," Sergei said.

"Of course we could," Ursula said. "Can't you feel them breathing with us?"

Sergei smiled. "Yes, I feel them all around."

66

Asya dreamed of bear. She opened her eyes to daylight and the sound of Panda's purring. She carefully moved the cat without waking her, got out of bed, and put on her clothes.

Usually when she dreamed of bear, she awakened frightened, her heart racing. Not today. Her daughter was long gone and now her granddaughter was in Siberia, too. What more did Asya have to lose?

She went outside into a bright blue day and stepped off of her porch and onto the ground. Northeast lay Mount Saint Helens and Mount Rainier, southeast Mount Hood. She could not see any of the mountains but she suddenly felt their solid presences through the soles of her shoes. She smiled and looked around. Her lawn and house were nearly surrounded by woods. If she walked in almost any direction, she would eventually run into someone else's house. Except north. North the woods went on and on.

She stared north. The evergreen woods looked dark. Shadows moved at the edges of the trees and her vision.

She was so tired of being afraid. It had not gotten her anywhere.

She had been alone for . . . ever. She strode toward the northern woods. A crow called out to her and she waved. An east wind cooled her brow. Her heart raced.

She stepped into the forest. The trees sighed a welcome. She kept walking. Deeper into the green gold darkness. Shadows moved all around her, shadows that took the shapes of deer, possum, a cougar. She kept walking.

Until she saw another shadow stopped and waiting for her. A bear. Staring at her. What should she do? Run? Climb a tree? Scream?

Her heart pounded.

Her chest hurt.

She fell to her knees.

The shadows stopped. The bear came to her side. Knelt next to her. Took her hand.

"I'm not afraid," Asya whispered.

"I'm glad," the bearman said.

"I'm old. It is time to die."

"You are not that old. You can be with us."

Asya glanced around. The forest was full of the People. She heard them, saw them, felt them in her blood.

"Have you been here all along?" Asya asked. "I've missed you."

The bearman laughed. "Yes. We have been here all along and we've missed you, too." He put his hand on her chest.

Her pain disappeared.

After a moment, the Bearman asked, "Are you ready?"

Asya nodded, and he helped her up.

"I think I am ready this time," Asya said.

She took the bearman's hand and followed the People deeper still into the forest.

67

Miriam and Bob sat in the lab together after hours.

"I should get home," Bob said. "I don't want to miss the kids' bed time."

Miriam glanced at the clock.

"Yeah, I should get going, too," she said, stretching. "Do you realize it's eight months to the day that Ursula disappeared? I can hardly believe it."

"And you're going back," Bob said. "Can you believe that?"

"There's something wild about Siberia that scares and intrigues me, but I want to be there when they repatriate the lady's body next month." Miriam sat forward. "Do you think the tattooed lady and Ursula are the same person? Her DNA does match the mummy's."

"It's impossible," Bob said. "I'll tell you this if you promise not to repeat it to anyone. One day when we were looking at tattoos of the Pazyryk man Ursula said that someday if she was really herself, she'd get a red tattoo on her butt, just like the lady's. Remember how odd and out of place that rose tattoo seemed on the lady? I think the tattoo was a message to us. Ursula wanted to tell us that she was living large, living a life of real passion, beauty, and love."

Miriam smiled. "Wouldn't that be nice if it were true?"

"I believe it is," Bob said. "Ursula's out of her cage and into the wild."

68

Sula pushed the embroidery needle into her daughter's skin. Ursula could feel her mother's breath on her back—could see Nikovotov pushing the tattoo needle into Sergei. She grabbed Sergei's hand.

"Good-bye, Mom," Ursula whispered. "See you soon. Good-bye, Niko."

The room tilted. Ursula closed her eyes.

After a few moments, she opened her eyes and looked at Sergei. Sula and Nikovotov were gone.

Sergei smiled at her.

"Do you think we're home?" she asked.

Ursula put her arms around Sergei. He kissed her lips and whispered in her ear, "I'm always home when I'm with you."

"I love you, too," Ursula said.

They went outside. To the south, Belovdia rose into the dusk. Across the plains, a fire burned. Drums beat. Dancers undulated and shook around the flames, each one of them moving, becoming a fox or a leopard, a wolf or bear. Man or woman.

Ursula felt a roaring inside of her, bubbling, gurgling, freeing her.

"Are you ready for this?" Sergei asked.

Ursula nodded.

They hurried toward the others. Opyea waved. Nels and Elio shouted to them. Ursula smiled. She did not know if this would be a short visit or a lifetime spent with the New People.

All she knew was that for now, she was going wild.

Kim Antieau has written many novels, short stories, poems, and essays. Her work has appeared in numerous publications, both in print and online, including *The Magazine of Fantasy and Science Fiction, Asimov's SF, The Clinton Street Quarterly, The Journal of Mythic Arts, EarthFirst!, Alternet, Sage Woman,* and *Alfred Hitchcock's Mystery Magazine*. She was the founder, editor, and publisher of *Daughters of Nyx: A Magazine of Goddess Stories, Mythmaking, and Fairy Tales*. Her work has twice been short-listed for the James Tiptree Award and has appeared in many best-of-the-year anthologies. Critics have admired her "literary fearlessness" and her vivid language and imagination. Her first novel *The Jigsaw Woman* is a modern classic of feminist literature. She is also the author of a science fiction novel, *The Gaia Websters* and a contemporary tale set in the desert Southwest, *Church of the Old Mermaids*. *Broken Moon*, a novel for young adults, was a selection of the Junior Library Guild. She has also written other YA novels, including *Deathmark, Mercy, Unbound, Ruby's Imagine,* and *The Blue Tail*. Kim lives in the Pacific Northwest with her husband, writer Mario Milosevic. Learn more about Kim and her writing at www.kimantieau.com.